SLIP CUE

Also by Joyce Krieg

Murder Off Mike

SLIP CUE:

A TALK RADIO MYSTERY

JOYCE KRIEG

THOMAS DUNNE BOOKS
ST. MARTIN'S MINOTAUR NEW YORK

THOMAS DUNNE BOOKS.
An imprint of St. Martin's Press.

www.minotaurbooks.com

Library of Congress Cataloging-in-Publication Data

Krieg, Joyce.
Slip cue / Joyce Krieg.—1st ed.
p. cm.
ISBN 0-312-32736-6
EAN 978-0312-32736-1
1. Women in radio broadcasting—Fiction. 2. Sacramento (Calif.)—Fiction. 3. Radio broadcasters—Fiction. 4. Talk shows—Fiction. I. Title.

PS3611.R54S57 2004
813'—dc22

2003069537

First Edition: July 2004

10 9 8 7 6 5 4 3 2 1

TO "THE GUYS" OF SACRAMENTO

ALLEN CHAMBERLIN, JOE SHIELDS, AND DAVID WALING

AND TO THE MEMORY OF

DAVE PALMER

(1962–2003)

SLIP CUE

1

IT WAS A SMALL THING, NOT MUCH BIGGER THAN A PARKING TICKET or an ATM receipt. A flimsy sheet of wire service copy with five lines of 10-pitch Courier type, the raw hole-punched edge of the tractor-fed paper trailing from one side.

If I had known then the dangers that scrap of paper would lead to—and the demons it would force me to dance with—I would have shoved it into the recycle bin and let the wire services cover the story.

I reread the bulletin that had just flashed over Associated Press and let the emotions come flooding back. And the memories. The night of the John Lennon shooting. The death of Princess Di, that freeway chase in a white Bronco. I felt a combination of dread, sorrow, and anticipation. Oh, hell. Scratch that. I was excited, dammit. I rode that adrenaline rush like a junkie, the incredible high of knowing a big news story is breaking. God, I love moments like this! Anyone who works in the news business will admit to the same, if they're honest.

America's latest celebrity bad girl had just escaped from jail.

The fact that she had local roots made the story all the juicier.

In the background, I could hear the thrum of afternoon traffic on Highway 160 beating its way past the bulletproof glass and through the walls of the on-air radio studio. Newspaper clippings and faxes cluttered the control console. The call-in lines blinked in two-beat harmony with a car dealer's jingle. "Save your dough, deal with Joe." A television monitor suspended over the console, the sound muted, carried the first game of the World Series.

"You're tuned to the Shauna J. Bogart Show," I said into the mike. "TNA—talk, news, and attitude—for Sacramento's drive home. We'll be right back after this."

I punched the button on the top cart deck, activating a promotional announcement for the sports talk show that followed my three hours of airtime. I handed the wire copy to my executive producer and gestured to the guest mike. "We'll break in with a bulletin as soon as I finish this stop set," I told him through the intercom.

A few months ago, I wouldn't have trusted Josh Friedman to nuke a bag of microwave popcorn without setting off a second-stage smog alert, let alone go on the air with a breaking news story. He was only a college intern, eager but green. That was before he proved to me how loyal and resourceful he could be. Okay, okay. The kid helped save my butt. Not only did Josh earn a fancy title for his efforts, but I wangled some money out of the boss to actually pay him to be my producer-slash-flunky.

"You're back with Shauna J. Bogart. Before we take your calls, Josh Friedman joins us in the Sacramento Talk Radio newsroom." I flipped the on-air switch to the guest mike and pointed a finger at Josh.

His student voice was rapid but steady. "A spokesman for the Monterey County sheriff has confirmed reports that the television star known as Jasmine has escaped from custody. She was being transported from a routine appearance in the courthouse in downtown Salinas back to the county jail when the escape occurred."

I picked up the remote and flicked the TV monitor to CNN.

Even with the sound off, I could follow the story from the on-screen images: The seventies-era album cover for *Jasmime Soup,* the singer at the peak of her rock diva glory, an exotic nymph in flowing rich hippie garb, surrounded by the symbols of the zodiac. If you listen to oldies radio, you can undoubtedly recite all three verses to her one big Top 40 hit, "Meet Me at the Casbah." Next came footage from her more recent incarnation as a sitcom star, playing the middle-aged earth mother to a Partridge Family–style band. Then Jasmine in handcuffs and jail overalls, defiant in front of the TV cameras. A map of Northern California, blinking buttons to indicate the Monterey Peninsula, scene of the crime, and the county seat of Salinas some twenty miles to the east. The *People* magazine cover—"From Songbird to Jailbird"—and the gritty black-and-white of the tabloid headlines—"Bad Trippin' with Jasmine."

Sex, drugs, and rock 'n' roll. It always sells.

"Repeating our top story, officials in Salinas confirm Jasmine has escaped from custody. Keep it tuned to Sacramento Talk Radio for the latest." Josh pointed, throwing it back to me.

No matter what, stay with the story. If a quarter century of working behind the mike has taught me nothing else, I've learned the importance of never letting anything stand in the way of a breaking news story. That, and never letting callers named for flowers or months get on the air.

"We'll go live to the network as soon as they have new developments," I told my listeners. "In the meantime, we're lining up phoners from Salinas, so don't go away."

WHERE THE HELL IS SALINAS, ANYWAY? My executive producer, tapping a message on the computer linking his call screener booth with the on-air studio.

Jeez, don't they make college students read Steinbeck these days? *East of Eden, Pastures of Heaven?*

SOUTH OF SILICON VALLEY, NORTH OF L.A. THE NATION'S SALAD BOWL. TRY DIRECTORY ASSISTANCE IN 831. I returned the message while keeping my ears tuned to Debbie from Carmichael on Line Two. Debbie claimed to have known Jasmine when she was just plain Cynthia Pepper, a B-plus-average student at El Camino High School.

"She was just the sweetest thing," Debbie said. "There's no way she could have done all those horrible things you media people keep saying she did. Just no way."

"I'm not saying you're wrong," I replied. "And I believe in innocent until proven guilty in a court of law. But you've got to admit it looks bad."

"Who's to say someone else didn't kill Johnny Venture? Jasmine could have just been in the wrong place at the wrong time. How do we know for sure?"

"If she really didn't do it, why break out of jail? Why not wait for the verdict and walk away a free woman?"

The callers pretty much reflected the tabloid court of opinion. Take your pick. Jasmine was a victim of male aggression who finally fought back. Or she was an innocent waif who got into something way over her head. Or a ruthless diva who would stop at nothing to make sure she stayed in the national spotlight. My attention darted from the callers to CNN, the program log, the control board, back to the screener booth. Judging from the body language coming from the other side of the glass—lots of palm slaps to the forehead—things were not going well, telephone-wise, between Sacramento and Salinas.

"No luck?" I asked Josh on the intercom during a commercial break.

"The sheriff's holding a news conference at five, so no one's saying anything 'til then."

"Live at five. How convenient for the TV cameras."

"The AP stringer's in the field and I can't track her down. The local network affiliate's on deadline and won't help."

"You tried the courthouse, of course."

"Can't get through. Every line is busy."

Truth is, it didn't mean squat whether we got anyone from Salinas to agree to talk to us on the air. We could simply have let the network run, any network, and the listeners would have known everything there was to know about Jasmine's jail escape. Or we could have kept reading wire service copy. But a live interview with someone on the scene creates the illusion that our station is one-up on everyone else. Even if all the interviewee is doing is parroting Associated Press copy.

"AP just sent over a longer story," Josh said.

"I'll throw it to you cold coming out of the last spot."

A taped announcement ended with a caution that my actual mileage will vary. I played my theme music, reintroduced the Shauna J. Bogart Show, announced the time and temperature, and let Josh take over.

"The escape apparently took place two hours ago," Josh read into the guest mike. "A van transporting Jasmine and four other female prisoners from the courthouse back to the correction facility was surrounded by armed men. Witnesses say the van was stopped at a traffic signal next to the Salinas rodeo grounds. The men forced the driver out of the van and took control. The van was last seen traveling at high speed on the Highway 101 northbound on-ramp. It was followed by a vehicle described by witnesses as a late seventies Chevy Impala. The other prisoners in the van have been identified as Ofelia Hernandez of King City and Irmalinda Guzman, Marcelina Villareal, and Bobette Dooley of Salinas."

The AP update ended by informing us that Jasmine had been in court earlier in the day for all of five minutes on a reduction-of-bail motion. The DA asked for a continuance, which the judge granted.

Meanwhile, Captain Mikey in the traffic chopper had a particularly juicy tie-up on U.S. 50 to warn us about, complete with alternate routes. That interruption gave me time to dash to my desk and pick up the latest *Broadcasting Yearbook*. I heaved the thick paperback through the door of the call screener booth. "Look up the jazz station in Monterey and see if you can track down Donovan Sinclair."

Josh gave me a quizzical look, but picked up the receiver and began flipping through the pages.

"Make sure he can go on the air with us before the sheriff's news conference," I added through the intercom as I popped the headphones over my ears and adjusted the mike.

Five minutes later, and a full fifteen minutes before the sheriff was due to face the press, Josh flashed a thumbs-up. SINCLAIR'S HOLDING ON THE HOTLINE. WHERE DO YOU KNOW THIS GUY FROM, ANYWAY?

JUST ONE OF THOSE RADIO THINGS.

One of the many things I love about this business is how everyone knows each other in the radio community. Go to any town in America and chances are you'll find a friend, someone you once worked with on the climb up or on the long slide down. Or at least someone who knows the same people you do, and shares your passion for and insider's knowledge of the most intimate of the communications media.

GOOD JOB, I added to my message to Josh.

"In case you've just joined us, repeating the hour's top story, the pop music star known as Jasmine, accused of homicide in the death of an elderly man in a Monterey Peninsula hotel, has escaped from custody," I told my listeners. "The correction facility van carrying Jasmine and four other female prisoners was hijacked by armed men while she was being transported from an appearance at the Monterey County courthouse in Salinas back to the county jail.

"The Monterey County sheriff is holding a news conference at five. Of course, we'll be carrying it live. In the meantime, exclusively for Sacramento Talk Radio, we bring you a live interview with a Monterey County insider, an eyewitness to the local scene."

Well, I didn't actually say he was an eyewitness to the escape, did I?

"This isn't about Jasmine," Sinclair said in a radio-announcer-school baritone after I'd introduced the Monterey disc jockey to my listeners.

"Run that by us again," I said.

"The jailbreak. It doesn't have anything to do with Jasmine. She was just along for the ride."

"What makes you say that?"

"Look at the scenario," Donovan said. "Two of those young ladies in the van had connections with local Latino gangs. The men who surrounded the van have been described by witnesses as Hispanic. They were driving a low-rider vehicle. When this thing shakes out, it'll turn out one of those guys was trying to bust out his girlfriend. Or kidnap some rival's girlfriend. Everyone around here knows this had nothing to do with some out-of-town celebrity suspect."

"No way!" I knew I was gushing, but I couldn't help myself. This was great stuff! I just hoped the hosts at the other local news radio stations were tuned in. Not to mention the news directors of the TV stations and the editorial staff at the *Sacramento Bee.*

"You know, Jasmine wasn't even supposed to be in court today," Donovan continued.

"I thought it was some routine motion for reduction of bail."

"The hearing was calendared for tomorrow. They moved it up at the last minute because the judge had some sort of personal emergency."

I managed to squeeze in one last traffic update before the top of the hour and the start of the sheriff's news conference. Off mike, I told Donovan he'd been terrific. "No one else has the Latino gang angle."

"You're pretty terrific yourself," he replied. "You're the only media person who thought to call a local insider like me instead of dealing with that circus over at the courthouse."

"How do you know all this stuff, anyway? You can tell me and still protect your sources. We're off the air now."

"You know the sheriff? We're real close. In fact, we had a little thing going on a few years ago."

I don't know what I expected from the Monterey County sheriff when the law enforcement officer appeared on the network TV screens at five. Typical small-town cop, I suppose. But the chief law enforcement officer for Monterey County wasn't fat or grizzled, didn't wear a rumpled suit covered with donut crumbs, and didn't speak with a cracker twang.

Sheriff Maria Elena Perez smashed a lot of stereotypes when she made her live, coast-to-coast debut, that's for certain.

"We're following up on several leads linking the hijacking of the correction facility van with Latino gang activity," she told reporters. "One of the prisoners who escaped was a known associate of the leader of a major Salinas street gang."

Thank you, Donovan Sinclair.

I opened the network pot, allowing the satellite feed to air live without interruption, and left the on-air studio for the newsroom, where I could watch four TV monitors instead of just one. ABC, CBS, NBC, and CNN brought me Maria Elena Perez in quadruplet: an unsmiling woman in her fifties wearing a simple dark gray suit, blue silk blouse, masses of black hair shot with gray caught neatly in a silver comb above each ear.

She spoke forthrightly, directly into the cameras. "I pledge the full strength of my department in tracking down and recapturing the escaped inmates, including the suspect known as Jasmine. We take it seriously when a jailbreak happens in Monterey County on my watch."

If she could make good on her pledge, I had an idea we'd be seeing more of Maria Elena Perez on the political scene in the years to come.

Josh Friedman joined me under the bank of TV monitors and handed me a slick four-color magazine. "It just came in today's mail." *Sacramento* magazine, folded open to the "Out and About in Sacramento" section, which had nothing to do with gay nightlife but instead chronicled the capital city's A-list social circuit. Photograph of a frizzy-haired woman in a slinky black dress standing next to a man in a tux. "Sacramento's celebrity couple to watch continues to be Shauna J. Bogart and Pete Kovacs. She's the top-rated afternoon radio talk show host, and he's the Old Sacramento antiques dealer and hot jazz pianist. We caught up with this busy pair at the opening night gala for the State Fair."

I reread the cutline and handed the magazine back to Josh.

Pete Kovacs. He'd called me just before the show, hoping we'd be able to get together this evening. He sounded serious, said he had something "important" to talk to me about, and something "interesting" to show me.

I was pretty sure I knew what Pete Kovacs wanted to talk about. And damned if I knew how I was going to respond.

The networks cut away from the news conference and back to filler material: stand-ups in front of the courthouse and the jail, maps with dotted lines showing the getaway route, more Jasmine career highlights. ABC had dug up footage from a headline performance at the Fillmore. Jasmine crooning the opening lines to "Meet Me at the Casbah."

Meet me at the casbah
The incense will light our way
It's twelve steps over a light wave
Then mellow out in a bright cave. . . .

Never did figure out what all that was supposed to mean.

I continued to stare at the bank of TV monitors and wondered, not for the first time, why none of the attention was focused on a meek man with a white beard, a quiet little fellow you'd never notice. Unless you listened to him, of course, and entered his private world. The man Jasmine was accused of smothering with a pillow in a cabin in a Monterey motor court.

An over-the-hill DJ named Johnny Venture.

2

I SLASHED MY SIGNATURE ON THE BOTTOM OF THE PROGRAM LOG and gathered up headphones, show notes, and the news clipping file. The six P.M. network newscast sounder boomed across the airwaves. The Jasmine jail escape was, of course, the lead story. No surprise there. I waited until the network newscaster moved on to the next item—car bombing in the Middle East, no big surprise there either—and allowed myself to savor the memory of my performance for the past three hours, highlights playing back in my mind like a tape slowly unspooling.

". . . Monterey County authorities say they have found a correctional facility van used in today's daring escape of television star Jasmine and four other inmates. It was abandoned next to a lettuce field near the community of Spreckels southeast of Salinas. Still no sign of the suspect. . . ."

". . . Sacramento Talk Radio has located Brianna Burke, who plays the part of the oldest daughter on *Yo Mama!* She has agreed to talk exclusively on the Shauna J. Bogart Show. Ms. Burke, what was Jasmine like to work with on the set? . . ."

". . . Okay, okay. I know Jasmine was overheard by a bunch of people in a hotel lobby telling Johnny Venture that she hoped he'd rot in hell just a few hours before she allegedly killed him. But that doesn't necessarily mean she was threatening him. It could have just been her way of flirting. . . ."

". . . This just in to the Sacramento Talk Radio newsroom. Our sources in Salinas say two of the women who escaped with Jasmine have been apprehended in the parking lot at a Salinas shopping mall. Stay tuned for an exclusive report. . . ."

". . . . Monterey County Sheriff Maria Elena Perez has just confirmed earlier reports that two of the inmates who escaped with Jasmine have been apprehended. We go live to the sheriff's office in Salinas. . . ."

". . . You heard it here first on Sacramento Talk Radio. The Monterey County sheriff has just revealed one of the inmates who escaped with Jasmine has strong ties with the so-called Mexican mafia. Ofelia Hernandez of King City, arrested on a charge of assault and battery, is still at large. So is Bobette Dooley of Salinas, who is facing charges of assault and disturbing the peace. . . ."

I heaved open the soundproof door of the on-air studio and did a little do-si-do around the sports talk guy whose show followed my three hours of airtime. Steve Garland was laden with headphones, notebooks, faxes, news clippings, stats books, and a super-sized bucket of soda from the convenience mart.

"Killer show!" he said to me by way of greeting.

I was in junior high, a gawky loner who spent her after-school hours listening to the radio and rereading back issues of *Mad* magazine, the year "Meet Me at the Casbah" charted as a Hitbound Sound on Top 40 radio. The seductive melody and enigmatic lyrics—what the hell was "twelve steps over a light wave" anyway?—made it one of those tunes that defined an era, just like "Stayin' Alive" time-stamps the disco era of a few years later. Or how all those "Yeah, Yeah, Yeah" Beatles tunes sum up 1964. I actually met Jasmine five or six years after *Jasmine Soup* went platinum. By then, I had managed to parlay my geek girl's knowledge of radio engineering, plus a naturally low-pitched voice and a talent for patter honed after all those countless hours glued to the radio, into a gig as the sole female DJ on the top-rated FM station in San Francisco. Jasmine dropped by the studio to plug the first of her many comeback attempts. I met a lot of stars on their way up and on their way down in those days, and my memories are somewhat vague: a coked-out, overly made-up, steel-edge woman, old before her time. But that description could fit most of the rock 'n' roll chicks from back in the seventies.

Interesting, how people's lives intersect for a moment, a day, or a year, and then take widely divergent paths, like two streams that flow together for a few miles, then split apart, one meandering through sunlit meadows and the other thundering down a rocky precipice. The gawky adolescent staring at the LP cover with its air-brushed photo of the rock star and dreaming of the day when she too would wear velvet, lace, and flowers in her hair and be adored by millions, becomes, in thirty years, the trusted voice of authority, reporting the humiliating downfall of her onetime idol.

My musings came to a halt at the sight of a long-haired man wearing a Boston Celtics sweatshirt sitting on top of my desk, his jeans-clad legs swinging over the side.

"How'd you get in here?" I asked.

"Is that any way for Sacramento's hottest celebrity couple to greet each other?" Pete Kovacs smiled and opened his arms for an embrace.

Pete Kovacs and I had hooked up this past Memorial Day weekend, when we shared a moment of terror on a balcony in Old Sacramento and managed to stop the last remaining family-owned radio station in the Sacramento market from falling into the hands of a big corporate chain. By the time the Fourth of July fireworks had exploded in the sky over Cal Expo, we'd become an item, trading phone calls every evening, spending most weekends together, even exchanging keys to each other's cribs.

Now the Halloween decorations were up in all of the stores, and he was saying he had something "interesting" to show me and something "important" to talk about.

If this "interesting" and "important" thing involved a diamond ring, I had no idea how I would respond.

I mean, I liked the guy. We were of the same mind on all the important stuff: politics (progressive), money (moderate conservatism), kids (he'd been there, done that; if my biological clock was ticking, I couldn't hear it), and pizza (cheese plus one topping, two at the most, and no "garbage," i.e., no pineapple, artichoke hearts, or free-range mesquite-grilled chicken). Our ages were a good matchup, me in my thirties (okay, thirty-nine) and Pete in his mid-forties. We agreed that any *Cheers* rerun with Diane automatically trumped a Rebecca episode, and we didn't snarl at each other over petty annoyances like the toilet seat being left up or down. We had fun hangin' with each other, and, well, we just looked like we belonged together, like that photo in *Sacramento* magazine.

I just wasn't sure if I was ready to commit to the whole marriage *megillah*. We hadn't been together all that long, really. We'd yet to survive the emotional HazMat zone of the Terrible Trio of holidays: Thanksgiving, Christmas, and New Year's Eve. Age and experience had taught me the wisdom of caution when it came to personal relationships. Like the old song says, fools rush in.

And yet . . . he made me feel good. Very, very good.

"Your boss's secretary was just locking up when I pulled into the parking lot," Kovacs said. "She waited and held the door open for me. I think she likes me."

"A woman of excellent taste," I said as I disentangled myself from his hug.

A cardboard file storage container squatted on the desk next to him. Not exactly the blue box from Tiffany that I'd secretly anticipated. "I thought you might find this interesting." Kovacs slid off the desk, dug into the box, and pulled out a bubble-wrapped package. He undid the plastic and let slip out a thin round disc roughly the size of a personal pizza. He held it reverently against the palms of both hands, careful not to let his fingers touch the surface.

"Gee, a 45," I said.

He peered at the words on the label. "The Dee Vines, recorded live at El Jay Records on Stockton Boulevard in 1961."

"Isn't that interesting," I said, trying to sound as if I cared. Sure, I remembered 45 rpm records. Even bought a few as a kid until my allowance grew big enough to cover the cost of LPs. In fact, *Jasmine Soup* was the first thirty-three-and-a-third in my collection.

Kovacs retrieved a cassette tape from the box. "I copied the 'Cruisin' on K Street' 45 onto tape. You've just got to hear this." He placed the cassette in the deck in one of the newsroom's editing stations and pressed the PLAY button. The sounds of four-part harmony crooning about the joys of teenagers with cars and crushes poured from the speaker. I'd not even been born during the doo-wop era, but to my untrained ear, the Dee Vines sounded at least as harmonious as the Platters. I had to admit, "Cruisin' on K Street" boasted cute lyrics and a catchy beat. Like they say, you could dance to it.

"Aren't they just great?" Kovacs said when the last note faded. "The granddaughter of one of the Dee Vines came by the store with this box a couple of weeks ago. She's trying to decide what to do with the old demo tapes and discs her grandpa left her. Is it worth trying to sell them, or should she donate the whole box to the city archives and take the tax write-off?"

"You're asking the wrong person. This is way, way before my time. I never even heard of the Dee Vines or this El Jay recording studio."

"From what the granddaughter told me, El Jay provided an affordable way for local bands, black and white, to make recordings back in the fifties and sixties, when it was possible for a group to actually have a regional hit without being on a major label."

"Yeah, and actually get some airplay on the local radio station," I agreed. I couldn't fault Pete for his intentions. This stuff actually *was* intriguing. But when a gal's expecting a ring—or at least a tennis bracelet—it's a bit of a letdown to be presented with a box full of dusty garage band tapes and discs.

The newsroom was deserted, silent except for the chatter of the police scanners. There was still a chance of turning the situation around. I threaded the fingers of my right hand into Kovacs's left-hand digits. "You said you had something important you wanted to tell me, remember?" I said in a seductive whisper.

"Oh, that." Kovacs didn't look pleased. In fact, he looked like he would have taken a step back, if the heavy wooden desk hadn't blocked his way. "You know that thing we were doing in San Francisco next week?"

"What about it?" I detached my hand, focusing on his use of past tense. *Were?* Yours truly was scheduled to be inducted into the Northern California Broadcast Legends Hall of Fame a week from Friday. Okay, it's not exactly winning a Peabody, but it meant a lot to me to get that kind of recognition from the radio personalities I'd idolized as a child.

"What if I have to cancel? It looks like something might be coming up."

I paused to remind myself that I was no longer fifteen, and this wasn't the Sophomore Sock Hop. "I can't pretend I'm not bummed," I said finally. "But I know you wouldn't bail out on me unless this 'something' really is important."

Kovacs let out a relieved sigh. "I'll make it up to you, I promise."

"I know you will, sweetie. In fact"—I gave him a quick squeeze—"I'll let you start tonight."

I stuffed a couple of press kits that I meant to glance at later into my backpack, grabbed my car keys, made for the door, then stopped midstride. "Damn. Almost forgot to sign off the logs." I did a 180-degree and headed for the on-air studio, Kovacs following.

A foot-wide ditch ran down the middle of the on-air studio. The station had been in shambles for weeks now, ever since the owner decided he finally had enough money in the budget to go digital. It was a development to which I had decidedly mixed feelings. I could well understand the lure of digital: one tiny CD replacing miles of recording tape, laptops taking the place of piles of paper. But I wasn't sure if I was ready to give up tape for good. I already missed records, those magic platters. And turntables, the subtle *thonk* of the needle making first contact with vinyl.

Sometimes, I feel as if I'm the only person left in radio who still knows how to do a slip cue.

I peered into the cavity at a small portion of the miles and miles of cable crisscrossing the floor, walls, and ceiling of the station. There's an old truism in radio about the chief engineer being the one person with job security, because only he (it's almost always a he) knows where all those wires go and how they're hooked up.

Kovacs caught up with me, stopping just short of the abyss. He still carried the cardboard file box, his fingers wrapped into the holes on each side. "Thanks again for being such a good sport," he said as soon as Garland segued into a commercial break and closed the mike.

"I already told you not to worry." I turned my back to him so I could slash my signature onto the transmitter log. "It's no big deal."

"For real?"

I took the box from his hands, placed it on the floor, backed him into a corner, put both hands around his neck, and drew him close. The sports guy held his palm up for silence and flipped a switch. The red on-air light filled the control room with a warm glow.

"For real," I whispered so the mike wouldn't pick up my voice. I gave Kovacs a kiss, long and lingering. My plan was to snatch my stuff and race over to his apartment, where we could start tearing each other's clothes off.

I would have made it, had it not been for the ringing phone.

Not the newsroom hotline, or one of the on-air lines, but the phone on my desk, its line connected to the station switchboard, which had closed down at least an hour ago.

"Yeah?" I said cautiously into the receiver.

"Shauna J. Bogart. This is Shauna J. Bogart?" Male, with an accent that sounded to me like it had originated south of the border.

"Who wants to know?"

"This lady wants to set up a meeting with Shauna J. Bogart."

"Shauna J.'s gone for the day. Try calling back tomorrow during business hours and ask her executive producer to check her calendar. Depending on who this lady is, of course."

"You'll want to meet with her when you know who she is."

"Yeah, well, lots of people want to meet with Shauna J. Bogart. How'd you get through to this number, anyway?"

The caller ignored my last question. "The lady told me to tell you to meet her at the casbah."

3

NO COPS.

Don't they always say that?

I scribbled as many notes as I could on the back of a discarded press release snatched from the pile waiting to be sent to the recycling bin. Intent on not missing a word of the caller's instructions, I actually scrawled NO COPS in all caps next to the instructions about where and when to show up. I folded the paper into quarters and slipped it into my backpack. He'd warned me I couldn't contact the authorities. But he didn't tell me I couldn't talk to Gloria Louise Montalvo.

I told Kovacs I'd meet up with him later, then rendezvoused with Glory Lou at the second-floor food court of Downtown Plaza. A shopping mall wouldn't have been my first pick as a place to meet a pal for dinner, but Glory Lou had insisted on not missing out on a big sale at Lane Bryant. And in defense of the Downtown Plaza food court, the lineup does include a branch of La Bou, a local bakery that makes a fabulous Chinese chicken salad.

"I need your advice," I said to Glory Lou after we'd carried our trays to a table overlooking the ground floor. "Will the station stand behind me if I manage to land an interview with someone who's in trouble with the law, someone on the lam, and I don't let the cops in on it?"

Gloria Louise Montalvo is more to me than just a news director. She's the closest thing I have to a best friend. No one would ever mistake us for sisters, though. Glory Lou is a towering, two-hundred-pound melting pot of ethnicity, while I'm five feet two inches of pure WASP. "Of course we'll back you up, hon," Glory Lou said. "Newspeople always protect their sources. It's a time-honored tradition."

"So I won't go to jail, then."

"I can't promise that. Journalists don't have the same privilege as doctors, lawyers, and the clergy. But we'll do everything we can to defend you, I can promise that." Glory Lou studied me with sharp brown eyes. "Any chance you'd care to share the identity of this fugitive from justice?"

"I'm not supposed to say. But it's big, really big. Someone who will guarantee the station a killer fall ratings book."

"Jasmine?"

"Jeez, keep your voice down." All I needed was some busboy who spends way too much time watching *America's Most Wanted* calling 911.

"Jasmine!" Glory Lou whispered, and reached across the table to squeeze my hand. "Way to go, girlfriend!"

"Yeah, well, I haven't exactly scored an interview with her. But a guy who claims to represent Jasmine says she wants to talk to me. I'm supposed to meet him tomorrow morning at eleven at Casa de Fruta."

"What's that, a bed and breakfast in San Francisco?"

I laughed for the first time that evening. "I keep forgetting, you didn't grow up in California."

We were silent while the busboy stopped at our table to pick up the plastic trays. "No disrespect, but why you?" Glory Lou paused between bites of a barbecued steak sandwich. "I know your show is hot, but wouldn't Jasmine want to tell her story to someone like Connie Chung? Why would she call a local radio talk show host?"

"Maybe she heard the show and liked it. Don't forget, she grew up here in Sacramento." I folded my notes and put them back in my backpack. I didn't really need them any longer, having memorized the date, time, place, and warning about no cops. And the other message I'd carefully jotted in pencil.

She knew Helen Hudson.

"How far away is this place where you're supposedly meeting Jasmine, hon?"

"At least a two-hour drive. A schlep, for sure."

"We'll have to get an early start, then."

"What's this 'we' business?"

"Lordy, you don't think I'm going to let you do this alone, do you?"

I nibbled on snow peas and grilled chicken and gazed over the food court railing at the mega-sized cartoon characters in front of the Warner Brothers store on the ground floor. I wasn't sure how I felt about her offer—or insistence—on coming along on the trip to Casa de Fruta. But I definitely trusted her when it came to matters of the heart. So I told her about Pete Kovacs, and his bailing out with only a vague reason on our date for the Broadcast Legends Hall of Fame ceremony, and the cardboard file box full of tapes and discs from some old recording studio. Like I said, when it comes to the important stuff, Glory Lou and I are tuned to the same frequency.

Glory Lou nodded slowly. "I think you handled it just right. You kept your dignity and let him think he's maintaining his independence. That's important to a man."

"I just wonder what this 'something' is that's come up all of a sudden."

"Sounds to me like he's lucked into something important with these old tapes, something that could really put his store on the map, just like the ratings are important to your career."

"Oh, well, it's not like this is the first time I will have gone stag to a radio industry event. I'll probably have more fun on my own."

Glory Lou reached across the table, helped herself to a snow pea I hadn't touched, and daintily crunched it between her teeth. "How about turning this into a winning situation for both of you?" she said when she'd swallowed. "Like you could book yourself for a whole weekend in San Francisco. Maybe Pete can meet up with you on Saturday night."

"Now why didn't I think of that?" I couldn't wait to finish dinner and race over to Pete's store in Old Sacramento and share the plan with him.

Glory Lou rose, slung a black leather laptop carrier over one shoulder, and picked up a shopping bag with the other. I hitched up my backpack and followed her to the escalator. She turned to look at me as we rode down to the ground floor. "As I live and breathe, it's never a dull moment in the news business. I have a feeling Jasmine is going to end up getting as much ink and airplay as O.J. Maybe even more."

"I think it's sort of sad," I said. "Here she's this washed-up has-been playing county fairs, Indian casinos, and seedy nightclubs, and then next thing you know, she lands the lead role on a summer replacement sitcom that turns out to be a huge hit. The network is all set to bring it back with new episodes in the midwinter season. Then this happens."

"Really. I wonder what will happen to *Yo Mama!* now." Glory Lou stepped off the escalator and strode in the direction of the elevators leading to the subterranean parking garage.

"I'm sure they've already written Jasmine out of the plot. Her career is finished, that's for certain. I mean, look at poor Tommy Chong, fired from *That 70s Show,* and all he did was sell glass bongs on the Internet."

"I guess Jasmine will go down in show biz history as just another one-hit wonder."

Just another one-hit wonder?

Glory Lou was only about eight years younger than I, but that was enough. Her childhood cultural icons were MTV, *Dynasty,* big hair, padded shoulders, and Molly Ringwald movies. She just didn't get the stars and the fads of those of us who went through high school in the seventies, just like I don't understand the Baby Boomers and their obsession with the Kennedy assassination, Woodstock, Vietnam, and psychedelic drugs.

Just another one-hit wonder!

It's like if Paul McCartney had recorded only "Yesterday," if the only tune Bing Crosby ever crooned was "White Christmas," if Patsy Cline had stopped with "Crazy" and never sung another note, wouldn't that achievement alone be worthy of pop culture immortality?

For us children of the seventies, "Meet Me at the Casbah" had the same grip on our collective heart.

Imitation gaslights cast circles of yellow over the darkened wooden sidewalks and western-movie-style storefronts of Old Sacramento. The tourist season had ended weeks ago, and the capital city's historic district, eight blocks sliced away from the rest of the city by Interstate 5, was practically deserted. Kovacs often shut his store early on slow nights in the off-season. But even if I found the "Closed" sign faceup at Retro Alley, I could still find Pete. He lived above the store.

The "Open" sign still faced the sidewalk. I peaked through the front window, where Jetsons-style lettering proclaimed:

RETRO ALLEY

Cool Stuff from the '50s '60s '70s
R. Peter Kovacs, Prop.

In honor of the season, a poster in the window announced a twenty percent discount on all Major League baseball memorabilia.

R. Peter Kovacs, Prop., leaned against a glass-topped sales counter. A cardboard box sat on top of the counter. I recognized the file box, or its twin, that he'd brought to the station earlier that evening. On the customer side, I spied the back of a female figure, long, sleek platinum hair, leopard-print sandals, white T-shirt cropped just below her bra strap, hip-hugging jeans so tight they could have been applied with an airbrush, bare midriff in between. A tanned and taut midriff. From the back view, I couldn't tell for sure, but I would have laid odds she had a pierced belly button. I would have, if I looked that tight.

I slipped into the store and ducked behind a circular rack holding vintage fifties bowling shirts just in time to hear the customer coo, "So this will be our little secret, then."

"You have my word I will treat this matter with absolute discretion," Kovacs replied.

"You're sweet. So we're on, then, a week from Friday."

Friday of next week! So this person—this Britney wannabe—was the "something" that came up preventing Kovacs from being by my side at the Broadcast Legends Hall of Fame ceremony.

Miss Bootylicious turned and catwalked out of the store. Yep, a tiny silver hoop dangled from her perfect little "innie" navel.

I strolled to the spot where she had stood next to the counter and began drawing circles on the glass surface with my right forefinger. "She was cute. If you go for that type, that is."

"You know my type," Pete said with a wicked grin. "I go for the brainy ones, especially the ones with a smart mouth as part of the package."

"Want to close early and open the package right now?"

His smile sagged. "Can't. There's a busload of spouses from the Bar Association conference due to arrive in Old Sacramento any second now. They've got credit cards, they're bored, just ripe for a little retail therapy."

"Maybe later, then."

· · ·

My apartment is only a ten-minute walk from Old Sacramento, but it hurtled me from the Old West into the dawn of the twenty-first century. More residential hotel than apartment complex, Capitol Square caters to the state government crowd: lobbyists, journalists, and more than a few officeholders. People with real homes somewhere else who need a furnished pad on a weekly or monthly basis.

Perfect for a radio gypsy.

I popped open a can of kitty tuna for Bialystock. Yeah, I was turning into one of those pathetic single gals with her cat. I fixed myself a gin and tonic and opened the sliding glass door leading to the balcony, letting in the blessedly cool breeze from the Delta. October is one of the few livable months in Sacramento, a break between the searing heat of summer and the onset of winter, when a thick mat of tule fog keeps the Central Valley in a ghostly, bone-chilling grip for weeks at a time. I seated myself at the glass-topped dining table that came with the place, took a long slug from my drink, and pried open the lid of an old cookie tin bearing a gaudy painting of a parrot. Helen Hudson used to store her costume jewelry in the tin. I use it for odds and ends that aren't quite important enough for my safe-deposit box but deserve to be stored someplace special.

Underneath the last letter my father ever wrote to me, a McGovern/Eagleton campaign button, and a roach clip, I found what I was looking for. A radio station Top 40 survey, dated August 29, 1974, and bearing the autographs of the station's talent lineup. I held the brittle five-by-seven tan sheet and studied the black-and-white thumbnail photos of the disc jockeys. I could still recall the day I collected those signatures, how thrilled I was to actually meet the voices I listened to on the radio every day.

Johnny Venture, seven to midnight.

The almost forgotten victim in the Jasmine case.

The man with the blow-dried hair in the Groovy Guys blazer bore little resemblance to the grizzled fellow whose picture was appearing in all the tabloids. But then, I'm not looking a lot like my high school yearbook picture these days either.

I took another stiff swallow and tried to imagine the scene, pieced together from police reports and eyewitness accounts.

Jasmine had traveled by car from her home in Santa Monica to Monterey the third weekend in September on her way to a concert, the first in a national tour with the *Yo Mama!* cast, at the San Jose Arena the following Tuesday. She'd decided to treat herself to a leisurely drive up the coast and a weekend relaxing in the coastal resort community before throwing herself into the rigors of a road tour. Johnny Venture, meanwhile, was in Monterey the very same weekend attending a quarterly board meeting of the Northern California Broadcast Legends. Both had ended up in the same quaint motor court on the edge of the downtown district. At least a half dozen guests in the lobby witnessed Jasmine chewing out Johnny Venture, screeching that she hoped he would "rot in hell."

The following morning, Johnny Venture lay dead in his bed, suffocated with a pillow. Jasmine was found passed out on the floor of the same cabin. She clutched the pillow in the manicured and beringed fingers of both hands.

I placed the Top 40 survey back into the tin, snapped the lid shut, and looked out the window across I-5 to the flickering lights of Old Sacramento. I knew from this distance I couldn't pick out the precise windows of Kovacs's building, but it was somehow comforting to imagine that I could. And that maybe, just maybe, he was peering out his window, squinting to pick up the light coming from my apartment.

I went back inside, flopped on the couch, turned on the TV, and flicked the remote. Larry King interviewing the Monterey County sheriff. A VH1 retrospective of Jasmine's career, cobbled together from a "divas of rock" special that I recalled from a few months back, plus footage from *Yo Mama!* A Channel 3 tease promising, "Details at eleven on the daring jailbreak by a pop music legend."

The local PBS station was in the middle of yet another pledge drive. I let my attention linger for a few moments on the fellow who hosted all the local beg-a-thons. He had a mellow voice, a full head of silver hair, and a lean body that looked as if he did a lot of yoga.

Cute, if you go for those earnest, scholarly types. He never introduced himself, so I always thought of him simply as Pledge Guy. "Call now with your one-hundred-dollar pledge," Pledge Guy told me, "and as your gift we'll send you *The Magic of Menopause* video and workbook."

I picked up the remote and hit the OFF button, pulled on a zippered sweatshirt, strapped on my Tevas, and hiked back to Old Sacramento.

Light poured from the open front door of Retro Alley, the only shop still illuminated this late in the evening. Two men stood in front of the door. I immediately recognized Pete Kovacs. As I drew closer on the nearly deserted street, I could make out the deep blue gleaming brass and polished leather of a Sacramento PeeDee uniform.

I hovered on the deserted wooden sidewalk, keeping my distance until I could figure out what was going on.

It didn't take long.

Chunks of glass sparkled in the glow of the street lamp on the sidewalk in front of Kovacs's store. More jagged shards of glass surrounded a melon-sized hole in the window, destroying the lettering announcing the location of R. Peter Kovacs, Prop. The poster advertising the sale on baseball memorabilia dangled from one corner of the shattered glass.

The only thing I couldn't tell for sure was whether the window had been broken accidentally or on purpose.

4

MY VINTAGE DATSUN 240Z CARRIED ME WEST ON HIGHWAY 152, away from the vast flatness of the Central Valley into the soft golden brown folds of the Coast Range. To my rendezvous with the man who claimed he could get me an interview with Jasmine, who allegedly had information about Helen Hudson.

My mother.

The gentle hills gave way to rocky outcroppings as the Z-car neared the summit of Pacheco Pass. The needle on the temperature gauge barely passed the midway point as my yellow sports car swooshed around an SUV still bearing the paper dealer tags. Not bad for a car that rolled off the assembly line about the same time I was signing up for my learner's permit.

Almost two hours from home and I could still pick up my station through a filter of high-pitched static on the Z-car's factory-issue AM radio. Normally on the open highway, I'd hook myself up to my Walkman—the CHP be damned—and crank up some cookin' road music, the Stones, Steely Dan, and Jimmy Buffett. But I didn't want to miss the latest headlines.

"The pop music star known as Jasmine is still at large," the network announcer told me, his voice zapping in and out as I passed under a set of power lines. "So are two of the other prisoners who escaped with her, Ofelia Hernandez of King City and Bobette Dooley of Salinas."

Through the rearview mirror I spotted Glory Lou's blue Camry a discreet two car lengths back just as I crossed the Merced/San Benito County line and cleared the summit. Barren gray rocks jutted from either side of the highway while a pair of hawks patrolled overhead in the October sunshine. Pacheco Pass is supposedly haunted by the ghosts of wayfarers killed by Mexican bandits back in the Zorro era. Personally, I figure if there are any screams to be heard or apparitions to be seen, they're of more recent vintage. Until the four-lane highway went in about ten years ago, Pacheco Pass, the only major route from the coast to the Central Valley between San Francisco and L.A., was one of California's most notorious Blood Alleys.

The new freeway bypassed Casa de Fruta, but CalTrans had been kind enough to build an exit for the venerable roadside attraction. A half dozen or so low wooden buildings squatted on the south side of the old two-laner, rechristened the Casa de Fruta Parkway. Business appeared brisk, Casa de Fruta being the only pit stop between I-5 and Highway 101, and I had to circle the parking lot twice before I found a shady spot. I killed the ignition just before the eleven A.M. network newscast kicked in on the car radio. Glory Lou's Camry pulled up just as I finished locking the Z-car.

I had no idea who I was looking for, although it was a fair bet, judging from his accent, he wouldn't turn out to be blond. Nor did I know where I was supposed to find him. The kiddie train ride? The coffee shop? The petting zoo? The rest rooms? God, I hoped not the last.

I had just started to inspect a pile of Halloween pumpkins at the front of the original produce stand that had spawned the train ride, coffee shop, et al., when someone grabbed my right arm.

"Don't say anything. Smile and pretend we know each other."

I pasted a phony grin on my face and studied my captor. Yeah, right. Like a white chick who's pushing forty is going to hang with a twenty-something homey. He wore khaki pants with pressed pleats, canvas shoes with intricately looped laces, and a black T-shirt bearing a full-color rendering of Our Lady of Guadalupe. Two teardrops were tattooed at the outer corner of his right eye. Symbolizing what? I wondered. Two years in prison? Two relatives killed in drive-by shootings?

"Who the hell are you?" I said softly as I hefted a pumpkin. Who knows, it might come in handy as a weapon. "And how did you know what I look like?"

"Shut up. I'm the one who gets to ask the questions. She sent me here to set up a meeting with you."

"Who's she?" I cradled the pumpkin in my arms as if it were a plump, well-behaved baby. Out of the corner of one eye I spotted Glory Lou pretending to inspect a gift basket filled with dried apricots, dates, and pistachios.

"Don't mess around with me. You know who she is."

"You're one of the guys who hijacked the county jail van, aren't you? What were you trying to do, bust out your girlfriend?"

He grinned, displaying even, white teeth from behind a wispy mustache that appeared as if it had been trimmed with pinking shears. "No prison walls are strong enough to capture our love."

Looked like I made the right move to appeal to his romantic side.

"And you-know-who was just along for the ride," I said. I tried to ignore Glory Lou as she peeked at us from behind an unfolded road map.

"She is a gift sent from the saints to bring us together. Love as true as ours will not stay behind bars."

Jeez, who comes up with this guy's lines? Some greeting card copywriter who overdosed on Godiva chocolates? "You won't even tell me your name. Why should I trust you?" I said.

"She told me to give you this."

Two Teardrops reached into his back pocket and handed me a sheet of white notepaper. I balanced the pumpkin in the crook of one arm so I could use both hands to unfold the five-by-seven page. A line drawing of a chubby angel filled the upper left corner. In the center, in strong forward-slanted letters, someone had penned one line in blue ballpoint ink. *Helen Hudson taught me everything I know.*

I nodded slowly and slid the note into my jeans pocket. "Let's go. Where is she, anyway?"

"Not so fast. Today was a test, to see if you could be trusted not to bring the cops. Tomorrow morning at eleven, at the factory outlets in Gilroy."

"That place is huge. How will I find you?"

Two Teardrops named a fast-food restaurant, then lunged through a hanging display of garlic braids, grabbing both my arms. I almost dropped the pumpkin. His face was so close to mine, the fruity-sweet scent of his cologne overpowered the odor of the garlic braids. "Next time, leave your fat friend at home."

"As I live and breathe, you're really serious about this," Glory Lou said. She leaned against the driver's-side door of the Camry, while I sat on the curb next to the Z-car at the rest stop back on I-5, where we'd agreed to regroup after my encounter at Casa de Fruta. "You're really going to go off with some gangster who may or may not be able to set you up with an interview with Jasmine."

"Lots of kids dress like he does." I almost had to shout to be heard over the thunder of big rigs and RVs on the interstate. "It doesn't necessarily mean he's part of a gang."

Yeah, right. Glory Lou didn't need to say it. I could see it in the smirk that crossed her face. "What kind of proof do you have that this upstanding young man really has access to Jasmine?" she said.

Helen Hudson taught me everything I know.

"He struck me as sincere, and the type who might hijack a van to bust out his girlfriend."

Glory Lou just gave me that "yeah, right" frown again.

"He's smart too. I mean, he figured out how to get through to my private line, after the switchboard was closed. I don't give out that number to anyone." Except Pete Kovacs, of course.

"T.R.'s not going to like it if you miss the show tomorrow." T. R. O'Brien was the owner of the radio station. My boss.

"He'll chill when he finds out what I've got. An exclusive interview with America's Most Wanted will guarantee us a killer fall ratings book, for sure."

I rose, stretched, and fished the keys out of my pants pocket. "One more thing," I said to Glory Lou. "When we get back to Sacramento, how much trouble would it be for you to check the police blotter for me?"

"Depends on what I'm looking for."

"Just a minor incident last night, I'd say around ten, in the nine hundred block of Second Street."

"That's Old Sacramento. In fact"—her voice took on a smug, know-it-all tone—"I'd say that sounds like the location of your sweetie's store."

"Just see what you can find out, okay?"

I must have sounded tense, because Glory Lou dropped the cutesy I've-got-a-secret attitude and became all business. "I'll do my best, hon."

I balanced a stack of a dozen or so "carts"—tape cartridges containing the sound effects, jingles, and sound bites I planned to use on my show—and navigated carefully from my desk to the control room. In another week or so, whenever engineering got finished installing all that new digital equipment, carts would go the way of the eight-track tapes they resembled. Carts, when they were first introduced some thirty years ago, were supposed to free us from mishaps caused by skipping records. But they had an interesting habit of jamming, misfiring, or simply devouring yards of tape. They tell us digital will liberate us from such annoyances. I can't wait for the first time the hard drive crashes.

"Is the gray-haired ponytail dropping by the station again tonight?" The stocky figure of Steve Garland, a yellow and brown bag clutched in one hand, blocked my path into the control room.

"Who?"

"You know. Old guys who insist on wearing their hair long, like they're still at Woodstock. Gray-haired ponytails. Your boyfriend."

"Oh, him." If Pete Kovacs harbored any secret desires, it was to be pounding out stride piano in a dimly lit, smoke-shrouded nightclub in Harlem in the twenties, not strutting around the Woodstock stage with Jimi Hendrix. "Why do you ask?"

Garland stuck his paw into the bag of peanut M&M's. "He and I had a little wager going over last night's game. He owes me twenty bucks. I warned him Boston's pitching wouldn't last, but would he listen?"

"Yeah, well, try calling him at the store."

"I did. No one picked up the phone."

The sportscaster held open the door to the control room for me, so that I wouldn't dump the precariously balanced pile of tape cartridges. "Watch your step," he said between candied crunches. "Engineering's still got the floor all torn up in there."

Glory Lou entered the control room at the start of the five o'clock network newscast. "Looks like your honey was the victim of a bit of misdemeanor vandalism, that's all," she said. She paused to consult scribbled notes in a spiral notebook. "Some kid tossed a rock through the window of Retro Alley just before nine last night."

"Is that all? I'm surprised the cops even showed up."

"They keep a pretty close eye on Old Sacramento. You know, make sure the tourists feel safe."

"Any idea who did it? Or why?"

"Probably just teenage vandals. Nothing had been taken and no one was hurt. His insurance will undoubtedly cover the cost of the window."

As soon as I said my good-byes to the listeners an hour later, I dashed over to Old Sacramento, to a familiar store in the nine hundred block of Second Street. A sheet of plywood had been nailed up to cover the broken window. I pushed open the door to the store and marched up to the counter.

A woman wearing a purple pantsuit, cat's-eye reading glasses, and sporting a mop of tight gray curls looked up from a computer monitor behind the counter. Penny Romswinkel, Kovacs's bookkeeper and all-around assistant.

"He's not around," she said before I could open my mouth to speak.

"Know where I could find him?"

She shook her head. "He packed an overnight bag and left around noon in his van. No, he didn't say where he was going. Just asked me to mind the store for the rest of the day today, tomorrow, and possibly the rest of the week." Mrs. Romswinkel tapped the tip of a pencil against the desktop.

I leaned against the glass counter and digested this information. So Kovacs wasn't just taking the evening off to jam with his band. He'd split, left town, vamoosed. Without telling me.

A rock, light gray, egg-shaped, worn smooth by centuries of caressing by the currents of the American River, not much bigger than a baseball, sat on top of the heavy wooden desk next to the computer. "Is that Exhibit A?" I asked, indicating the rock.

"I'm afraid so." Mrs. Romswinkel rose from the desk and faced me from across the counter. "Just between us, I'm sure this business with the broken window is why Pete decided to disappear for a few days. He's been under a lot of pressure lately, and this was just the last straw."

5

THE DAY PROMISED TO END WITH ME EITHER BEING ON TELEVISION, in jail, or running for my life.

I didn't have a thing to wear.

One of the many things I love about radio is that it doesn't matter what you look like. During Sacramento's five-month summer season, I usually wear loose gauze skirts in an ethnic print, a T-shirt, and my trusty Teva sandals. If I'm having a good day, the T will even color-coordinate with the skirt. In the winter, I bundle up in jeans, pullover sweaters, and UGG boots, the name of which pretty much sums up my take on Sacramento's climate.

Which leaves a spring season of roughly two and a half months and a six-week-long fall when you can dress in what would be considered normal, everyday attire in more civilized climes.

Mid-October is still shorts season in Sacramento, but for all I knew, Jasmine could be holed up in some beach shack in Monterey, where if the temperature gets above seventy degrees, they call it a heat wave. Bare thighs mottled with goose bumps never looked particularly fetching on television. Jeans? Don't they say not to wear jeans on prison visits, for fear of being mistaken for an inmate? Forget jeans.

I finally settled on a pair of navy canvas slacks topped with a red-and-white-striped cotton knit top. A nice patriotic touch, should I end up on the six o'clock news. And the dark slacks should have a slenderizing effect. In the back of my closet I unearthed a pair of dressy black leather flats that, I hoped, wouldn't slow me down too much if I had to make a run for it. I slipped a new notebook, two pens, and the usual girl stuff, lip gloss, mascara, and hairspray, into my backpack. You know, in case the TV people showed up.

After adding an extra helping of kibble into Bialy's dish, I snatched the keys to the Z-car from their usual hiding place underneath the front section of the latest *Sacramento Bee* ("Search Continues for Jasmine" above the fold on the first page) on the dining table. I gave the cat one last scratch behind the ears, double-checked the deadbolt on the front door, and emerged in the early morning sunshine for my date with Two Teardrops at the factory outlets in Gilroy.

This time, he'd brought a companion. The friend was dressed in identical gangbanger attire, but while Two Teardrops was slender and almost waiflike, the new guy had a build hefty enough to qualify for the security staff at a Stones concert. His complexion was in desperate need of the services of a good dermatologist, which probably explained the absence of tattoos on his face. Too bumpy.

No fair, I thought. Two Teardrops gets to bring a friend, but I have to leave Glory Lou at home.

We stood in front of a Pontiac Catalina. The land yacht looked like it might have started life some shade of blue, but decades of sun, plus generous applications of Bondo, had turned the color into a mottled gray. The new guy popped the trunk lid. "Get in."

It looked like the kind of place where a family of banana slugs would feel right at home. A dank, loamy smell arose from a pile of something soft and brown—potting soil?—in one corner. A ratty yellow blanket with a crusted reddish stain along one edge covered most of the spare tire. An empty bottle of Jose Cuervo sat on top of a set of snow chains, and a pair of crumpled boxer shorts snuggled next to the chains.

"Forget it." Just looking into that trunk and inhaling, I probably needed a tetanus shot. "I'm not getting in there, no way."

Two Teardrops gave his pal a "see, I told you so" look.

The new guy said nothing, just tried to grab my tape deck from my shoulder strap and started pushing me toward the gaping maw of the Catalina, like he was in the SLA and I was Patty Hearst.

I yanked the tape recorder back with a lurch. "How am I supposed to interview Jasmine without the tools of the trade? The tape deck stays with me. And you're not putting me in the trunk, no way." I gestured toward the adjoining parking slots, where two nearly identical SUVs had just pulled up and disgorged a pair of mothers and their toddlers. "Like you really think you can force me into that trunk without someone noticing and calling the cops."

I was gambling on the other customers being willing to get involved, assuming I could distract them from their visions of jumbo burgers and supersized sodas long enough to pay attention to my plight. In the distance, the traffic on Highway 101 kept up a steady roar, while closer a tinny voice asked if there would be any fries with that order.

My two new male friends looked at each other and shrugged. I could almost see the mental process at work.

"Why don't you blindfold me and put me in the backseat," I said. "I promise I won't look."

The two conversed in Spanish while I watched a tour bus pull up to the discount panty hose place. Two Teardrops turned to me and nodded.

"One more thing," I said. "I've been on the road for three hours. We're not leaving until I visit the john." I had an idea it was going to be a long ride to Grandma's, and Daddy wasn't going to stop the car until we got there.

. . .

A sign next to the mirror in the fast-food restaurant's ladies' room urged me to *lave sus manos* before returning to work. I dutifully wiggled my fingers under the running water just as the two young mothers from the SUVs in the parking lot entered with their toddlers. The women were dressed in the California suburban mom uniform of athletic shoes, synthetic bicycle shorts, and oversize designer T-shirts.

I balanced the tape deck on one arm and pulled a paper towel from the dispenser as I watched the moms trundle their little boys into the side-by-side stalls. What must their lives be like, these stay-at-home moms? Women with the luxury of time to spend an afternoon lunching with a friend and cruising the mall. I pictured an endless round of Gymboree and pediatrician's appointments, and, later on, trips to Little League games and the orthodontist. Sometimes I wondered if I'd made the right choices in my life, if I was going to be sorry when I was the only lady in the old folks' home with no pictures of great-grandchildren to share. But most times I was glad my life had turned out the way it had, and wouldn't think of trading places with a mom from the 'burbs.

And I was especially glad I'd made it into the ladies' room before they had. Have you ever waited and waited in front of a locked stall, desperately needing to use the facility, listening to someone beg her little tyke to "tinkle for Mommy"?

"Did you hear?" One of the moms said to the other from inside the stall. "The radio was just coming on with a bulletin. They just caught Jasmine."

Oh, hell.

"I heard it too, but it wasn't Jasmine," her friend replied. "You know those Mexican girls who escaped with her? The last one just turned herself in. I heard it on KGO."

Ofelia Hernandez. Almost as bad. Without his ladylove, would Two Teardrops have any interest in helping Jasmine? Or me? Forget help. Would he even care about keeping us alive?

. . .

Two Teardrops and his friend leaned against the driver's door of the Z-car, dashing any thoughts of escape. Oh, well. In for an inch, in for a mile, and all that. Apparently Two Teardrops wasn't aware his girlfriend was back behind bars, so that might buy me some time. Still, I wasn't looking forward to being there when he found out.

"Just one more thing," I said. "If we're going to be traveling companions, let's at least be on a first-name basis. I'm Shauna J." I held out my hand to Two Teardrops.

"Luis," he replied. He jerked a thumb toward his friend. "That's Hector."

Hector's cratered face broke into a grin as he handed me a red bandanna. Just ducky. I'll fit right in with the rest of the gang with my colors when the cops show up.

I slid into the backseat of the Catalina, took one last peek at my watch, and dutifully tied the red bandanna over my eyes. Hector—I think it was his thick fingers—checked the knot and ordered me to lie down on the cracked vinyl.

The Catalina's heavy engine roared to life. We made two lefts, then the car picked up a steady speed, no stops. Got to be 101, and judging from the bumps and curves, we were heading south, out of Silicon Valley and through the Coast Range toward Salinas.

Luis and Hector kept up a steady patter of conversation in Spanish, while the radio blared mariachi music. I didn't think I heard anyone say "Ofelia" either from the front seat or the radio, but it was hard to tell for sure. I promised myself if I got out of this in one piece, I'd call adult ed and sign up for Spanish classes, first thing.

The Catalina slowed, made a gradual right turn, then picked up speed again. Another freeway? We hit a row of several nasty potholes, one of which jarred my head against the door handle. Ouch! At least Johnny Venture got to spend his last hours in bed in a Triple-A-approved motel room, not tossed around as if on a tawdry amusement park ride, with nothing but a Mexican radio station and panicky thoughts for companionship.

Helen Hudson taught me everything I know.

That's why I was putting myself through this.

The car slowed, made a soft right, then two hard rights, a lurching stop, a left turn. A crunch of gravel and the engine died. Four rough hands helped me out of the car. I felt a rush of damp air, a good twenty degrees cooler than the temperature in Gilroy, and smelling of the ocean.

Luis and Hector took me by each arm and led me along what felt like a dirt path and up two low steps. I prayed that Jasmine would be there, wherever we were going, and that we'd get the interview in the can before my two captors found out about Ofelia Hernandez. I clutched the tape deck tighter and made one more request to the gods that watch over media people: Forget the interview. Just get me the hell out of here!

I heard a flimsy door swing shut and inhaled the stale aroma of cigarette smoke, pot, onions, and cheap scented candles.

Someone slipped the blindfold over the top of my head. I took another look at my watch. Forty-five minutes. I was pretty sure Hector and Luis had taken a straight route at a steady sixty-five or so, except maybe right at the end. I also figured they probably threw in an extra turn or two, just to confuse me.

My eyes adjusted to the dim light. I found myself inside a small, shabby trailer. It had the look of a place that had once been tidy, cared for, but was rapidly declining to the point where it'd soon resemble the trunk of the Catalina. Frilly pink curtains were duct-taped around the edges of the window frame, so no one could look in—or out. A carved wooden angel positioned above the door stared disapprovingly at a pile of food-encrusted dishes in the tiny kitchen sink. The minuscule living room was dominated by two posters of more chubby, WASP-ish angels. "This Home Guarded by Angels" and "Angels Fly Because They Take Themselves Lightly." Give me a break.

A young woman sat on the couch watching a rerun of *Columbo* on cable. It didn't appear to be the sort of station that would break in with a news bulletin, unless it was of the natural-disaster, we're-all-going-to-die-now type. She took one look at the three of us and burst into tears.

She was too young and too plump to be the missing TV star. And she was way too blond and pale to be someone named Ofelia Hernandez.

"Where is she?" Hector demanded, grabbing the sobbing woman's arm.

"Hey, keep your hands off my girlfriend!" Luis began tugging on the back of Hector's shirt.

Girlfriend?

Hector backed off, spotted a pile of orange fabric lying on the floor, scooped it up, and waved it under the girl's face. It was a jumpsuit, with black letters stenciled on the front and back: "Monterey County Jail." "Where the hell is she?"

The girl turned a pleading face streaked with blue eye shadow toward Luis. He opened his arms and gathered her up. "Bobette, baby, it's okay. Everything's going to be all right, I promise."

Bobette, baby? Bobette Dooley? The fourth inmate who'd escaped with Jasmine? This was the love of Luis's young life?

She continued to weep. Not so much of a Lucy Ricardo wail as a quivery Laura Petrie snivel. In between sobs, she told the story. "I kept my eyes on Jasmine all the time, just like you said. And I held the gun, just like you showed me."

A gun. Oh, great.

"She said she needed to use the bathroom. She acted weak and said she was sick, dizzy. So I kind of let her lean against me, trying to help, you know? Then all of a sudden, she goes all *Charlie's Angels* on me. She kicked the gun right out of my hand. I didn't know a woman as old as her could kick that hard."

Bobette wiped her face with the sleeve of a commemorative T-shirt from the Salinas Rodeo. "She ordered me to hand over all the cash. Eighty bucks at least. Then she made me find something for her to wear. She took one of Aunt Velma's favorite sweats." She looked nervously at Hector. "She got your pickup."

"You gave her the keys to the four-by-four?" Hector roared, and made another lunge for the hapless Bobette. She threw herself back into Luis's arms and turned up the weeping. Hector tore one of the frilly curtains off the rod to look out into the backyard and prove to himself that his pickup truck was, indeed, missing. I followed his gaze out the window. Gray skies, no trees, just a pair of smoke-stacks on the not-too-distant horizon.

Luis maneuvered Bobette back to the couch. He sat next to her, kissed her hands, stroked her hair, and made lots of "it's okay, baby" noises.

I waited for her latest convulsion of tears to slow to a trickle, then wondered out loud, "What were you in jail for, anyway?"

"Resisting arrest," she said. "Assaulting a police officer. And shoplifting."

"A home pregnancy test kit," Luis added proudly.

"Are you?" I had to ask.

"Two months along," she managed to say before the water-works began flowing again. Hector, meanwhile, kept pacing and muttering about how he couldn't believe how Bobette was so stupid that she'd give up the keys to his pickup.

Jasmine was out there somewhere in a decent set of wheels, new threads, a weapon, cash, and a head start of at least an hour. Not bad.

And what happens to the hostage talk show host?

"We gotta get rid of her," Hector said, jerking his head in my direction.

I took that as my cue to take command of the situation. "Of course you do," I said soothingly to Hector. "But why waste this opportunity? Luis and Bobette, you've got a terrific story to tell. It's got it all: romance, excitement, danger. If you just let me ask you a few questions while the tape is rolling"—I paused to fiddle with the tape deck and microphone—"I'm pretty sure this will make the national network news once I put it out over the air."

The two lovebirds looked at each other, and Bobette squealed with excitement. I could just see her imagination at work, picturing an intimate conversation with Oprah, turning on the tears for Barbara Walters.

Of course they said yes. They always do. No one can stand the thought that they might be missing out on their fifteen minutes of fame.

I let Bobette and Luis ramble on about how they met (in church, Luis was just coming in for mass for someone named Armando, while Bobette was coming out from confession), the dress Bobette made and the limo Luis hired for her senior prom, and how, honest, she'd never done anything like that before when she was busted for shoplifting. I felt as if I'd stumbled onto a community theater production of *West Side Story*.

Luis confirmed what everyone had suspected. The hijacking of the corrections facility van had nothing to do with Jasmine. He was just trying to bust his girlfriend out of the slammer.

"When you realized what a prize you had, you figured you could use Jasmine to your advantage," I prompted.

Luis answered in the affirmative. "We couldn't take her to my house, or to Bobette's. The cops, they were everywhere. Then Bobette remembered her great-aunt Velma and her trailer."

"We got lucky," Bobette said. "Aunt Velma happened to be away on a bus trip to Branson with the ladies from church."

"How convenient for you," I said. "But for real, kidnapping is a serious offense. We're not talking a few months in the county jail here."

"Not the way we had it worked out," Luis said. "See, we made a deal. Jasmine had this thing about talking to you, and only you."

"She kept saying if she could just explain to someone who might understand, then maybe they'd let her go and find the real killer," Bobette put in.

"And she said this talk show host named Shauna J. Bogart in Sacramento was the only person in the media she could trust," Luis finished.

Sure, because Shauna J. Bogart is the only person who cares about a washed-up torch singer named Helen Hudson. Not that I could fathom any connection between my mother and her schmaltzy love songs from the forties and fifties, and a rock diva of a generation later.

"Let me see if I got this right," I said. "The deal was, you'd bring me here to get Jasmine's story. In return, she wouldn't rat you out to the cops."

Luis nodded. "Pretty good plan, wasn't it?"

Sure, until the key player changed the rules and decided to make a run for it.

I asked what Jasmine had done with herself during her two days of captivity. "Listened to the radio, mostly," Bobette replied. An off-brand boom box sat on top of a small bookcase.

How did she act? What was she like? "The bitch wouldn't stop whining. At least it's quieter around here now that she's gone," Hector contributed.

"Did she ask for anything before she left? Road maps? Food? Did she give you any idea where she might be going?"

"It was weird," Bobette said. "Isn't the guy dead already?"

"What are you talking about?"

"She said she was going to go find Johnny Venture."

6

IT WASN'T DIFFICULT TO CONVINCE LUIS TO GIVE ME A RIDE BACK to the fast-food restaurant in Gilroy. "The sooner I can get back to the station and put this tape on the air, the sooner the networks will hear it." I let his imagination fill in the rest.

Bobette decided to come along for the ride. After all, there was no one left for her to guard in the trailer. Last time I saw Hector, he was in the backyard, hot-wiring Aunt Velma's Honda Accord. I let Luis tie the blindfold over my eyes and guide me to the backseat of the Catalina, not letting on that I was positive I knew where I was.

"You should think about visiting Planned Parenthood," I told Bobette as I felt the car pick up speed on Highway 156. Before she could protest, I continued, "They won't force you to have an abortion, I don't care what you've heard. They'll help you even if you decide to keep the baby. You need to get medical care. And for God's sake, lay off the cigarettes and the dope."

I waited for this bit of big-sisterly advice to sink in, then made another appeal to Luis's machismo. "That was pretty clever, how you figured out how to call me on my private line at the station after the switchboard had closed for the night."

"That was easy." I could just picture Luis grinning behind the wispy mustache. "The station has one of those numbers that ends in a bunch of zeros, right?"

"Eight thousand, sure. For the business line."

"And you've got an extension with three numbers, right?"

"Uh-huh." To get through to my desk, you dial the business line that ends in eight thousand and the receptionist comes on the line. You ask for me and she patches you through to my extension. "Only the switchboard was closed, the receptionist had gone home," I reminded Luis.

"Don't need no receptionist," Luis said. "I just dialed your exchange, then eight, and started punching in numbers. Right away, I figured out all the extensions at your place start with a two. I knew if I just kept punching numbers, eventually I'd get your desk."

"Jeez, that must have taken forever!" How many of my co-workers had found mysterious hang-ups on their phones the following morning, I wondered, and how had Luis figured out how to make all those calls without running up a huge long-distance bill? On second thought, I really didn't want to know. Still, it was a handy trick. I wondered if it would work at the White House.

"Nah, it was no big deal," Luis said.

Having run out of conversational gambits with Luis and Bobette, I took to speculating where Jasmine might be. If I were in her situation, I'd head for Santa Cruz. The funky beach and university town is only about a half-hour drive from the trailer and with a large population of surfers, slackers, druggies, and anarchists left over from the sixties, she'd be sure to find refuge. She'd have to trade in Aunt Velma's velour sweats for jeans and a sweater if she was going to blend with the locals, however. Yeah, Santa Cruz definitely bore checking out.

Luis deposited me at the Gilroy factory outlets exactly forty-five minutes after we'd left the trailer. I wished him and Bobette the best.

"Just don't forget, you promised to put us on the radio," he said in return.

The Catalina disappeared back toward the southbound freeway ramp, but not before I made a mental note of the license number. Sure, the plates were probably stolen. But still, you never knew what might come in handy.

"You did what?" The dismay in Josh Friedman's voice cut through the static in the cell phone connection.

"I did what I had to do." I crooked the phone between my left shoulder and ear and steered the Z-car over the top of Pacheco Pass. "Stop wigging out and get Glory Lou for me. The show starts in less than a half hour."

"You're joking, right?" Glory Lou said a few moments later. "Tell me you didn't let the cops in on this."

"Look, I'm not one of those mad dog reporters, okay?" I spent most of my career as a DJ in rock radio, a mere spinner of platters, a purveyor of light chatter. The news was a five-minute break that allowed for a quick dash to the john. I ended up in talk radio when T. R. O'Brien remembered tuning me in, one of a handful of female DJs in the nation, on a regular basis on a wild, anything-goes FM station in San Francisco. Fifteen or so years later, in search of that elusive "compelling" talent for his afternoon slot, he tracked me down at an oldies station in Seattle and talked me into making the switch from music to talk radio. "Shoot, talk radio's just the same as those free-form FM stations back in the seventies, just no records," he told me. "Haven't you always wanted the freedom to say whatever you want?"

T.R. knew my weak spot. The corporate clones had long since sucked all of the creative juice out of FM radio. Reading prescripted liner cards and playing a predetermined list of tunes was about as creatively satisfying as punching out circuit boards or cleaning teeth for a living. So I told T.R. I'd give talk radio a chance, packed up my rain slickers, and followed the U-Haul down I-5 from Seattle to the California state capital.

Like T.R. promised, it wasn't all that difficult to make the transition from music DJ to talk radio host. It's all show business. I've always been grateful to the man who rescued me from ever again having to play "Stairway to Heaven."

But still, I must have missed one of the lectures in Talk Radio 101 because, sorry, Shauna J.'s just not going to risk wearing an orange jumpsuit and choking down watery mashed potatoes off a tin tray just to cover the collective asses of Luis, Bobette, and Hector. Well, Luis and Bobette, maybe. But definitely not Hector.

I told Glory Lou to put Josh back on one of the extensions. "I know a reporter's supposed to always protect her sources," I said to both of them. "But we're talking about aiding and abetting in a felony case. Withholding evidence. Anyway, I didn't give them my name."

I mean, what's the big deal? The Monterey County sheriff would have found out everything the instant I went on the air. At least this way I might score a few brownie points for having notified her before hitting the airwaves. Even if I did do it anonymously. And I had an idea that it might be helpful later on to have a few markers to collect with Sheriff Maria Elena Perez.

"We've got a show to do," I said. "Glory Lou, you host from the control room, play the spots, and do the intros into the stop sets. Josh, get ready to roll the tape. Soon as I get to the truck stop at Santa Nella, I'll find a pay phone with a decent line and start feeding audio. Glory Lou, you stand by to fill."

The two made affirmative answers. "You guys'll have to take it out of delay," I continued as the Z-car sped past the San Luis Reservoir, a vast sheet of gunmetal blue against the brown hills. "I'll take my cues off the radio."

Like most talk stations, our programming isn't "live" in the purest sense of the word. It's automatically taped and delayed for seven seconds, giving us time to bleep out obscenities or, more likely in these PC days, slurs concerning ethnicity or sexual orientation. If we were to keep the station in delay, I'd sound as annoying as those callers who refuse our repeated instructions to "turn down your radio."

"One more thing," I instructed Josh and Glory Lou. "When the people from TV and the newspapers start calling, tell them I'll be available to the media at the station at five-thirty."

"Epic!" Josh said.

"Better yet, call them and let them know."

"Manhunt widens for Jasmine. Authorities say there are no new leads," the network newscaster told me from the car radio just as I exited I-5 and pulled up to a truck stop in Santa Nella. I parked between a humongous RV with a Good Sam Club sticker and a Ryder truck with Utah plates. Something about these places always makes me feel like I should start humming "Six Days on the Road," pepper my talk with Citizens Band radio lingo, and buy a set of Mr. Natural mud flaps. I was just happy to find a pay phone in a real booth with a door that closed. And that didn't reek too badly of cigarette smoke.

After looking around to make sure no one was watching, I placed a collect call to the station, then unscrewed the mouthpiece and attached to it a pair of alligator clips. I plugged the other end of the clips into the tape deck and punched PLAY. With any luck, the station would have a broadcast-quality copy of my interview with Luis and Bobette.

"Got it!" Josh said when the interview ended. "This is sweet."

Sweet, for sure. Josh and Glory Lou played the entire Luis/Bobette interview coming out of the three o'clock network newscast. No new leads in the search for Jasmine? Hah!

Luis described the hijacking of the corrections facility van, and Bobette told how Jasmine fled in Aunt Velma's pantsuit and in Hector's pickup, while I gave a running commentary through the cell phone as I cruised north on I-5. Normally I would have felt like pathetic yuppie scum, driving and talking into one of those things, but today I didn't care. I kept one hand on the steering wheel and the other on the cell as I chatted with my listeners about the initial phone call from Luis, the first meeting at Casa de Fruta, the ride in the Catalina, and the trailer in Castroville.

Shortly after four, the network interrupted with a bulletin. Hector Sandoval, twenty-two, of Salinas, had been captured by the CHP after Aunt Velma's Honda had conked out on Highway 156 only a few miles out of Castroville. When the patrol nabbed Hector, he had the hood up and was fiddling with a busted fan belt at the side of the road.

"CNN's holding on Line Two," Josh said during the next break. "Do you want to go with them next?"

Yeah, right. Like I'm going to tell CNN they'll have to wait their turn behind all my regular callers. CNN! I'm all but hyperventilating. What's next? *Good Morning America, People,* maybe even a mention in the "Street Talk" column in *Radio and Records?* Now that would be sweet, as Josh would say.

I repeated my story for the CNN reporter as I continued to pilot the Z-car on the long, lonely stretches of I-5. I pictured the truckers and the snowbirds in their RVs tuning in and hearing the tale, not realizing the show was unfolding in the low-slung yellow sports car sharing the ribbon of asphalt.

CNN signed off and Glory Lou segued into a report from the traffic chopper. I plugged the cell phone into the battery charger, sat back, and pushed the gas pedal to the floor to pass a pickup truck with an In-N-Out Burger bumper sticker. Someone had taken a pair of scissors and cut the "B" and end "r" from Burger. I laughed out loud and waved at the driver through the rearview window. This could turn out to be one of the greatest days of my career!

The media pack was ready to ambush me the instant I drove into the station parking lot. Now I know what it feels like to be a White House intern. I never even made it into the building, but I did at least manage to maneuver the media beast to the Sacramento Talk Radio sign next to the front door. T.R. O'Brien would be pleased that I managed to get the call letters on nationwide TV.

By this time, I'd told the story so many times I had it down to a script. But the *Sacramento Bee* reporter hit me with the one question for which I had no ready-made answer. "Out of all the hundreds of reporters and talk show hosts, radio and TV and print, that Jasmine could talk to, why did she choose you?"

I gazed into the cluster of cameras, microphones, and notepads writhing before me like a basket of snakes. I knew they wouldn't buy the answer I'd given Glory Lou two nights ago, that Jasmine must have picked up the show during visits to her hometown and liked what she'd heard.

"She and my mother had some connection," I said. "They apparently worked together a number of years ago." That was as far as I was going to take it. Truth was, I didn't know much more than that.

The media pack departed shortly after six. Josh and Glory Lou, who'd been watching from the control room window, greeted me with hugs and cheers as soon as I entered the newsroom. Steve Garland flashed a thumbs-up through the tiny round window in the on-air studio door, and T.R.'s secretary told me the boss wanted me to meet him at the Salt Shaker as soon as I had a chance.

At least two dozen drinking establishments are within staggering distance of the station, but T.R. and his imbibing buddies favored the Salt Shaker. I'm guessing the ambience reminded them of the cocktail lounges of their youth: lavish with mirrors, neon, and crushed velvet. Just imagine it's 1961, and Sinatra is going to come striding through the doors with Angie Dickinson hanging on one arm. Ring-a-ding-ding.

T.R. sat by himself at the bar, his cowboy-booted feet wrapped around the chrome legs of the barstool. Good. I was afraid he might be hanging with the guys from the sales department. Get two or three of them together with their powers of persuasion and relentless chutzpah, and the next thing you know, I'm agreeing to do a live broadcast at the grand opening of a strip mall in Stockton. A TV set positioned above the bar, the sound muted, replayed my impromptu meeting with the media from an hour ago. God, if only I'd had a chance to use some of that makeup I toted around before the cameras pounced. Or at least run a brush through my hair.

T.R.'s leathery face creased into a grin when he saw me in the dim light. "You done great! Killer!"

I ordered a gin and tonic and let T.R. put it on his tab. I swear, before I moved to Sacramento I hardly ever touched the hard stuff. My first month in the California capital, I was roped into being a celebrity judge at a big charity wine tasting. Outdoors, in June, in the middle of the afternoon. At least ninety-five degrees. I'd never been so hungover in my life. Then I remembered the British colonists in India, quaffing their gin and quinine water on the veranda every afternoon. I figured they must have been on to something.

"You were killer," T.R. repeated as he lifted his second scotch and water with his good right hand. The left consisted of a metal hook, the souvenir of a land mine in the Korean War. "In fact, you were so terrific there's a very special lady who'd like to have a little chat with you."

Katie Couric? Diane Sawyer?

"Cool! Who might that be?"

"The Monterey County sheriff."

"Oh."

"Miz Perez called me right after you made that anonymous phone call to the sheriff's department this afternoon from the car."

I set my drink down so hard an ice cube bounced out and landed in my lap. "How'd she figure out it was me so fast?" I brushed the frozen water off my lap and onto the purple carpet.

"They've got some sort of equipment attached to their phone system, traces the numbers of all the incoming calls. Once they had the number of your cell phone, it was easy enough to track the ownership back to the station."

"Damn." Did I feel stupid or what.

"Hey, don't feel bad. You didn't think you could keep the cops out of this, did you?"

"I guess not." I traced my finger around the rim of the glass. "I just didn't think they'd latch on to me this fast."

The TV above the bar had switched from my news conference to a live shot from the trailer in Castroville, now wrapped with yellow crime-scene tape. Not even Aunt Velma's angels could protect the trailer from the mess that Luis, Hector, and Bobette had made, and now the cops.

"Look at it this way. It's a big compliment, in a backhanded way," T.R. said. "That lady sheriff is coming all the way up to Sacramento, just to chew the fat with you and me."

"She's coming here?"

"Tomorrow morning at eight, the Nisenan Club."

We traded theories as to the real reason the Monterey County sheriff felt the sudden urge to spend a Friday morning in the capital city with a local radio talk show host. It was hard not to fear I'd end up in the same cell that once housed Jasmine, charged with aiding and abetting.

"Look on the bright side," T.R. said. "Maybe all she wants is to finagle a guest spot on your show."

Sacramento—San Francisco—L.A.—Monterey—Salinas.

I sat at the dining table and traced the Jasmine saga on an auto club map of the Golden State.

My eyes swept its towns and cities, picking out Santa Cruz at the north end of Monterey Bay, where my hunch told me Jasmine would go if she were on the lam. South of Monterey, in Big Sur, the territory was too sparsely populated, too rugged, to serve as a diva's hideout. After all, we are talking about a gal who undoubtedly can't be separated for too long from her cell phone, her therapist, or her masseuse.

For years, the Sutter Club dominated the power axis of old families and old money in Sacramento. Like many organizations of its type, the Sutter Club, until recently, didn't exactly roll out the welcome mat for prospective members with two X chromosomes or skin of dusky hue. To take up the slack, several newer social clubs popped up in the capital city, the sole criteria for entry being a checkbook fat enough to meet the hefty membership fees. The Nisenan Club—named for one of the indigenous tribes Captain Sutter and his troops managed to subjugate—was one such establishment.

I met T. R. O'Brien at the entrance of a Capitol Mall skyscraper a few minutes before our eight o'clock appointment with the Monterey County sheriff. We rode the elevator to the twentieth floor and emerged in an expansive lobby. Judging from the decorating scheme—light woods, fabrics in peaches, mauves, and aquamarines—the female members of the Nisenan Club were calling the shots. I recognized several works by well-known contemporary artists from the Sacramento area, a Gregory Kondos oil of the Delta and a Robert Arneson sculpture. Before I could explore, the headwaiter whisked us to a table with a jaw-dropping view of the American River, the eastern suburban sprawl, the foothills, and, in the distant horizon, the jagged peaks of the Sierra, tipped in orange by the early morning sun.

Two women and one man stood next to the table. I recognized the woman facing us, even though she wasn't wearing her robes. Minta Patrick-Moore of the Superior Court bench, our sponsor at the Nisenan Club. She introduced her guests, Monterey County Sheriff Maria Elena Perez and a bony, dour-faced man named Oakley Plummer III, chief deputy district attorney for the county of Monterey. "I'll be in the workout room," Patrick-Moore told Perez. "Give me a call if you need anything. And be sure to put everything on my tab."

Sheriff Perez shook my hand and studied me carefully, as if deciding whether I would be a worthy opponent. Or as if she were memorizing details, in case she had to issue an APB later on. Then she smiled, we both did the nice-to-meet-you routine, and let the waiter pull out our chairs and place napkins in our laps.

The sheriff ordered a bowl of fresh fruit, a whole-grain bagel, no schmear, decaf. I should have showed similar caloric restraint, but I hardly ever get invited to high-toned joints like the Nisenan Club. So I ordered eggs Benedict.

I've been to enough restaurant meetings, though, to know how the ritual works. We'd engage in polite small talk until well into the meal. Only then would Monterey County's head law enforcement officer tip her hand as to the real reason she wanted to have breakfast with a local radio personality in a city four hours' drive away. So we exchanged pleasantries about the weather, the merits of various driving routes between Sacramento and the Monterey Peninsula, and shared stories about her onetime squeeze and my old radio pal, Donovan Sinclair.

"I know you're probably wondering what happened to our relationship," Perez said. "The simple fact is, we realized after a few months that we just made much better friends than we did lovers."

The waiter cleared our plates just as I was sopping up the last of the to-die-for Hollandaise sauce. "You've done a remarkable job of investigation," Perez said. "Congratulations."

"Just lucky."

"Luck, plus determination, tenacity, timing, and street smarts. Those are traits I admire in others, and in myself." The sheriff leaned forward and her gaze drilled into mine. "But Jasmine didn't decide she wanted to meet with you just because you're good at what you do."

"It's like I told the media last night," I said, returning her stare. "She and my mother were apparently friends, a long time ago. Way back before I can remember. She trusts me because of that old friendship."

"Tell me about your mother."

I glanced over at T.R., who gave one tiny nod. "She was a nightclub singer, back in the fifties," I said. "Helen Hudson. She put out a few records, played a lot of clubs on the West Coast. You've probably never heard of her."

"Is she still with us?"

"She died when I was twelve."

"I'm so sorry."

"I spent most of my time with my father," I said with a shrug. "I barely knew her, really."

Oakley Plummer, III, who thus far had attacked his Denver omelet in silence, decided this was the moment to jump into the conversation. "We understand a friend of yours might be having a bit of unpleasantness. Owns a store in Old Sacramento."

Why would an assistant deputy DA way down in Monterey even know about an incident of petty vandalism? If he was trying to intimidate me, he picked the wrong person. "What the hell are you talking about?"

"Now, now," Perez said. "We heard about the trouble at his store the other night through our contacts with local law enforcement here in Sacramento. We're concerned, that's all."

Did I sense a game of bad cop/nice cop? Damned if I was going to play along. I took a sip of water, dabbed my lips daintily with the heavy cloth napkin, and fixed my mouth into a smug smile. "Then you should know that the cops think it's just a random act of vandalism. Probably just kids."

"He's been gone for two days now, hasn't he?" Plummer said. "Didn't tell you or his assistant where he was going."

"Like I said before, what the hell are you trying to get at?"

"You're right, the local police surely have the situation well in hand," Perez said. "Our concern is the Jasmine case. The suspect trusts you. She's tried to set up a meeting with you before, and may very well try again."

"She might," I agreed.

"I'd like to propose a little arrangement. You continue your investigation. If Jasmine calls you, or if you discover any other information that may be helpful, you call us first, before it goes on the air."

"And in return, you'll let me have first crack at any information you may uncover."

"No, in return we won't charge you with interfering with an investigation, or aiding and abetting. We won't even charge you with being an accomplice, even though we could and should." This from Plummer, loud enough that several diners at nearby tables turned their heads our way.

Now it was the sheriff's turn to give a smug smile. "I'm sure it won't have to come to that. There's no reason why we can't come to an understanding. You continue your investigation on your own, just as you've been doing. The only difference is, you report to us on a daily basis. As long as we agree our priority is returning Jasmine to custody."

"I'll have to think about it. I mean, I have a three-hour show to do every day and we're in the middle of the fall ratings book." I looked at T.R.

"It's up to you," he said. "Don't worry about the show. We'll cover for you. Whatever you decide to do is fine with me."

I fidgeted and took another sip of water. No matter what, it would be the biggest story of my career. "Newspeople aren't supposed to collaborate with law enforcement," I said, thinking out loud.

"Get real," Plummer said. "For all we know, Deep Throat was an officer with the D.C. cops."

"No one will ever find out I'm feeding tips to you?" I directed my question to Perez, ignoring her partner.

"Never."

I studied T.R.'s impassive face, then returned to Perez. "You've got a deal."

The three of them sighed, letting out air and tension, and relaxed in their chairs. A moment later, I realized I'd done the same.

We discussed details and exchanged private phone numbers. Perez finished her decaf, returned the delicate china cup back to its saucer, then said to me, "Just curious. What do you plan to do first?"

"That's easy. I'm going to do what Jasmine told Bobette Dooley she was going to do just before she took off."

"What's that?"

"I'm going to go find Johnny Venture."

7

I GRABBED THE SHEET OF COPY PAPER JUST AS THE PRINTER SPAT IT out, and clutched it in my left hand. My right hand was wrapped around three audiocassettes containing highlights of the Luis-Bobette interview, my news conference, and the running commentary I'd made from the cell phone as I cruised up I-5 the previous afternoon.

Exclusively on Sacramento Talk Radio . . . the only newsperson in the nation with the inside track to the Jasmine saga . . . don't miss a minute as the drama unfolds . . . no one gives you coverage of today's hottest story like Sacramento Talk Radio . . . the Shauna J. Bogart Show, this afternoon and every weekday afternoon from three to six. . . .

I could just hear it. Our production director has pipes like a young James Earl Jones and would lend the perfect voice of authority to the intro and out cue. I'd written four different versions of the copy, the usual sixty and thirty seconds, plus a fifteen-second drop-in and a two-minute filler piece. Terrific copy, the taped highlights from yesterday's show and sound bites from Luis and Bobette, mixed with sounders and special effects from our digital production library. Now I just needed to get the thing produced and on the air.

The red light blazed above the closed production room door: RECORDING. In other words, KEEP OUT. Nuts. I looked through the round, double-paned window on the door. The production director faced me from behind the controls. Two men and a woman had their backs to me. I recognized the salon-styled hair and the back of an Armani knockoff jacket belonging to one of our sales guys. Double nuts.

I bounced on my toes and waved, trying to get LeVon Rogers's attention. The production director nodded, flicked off the mike switch, automatically dousing the red light, and opened the door an inch.

"I know this is last-minute, and I'm sorry," I whispered. "But it's urgent. I've got to get this promo on the air right away."

"Can it wait another hour or so? We're in the middle of cutting a spot that's got to go on the air tomorrow." He rolled his eyes. I returned a sympathetic look.

If you started a list of thankless jobs in radio, the production director would easily come out tops. Well, maybe he'd have to duke it out for number one billing with the traffic coordinator, the person who puts the daily program logs together and decides when the sponsors' commercials are going to run. The production director is inevitably a former DJ, lured away from the on-air studio by the promise of regular eight-to-five hours, as well as an escape from the tyranny of the ratings book. In exchange, he gets to spend his days toiling to the whims of the sales department. Once in a while, he lands a creative, satisfying project. Like my promo.

The sales guy nudged LeVon Rogers out of the way and stuck his head out the door. "Can't you see we're trying to get a spot on the air?" He was new, Fred something.

"Can't you see we're in the middle of a breaking news story?" I responded.

"Don't you have your own production studio in the newsroom?"

"Yeah, but it's not digital and it doesn't have all the special effects you guys have." And it didn't have LeVon Rogers and his voice of authority.

"Hey, there, little lady. What's the problem?" A cracker accent boomed from the back of the production room. I peered over Fred's shoulder and traced the voice back to a tall, rough-hewn man with a full head of gray hair and a bushy handlebar mustache.

Every city has one. Usually a car dealer, or one of those personal injury lawyers. They insist on voicing their own radio spots and starring in their own TV commercials. By sheer repetition and a large helping of moxie they manage to turn themselves into local celebrities. Lloyd Ellwanger, owner of the Mine Shaft Restaurant chain, was Sacramento's contribution to their ranks.

"Shauna J. Bogart! My favorite talk show host!" Ellwanger bellowed. "Does this mean you're finally consenting to appear in a spot with me?"

I don't do commercial endorsements. I don't need the extra dough that badly, and I figure it weakens my credibility. Course, no one's ever tempted me with really big bucks. But a regional restaurant chain would hardly have that kind of money, so I used the line I generally employ to gently fend off such requests. "Love to, but you'll have to check with my agent." Not that I actually have an agent, but it usually scares them away. And sounds impressive as all get-out.

A woman in a pink designer suit, dripping gold chains and bracelets, brown hair sculpted in a perfect bouffant helmet, elbowed her way to the doorway. "I'm terribly sorry, but we're on a tight schedule." She didn't sound sorry at all. Just abrupt and full of herself. She handed me a business card announcing herself as Cherise Rose, president of Rose and Associates: Advertising-Marketing-Public Relations. It featured, you guessed it, a line drawing of an American Beauty in full bloom.

"Aw, let the little lady come in and do what she needs to do," Ellwanger said. "We just wasted the last two hours. So what if we have to wait a few more minutes? Anyways, I could use a break."

"We wouldn't have wasted all this time if you'd just gone along with my original concept," Rose said. "It's hot, I tell you. Red-hot."

Ellwanger's mustache drooped in a frown. "I thought we already settled that."

"What better way to launch your expansion into Southern California than with a campaign that's sure to create buzz?"

"Nope. Ain't gonna happen."

"Just a few creative differences here," Rogers said. He stretched and rubbed the palms of both hands over the broad expanse of his forehead. "Give us another half hour and we'll have it wrapped up. Your promo is next thing on my list. Promise."

I knew when I was outnumbered and outgunned. Might as well make a graceful exit. "Sure, no problem. Have fun in there, kids, and try not to break anything."

I logged on to one of the newsroom computers and began trolling the sites that feature directories of personalities from radio's other Golden Age, the mid-fifties to the mid-seventies, when the platter chatter really mattered, and a popular disc jockey played second only to God in the influence he had over teenagers' lives. Searched through the 411 about a DJ named Johnny Venture. Clicked through LA Radio People, Boss Radio Forever, Uncle Ricky's Reel Radio, 440: Satisfaction, Radio and Records Online, Corey Dietz's Planet Radio. Plus a Google search, natch.

A half hour later, I studied the notes on Johnny Venture that I'd cobbled together from my Internet research:

Born Anton Greb in 1937 in Modesto, about an hour's drive south of Sacramento in the bottom half of the flat expanse of California's Central Valley. Graduated high school, attended one year at Modesto Junior College, two-year stateside stint in the Army, where he was assigned to the communications shack and got nibbled by the radio bug. First gig, overnights in Fresno, detour to San Luis Obispo on the coast, then in 1964 landed a spot on a Top 40 station in Sacramento, where he first adopted the Johnny Venture moniker. Sacramento lasted until '69, when he took the Johnny Venture shtick to San Francisco, and the girl who would become Shauna J.

Bogart nabbed an autograph during a personal appearance at the Cow Palace auto show.

Fired along with the rest of the air staff in 1978, when Top 40 radio gasped its last breath, a victim of FM and changing musical tastes. In other words, disco. Four years at an ad agency, then reinvented himself as Sebastian Drake and managed to find work at a Big Band/nostalgia station. That lasted until 1994, when the local owners sold out to a conglomerate and the station went satellite. Two years of unemployment, then back home to Modesto to host the morning show for an oldies-but-goodies station. Back to the hyper-personality of Johnny Venture, only this time around, the commercials were for Viagra and bladder control products instead of zit cream.

Then he got elected to the board of the Northern California Broadcast Legends, attended a directors' gathering in Monterey. And met up with a TV star named Jasmine.

I printed out my notes, logged off the computer, and interrupted Glory Lou in her office just as she was sliding a new photograph of one of her innumerable nieces and nephews into a frame shaped like a school bus.

"If I'm going to be spending time in the field, I'm going to need wheels," I said.

She finished pressing down fasteners with perfectly polished nails and looked up. "That antique sports car of yours would hardly be inconspicuous for undercover work," she agreed.

"Plus I really don't want to be cranking up that much mileage. Those two trips to the central coast two days in a row are the most highway driving she's seen in years." I sank into the guest chair and propped my sandaled feet against the side of Glory Lou's imitation oak desk. The news director rarely has clients to impress, so management generally skimps on the decor and saves the good stuff—i.e., the real wood—for the sales department.

Glory Lou carefully positioned the frame in a cluster of similarly displayed photographs of her nieces and nephews on the back wall of her office. "You need something that won't draw attention to yourself, yet something loaded with all the equipment. Take the U.V." She tossed a set of keys toward my outstretched arms.

News departments don't have cars, trucks, vans, or airplanes. They have News Units and News Flights. The van becomes the Incredible Prize Patrol. The latest in our little fleet was a plain white Volvo sedan, void of any station logos or call letters, for use when a low profile was called for, but still equipped with police scanner, two-way radio, tape deck, and cell phone. The Unmarked Vehicle, or U.V.

"Might as well let you have this too." She shoved a plastic card across the desk.

I picked up the card, recognized the logo of a major gas company.

"Lordy, just don't go over the limit or O'Brien will toss me out of this cozy new office for certain," Glory Lou said.

"Johnny Venture was an angel." Sharon Vanderwahl, the program director of the Big Band/nostalgia station he'd worked at in San Francisco, and the first call-in guest on my show. I'd tracked her down by looking up San Francisco radio stations in *Broadcasting Yearbook*. "He was a joy to work with. Always reliable, always delivered the numbers, and always the first to volunteer for whatever charity assignment happened to cross our desk."

"And he was with your station for, what, over fifteen years?"

"Yeah. Hard to believe in this industry, isn't it? It shows you what a talented and terrific guy he really was."

"And you worked with him all that time?"

"Heavens, no. I transferred to San Francisco in 1992, when Amalgamated Broadcasting merged with Federated."

"Still, you're another survivor. Over ten years at one station, that's impressive in this industry."

"Yeah, well, now I'm in charge of the programming for eight Federated stations, and basically it means making sure we're getting all the local sound drops in the right place in the satellite feed." Vanderwahl sounded wistful.

A message from Josh in the call screener's booth scrolled across the control room monitor. BRENDA IN FOLSOM ON LINE FOUR. CLAIMS SHE'S JOHNNY VENTURE'S EX-WIFE.

"For real?" I said after introducing Brenda to the listeners. "You were once married to Johnny Venture?"

"From June to November back in the sixties." The voice was tight, barely controlled anger. "Trust me, the man was no angel."

"How do you mean?"

"It's the usual story. He's the popular radio personality and I'm just a kid hanging around the station. I end up in the family way, and in those days, marriage was the only alternative. Our baby was stillborn"—Brenda paused to compose herself—"and less than a week later, I caught him at the Woodlake Inn, cattin' around with a stewardess."

"Ouch. Still, it was, like, forty years ago."

"Yeah. That's what my therapist keeps telling me."

The next guy on the line called himself Lars from South Natomas. "About that last caller, I don't know where she's coming from."

"In what way?"

"I knew Johnny Venture back in those days. Lots of us did. The Johnny Venture we knew wouldn't have been playin' on that gal's team, if you know what I mean."

I'd been pacing in front of the microphone in the control room, like I usually do. Standing, moving, keeps my energy up and dissipates nervous tension. I stopped midpace to avoid taking a swan dive into the open trench with its tangle of cable. "Are you hinting at what I think you are?" I asked Lars.

"The love that dare not speak its name. Gay. Homosexual. Queer. Fa—"

I slammed my fist against the censor button before Lars could finish the slur I was pretty sure he was about to utter. With my other hand, I signaled a thumbs-up to Josh. This was great radio!

"Who cares whether Johnny Venture liked boys better than girls?" This from Miranda on a cell phone. "I grew up listening to his show back in the sixties and he was dynamite. He was my favorite DJ, me and all the rest of the kids at McClatchy High. I still remember the night he emceed the Halloween dance. I swear, he wasn't coming on to any of the boys—or the girls. He was a professional act all the way."

I fidgeted through a commercial break and a visit with Captain Mikey in the traffic chopper. Josh buzzed me on the intercom. "Some lady named Mrs. Popsicle wants to talk to you off the air. She says it's important."

"Mrs. Romswinkel?"

"Could be."

"Put her through."

"Do you think you could stop by the store after the show?" Pete Kovacs's assistant normally spoke with brassy confidence, but today Penny Romswinkel's voice had a quaver.

"Sure, no problem."

"Could you come over right away? I mean, as soon as you finish?"

"What's up?"

Her voice dropped to a whisper. "There's something I think you should see."

I had just enough time to squeeze in one more call before the six o'clock network newscast heralded the end of my show. "Vance from downtown Sac, you've got forty-five seconds."

"Then I won't waste it." I had no idea who this Vance might be, but I immediately recognized the pipes of someone who'd spent a lot of years in the industry: the deep pitch, the perfect enunciation, the absence of hesitation or stumbling. Most callers panic when you tell them they have less than a minute. Pros know you can pack an amazing amount of fact and opinion into sixty seconds.

"I just thought you should know," Vance from downtown Sac continued.

"Know what?" I prompted.

"This Johnny Venture you've been chatting about all afternoon?"

"Go on." I kept one eye on the second hand as it made its arc to the top of the clock.

"You're talkin' to him."

8

I DRUMMED MY FINGERS AGAINST THE STEERING WHEEL OF THE Volvo, waiting for the light to change at Tenth and I streets. I'd been snared in the final throes of the Friday night commute, a sluggish river of traffic struggling to squeeze its way out of downtown. I willed myself to relax in the bucket seat and not to obsess about Mrs. Romswinkel, and why she wanted me to come by Pete Kovacs's store as soon as I got off the air.

Twenty-five minutes after bolting from the station, I finally eased the U.V. under I-5, out of the downtown jumble of state government high-rises, and into Old Sacramento. The historic district was serene, a welcome oasis after the chaos of downtown in the lull between school field trips and senior citizen bus tours in the daytime and the diners and club-hoppers in the evening. I was lucky enough to snag a parking spot just a block down Second Street from Pete's store, and to find a couple of quarters at the bottom of my backpack to stuff down the throat of the parking meter.

A bell tinkled as I pushed open the door to Retro Alley. Mrs.

Romswinkel looked up from a ledger where she'd been entering figures with a No. 2 pencil, like they'd never invented Quick Books.

"I'm so glad you're here." Mrs. Romswinkel pushed the ledger aside and handed an envelope across the glass counter to me. "This came in today's mail."

A white #10 envelope, addressed simply to Owner, no return address. American flag stamp, local postmark from the previous day.

"Go ahead, look," Mrs. Romswinkel told me.

I pulled up the already-torn flap and slid out a single Polaroid photograph of Pete Kovacs, standing next to his van at a gas station, brown hills in the background, and a green triangle of a highway directional sign on one corner. Ballpoint lettering on the white margin proclaimed: *You can run, but you can't hide.*

I put the Polaroid in the envelope and passed it back to Mrs. Romswinkel. "You'd think whoever sent this might have been able to come up with a threat a little more original."

"I'm afraid it might have some connection to the vandalism the other night." She gave me a worried look. "What do you think?"

"I'd still like to think the vandalism was just kids."

"I suppose you're right. But then, take a look at this." She passed a sheet of business stationery to me. "I found this today when I was going through a stack of Pete's correspondence."

The stationery was thick and creamy, and carried lacy old English lettering announcing the law offices of Gerstl, Gourlay, Karrer, Nowicki and Irwin.

" 'Dear Mister Kovacs,' " I read aloud. " 'You are in possession of a box of material pertaining to the career of a recording group known as the Dee Vines. This box, and the material therein, is the property of our client. We will be sending our paralegal, Ms. Rosenbloom, to your place of business to collect our client's property in the next forty-eight hours. I advise you to cooperate fully to avoid any legal action.' "

The letter was dated two weeks prior and signed by one Alexander Brown-Ward, associate counsel.

"You tried calling the number on the letterhead, of course," I said to Mrs. Romswinkel.

"Of course. A disconnect message."

I studied the law office address on the ornate letterhead. "2801 L Street. Isn't that Sutter's Fort?"

Mrs. Romswinkel snatched the letter back from me and focused her reading glasses on the letterhead. "Well, shoot."

"It would be easy enough for someone to fake something like this on their home computer. All you need is some expensive paper and a laser printer."

"But why? And don't tell me it's just kids." Mrs. Romswinkel's face crumpled and she appeared dangerously close to tears. "He just takes off with no warning, and then there's the rock in the window, and the photograph, and now this. What does he expect me to do?"

"C'mon, why don't you close up early tonight, and I'll buy you a glass of wine."

Fat City always makes me feel as if I've stepped into a Barbary Coast saloon, circa 1906. Lots of stained and beveled glass, Tiffany-style lamps, dark woods, and a bar, so the story goes, imported from Leadville, Colorado. Picture it's the night before the Big One, and Jeannette MacDonald is going to waltz in any minute now and start belting out the chorus to "San Francisco."

The evening was still young enough that Mrs. Romswinkel and I were able to commandeer a table in a quiet corner. I took a sip of white wine and watched the shadows deepen on the Old Sacramento boardwalk. In another couple of weeks, we'd fall back to Standard Time and this was how dark it would be when I got off work. That thought depressed me so much I took another swallow of wine.

"Why do you suppose Pete took off?" I asked Mrs. Romswinkel. "I mean, he comes by the station Monday night to show me this box of old 45s and photographs. I didn't think it was any big deal at the time."

"All I know is, someone related to the owner of the El Jay studio—the granddaughter, I believe—came by the store a couple of weeks ago with that box of old recordings. She wanted to know if Pete would be interested in buying them. He acted like he could take it or leave it, but I could tell he was excited. That finger thing."

"Finger-spitzengefuhl," I said. Pete told me once about a perceptible tingling in the fingers that collectibles dealers instinctively feel when they know they're on to something big. The term originally applied to the discovery of centuries-old books and manuscripts in Europe. But even though Kovacs dealt in mid-twentieth-century collectibles and kitsch, he knew what finger-spitzengefuhl felt like.

If his instincts kicked into high gear over the El Jay stuff, there had to be something way more interesting in that box than just a bunch of dusty old discs and photographs.

"What did this granddaughter look like? Any chance she was young, blond, cute figure, tight jeans?" I hoped I sounded businesslike, and that Mrs. Romswinkel wouldn't catch any hint of jealousy in my voice.

"I never saw her." Mrs. Romswinkel paused to reposition her narrow tortoiseshell glasses on the bridge of her nose. "She came in when I was on my lunch. I just saw how excited Pete was about the stuff in that box. But I think I do know who you're talking about."

"Oh?" God, I hoped I sounded cool.

"The very same afternoon that Pete got the box of tapes, he started making phone calls. About a week later, a young lady that sounds like your description stopped by the store—several times, actually. Most of the time, she had a fellow with her."

"Any idea who they were, or where they were from?"

"All I know is, Pete took off with them at least three times that I can remember, maybe more. They'd disappear for hours, leaving me all alone in the store." She pursed her lips together in the start of a pout.

I reached across the round cocktail table to place my hand over Mrs. Romswinkel's gnarled fingers. "I know he appreciates your loyalty."

"Just good old Penny Romswinkel, that's me."

"He'll make it up to you when he gets back. I'm sure of it."

"I just wish I knew when that's going to be."

The telephone answering machine was blinking in triplicate as I entered my darkened apartment. I groped to punch the PLAY button and felt something warm and furry brush against my ankles. Bialystock, wondering why I waited so long to come home and feed him.

Three messages, all from the same person, all bearing essentially the same message. Normally, I'd wait until the weekend was over to deal with job-related calls. But not when they come from the boss.

"You managed to scoot out of the station mighty fast tonight." T. R. O'Brien's raspy twang picked up on the first ring. In the background, I could hear the yipping of Yorkies and what sounded like a Willie Nelson record.

"Yeah, well, I had things to do." Since when did he turn into a clock-watcher?

"Hey, don't you fret none. I just wanted to pass on a bit of advice about that last caller of yours."

I had to pause for a moment to recall the last listener I'd put on the air. "Vance from downtown Sac? What about him?"

"He's an old pal of mine."

"Really. I just assumed he was another nutcase."

"Vance Ballard. Name ring any bells?"

I carried the cordless phone to the couch and stretched to allow the cat to crawl onto my belly. "Maybe, maybe not. Owns an ad agency here in town, something like that?"

"Recording studio." T.R. paused, and I could hear the click of a lighter and the inhale of smoke. "Been on the local media scene almost as long as I have."

That would have made it at least forty years, almost fifty.

"The point I'm tryin' to make is," T.R. continued, "Vance Ballard could be a crackerjack source of information, not just about

Johnny Venture, but about the whole local music scene. Shoot, he probably knew Jasmine back when she was just a kid named Cynthia Pepper and trying to break into the business."

Normally, I avoid having to do face-to-face meetings with fans, especially those who actually call the show. Too much chance for dashed hopes and disappointment—"You don't look anything like I thought you would"—not to mention the very real possibility the listener could turn out to be certifiably *non compos mentis*. But this Vance Ballard, at least the way T.R. described him, sounded more like a colleague than a fan. "What's his number?" I lifted Bialystock to the floor and rose from the couch in search of a scrap of paper and something to write with.

"Already taken care of. He's expecting you to meet him tomorrow morning at ten at Ballard Productions."

I could have walked the dozen or so blocks from my apartment complex to the address T.R. had given me, but I wanted to get used to driving the Unmarked Vehicle. Like many one-industry towns, Sacramento's downtown district goes into hibernation whenever the factory is closed. Weekends and holidays, or whenever state government takes the day off, the streets are all but deserted, giving me the perfect opportunity to practice driving a vehicle a lot newer, bigger, and higher off the ground than I was accustomed to.

I parked the white Volvo in front of a flat, windowless warehouse and next to a late-model silver Lexus that I assumed belonged to the owner of Ballard Productions. An industrial-strength door sealed the one entrance to the studio. I pushed the intercom button, spoke to a metallic voice, waited for the required electronic belch, and heaved the door open.

I stepped over the threshold and into five decades of Sacramento music history.

Framed posters everywhere: black block type, starbursts, and grainy black-and-white photographs advertising all-but-forgotten

R&B acts of the fifties, the Beach Boys at Memorial Auditorium in 1964, the late sixties "happenings" bursting into color and swirls, the classic Art Nouveau Tower Records calendars from the seventies, fliers for glam eighties rock bands giving way to the gritty grunge of the nineties, boomeranging full circle to Retro, all pinks and aquamarines, daisies, polka dots, and polyester. I even spotted a poster advertising Helen Hudson's appearance at the Blue Door nightclub back in 1963.

"Kinda makes up for not having a view, doesn't it?"

I jerked my vision away from the Tower Records calendar for 1975 and located the owner of the voice in the shadows behind the deserted reception desk.

"Vance Ballard." He stepped forward into the lobby and offered a hand. Around T.R.'s age, I'd say, which would have meant pushing seventy. Tufts of white curls peeked out from under a Greek fisherman's cap that, I was willing to bet, covered a hairless dome. Blue and orange Hawaiian shirt worn on the outside, not quite hiding a small potbelly, khaki slacks, flip-flops.

I returned the hand clasp and gave my name. "Thanks for taking the time to see me on a Saturday, Mr. Ballard. Or should I say, Mr. Venture?"

Ballard snorted a laugh and said I should follow him to his office. Ballard Productions was a virtual duplicate of every radio station I'd ever toiled in, a maze of narrow corridors and tiny rooms with red lights over the doors. Ballard ushered me into a corner office, probably the largest room in the building, and indicated I should sit in a butterfly chair covered in leopard-print fabric.

"Can I get you something to drink? Water? Soda? Juice?" He bent to open a dorm-room refrigerator. Cute tush for an old guy.

"Water's fine."

Ballard took two bottled waters from the fridge, twisted open both caps, and handed one to me. He pulled the handle of a file drawer while I studied walls just as busy as those in the lobby. Mostly framed certificates instead of posters, awards for production work from the Sacramento Ad Club, so numerous the frames overlapped. A half dozen or so gold records were mixed in with the certificates, but either they were too far away for me to make out the lettering, or my eyes were starting to go.

"Handsome devil, wasn't I?" Ballard handed me an eight-by-ten black-and-white photo in a protective plastic sleeve. Skinny young fellow with a butch-waxed pompadour seated in front of a radio mike, one hand on the turntable. "Check out the back."

I flipped the photo over to find a scrap of browned paper under the plastic cover. The *Sacramento Bee* radio listings for a September date in 1958.

"See that?" Ballard said. "Johnny Venture and the Lucky Lager Music Box, eight to midnight? That was me. I was the original Johnny Venture."

I nodded slowly, turning the plastic sleeve from one side to the other. Johnny Venture was a saint. The devil incarnate. Gay. Straight. Six feet under. Sitting right in front of me.

"There were a whole bunch of Johnny Ventures, weren't there?" I said. "When one Johnny Venture would leave the station or get fired, the next guy who came along would become the new Johnny Venture? The kids were so naive they never figured it out?"

"Just about. Usually they'd wait six months or a year for the listeners to forget exactly what the old Johnny Venture sounded like, then, like magic, Johnny's back! As long as he had the same line of patter, it really didn't matter who was playing at being Johnny Venture on any particular day."

"For real?"

"It wasn't all that unusual back in Top 40 radio. A fellow gets hired at a new station in a new town, first day on the job he's told, 'Your air name is going to be Tommy Hawks, or Bob Saint John, or Dan the Duke Kelly, or—' "

"Got it."

"Like, your name's not really Shauna J. Bogart, right? Let me guess: Gertrude Hagenfuss? Sheila Lumpkin? Ida Mae Hickenberry?"

"But at least there's only one Shauna J. Bogart." I ignored Ballard's attempt to pry into my private life. "How many Johnny Ventures do you suppose are out there?"

"Hard to tell. I lasted two years. Then I got drafted, and when I finally managed to get myself discharged"—Ballard paused to make a face, eyebrows joined, frowning, teeth bared—"honorably, I might add, I opened the studio. I figured there was a lot more money to be made behind the scenes. Looks like I made the right decision."

"So you're not the Johnny Venture that Jasmine would be looking for?"

"I seriously doubt it. She would have been just a kid when I was doing the Johnny Venture shtick. I never even met the lady."

"Still, you never know." I slid the plastic sleeve with the photograph and *Bee* clipping onto Ballard's desk and took a sip of water.

Ballard put his feet up on the desk, leaned back in his leather executive chair, and clasped his hands behind his head in a show of nonchalance. "Let's just say I don't think I need to hire a bodyguard anytime soon."

"Wouldn't you think some of these other Johnny Ventures would have come forward, given all the publicity in the Jasmine case?"

"You'd think," Ballard agreed. "But go figure: Some of them are probably dead, some of them have probably moved across the country. Some of us may have gone on to other successful careers and may not want our youthful indiscretions exposed. We've got wives and grandchildren to protect. Plus we all had to sign nondisclosure and noncompete contracts."

"That figures." Nothing Ballard told me about the early days of Top 40 radio would surprise me at this point.

"Yeah. Ask me why I got out of radio and into something more legitimate. All of us had to sign a statement that we would never let on that we weren't the only Johnny Venture or take the name to a competing station in the same market."

"Jeez. It's like you were just pawns on a chessboard." Some days, especially during those agonizing waits for the ratings book to come out, I knew exactly how Vance Ballard must have felt.

"Tell me about it."

I crossed and uncrossed my legs, trying to get comfortable in the metal-and-canvas butterfly chair. "So what you're telling me is . . ."

"Yeah. A real corker, isn't it?"

Odds are, Jasmine—or someone—killed the wrong Johnny Venture.

9

SO RADIO IS A SLEAZY BUSINESS.

Tell me something I don't already know.

The thing about radio, it's just so simple. You're not manufacturing anything, or providing any sort of hands-on service that people really need like, say, a supermarket or a hospital. You don't require inventory, a factory, supplies, or a college-educated staff. All it takes is an FCC license, electricity, a minimal investment in equipment, and a few guys with deep voices.

That, and a heaping helping of imagination.

But still, it's true: Owning a broadcast license *is* like having a license to print money. I'll bet the day Guglielmo Marconi, the father of radio, first hurled a wireless signal into the ether, some sharpie said, "By cracky, we ought to be able to get the rubes on Tin Pan Alley to *pay* to have their newfangled gramophone records played over the air!"

I'd gotten into the business just at the end of the reign of the DJ, when every town in America had a Johnny Venture type who actually was a local celebrity and had the power to make or break a new record. My memories of that era come from the perspective of the fan, the kid huddled under the covers late at night with the transistor radio glued to her ear. Those hipster voices, creating an imaginary grown-up world of fast cars, swingin' parties, bachelor pads, secret in-jokes, where the beat goes on and never stops. A world far removed from middle school cliques, overdue homework assignments, and a pubescent body I could no longer trust, or some days even recognize.

The door to Vance Ballard's office opened halfway and a young male body leaned in. I recognized Brandon Nguyen, a freelance engineer we used on a regular basis at the station, and waved a hello.

Nguyen returned the gesture and said to Ballard, "You told me to let you know when Ms. Rose arrived."

Ballard nodded a thanks and turned to me. "I just need to hold her hand for a few minutes. You're welcome to come along for the ride."

I followed Ballard and Nguyen through the labyrinth and into a sound booth where Cherise Rose paced. The ad lady was dressed in what I'm sure she considered weekend casual, white linen slacks, blinding white sneakers, pink polo shirt, white fisherman knit sweater tossed over her shoulder. My weekend casual outfit was an exact match of that being worn by Brandon Nguyen, which is to say jeans, T-shirt, and well-worn sneakers. The only thing keeping us from looking like a his-n-her portrait were the messages on our black T-shirts. Brandon's promoted the world tour of some hip-hop group I'd never heard of, while mine proclaimed, "Friends don't let friends vote Republican."

Ballard's studio was, of course, totally digital, so I concentrated on picking up tips that might be helpful in making the impending transition from tape. Still the same flashing lights and buttons to push as far as I could see, plus data to be read on a monitor and instructions to input on a keyboard. Cherise Rose's project turned out to be another incarnation of the new advertising campaign for the Mine Shaft Restaurant chain and its expansion into Southern California.

One speaker blared the thunka-thunka beat of the jingle:

Let's all go to the Mine Shaft, woo, woo
Let's all go to the Mine Shaft, woo, woo
Get us a slab of ribs at the Mine Shaft, woo, woo
It's all happening at the Mine Shaft, woo, woo, woo, WAH!

From the other speaker, the voice of the announcer with various versions of the closing line—the outro:

"Opening next week in Century City, Reseda, Duarte, San Dimas . . ."

"Opening tomorrow in Century City, Reseda, Duarte, San Dimas . . ."

"Grand opening today in Century City, Reseda, Duarte, San Dimas . . ."

"Now open in Century City, Reseda, Duarte, San Dimas . . ."

Cherise Rose stopped her pacing. "Is this the best you can do? You dragged me in here on a Saturday for this crap?"

Her attitude made me cringe, but I had to admit, Rose had a point. That jingle was lame, woo, woo, woo, WAH. Especially for a market as sophisticated as Los Angeles.

"C'mon, Cherise, you gotta admit, you didn't give us a whole lot of time," Ballard said. "But, hey, we want our clients to be happy. What if we add some more reverb to the music bed? It might just give it the punch we need."

I could see this was going to be a long session, so I told Ballard I could find my way to the door.

"High-maintenance," he said to me in a soft voice as he held open the door to the sound booth.

"Aren't they all." I tried to put as much sympathy into a whisper as I could.

Not quite noon. I supposed I should call my contact at the Monterey County Sheriff's Department with the news about the multiple Johnny Ventures. But their only concern was tracking down Jasmine and tossing her back into their slammer. Seemed to me the investigation into the death of Johnny Venture belonged to the law enforcement agency where the crime occurred. In other words, the Monterey Police Department.

Still, the Johnny Venture clones would undoubtedly prove helpful in getting a bead on Jasmine's whereabouts. Hadn't her parting words to Bobette been that she was going to look for Johnny Venture? Sounded like Jasmine wasn't even after the dead man; her enemy just happened to have worn the name.

Part of me itched to climb into the Volvo and drive to the coast, Santa Cruz, where my instincts told me Jasmine might be holed up. I was all but positive that T.R. and Glory Lou wouldn't care about a one-night hotel bill, if my hunch was right. Still, I could just as easily spend the night at home and get up early Sunday morning to make the drive to the coast.

Anyway, if the answer to the Jasmine puzzle hinged on locating the "real" Johnny Venture, then the clues might just as well be lodged in the town where the rock diva grew up and all these Johnny Ventures once worked. Right here in River City.

I steered the Volvo eastbound on Highway 160, across the American River, past the city limits, and into the suburban sprawl that surrounds the capital city on three sides. Vast stretches of unincorporated county land, a flat landscape of tract houses, expressways, strip malls, auto dealerships. I pulled into the empty parking lot of El Camino High School ten minutes after leaving downtown.

There's nothing quite as lonely as a school with no kids. I crept through the vacant corridors, trying to conjure up the sights and sounds of the crush of hundreds of teenage bodies in the scramble between classes. Only the smells remained: stale milk in cardboard cartons, sweaty gym socks, the fruity-minty stench of hundreds of cuds of discarded gum, and the underlying reek of rampaging hormones.

The campus consisted of a series of low-slung cement classroom buildings fanning out from a central quad. It wasn't a stretch to imagine myself as the girl who would become Jasmine in such a setting. El

Camino was that close of a match to the high school I attended in San Jose. Which is to say, it looked the same as every other high school in California that had been put up in the fifties and sixties. Was there some sort of central bureau, I wondered, that drew the blueprints and sent them to every school district in the state? Whose idea was it that every high school campus had to be barren and bland, devoid of any sparks of creativity, inspiration, whimsy? Was it part of a vast conspiracy to stamp out individuality, replace it with despair and ennui, so that a few years later, the graduates would march dutifully off to their cubicles in the state office buildings downtown?

Yet Cynthia Pepper had managed to resist the programming and make herself over into Jasmine. Just like the girl who would become Shauna J. Bogart.

I wandered past a hand-painted banner urging us to "Beat Bella Vista!" and tried to dredge up from my memory as many details as I could about Jasmine's Sacramento connections. Her mother, a secretary turned housewife, had succumbed to breast cancer about ten years after "Meet Me at the Casbah" had topped the charts. The father, a retired military pilot, had remarried and relocated to, I think, Oregon. No siblings. Her former classmates at El Camino recalled her as "quiet" and "sweet." The only activities listed below her picture in the school yearbook were Glee Club and Madrigals.

The *Bee* and the Sacramento TV stations had already scoured the scene, searching for that elusive and all-important "local angle" to the Jasmine story. The amateur musician dad, playing reeds in a Dixieland band, brings the daughter along to a Sunday night gig at Shakey's Pizza Parlor. Slow night, Dad invites kid to sit in with the band, sing a few bars of "Keepin' Out of Mischief Now." By the time her junior year of high school ends, Cynthia Pepper is the band's regular vocalist. Local record producer happens to be in the audience one night, asks her to help out with a demo tape he's been trying to put together for a little number he's recently written.

That little number just happened to be "Meet Me at the Casbah."

They never did get around to making a master recording. The

demo tape was an instant hit, snapped up immediately by the hometown radio stations. Within weeks, it landed on the playlists of the San Francisco and L.A. stations and got picked up by a major label. Cynthia Pepper became Jasmine. A star.

I stuck my hands into my jeans pockets and aimlessly kicked a pebble down the cement hallway of the science and math wing. If the spirit of the girl who would become Jasmine lingered in these corridors, it had already been picked over and stripped bare by the media. There was nothing new for me to find.

Hang the expense. I detoured back to the apartment to throw a toothbrush, clean underwear, a spare T-shirt, and a sweater into an overnight bag, and to set out extra bowls of kibble and water for Bialy. Within forty-five minutes I was back in the Volvo, merging onto I-80, a straight ninety-mile shot to San Francisco.

It took me another half hour to cross the City by the Bay. Late afternoon fog billowed in white drifts through the Golden Gate as I pulled into the military cemetery at the Presidio on the western edge of the city. I parked in front of a white stucco office building.

Closed.

Just my luck.

Hundreds of headstones marched in precision over gentle green hills. It would take hours, well past dark, to walk through the place and scan every name. I'd been banking on the office being open on a Saturday afternoon, or at least a map and directory being posted to help the living locate the permanent residents.

A yellow taxi swept through the massive wrought-iron gates of the cemetery, chugged up the hill, and parked. I watched the driver help a stooped woman out of the cab. She wore a black plastic trench coat and a paisley head scarf and used a cane to help herself totter the few feet to a grave. She stood silently while I hiked up the hill, hovering to maintain a respectful distance. I waited until she turned to hobble back to the idling taxi before approaching her.

"Excuse me, I'm so sorry to intrude. . . ."

She studied me through thick glasses. I could detect only curiosity in her stare, none of the typical big-city wariness of strangers. "I don't believe I've seen you around here before," she said.

"This is my first time."

"Looking for a new arrival?"

"Yeah."

"Try down by the parking strip." She used the cane to point to a line of headstones hugging a curb at the foot of the hill near the office and the cemetery gates. "They ran out of space for proper burials years ago, but they'll still take ashes, if you don't mind them being in the parking strip."

I thanked the woman and helped her into the cab. Before I started the walk back down the knoll, I glanced at the grave she had just visited. Raymond Culbertson, 1922–1978, U.S. Navy. Served his country in World War II and Korea. I thought briefly about the woman and wondered how often she made these trips to the cemetery to visit good ol' Ray.

Even on the parking strip, the headstone belonging to PFC Anton Greb, U.S. Army, occupied prime real estate. The orange south tower of the Golden Gate Bridge peeked through the fog, and the moist air coaxed out the aromas of pine and eucalyptus. I planted my feet on the narrow road next to the parking strip and gazed at the letters chiseled into the marble slab, as if I could somehow conjure those scoops of ashes and bits of bone back to life.

Anton Greb. Sacramento's Johnny Venture from 1964 to 1969. San Francisco's "Johnny" from '69 to '78.

Cynthia Pepper wasn't even traipsing the halls of El Camino High School and singing at Shakey's Pizza Parlor until the early seventies. So it was unlikely her rising star intersected with this particular Johnny Venture, at least not in his Sacramento radio days. Did the connection happen in San Francisco, as "Meet Me at the Casbah" was about to break nationwide? Or was it a year later, or the years after that, as Jasmine made the rounds, flogging follow-up releases destined to end up in record store bargain bins, barely cracking the Billboard 100, never coming remotely close to the success of "Meet Me"?

Could be it was all just a fluke, a foul-up of cosmic proportions. Anton Greb might have simply made one huge error in judgment a few years ago when he resurrected the Johnny Venture persona at the oldies station in Modesto. If someone in Northern California was looking to exact revenge on a DJ named Johnny Venture, wouldn't it stand to reason the only guy still using the name on radio would be the first in the line of fire?

I realized I had turned myself into a duplicate of the Widow Culbertson, standing over a grave and trying at some level to make contact, engaging in one-way dialogue for all eternity. I thought about the emotional ties that would spark such devotion, visiting the final resting place of a mate dead for nearly a quarter century, what—every Saturday? Once a month? On birthdays, anniversaries? Or whenever her apartment became unbearably lonely?

Emotional ties can work both ways. Something must have happened—a deal made, promises exacted, drugs or money or sex changing hands—between a rising young rock star calling herself Jasmine and a DJ named Johnny Venture. Something so important—or so terrible—that a quarter century later, the forces of revenge and retribution still hurtled through the universe, at long last finding their target.

Anton Greb could have been an innocent bystander.

Or he could have gotten exactly what he deserved.

10

THE THING ABOUT MOTELS IS, THEY'RE NOT MUCH FUN IF YOU'RE alone.

The sun had just finished its disappearing act into the fog bank on the western horizon when I left San Francisco and buzzed down the coast on Highway 1 toward Santa Cruz. Rather than negotiate the aptly named Devil's Slide in the dark, I promised myself to do the responsible thing and stop at the first motel I came to that had a "Vacancy" sign and didn't look too Norman Bates-ish. The Sea-Vu Motor Lodge in Pacifica fit the bill.

I slid my AmEx card across the Formica registration counter and grunted an affirmative to the clerk when he asked me if I required just one key. What would have been a hoot, with the right person to play along with, was just tedious, bordering on depressing, when traveling solo. I couldn't help thinking about the last time Pete Kovacs and I checked into a motel, this past summer up at Tahoe. He put on his fake Hungarian accent, while I pretended I had just picked him up in front of the dollar slots at Harrah's. There's just something so deliciously sleazy about motels, you know? Even the ones listed in the Triple A guide that call themselves motor lodges. As far as I'm concerned, if you can park in front of your room, it's a motel.

After six or so hours of fitful sleep between scratchy sheets, never quite succeeding in blocking out the din of traffic on Highway 1, I showered, dressed, helped myself to a cup of scalding coffee and a cold Danish from the Sea-Vu's free continental breakfast, and fired up the Volvo for the drive to Santa Cruz.

No sooner had Pacifica faded in the rearview mirror that I realized I'd made the right decision to stop for the night when I did. For one thing, this stretch of Highway 1 proved to be a lot more hilly and twisty than I recalled. But more important, it was a glorious morning, no fog, just sapphire skies, the Pacific crashing on the right, fields of artichokes and brussels sprouts lining the coastal hills on the left, narrow band of asphalt in between. Pickups and vans filled every turnout as I drew close to Mavericks, one of the world's most famous—and treacherous—surf spots. I kept both hands on the wheel and made darting glances at the dirt shoulder. There was always a chance one of those dudes wouldn't have his beach towel wrapped tightly as he wriggled out of his street clothes and into his wet suit. Let's just say there's an interesting variety of scenery to enjoy on Highway 1.

It was still early enough for folks to be in church when I reached the Santa Cruz city limits sign, which informed me that I was entering a nuclear-free zone, and that courteous drivers shared the road with bicyclists. Good old tie-dyed Santa Cruz. In a contest with Berkeley, it'd be a toss-up on which city leans farthest to the left. In Santa Cruz, you'll find not only the liberal university element, but also the laid-back surfer crowd, aging hippies, and a fair helping of bikers, slackers, and drifters to add to the mix.

Jasmine—if, indeed, she was here—couldn't have picked a better place to stash herself.

I located a Kinko's, ran off a hundred fliers, purchased thumbtacks and clear tape. I figured my hand-lettering on the fliers urging Helen Hudson to phone home, followed by my cell phone number, would add a homespun folk art touch that Santa Cruzans would appreciate. I spent the next couple of hours tromping through bookstores, head shops, Laundromats, and coffeehouses in the downtown district, posting the handbills on every community bulletin board I could find. I was glad I had paid a few pennies extra to copy the fliers onto orange paper, making them stand out among all the notices for roommates, lost cats, used vehicles ("runs great!"), and "lose thirty pounds in thirty days."

I didn't know a soul in Santa Cruz, and needed to find someone who could give me the skinny on the local landscape. I knew just where to look. A clerk at Bookshop Santa Cruz was kind enough to loan me a phone directory and give me directions to the address I wanted.

After ten minutes of maneuvering on city streets, I spotted a needle of steel poking through the branches of a eucalyptus grove. I turned into a packed-earth parking lot in front of the curvy Art Moderne building on the edge of a saltwater lagoon. The home of the one commercial radio station in Santa Cruz. The tower itself was planted in the middle of the marsh, the salt water providing an ideal natural conducting medium for the copper wiring. Two other vehicles in the parking lot: a rusted-out Toyota Tercel covered with surfer decals, and a sleek Mercedes convertible, fire-engine red, vanity license plate TUNE IN. It didn't exactly take a Rhodes scholar to figure out which one belonged to the weekend DJ and which was being driven by someone in sales or management.

Radio is the original 24/7 business. You can always count on someone being on duty. And that someone is usually hip to the local scene. Whether you're trying to track down a safe house, a pot dealer, or a club that isn't picky about checking IDs, chances are one of the guys or gals at the radio station will point you in the right direction. Even if it's only the weekend DJ. Especially if it's the weekend DJ.

I pushed open the glass door and stepped into a lobby that looked as if it hadn't been redecorated since the seventies. We're talking avocado-green shag carpet, couch covered with nubby rust-colored fabric, grass cloth wallpaper, bronze metal wall sculpture of seagulls, clump of macramé clutching an overgrown spider plant. I was about to tiptoe past the vacant reception desk in search of lights and sounds when a side door opened.

"Can I help you?" The voice was male, hearty, smooth, with perfect enunciation.

It was also vaguely familiar. I was pretty sure I'd heard that very voice on my own airwaves within the past few days. Donovan Sinclair, the Monterey DJ who'd filled me in on the connection between Jasmine's jail break and the local Latino gangs.

I turned in the direction of the voice and saw a slender man, sixtyish, graying goatee, and hair scraped back into a ponytail knot. Clothes that matched a driver of a Mercedes: black sweater that looked to me like cashmere, neatly pressed black slacks that didn't come off the rack at Men's Warehouse, black tasseled loafers that probably bore some fancy Italian name.

Donovan Sinclair?

Last I'd seen him, maybe fifteen years ago at a staff reunion for a station I'd once worked at in San Francisco, he'd been running his own personal Jerry Garcia look-alike contest, all roly-poly, shaggy, and rumpled.

"Shauna J. Bogart." I stuck out my hand for a shake. "From Sacramento? Used to work with Dr. Hipster and the gang in San Francisco? Didn't you used to be Donovan Sinclair?"

"Sure, sure." He returned the handshake. "I'm still your Big Daddy Donovan. Maybe not just as big."

"I'll say. You look terrific! What's your secret?"

"No secret. Diabetes. Got diagnosed exactly one year and four months ago. Talk about a wake-up call. I cleaned up my act, dropped eighty pounds."

"Good for you! And treated yourself to a brand-new look." I jerked my thumb in the direction of the glass door and the Mercedes in the parking lot. "That your ride?" I was still trying to take it all in, the small-town radio personality, the weekend DJ, dressed in designer threads and tooling around town in an expensive sports car.

"You betcha. And this is mine too." He swept open both arms, taking in the entire building. "Bought this baby two years ago. I own the stick in Monterey too, and one in San Luis Obispo."

The stick. Radio slang for the tower, the physical embodiment of the station. You haven't lived until you've been in a room full of station owners talking about the size, number, and location of their sticks.

"I'm impressed." What on-air talent hasn't dreamed of one day owning the whole station, calling her own shots, controlling her own destiny?

"So what brings my little Shauna J. all the way to Santa Cruz?" Sinclair indicated the couch and seated himself. "Still working the Jasmine story?"

"You got it." I showed him one of my fliers. "See, I'm thinking this is a message only Jasmine would get, if she sees it, and she might be curious enough to call. Or desperate enough."

Sinclair took the orange sheet of paper from my hand and studied the wording. "Helen Hudson, phone home. Helen Hudson? The old nightclub singer?"

"Yeah."

"What's her connection to the Jasmine case?"

"Can you keep a secret?"

"Hey, who loves ya, baby?"

"Helen Hudson was my mother, see?"

"I didn't know that. For real?"

"For real. Jasmine and now you are among the very few people who are aware of that. Jasmine apparently had some connection with my mother early in her career. That's why she tried to get in touch with me in the first place."

Donovan nodded slowly. "Very clever idea, those fliers."

"I've already put these up all over downtown. I was wondering if maybe you could have one of your announcers put the same message out over the air. Also if you could give me some leads on other places around here where someone like Jasmine might see my flier."

"You really ought to drive up Highway 9 to Felton, Ben

Lomond, Boulder Creek. Some pretty strange cats live up in those hills."

I considered Sinclair's advice. Highway 9 would take me north and east, into the Santa Cruz Mountains, toward Silicon Valley and away from the coast. I had been planning to continue driving south on Highway 1, back to Castroville and on to the Monterey Peninsula, before I had to loop back to Sacramento. Still, my recollection of teenage forays into the redwood-forested hills between San Jose and Santa Cruz matched Sinclair's description: a strange brew of druggies, computer millionaires, and granola crunchers. Highway 9, and the communities that dotted the mountain road, might prove interesting.

"I was planning to keep driving down the coast, see if anyone in the Monterey Police Department would talk to me," I told Sinclair. "I'm curious about something."

"I'll bet you are."

"Just wondering if they tested Jasmine for any drugs in her system when she was arrested. I'm sure they did, but I just can't recall, and can't find anything online or in the news."

"There won't be anyone at that small-town police station authorized to talk to the news media on a Sunday." Sinclair rubbed his hands together. "I'll be heading back home tonight. Why don't I check with them tomorrow and give you a call."

"That'd be terrific."

"And give me some of your fliers. I'll put them up for you all over the Monterey Peninsula. I'll even stop in Castroville on my way home. You never know, Jasmine may have figured she was safer hiding out there instead of hitting the open highway."

I felt a glow of gratitude and warmth. This is one of the many things I love about radio, the instant camaraderie and the insider's willingness to help out another insider. "I don't know how I'll ever thank you." I removed twenty or so fliers from the stack and passed them to Sinclair.

"My pleasure. Whoever finds Jasmine first takes the other out to dinner. Deal?"

"Deal." We sealed it with a handshake, an exchange of cell phone numbers and e-mail addresses, and promises to check in with each other the following day.

I backtracked through central Santa Cruz, north on Ocean Street past the county courthouse and a string of motels and fast-food joints, and made a dogleg onto Highway 9. Within minutes, I left the sunny beach town behind. I steered the Volvo up a narrow two-lane road carving a serpentine route through a dark redwood canyon. Shards of sunlight occasionally pierced the murky forest canopy. I groped at the still-unfamiliar dashboard to flick on the headlights, even though sunset wasn't due for at least another four hours. The San Lorenzo River slithered through culverts and seeped across rocks far below the shaded roadbed. In a couple of months, the winter rains would turn the peaceful stream into a frothing torrent and I knew I could count on stories crossing the wires of mudslides and flooding in the Santa Cruz Mountains. That and the earthquake faults that riddled the hillsides made me wonder if there might be some natural magnet that drew more than your average number of unstable personalities to this particular region of Northern California.

I pulled over to tack up a flier at every coffeehouse, yoga studio, natural foods store, and day-care center in the rustic Grimm's fairy tale hamlets that dotted the highway. Outside Ben Lomond, I spied a collection of Harleys, SUVs, vans, and assorted luxury cars parked at odd angles on the dirt shoulder of Baxter's Riverside Resort. The weather-beaten sign boasted "Swimming—Cabins—Restaurant—Cocktails—Since 1949." The marquee announced that Vonda Sue Weaver would be appearing this weekend "live and in person!" on the lawn. I slowed down enough that I could see the rusted holes where neon tubing had illuminated the sign back in the fifties, and managed to wedge the Unmarked Vehicle between a pair of Hogs and a Porsche with a license plate frame from a dealer on Stevens Creek Boulevard, Silicon Valley's auto row. I followed the sounds of amplified guitars and applause around a version of someone's Disney-esque dream of a Swiss chalet—all peaked roofs, curly wood trim, and window boxes filled with plastic edelweiss—to a meadow sandwiched between the lodge and the redwood-lined river. Several hundred bikers, neo-hippies, geeks, and cowboy-wannabes lounged on blankets and in aluminum lawn chairs, all focused on a female figure and a five-piece band on the stage.

The name Vonda Sue Weaver rang some vague chimes. She had a hit, or maybe two, in the mid-seventies, back when a country artist could still count on getting airplay on Top 40 radio if her record sold enough units and had crossover appeal. I crept along the edge of the crowd toward the stage, contemplating the strange twists and turns her career must have taken, from the Grand Ole Opry to playing a free show during the off-season at a dump like Baxter's. I lowered myself onto a square foot of unoccupied turf on the outskirts of the crowd, hoped I wouldn't end up with grass stains on my best pair of white slacks, and watched two guys stumble from the back door of the lodge, each balancing a pitcher of beer. That violation of ABC regulations, and the wafts of marijuana smoke hovering over the lawn, drew me to conclude that the Santa Cruz County sheriff made only sporadic visits to this corner of Highway 9, if at all. Not that it mattered to me.

Vonda Sue Weaver announced a tune called "Honky Tonk Honeymoon" as her next number. Judging from the whoops and whistles, it must have been her big hit. She wore the country girl singer's uniform of tight jeans, pointy-toed boots, cowboy hat with feathered band perched atop fluffy hair the texture and color of cotton candy, more feathers dangling from earrings, and a boldly cut ruffled blouse with a lace inset strategically placed where cleavage reached the danger zone. The boys in the band were similarly attired except for the feathers, and they'd swapped the blouse for striped shirts with pearl buttons. All but the mandolin player, who wore a Dixie Chicks road crew T-shirt.

Country music isn't exactly my thing—all those twangy guitars, and all that heartache—but I had to admit, Vonda Sue Weaver knew how to sell a song and work a crowd. I even found myself clapping in time to the chorus of "Honky Tonk Honeymoon" with the rest of the gang. Again I wondered: What was a talent like this doing working a loser gig like Baxter's Riverside Resort? I knew the answer as soon as I'd articulated the question: timing and luck. The breaks of the toughest business in the world.

Vonda Sue tossed her head back and wailed into the handheld microphone to finish the tune, then waited until the strategic moment when the applause was just starting to fade to announce the band would be back after a quick break. I rose, stretched, wiped grass clippings off the seat of my pants, and threaded my way through the crowd toward the lodge in search of a likely spot or two to post my fliers.

No community bulletin board in Baxter's front office, just a clerk who barely looked up from her PlayStation to nod in my direction. The barroom was so covered with autographed photos of down-on-their-luck entertainers who'd played Baxter's—everyone from Scatman Crothers to the Statler Brothers to Maria Muldaur—there wasn't a spare patch of wall to fit a flier. If I'd had time to study the publicity pix carefully, I was willing to lay odds I'd find a shot of Helen Hudson, circa 1965.

That left just one logical place to post a flier. The women's john.

I punched my last four thumbtacks through the orange paper onto a piece of wood paneling right next to the "feminine products" machine. One of the stalls opened and a cowboy-hatted figure sashayed out. Vonda Sue Weaver, live and in person. Like most performers, she looked tinier in person than onstage, shorter even than my five-foot-two. Older too, pushing fifty I'd say, judging from the crow's feet and the feathers of scarlet lipstick around her mouth.

"Hey, great show," I said.

"Glad you like it," she whispered. "Sorry. Gotta protect the voice. Nodes, you know?"

"Sure, I understand." There were days when I could manage only a croak for casual conversation, preserving the vocal cords for what counted. Those three hours on the air.

"Doc says I should have them taken out. But a girl's gotta make a living, you know?" Weaver stood in front of a cracked and stained mirror to fluff her hair and readjust the hat, then froze. She turned, stared at the orange paper, and mouthed the hand-lettered words: *Helen Hudson, Phone Home!*

"Helen Hudson," she wheezed. "I haven't thought about her in years."

"What about her?" I was instantly on edge.

"Helen Hudson taught me everything I know."

11

A HEAVY HAND POUNDED ON THE BATTERED DOOR SEPARATING THE women's rest room from the bar. A gruff male voice shouted an order.

Vonda Sue Weaver flashed me a fake smile. "Sorry. Show time." She turned, pushed open the door, and trotted through the half-filled bar toward the entrance to the outdoor stage.

"Wait!" I pushed my way through the cheap laminated wood tables in the dank, sour-smelling saloon. I caught up with the country singer just as she emerged into the dappled sunlight of the lawn. "What's this business about Helen Hudson teaching you everything you know?"

She ignored me and continued to prance toward the stage. She gave a Miss America wave to the crowd, sending them into a frenzy of hand-clapping.

"Give me a break." I sprinted past Weaver and blocked her way to the stairs leading to the stage. "Helen Hudson taught you everything you know? What the hell's up with that?"

She favored me with another movie-star megawatt smile, as if she were dealing with just one more groupie. "Camp Melody. Summer of 1970." Then she gave my shins a quick kick with her pointy cowboy boot, never dropping the grin or taking her eyes off the audience, shoved me aside, and mounted the stage.

I had plenty of time to ponder Weaver's tidbit of information during the three-and-a-half-hour drive back to Sacramento. I'd never heard of Camp Melody, never recalled my mother mentioning such a place. Summer of 1970? I would have been still in elementary school. I dredged up a scrap of shadowy memory of spending a few days with Helen Hudson in her tiny West Hollywood apartment just after school let out for summer vacation. Then I was hustled back up to my dad's place in Silicon Valley so Miss Hudson could continue her career of summer stock and resort gigs like Baxter's.

I couldn't ask Helen Hudson about Camp Melody in the summer of 1970. She'd died a couple of summers later, the victim of an accidental fall on the crumbling oceanside bluffs northwest of Santa Barbara. My dad was likewise unavailable for consultation, a bum ticker sidelining him for eternity about fifteen years ago.

What did Camp Melody—and Helen Hudson—have to do with Jasmine, the on-the-lam comeback kid? I tried to patch together a link. Jasmine and Vonda Sue Weaver looked to be roughly the same age, and I fixed their hits, "Honky Tonk Honeymoon" and "Meet Me at the Casbah," as breaking on the Billboard charts within a few months of each other in the mid-seventies. Both singers would have been teenagers in 1970. Did their parents drag the two of them to some pathetic resort named Camp Melody that summer, and did they have some sort of encounter with the resort's headliner? A has-been warbler named Helen Hudson?

I slid a CD into the Volvo's in-dash player as the white sedan crested the Altamont Pass separating the San Francisco Bay area from the vast Central Valley. There really are two Californias, but they aren't split north-south as everyone likes to think, but east-west. The western half, the coast side, is what most of the world pictures when it imagines California: Hollywood, surfing, Silicon Valley, the Golden Gate Bridge, and all those kooky left-wing hippie leftovers. The unending expanse of prairie to the east is the home of corporate agribusiness, descendants of Steinbeck's Dust Bowl Okies, Republicans, fundamentalist sects, and the state capital. Sacramento. My current hometown.

Hundreds of high-tech, power-producing windmills sent long shadows slanting over the hills of the Coast Range in the fading sunlight as the U.V. drifted downhill toward the valley floor. Helen Hudson's torchy contralto poured from the speakers. Her recordings were, of course, long out of print, available only in used record stores and on eBay, but I'd recently figured out how to transfer those dusty LPs to compact discs. Well, figured it out with a little help from Josh Friedman. Hudson's playlist had been growing mold even when she first recorded it in the fifties and sixties. "St. James Infirmary Blues." "After You've Gone." "Always." For years, this rock 'n' roll chick had wanted nothing to do with those sappy old standards. Now, with the distance of years, I could appreciate Helen Hudson's sense of style, her vocal salesmanship, and her sheer determination. Still, all it got her was the chance to dance on the flickering edges of fame, never fully savoring its fire. Just like Vonda Sue Weaver. And Jasmine, until the fluke of a hit TV sitcom and then a sensational crime plucked her from the embers of fame and flung her into the pit of notoriety.

I pulled over at a truck stop outside of Tracy to gas up the Volvo. This could have been the very station where Pete Kovacs had filled his van and someone snapped a Polaroid. I imagined him unscrewing the gas cap, sluicing the squeegee across the windshield, while someone spied on him, shooting those Polaroids and sending one to Mrs. Romswinkel.

I glanced around and didn't see anything sinister, just a van with the name of a Baptist church in Oakland painted on its side parked next to the rest rooms. A grizzled fellow in a camper truck with Oregon plates was gassing up while his gray-haired female companion washed the windshield. Still, I didn't even bother to wait for the automated gas pump to spit out a receipt. I just unhooked the nozzle as quickly as I could, hustled back into the driver's seat, and floored it back to northbound I-5.

Pete Kovacs! Where the hell was he? It was rare for us to go more than twenty-four hours without exchanging a giggle, a phone call "just to hear your voice," or some cuddling. By this time tomorrow evening, it would be exactly a week since I'd last had an in-person conversation with my boyfriend.

I didn't even wait to unpack my overnight bag when I arrived home, just picked up the phone and dialed Mrs. Romswinkel.

"I haven't heard from him," she said as soon as I identified myself. "How about you?"

"Nothing, nada, zip." I was about to wind up the conversation, then acted on a hunch. "You ever hear of a place called Camp Melody? I think it was a resort or a music club of some sort back in the seventies." Mrs. Romswinkel's husband was a musician, playing tuba in Pete's band. So she might have a lead.

"Just a moment, let me ask Herman." A clunking noise indicated Mrs. Romswinkel had set down the receiver. A few moments of muffled silence, then she came back on the line. "He's not sure, but he thinks it might have been a music camp for kids. He says you might want to check with Zack's Music City."

I was still wondering about Pete Kovacs the following morning when I did my usual workout in the Capitol Square swimming pool. I swim laps not so much for physical fitness, but to calm and center myself for the upcoming three hours on the air. In the chlorinated depths of the pool, I hear nothing but the rhythmic sounds of my strokes and have no company except my own thoughts. But try as I might this particular morning to concentrate on the show, I could only thrash about, curiosity amping up to anxiety over Pete. I gave up and climbed out of the pool, covered my tank-suited torso with an oversized T-shirt, slipped into a pair of flip-flops, grabbed my keys and a towel, and headed down a curving, shrubbery-lined cement path toward the mailboxes.

Capitol Square takes up nine city blocks in downtown Sacramento that had been leveled during the same urban renewal project that transformed the city's seedy West End into the Old Sacramento historic district. The apartment complex landscaping had grown lush and jungly over the years, softening the boxy midcentury architecture. I cover the equivalent of six city blocks, round trip, on my daily hike to the mailboxes. During those chilly winter months, when only the polar bear types brave a dip in the outdoor pool, the trip to the mailbox is the only exercise I get. That, and pacing in the control room.

"I was the one who called the police." The wife of Assemblyman George Gargoolian (R-Fresno) blocked my way. She wore a muumuu, floppy straw hat, and full cocktail party makeup, and cradled a squirming dachshund. "Schatzie and I were just starting our walkie."

I see Mrs. Gargoolian and Schatzie pretty much every morning. Almost all of the other tenants at Capitol Square work an eight-to-five shift in a state government building. Middays, I have the place to myself, just me, a couple of local evening news anchors, and the occasional legislative spouse who manages to tag along to the state capital instead of staying stashed in the home district. I usually tried to avoid contact with Mrs. Gargoolian. She was lonely and wanted to gab, while I cherished those moments of solitude at the pool.

"I beg your pardon?" I said.

"Didn't you hear the sirens?"

When I was deep in swimming mode, a Van Halen concert could have been going on one block over, and I wouldn't have heard a note. "What sirens?"

"I knew something was wrong the minute I saw the patio gate was open over in the Fremont Wing. And the broken flower pot. Then I saw this young man running from the patio toward Crocker Park. That's when I grabbed my cell phone and dialed 911. Didn't I, Schatzie?" She tapped her index finger on the dog's pointed nose.

"Good for you for getting involved." I maneuvered my way past Mrs. Gargoolian and Schatzie and continued toward the bank of mailboxes in the center of the complex. It wasn't even worth calling the newsroom to tip them off to the story. In Sacramento, drive-by gang shootings and stabbings at Folsom Prison are considered minor stories. Our news department uses generic, fill-in-the-blanks copy to save time. An apartment house burglary would hardly rate a one-inch article in the *Sacramento Bee*. In fact, I was surprised the Sac PeeDee even bothered with a siren when they sent over a cruiser. Unless they thought the tenant was in danger.

I turned the key in the imitation brass mailbox bearing my apartment number and pulled out a Sharper Image catalog, my SMUD bill, and an envelope promising me, in two-inch type, zero percent interest for one year. A piece of card stock fell from between the glossy pages of the catalog and the window envelopes. As soon as I scanned the message, I scrambled for a phone. Didn't even bother running back to my apartment, just barged into the rental office next to the mailboxes and grabbed the phone from behind the counter before the manager could object. I tried to calm my breathing as I punched in the number to Pete Kovacs's store.

"I got one too," Mrs. Romswinkel said. This time, she didn't even wait for me to finish babbling a greeting. "I just left a message on your machine."

"What did he say to you?"

"Only that he's fine, and that he appreciates my watching the store while he's gone, and that he should be back home in another few days. How about you?"

"Pretty much the same, except the part about watching the store."

Actually, my card contained one more feature I didn't share with Mrs. Romswinkel, a series of dots and dashes that ran across the bottom and halfway up one side.

.- .. -. - / -- .. ... -... . .... .- ...- .. -.

Early in our relationship, we accidentally discovered that we both had learned Morse Code as youngsters, Pete as part of his Eagle Scout requirements and me due to my fascination with all things radio, including ham operations. We also discovered it was a skill you never really forget, just like riding the proverbial bicycle. We'd latched on to Morse Code as our own private message system, a form of communication so archaic few knew how to translate it. Perfect for sweet nothings, mash notes, and the just plain lewd innuendo, especially when out in public.

I substituted the letters represented by the dots and dashes and smiled. *Ain't Misbehavin'*. Typical Pete, taking the title of an old Fats Waller tune to assure me he wasn't up to any hanky-panky. I flipped the postcard back and forth in the fingers of my right hand, while my left clutched the receiver. From behind her desk, Myrna, the apartment manager, studied me with lips pursed in disapproval, taking it all in: frizzy hair dripping onto a beach towel wrapped around my shoulders, the soggy T-shirt with its slogan urging us to hang loose in Hawaii, the flip-flops that left a trail of squishy footprints on her carpet.

The front of the postcard bore the logo and color photo of a generic chain motel, a two-story cement slab that seems to occupy the off-ramp of every interstate in America. A cut above the one that promises to leave a light on for you, but just barely. The reverse had a Los Angeles postmark from Friday, three lines written in blue ballpoint ink, and Pete Kovacs's signature.

"Do you think it's real?" Mrs. Romswinkel said to me through the phone.

"I think so." I reread the message and studied the signature. The penmanship looked genuine, and I couldn't detect any sinister meaning in his coded message. I felt my spirits lift in relief after my frenzy of worry in the pool. But why didn't he just tell us where he was? And why was he staying away so long?

"I hope so," I added.

"You and me both."

Capitol Square recently got a new corporate owner whose marketing manager thought it might be a classy touch to name the various buildings after figures from California's political history. Thus, the Fremont Wing, Earl Warren Tower, Sutter Square, and my own Hiram Johnson Block. Wisely, the marketing wizards chose to confine the honor to persons who had departed the scene decades ago. The thought of having to direct visitors around, through, or to a Ronald Reagan Wing was too horrifying to contemplate.

I took the long way back home just to see if anything exciting really was going on over at the Fremont Wing as Mrs. Gargoolian had said.

I found her fluttering in front of an end unit of the row of town houses that made up the Fremont Wing. A patrol car straddled the sidewalk on Third Street. She shifted the dachshund into the crook of one arm and gestured with the other toward two uniformed city cops. "They're going to put me in their report, I'm sure of it. The police always make notes about citizens who witness crimes. I saw it on *Diagnosis Murder*. I wouldn't be surprised if they call me in for questioning. Won't that be exciting?"

"You bet," I said. "So you actually saw some guy running from the patio?"

She nodded, sending the brim of her straw hat flopping in the breeze. "He was young, tall, over six feet, and—" She stopped and groped for the right word. "African-American."

In her youth, the politically correct term was probably "Negro."

"He wore black jeans and a black nylon jacket." Mrs. Gargoolian already sounded as if she were quoting from the police report. "Oh, yes, white sneakers, those big fancy expensive kind all the young people like."

A hulking, uniformed figure lumbered up the sidewalk toward me and Mrs. Gargoolian. Victor Pahoa, part of the private security force that guarded Capitol Square, 24/7. "Chee, that was one dumb crook," Pahoa said.

"How do you mean?" I said.

"That apartment? No one's living there. Nothing in it worth

stealing, 'cept a crummy TV set bolted to the wall. And the guy didn't even get that."

"That's because I practically caught him in the act," Mrs. Gargoolian said.

"What do you mean, no one's living there? It's got a TV set and flower pots on the patio." I addressed the question to Pahoa, ignoring Mrs. Gargoolian's preening.

"The Fremont Wing's all short-term rentals. Folks staying in town for just a week or two. Maybe they want a place with a kitchen, something that feels more like home than just a hotel."

Now that Pahoa mentioned it, I did recall seeing short-term rentals being promoted in Capitol Square's usual newspaper advertising. "I'll bet you've seen your share of important guests, then."

Pahoa grinned, revealing a row of square white teeth set in a face that would have blended well in a tiki lounge. I knew the security team wasn't supposed to divulge information about the VIPs they helped protect. But talk radio had taught me how to be a good listener, and an even better dispenser of advice, and over the past months I'd given plenty of both to Victor Pahoa when he was having troubles with his girlfriend, his various aunties, or his classes at Sacramento City College.

"We have a bunch of performers every summer for the Music Circus. There was this one guy we had a week last summer, famous singer, you know that musical about King Arthur?"

"Robert Goulet?" Mrs. Gargoolian put in. "My, that must have been exciting!"

The arrival of one of the city cops interrupted our chance for more celebrity dish. I recognized Sergeant Donette Mitchell, who'd helped extricate me from a sticky situation on a balcony in Old Sacramento the previous May.

"You're just the person who can help us out," she said after we'd exchanged greetings. "I was thinking you could help us determine what this might be."

She opened a nine-by-twelve brown envelope bearing an official-looking stamp and slid a slender object onto a matching envelope, careful not to touch it. "We found this on the ground next to the patio door."

It was gray metal, roughly the size and shape of a CD jewel case. A loop of recording tape stretched from edge to edge on one side.

"Can you turn it over?" I asked.

Mitchell slowly slipped the item from one heavy envelope to the other, as if she were separating an egg. I watched, then asked if she would mind loosening a screw at the top. "Will it help you make an identification?" she asked.

"I believe so."

She placed the envelope with the object onto a bench, donned a surgical glove on her left hand so she could hold the item steady, and undid the screw with the tip of a penknife. Pahoa, Mrs. Gargoolian, and I clustered around the bench and stared as the top panel slid open, revealing a capstan and a coil of tape.

"Well, I'll be damned," I said.

"What's that, Ms. Bogart?" Mitchell said.

"It's a tape magazine from a MacKenzie Repeater."

"Say what?" This from Victor Pahoa.

"Radio stations and recording studios used this gizmo for sound production in the late fifties, just before the invention of the continuous loop tape cartridge. You know, the eight-track."

The three gave me blank stares.

"Remember those cool jingles and sound effects at the old Top 40 stations? The reverb, the synthesized wall of sound? They were all made possible by the MacKenzie Repeater."

Pahoa, Sergeant Mitchell, and Mrs. Gargoolian continued with the dumbfounded act. The two uniforms were too young to remember Top 40 radio and Mrs. Gargoolian too old to have been a listener. Oh, well.

I gave the tape magazine a reverent look. "The MacKenzie Repeater was on the market for only a couple of years," I said. "You don't see many of these around any longer. Just in museums, and in a few private collections."

In fact, I'd only seen a MacKenzie Repeater once in my life. As far as I knew, it was the only one left in Northern California.

It reposed in a glass case in Pete Kovacs's store.

12

"WHAT DO YOU MEAN, YOU NEVER EVEN NOTICED IT WAS MISSING?" I stood in front of the glass display case in Retro Alley, arms folded across my chest, and glared at Mrs. Romswinkel.

As soon as I spoke, I regretted my impatient tone. Penny Romswinkel visibly drooped, drawing herself inward in the swivel chair behind the sales counter.

"Hey, I'm sorry," I said.

"I'm doing my best, I really am," she said. She tried to sound assertive, but I could tell she was holding back tears. "Keeping the store open, paying the bills, dealing with all of his online business, and then that strange mail and the rock through the window. I'm worried sick about Pete."

"Of course." I slipped behind the counter and gave Mrs. Romswinkel's plump shoulders a hug.

Around fifteen years ago, Pete Kovacs had the uncanny good sense to start buying up collectibles and kitsch from the middle decades of the twentieth century, back when no one else cared about that stuff. The days when you could find goodies like lava lamps, kidney-shaped coffee tables, bowling shirts, polyester leisure suits, and record albums with groovy covers at garage sales, flea markets, and even the city dump are long over. The results of Kovacs's prescience stared down at Mrs. Romswinkel and me from every shelf, rack, and corner of Retro Alley. It was one of the hottest and most profitable stores in Old Sacramento and an even more lucrative Web site. Even more to the point when it came to my love life, Pete Kovacs managed to avoid coming across like a nerd in a business barely one rung above comic book dealers and Trekkies. In fact, he was downright cute in a Ben Stiller kind of way, even though he did play piano in a Dixieland band, which normally would have sailed a guy off the charts when it comes to uncoolness.

I turned my attention back to the glass case, where Kovacs kept a collection of midcentury electronic gadgets. There, between the sixteen-inch transcription turntable and the Japanese transistor radio, still in its original box, should have stood the centerpiece of the collection. A case covered in brown leatherette, about fifteen inches square, ten slots, ten metal magazines, ten on-off switches. The MacKenzie Repeater.

An empty square delineated by a faint outline of dust was all that remained.

I swung by the station to pick up a tape deck, then made a ten-minute drive to an address in the depths of Sacramento's unincorporated suburbia, perhaps a mile or so away from El Camino High School. I pulled into a potholed parking lot littered with fast-food containers, parked under one of the few light fixtures that wasn't bent or broken, double-checked the lock on the Volvo, and crossed the asphalt toward the cluster of stores that made up the almost-deserted shopping center, Brite Way Plaza.

Places like this—loser shopping malls, abandoned movie theaters, lost-cause amusement parks—always fill me with a vague sense of sadness. Perhaps it has to do with coming face-to-face with something that had been fresh and new in my lifetime becoming old and irrelevant before its time should have been up. I could just picture the excitement that must have surrounded Brite Way Plaza when it first opened circa 1975, the searchlights, the full-page newspaper ads, the babes from the local modeling agency handing out entry blanks for hundred-dollar shopping sprees at Weinstock's Department Store. Then the slow decline, as small open-air centers like Brite Way got steamrollered, first by huge enclosed malls, then by the big box chains. Any day now, I expect to see the bulldozers leveling Brite Way Plaza to make way for yet another Wal-Mart.

About half the stores were empty, papered-over windows staring at me with a sense of futility. The others were occupied by mom 'n' pop businesses taking advantage of the cheap rents: a donut shop run by Cambodian refugees, a children's formal-wear store featuring pint-sized tuxedos and ruffled dresses suitable for confirmations and *Quinceanera,* a baseball card trading post, a used paperback emporium, and a place calling itself The Joy of Cross-stitch.

I headed to a corner spot at one end of the mall, to a yellow and red vinyl banner announcing the location of Zack's Music City. Above the banner, I could just barely make out the faded lettering on the wooden facade revealing the identity of the original tenant, Joseph Magnin. I felt another wave of poignancy. I'd picked out my first dressy, grown-up gown and heels for the eighth-grade graduation dance at Joseph Magnin's flagship San Francisco store. There was a time—mid-sixties to mid-seventies—when JM carried the kickiest threads in Northern California. Today, it felt like I was the only one left who even remembered. Or cared.

Zack's Music City looked relatively prosperous in contrast to its neighbors. The store was clean, brightly lit, and stocked with merchandise: an entire wall of guitars; display cases full of reeds, pads, and oils; and racks of sheet music, everything from the Carpenters' greatest hits to Celine Dion's latest. I was the only customer, but I was willing to lay odds that when school let out later in the afternoon, the aisles would swarm with garage-band wannabes, junior Juilliards, and maybe even the next Wynton Marsalis. Come Saturday morning, I could just picture Zack's being taken over by an older crowd, lawyers, legislative analysts, and stockbrokers, musical weekend warriors clinging to that teenage dream of someday playing a club date in a band.

"Help you find anything?"

I turned in the direction of the voice, to the man standing behind the sales counter.

"I'd like to speak to Zack if he's around," I said.

The man gazed at me with suspicion, as if I were going to try to sell him something. "You're lookin' at him," he said. "Zack Klemp."

I put him in his mid-fifties, a slender fellow just under six feet tall. Even though the outdoor temperature was well into the seventies, he wore a thick flannel shirt and a drab olive fleece vest. He had a cap of frizzy red hair streaked with gray, green eyes behind round, wire-rimmed glasses, and a ginger mustache. In another fifteen years or so, I'd probably look about the same. Minus, I hoped, the mustache.

I identified myself and exchanged the usual banter about how I didn't look anything like I sounded on the air. "I was told you might be able to tell me something about a place called Camp Melody." I reached down to the tape deck that hung from my shoulder and pressed the RECORD button.

Zack gave the tape deck a wary look and put his hands on his hips. "Is this going to be used on the air?"

"Right now I'm just doing background research for a major investigative news story. Top secret, hush-hush. Of course, if we use your information, I'll be sure that Zack's Music City gets mentioned."

"Well, that's okay, then." Zack relaxed his protective stance and let out a loud sigh, like a balloon rapidly deflating. "How can I help you?"

"Camp Melody?" I prompted.

"Oh, sure. I attended Camp Melody as a student when I was between my junior and senior years of high school. That would have been"—he paused to mentally calculate—"the summer of 1965. Later on, I worked there as a counselor while I was in college."

"Any chance you were there during the summer of 1970? I'm

specifically trying to get information on someone who might have been on the faculty that summer."

Another pause as Zack's mental gears clicked into place. "Don't think so—1970 was the summer I toured with 'Up With People!' "

Damn. Well, it had been a long shot. Still, I decided I might as well get as much information as I could from Zack. "What was Camp Melody, exactly?"

"I thought you knew all about it."

"I just heard it was some sort of music camp for kids."

"Some sort of music camp for kids, and then some. Camp Melody took only the very best, the most promising high school students from all over the Central Valley. I can't even begin to tell you the number of entertainers who got their start at Camp Melody: studio musicians, concert performers, even Broadway chorus singers. Everything was just top-of-the-line at Camp Melody: the students, the faculty, the location, even the food."

"So this was some sort of private camp?"

"No, that was the real beauty of it. Camp Melody was run by a consortium of school districts in the Central Valley. All you needed to qualify was talent. The school system took care of the rest."

"Gosh, sounds fabulous. Where is this Camp Melody, exactly?"

"Up by Donner Summit, off Interstate 80 near Squaw Valley." Zack paused to pull on his mustache. His voice took on a pensive tone, underscored by sarcasm. "Course, you wouldn't want to go looking for it now. Camp Melody's been closed since around 1980."

"You're kidding." How could a resource that sounded so wonderful just disappear?

"Just one of the many victims of Proposition 13."

Music and art. Always the first things to go when the school districts have to cut their budgets.

"Last I heard, some new owners came in and turned it into a rehab center," Zack added.

"A sign of the times, for sure." I turned off the tape machine and reached across the counter to shake Zack's hand. "Thanks, you've been helpful."

"If you're really interested in Camp Melody, you might want to try the Internet," Zack said. "I hear there's at least one tribute site out there. Course, you'll want to make sure you spell it right in the search engines."

"How's that?" I dug into my pocket, pulled out a business card, flipped it over, and snagged a pen from Zack's counter.

"I'd better show you."

I handed the pen and card to Zack and studied his hands as he carefully etched the letters onto the card: Camp Mel-O-Dee.

"Someone from the Monterey County Sheriff's Department has been calling for you at least every half hour." Glory Lou shoved a fistful of pink phone message slips into my hand as soon as I entered the newsroom.

"She can cool her jets for a few more minutes." I placed the tape deck on my desk and shrugged out of my backpack.

"You were the one who made the deal with her, not me."

I seated myself and made a show of shuffling through the phone messages and smoothing my hair, as if I didn't really care whether Sheriff Perez was gunning for me. Then I lifted the receiver and punched in a number in the 831 area code. As soon as I identified myself, I heard a series of clicks and then the voice of Maria Elena Perez herself.

"You're supposed to be checking in with us at least once a day."

"Yeah, well, I've been out in the field. Investigating, you know?"

"We haven't heard from you since Friday," she persisted.

"Hey, isn't a girl allowed to take the weekend off?"

"I'm not sure you understand the gravity of your situation. Perhaps I should spell it out."

I bit back several sarcastic responses. "I understand." I spoke in as bland and pleasant a tone as I could force myself to generate. "No need to get all technical between two professional partners, right?"

"Just cut the crap and tell me what you've been up to since Friday."

Every instinct in me longed to verbally bitch-slap the Monterey County sheriff. How dare she horn in on *my* story and *my* investigation? I reminded myself of the little issue of interfering with a law enforcement investigation, and how I'd probably end up sharing a jail cell with Bobette Dooley if I didn't become a bit more cooperative. So I lobbed a juicy tidbit her way: my meeting with Vance Ballard on Saturday, and the multiple disc jockeys calling themselves Johnny Venture. Judging from the silence on the other end of the line, Perez was probably honing in on the same conclusion I'd come to on Saturday: Jasmine could very well have offed the wrong man, another disc jockey who happened to call himself Johnny Venture.

"I've invited Vance Ballard to be on the show this afternoon," I told Perez. "Just tune me in, and you can hear him repeat the story he told me on Saturday, live and in person."

"I seriously doubt I could pick up your little station way down here in Salinas."

"No problem. We've got streaming audio on our Web site." I gave her the station's URL. "In fact, I'd suggest you log on and listen every afternoon. Anything I come up with on the Jasmine case, I'll be sharing with my listeners."

I fought back the urge to add: *Before I share it with you.* No sense antagonizing a lady who carries a gun and knows how to use it.

I arranged tape cartridges, newspaper clippings, and a notepad on the studio console, and helped Vance Ballard settle into the guest chair in preparation for the show. Josh Friedman rang me on the intercom. "Got time for a call before the show? That Sinclair guy from Monterey is holding on the hotline."

For a call from Donovan Sinclair, I always have time.

"Your fliers are up from Castroville to Carmel and beyond," he said. "If your gal is anywhere on the Monterey Peninsula, we've got her covered."

"Fabulous! You are the best."

"And I checked with my contacts over at the jail who originally booked Jasmine when she was arrested, just like I said I would."

"And . . . ?"

"She tested positive for alcohol and cannabis."

"Anything else?"

I could hear a faint rustle of paper, as if Sinclair were checking his notes. "Something called Premarin."

So Jasmine was going through The Change. "That's it?"

"That's it."

I had one ear cocked to the phone, and the other checking the network. In another sixty seconds, the top-of-the-hour news update would wind down and the jingle signaling the start of my three hours of airtime would kick into gear. I barely had time to thank Donovan Sinclair for coming through for me once again.

Too bad the information he supplied wasn't what I'd been expecting—or hoping—to hear.

Just as I thought, Vance Ballard turned out to be the perfect talk radio guest. Even though his disk jockey days were long behind him, he still remembered how to put that extra *oomph* of personality into his voice as soon as the mike was hot, how to talk up to the clock at the start of a commercial break, and how to always leave the listeners wanting more. He also turned out, just as I had suspected, to be utterly bald underneath the Greek fisherman's cap, which he doffed to slip on the headphones.

Ballard managed to sum up the story of the more-than-one Johnny Venture during the first half hour of the show, while I prompted with questions as if it were new information for me as well as the listeners.

"Just purely for speculation," I said into the mike, "what connection could there be between a rising young rock star like Jasmine and one of these Johnny Venture disc jockeys?"

"For starters, there's always payola," Ballard said.

Bingo! Just the answer I was anticipating. "Pay for play," I said.

"The recording artist or the record company supplies the disc jockey with cash, or a trip to Hawaii, or merchandise. The DJ gives the record an extra push on the air to make it a hit."

"Back in my day, it was usually hookers or drugs first, then cash."

"Ass, grass, or cash. Nothing gets played for free."

Payola. Everyone thinks it's illegal, but what's actually against the law is for the radio station to accept a gratuity from a record company and then not disclose it to the listeners. Trouble is, most stations don't want to have to make an announcement after every song to the effect that the tune you just heard has been paid for by a major label. Thus rose the middleman, the independent record promoter who takes the funds from the record companies and funnels it into the radio station. Or, these days, wires the money directly into the accounts of a handful of huge chains that own the bulk of the nation's radio stations.

I summarized the situation for the listeners and added, "The days when an individual disc jockey could actually choose the records he wants to play are long gone."

"But there was a time when the local DJ really did have that kind of power," Ballard said. "With the right kind of enthusiasm, and enough airplay, a popular local disc jockey really could guarantee a record would place on the regional charts."

"So let's say Jasmine made a deal with one of those Johnny Ventures, offering sexual favors in return for airplay. Maybe it was for her follow-up release to 'Meet Me at the Casbah.' Maybe he didn't come through, and the record tanked. Maybe that's why she decided to get revenge after all these years."

"That's a possibility," Ballard said. "But there's one thing you have to keep in mind."

"What's that?"

"No amount of plugging and promotion is going to turn a record that's dog poop into solid gold."

"You think so? I always believed that if a DJ played a record often enough, the kids would race out to buy it, no matter how bad it was."

"No way. All a DJ can do is give an extra push to something that's already hot to begin with."

"So you're saying one of those Johnny Ventures could have done his best to make Jasmine's second release a hit and it still wouldn't do any good?"

"Absolutely."

"Then why would Jasmine want to kill him twenty-five years after the fact?"

"I would say that's a question only Jasmine can answer."

I glanced at the second hand on the studio clock. "We'll be back with your calls right after this traffic check."

"Great stuff!" I told Ballard as I removed my headphones and backed away from the mike. "Just between us: Do you think Jasmine was involved in some sort of payola scheme back in the seventies?"

"All I can say is, there was a reason she was known in the industry as Juicy Jasmine." Ballard was silent for a moment and stared out the studio window at the blur of traffic on Highway 160. "One of the things I've always regretted is that Ballard Productions didn't discover Jasmine and launch her career. My company could have used the money. And things might have turned out better for her."

I looked up from the program log, where I'd been checking off the list of commercials as they aired. "I've been wondering about that. Who produced that demo tape of 'Meet Me'?"

"Those sleazebags over at El Jay."

13

I STOOD IN FRONT OF A MAP OF SACRAMENTO MOUNTED ON THE newsroom wall and traced Stockton Boulevard with my index finger, from the thoroughfare's downtown headwaters through the southern suburbs until it merged with Highway 99 and fell off the bottom edge of the known universe.

"I think I know that place you're looking for." Josh Friedman sidled next to me.

"Vance Ballard told me he couldn't remember exactly where the old El Jay studio was located, just somewhere on Stockton Boulevard between Broadway and Fourteenth Avenue." I stabbed the intersection of Stockton and Broadway with my finger.

"There's this dance club in an old recording studio on Stockton Boulevard just up from Fourteenth. The Attention Deficit Zone."

I'd heard of the place, one of those clubs that advertises in the back pages of the *Sacramento News and Review* and on fliers tacked to telephone poles around the Sac State campus.

"What do you expect to find there?" Josh added.

"Pete Kovacs has a box of old recordings made at El Jay and he seemed to think they were pretty important. Jasmine cut her first demo tape out at El Jay. It's worth checking out."

"Are you sure you're up for this? I mean, the Attention Deficit Zone isn't exactly your type of crowd."

I turned from the map to face Josh. "I've been out clubbing before. I know what to expect."

"Oh, sure. I'll bet the last time you went to a dance club, they had one of those lighted disco balls and all the guys were trying to do the Hustle in their white John Travolta suits."

"How old do you think I am, anyway!" The truth is, the kid had a point. Much as I liked to think of myself as a hip and happenin' rock 'n' roll chick who would never grow old, lately my social life had consisted of parties likely to end up in the "Out and About" column in *Sacramento* magazine. Charity balls, political receptions, grown-up soirees just like my dad used to attend.

"I suppose this is one of those 'rave' places where they slam dance and all that," I said.

Josh rolled his eyes. "I'd better go with you."

My college student intern/producer repeated the eye-rolling routine when he stopped by my apartment to pick me up at eight-thirty. "What?" I said. "What's the problem?"

"Nothing." But he was smirking and shaking his head.

Pete Kovacs had said I looked fabulous when I wore the same outfit a few weeks ago when his band played at a Folsom Chamber of Commerce barbecue. Skinny black velveteen jeans, satin blouse in a light peach color, unbuttoned far enough to show just a hint of lacy bra in a similar peachy tone. I'd even fluffed up my hair and slicked on mascara and lip gloss.

I gazed out the passenger side window as Josh drove his Geo Metro down Stockton Boulevard past blocks of cement, steel, and glass monoliths that housed Sac Med Center, the huge University of California teaching hospital. The drab government buildings gradually yielded their turf to Oak Park, one of those districts that civic leaders like to point to as having "potential," ripe for revitalization. I'd heard it had been a swank neighborhood at the turn of the last century, Sacramento's first suburb, but its fortunes fell when the freeway amputated it from the rest of the city back in the fifties. Tonight, I couldn't see much in the way of this alleged potential in the boarded-up Victorians, rubble-strewn lots, and empty storefronts with barred windows.

"Good show today," Josh said. I wondered if he was trying to make up for his lack of enthusiasm about my outfit.

"Thanks. I just wish the hunch I had about Jasmine's drug test had panned out."

"How's that?"

"I thought for sure they would have found a date rape drug in her system."

"Roofies, you mean."

"Roofies?"

"Roofies, rophies, roofenol. Those are the street names. Manufactured under the name Rohypnol. A legal sleeping pill in Europe and South America, illegal in the U.S. Highly potent when mixed with alcohol. You slip it in a girl's drink and a half hour later, she's passing out."

"Doesn't it seem plausible that maybe that's how Jasmine woke up in Johnny Venture's hotel room the next morning? She claims she had no idea how she got there or what had happened."

Josh continued to head south on Stockton Boulevard. I spotted a few signs of life, Asian and Mexican restaurants, grocery stores, and video-rental places, new waves of immigrants making their own potential out of the cheap real estate.

"Yeah, except for one problem. Roofies aren't detectable by any drug test. They don't stay in your system long enough. That's why date rape cases are so difficult to prove."

"You seem to be an expert. I suppose they put all of you college students through an orientation on the dangers of things like this during your freshman year."

"College?" Josh paused to snicker. "Try seventh grade."

I felt around a million years old.

A cluster of young people spilled out onto the sidewalk in front of a building near the northwest corner of Stockton and Fourteenth. Strings of multicolored Christmas lights outlined a painted wooden sign over the door: Attention Deficit Zone. I could tell the building had been a beaut once, Art Deco lines topped with a triple-tiered wedding cake tower, but years of neglect plus a dun-colored paint job did little to bring out the structure's charm.

Josh made a right onto Fourteenth, entered a potholed parking lot, and managed to squeeze the Metro between a beat-up Ford Ranchero and a new Beemer. As we neared the entrance to the club, I dug into my evening bag for my ID, but the doorman lowered the velvet rope and waved me on through.

"Don't feel bad." Josh shouted to be heard over the thunder of the *thunka-thunka* music. "They're only trying to keep out the under-eighteens. This is a no-alcohol dance club."

There went my plan to attempt to order a Ritalin cocktail at the Attention Deficit Zone.

I looked around in the pulsating light for a band, but saw only writhing masses of dancing teens and early twenty-somethings. Now I understood why Josh had found my outfit a bit quaint. The girls' clothing consisted of form-fitting slacks in slinky knit fabrics, cut so low they were within inches of revealing all, topped with skimpy, midriff-baring tanks and camisoles. I mean, I'm all for the sexual revolution, but these girls were out on the front lines. The boys wore Josh's uniform of baggy canvas pants ending just below the knee, high-top sneakers, and sloppy T-shirts bearing manufacturers' logos from the holy trinity of boards—surf, snow, skate—sacred to the male teenager's soul.

Josh wove a path through the crowd and out an emergency exit in the back. "See?" He pointed to a worn metal sign on the door. I could barely make out the chipped paint of the lettering in the faint light provided by a naked bulb above the door.

EL JAY STUDIOS

"The Sounds of Sacramento"
Shipping and Receiving

"Can I help you young folks with anything?"

I turned in the direction of the gruff bellow and made out a tall, gray-haired fellow loping toward the door.

"Shauna J. Bogart?" He said in a puzzled tone as he drew close enough to place me. Almost simultaneously, I recognized the Yosemite Sam mustache of Lloyd Ellwanger, owner and commercial spokesman for the Mine Shaft Restaurant chain.

"Just checking out something for a possible future show topic," I said. God forbid he should think I was trolling for young meat. And along those lines, what was *he* doing at an underage dance club?

"If you're looking for clues about the Jasmine case, you're out of luck, young missy."

"Oh?"

"A little lady from one of those TV tabloid shows came by here this morning. We scoured the place top to bottom, but the fellow who owned the old recording studio must have taken everything with him when he left. No tapes, no contracts, no files, no nothin'."

"What's your connection?" I shifted into the circle of light by the back door so I could study Ellwanger more closely.

"One of my many commercial real estate investments. The club is just a little family project."

"No kidding." I was having trouble picturing the grizzled cuss in the role of teen dance impresario. We're not exactly talking Dick Clark here.

"Damn straight. My two daughters and my son knocked out all the old walls, rewired the place, and got it up to code. I've got one grandson working the door tonight, and another one selling soft drinks. Just between us"—Ellwanger stooped so he could whisper—"we haven't made a dime, but I figure it's worth it. This little joint has brought the family together and it gives the youngins something to do."

"You must be very proud of them."

"Damn tootin'." Ellwanger slapped his thigh. "Say, did you happen to catch my granddaughter spinnin' the disc?"

A teenage female disc jockey. This I had to see. Ellwanger led the way back into the club, cutting a path through the gyrating throng until we landed in front of a waist-high partition that sectioned off one corner of the dance hall. On the other side of the flimsy barricade, a girl with brown hair streaked with neon-yellow highlights and a pair of headphones around her neck perched on a stool. Her purple T-shirt announced that she was a member of the Phemmes, the Feminist DJ Collective. On the counter in front of her I recognized a mixing board, microphone, stack of LPs, and two turntables.

Turntables! I thought they'd gone the way of working pay phones, typewriter ribbons, and Betamax tape. Extinct fodder for eccentric collectors like Pete Kovacs.

Ellwanger shouted introductions. Allison someone. She waved a hello and acted as if she'd heard of me, then returned her attention to the turntables, where one LP spinned, blaring over the club's sound system. I watched, fascinated, as Allison placed a vinyl disc on the second turntable and rotated it by hand under the stylus until she hit the very first note. Then, carefully holding the LP in place with her thumb, she flipped the power on the mixing board to the second turntable. The instant the notes on the *first* record ended, she deftly lifted her thumb off the *second* vinyl disc, creating a seamless flow of music from one tune to the next.

We didn't know about mixing or scratching when I learned that trick. We called it slip-cuing a record. To this day, my all-time favorite segue is the last thundering beats of the Beatles' "A Day in the Life" flowing into the opening tones of Yes's "Roundabout."

I hadn't a clue of the name of either pounding guitar and drum-laden tune Allison had just punched through the club's amplifiers and out the speakers. I just knew I had just watched a teenage girl perform a perfect slip cue.

For the first time that night, I didn't feel like a dinosaur.

Just as Zack at the music store had predicted, I found the Camp Mel-O-Dee tribute site on the first try after entering the correct spelling in the Google search bar on my home computer. I scrolled through photographs of pine cabins, band practices, and outdoor stage performances of *Oklahoma!* and *Fiddler on the Roof* until I found the page with the faculty members.

There she was, sandwiched between a former clarinetist with the Lawrence Welk TV orchestra and the guitarist with a one-hit surfer band: upswept hairdo, dangly rhinestone earrings, thick, camera-ready makeup. Helen Hudson, vocal music, 1968–1973.

In the twelve years that I'd known my mother, I never recalled her once mentioning teaching at a kids' music camp. She'd always led me—and, as far as I knew, my dad—to believe she was spending her summer months performing at resorts and nightclubs, or appearing in some theater-in-the-round on the East Coast.

I continued scrolling and scanning text, searching for Helen Hudson's name on the message boards. It wasn't difficult to find. ". . . the best and most compassionate voice coach I've ever had . . ." ". . . Helen Hudson generously gave me the confidence to pursue a career on stage . . ." "I credit Helen Hudson and her creative approach to teaching with my successful career as a studio backup singer . . ." ". . . Helen Hudson taught me everything I know."

Helen Hudson? The tyrant who dragged me, terrified, onstage when I was only seven, determined to turn me into one half of a mother-daughter act? Helen Hudson, who never let me forget she was up for a part in a Doris Day picture until she popped up preggers with me? Helen Hudson—compassionate, generous, creative?

I clicked back to the faculty photographs. No question, it was the same Helen Hudson.

Next I hit the page of "Distinguished Alums." A young Vonda Sue Weaver was easy to pick out, sporting that cowboy hat with the feathers even back in 1970.

Another photo from the 1970 summer class made me pause. A sad-looking young woman with limp hair and too much eyeliner. "Cynthia Pepper, summer of 1970," the caption told me. "She changed her name to Jasmine and sold a million-plus copies of 'Meet Me at the Casbah.' "

And Helen Hudson taught her everything she knows.

Mrs. Gargoolian and Schatzie managed to block my way before I covered even half the distance between my front door and the gate to the swimming pool. I craved nothing more than solitude. I ached to slide into the cool water and move my arms and legs in harmony, blast the fog out of my brain brought on by a too-late night of Web crawling. I made an attempt at detouring past the muumuu-clad elderly woman, hoping to get away with nothing more than a quick hello.

"They're calling off the investigation!" She planted herself and the dachshund solidly in front of me on the curving cement walkway and let out a wail.

"What investigation?" I started to say before I remembered the break-in at the short-term rental the previous morning. If it hadn't been for that tape magazine that I was pretty sure came from Pete Kovacs's collection, the incident wouldn't have even registered in my memory bank.

"I was just talking to Myrna in the manager's office. She says that the tenants claim nothing is missing and they're not even interested in filing a police report." She pouted her orange-painted lips.

"Who's renting that unit, anyway, did Myrna say?" It occurred to me that if I could locate the tenant, he or she might be able to tell me how a tape magazine from a MacKenzie Repeater ended up outside the patio door, and how Kovacs might figure into the picture.

"Schatzie, get your nose out of the pansies this instant!" Mrs.

Gargoolian gave the leash a quick tug. "Some organization calling itself Advanced Legislative Dynamics. That's what Myrna tells me, at any rate."

"A lobbying group, I suppose." I shifted my beach towel from one arm to the other and wondered what a state capital lobbyist would need with an antique piece of broadcast equipment.

"I suppose." Mrs. Gargoolian continued the dejected act for another moment, then straightened and clapped her pudgy hands, sending her hat brim flapping and Schatzie jittering at her ankles. "Guess what I saw over at the Earl Warren Tower last night!"

"Thanks, but I've really got things to do. Deadlines, you know?" I tiptoed as best I could in flip-flops through the flower bed, past the woman and her dog.

"I think I saw a call girl coming out of one of those penthouses. Don't you think that might make an interesting topic for your show?"

"Some other time." I pushed open the wrought-iron gate to the pool area, then turned to give Mrs. Gargoolian the thumbs-up sign. "But you go get 'em, Mrs. G.!"

"Man, I wish I had something strong to put in this brew to get me through the day."

"How's that again?" I removed my head from the refrigerator in the Sacramento Talk Radio break room, where I'd been scrounging for a box of Chinese restaurant leftovers I'd hidden a few days ago, and faced the speaker, LeVon Rogers, pouring himself a mug of coffee.

"Cherise Rose and Lloyd Ellwanger are coming in this afternoon with yet another version of that Mine Shaft commercial." He made a face.

"Ouch." I returned the grimace in sympathy. "I heard her working on the latest over at Ballard's studio Saturday morning. It's a bow-wow."

Rogers gulped a mouthful of coffee and made another sour face. "What I don't get is, they had a cute jingle in the works, catchy tune.

Then just like that"—he snapped his fingers—"she and Ellwanger decide to can it. Just like that." His fingers snapped again.

"Creative differences," I said, recalling the scene in Rogers's production studio the previous week.

"Want to hear what they were working on? The original version, I mean?"

I really should have been prepping for my upcoming three hours on the air. But LeVon Rogers was a good guy, one of those behind-the-scenes toilers, like the boss's secretary and the chief engineer, who can make us on-air folks sound even better. Giving LeVon Rogers a little attention was an investment of time sure to pay off later on.

I followed the production director through the mazelike corridors of the radio station and into a recording booth. I waited for him to rack up a tape, then remembered that the production studio had already gone digital. Rogers's long, brown fingers tapped instructions into a keyboard, and the next thing I knew, I heard perky singers through the speakers. "Cruise on over to the Mine Shaft . . . you're right at home at the Mine Shaft . . ."

Rogers was right. It was a catchy tune, light and uptempo, with a slight calypso beat. Something hard to get out of your brain after hearing it three or four times on the radio driving to work. The perfect advertising jingle.

And—I was almost certain—I'd heard it before.

I stood next to Rogers and watched graphs and text dance on the computer monitor. "Can you make it slower?"

Rogers looked puzzled, but punched more instructions into the keyboard. More music—or something similar to music—emitted from the wall-mounted speakers. The singers sounded as if they were underwater, the notes drawn out painfully slow, the melody reduced to mud.

"A bit faster," I said. "And can you lose those bongos, or whatever they are, on the backbeat? That reggae-sounding stuff."

Once more, Rogers's fingers flew across the keyboard, the graphics on the monitor altered their patterns, and sounds poured from the production room speakers.

This time Rogers had managed to goose the jingle up to ballad speed, and the vocalists were making tones that sounded almost normal, not as if they were awakening from anesthesia. The melody was clear and easy to follow.

I leaned against the spongy soundproofing of the studio wall. "Like our friend Glory Lou would say, 'as I live and breathe,' " I whispered.

"How's that again?"

"I think I've heard that tune before, that's all. Burn me a copy, okay?"

I'd heard that tune before, all right.

Pete Kovacs had played it on tape for me during his last visit to the station. A copy he'd made of "Cruisin' on K Street," the Dee Vines' big hit on their 45 back in 1961.

The record Pete Kovacs had unearthed in that box of memorabilia from the old El Jay recording studio.

14

I STOPPED AT MY DESK JUST LONG ENOUGH TO GRAB KEYS AND A file folder, and to look up an address in the yellow pages. Traffic into downtown was light just after the lunch hour. The U.V. shuddered to a halt in front of an address on J Street just ten minutes after I peeled out of the Sacramento Talk Radio parking lot.

Sacramento's Midtown district, Lavender Heights to the locals, is the closest thing the capital city has to Castro Street, West Hollywood, or Dupont Circle. A neighborhood of boutiques, alternative bookstores, trendy restaurants, and dance clubs had also drawn mainstream businesses hoping to horn in on the cutting-edge image. Firms like Cherise Rose's advertising agency.

I snatched the file folder, trotted up a flower-lined sidewalk—roses, of course—and took the stairs two at a time. Rose and Associates had taken over a Victorian mansion and painted it various shades of pink with white and gold trim. More pink roses of the climbing variety entwined themselves through the hand-milled porch railing. A wicker love seat on the porch held a male and female mannequin, each dressed in Gay Nineties garb and locked in a smooch. Given the neighborhood, I figured it should have been a same-sex couple. Scratch that thought. Too over-the-top for even the most flamboyant denizens of the neighborhood.

I flung open the carved wooden door inset with a stained-glass version of the Rose and Associates logo, barged past the receptionist before she could object, and bounded up the stairs to the corner office with the bay window, where I was pretty sure the boss lady would have ensconced herself.

Cherise Rose's hand froze in the middle of relining her lips. She capped the pencil and dropped it into a designer purse atop her dainty antique desk. Rose's office decor carried out more of the faux good ole days theme: oriental carpet in pink tones, white wicker guest chairs, calico wallpaper, trailing greenery, and—yes!—a Thomas Kinkade print of a rose-covered country cottage in a gaudy gold frame.

"Excuse me, do you have an appointment?"

I planted myself firmly in front of her desk, legs apart, arms folded across my chest. "Nope."

"Then I'm afraid you'll have to leave." She smiled, but her voice dripped with frost.

"I don't think so. Shauna J. Bogart, Sacramento Talk Radio, and no, I'm not rolling tape and this isn't on the record—at least, not for now."

"How did you get past the receptionist?"

"Just tell me everything you know about that old record by the Dee Vines and the Mine Shaft jingle." I itched to fling the contents of the file folder in her face, but kept it clutched under one arm. For later.

Rose looked me over from across the gewgaw-strewn desk and steepled her fingers. "My agency places several hundred thousand dollars' worth of advertising on your radio station every year. I don't think T. R. O'Brien is going to be very pleased when he finds out I caught one of his employees trespassing into my office and harassing me."

"Fine. Pick up the phone and call him." I lowered myself into one of the wicker chairs.

Her penciled eyebrows furrowed in thought. "What is it, exactly, that you want to know about the Mine Shaft campaign? Off the record, I believe you said."

I flung one leg across the arm of the wicker chair, as if settling in for a good long stay. "Now that's the spirit! I just knew we'd get along. You and Lloyd Ellwanger were planning to get the rights to 'Cruisin' on K Street' and use it as the theme song for the expansion of his restaurant chain into Southern California, weren't you? Then all sudden-like, it's off. What happened?"

"Is that all?" Rose made a laughing sound without a hint of genuine humor. "We like to keep these things under wraps until the campaign is ready to break, but yes, at first my client and I were both very enthusiastic about using 'Cruisin'' for the new Mine Shaft jingle. But we test-marketed it with focus groups and it just didn't go over as well as I'd hoped. It took a bit of persuasion on my part to convince my client that we needed to seek a new direction, but he finally saw the wisdom of my advice."

That wasn't quite the version of the clash over "creative differences" I'd witnessed in the station production room last Friday afternoon. Seemed to me it was Ellwanger who was hankerin' to ditch the concept and try something new, while Cherise Rose clung to the old plan.

I opened the file folder and dealt two items onto Rose's leather desk blotter. A Polaroid photo and a letter on law office letterhead threatening Kovacs with legal action if he didn't give up that box of memorabilia from El Jay. "That was a cute touch, using the address of Sutter's Fort for your phony law firm, wasn't it, Ms. Rosenbloom?"

It was one hundred percent bluff, but my instincts told me it was worth seeing how the ad lady would react.

She drew in air sharply and stood. "This conversation has officially ended. Get out now before I call 911." Her voice never lost the polite business-school tone, but she bit off each word as if she wanted to spit it out.

"I'll bet you also had something to do with that rock going through the window at Retro Alley."

That last accusation seemed to crack Rose's icy facade. She grabbed the designer handbag and stepped over to the wicker chair where I continued to lounge. I even wagged my lower leg over the chair arm a few times to emphasize my nonchalance. Rose responded by raising the bag over her head like a weapon.

Now, I suppose the purse could have done some damage, especially if she'd filled it with a roll of quarters along with all that makeup. The corners of the miniature pink leather satchel were reinforced with gold-colored metal and could conceivably draw blood if one of them jabbed me in a tender spot. Still, I was at least ten years younger than Cherise Rose, and though she kept herself in good enough shape to fit into designer threads, I was willing to bet I sported more muscle per square inch, thanks to all of that swimming. Plus, she was handicapped by wearing a wool suit with a narrow skirt and pumps, while I had on my usual loose slacks, cotton top, and river sandals.

I hurtled to my feet and grabbed Rose's upraised wrist with both hands, squeezing until she gave a little yelp of pain and dropped the purse.

"Don't make me do that again," I said as I dusted off my hands and returned to the wicker chair.

Rose answered with a whimper and slunk back into the chair behind the desk. "You want money, I suppose."

"Nope, just answers. Well, maybe a check to cover the cost of a new window for Pete Kovacs's store. Now start talking. If you can convince me you're telling the truth and not holding anything back, it'll never go beyond this room."

"It was Ellwanger's idea, not mine, to use 'Cruisin' on K Street' as the new theme song for his restaurant chain." Rose continued to rub her wrist as she spoke. "But I immediately saw the merit. Those commercials that use classic pop music almost always do well, profitwise. The song was a big hit in the Sacramento area, and I'd hoped the tune might work in L.A. as well."

Personally, I find myself cringing whenever I hear one of my favorite songs from when I was a kid being used to peddle laundry detergent or soda pop. I was glad Janis Joplin wasn't around to hear "Oh Lord Won't You Buy Me a Mercedes Benz" in those commercials for guess which luxury car company. But like Rose said, some people must like those damn commercials and buy the products or the advertisers wouldn't keep using the tactic.

"You were lying about the focus groups a few minutes ago, weren't you?"

"Lying is such a hostile word."

"Well, were you?"

Rose chewed off a layer of pink lipstick. "Oh, all right. The focus groups loved the new jingle. It tested right off the charts."

"So then what happened?"

"Ellwanger said he'd have his attorney negotiate with the owner of the publishing rights. I was pleased, because it meant one less detail that I had to attend to."

"Keep talking," I said.

"Just as we're about to launch the campaign, Ellwanger's attorney says a slight problem has developed. There's some doubt over the legal ownership of the song, or some such nonsense, and it seems to hinge around some old records and tapes that belonged to one of the original El Jay recording artists."

"And that box of records and tapes just happened to end up in the hands of Pete Kovacs," I prompted.

"Ellwanger hinted to me that if 'someone' could convince Kovacs to give up those recordings, then our problem would be solved, and we could proceed with the launch of our new advertising campaign."

"Back up a second. How the hell would someone like Lloyd Ellwanger know anything about Pete Kovacs having that box?"

"I would assume when Ellwanger got in touch with the licensing agent for the song, or the holder of the legal rights. Is this really important?"

"I'm the one who decides what's important and what's not. So you took it upon yourself to be the 'someone' who would pay a visit to Kovacs and try to coerce him into giving up the recordings."

"He's a very stubborn man, your Pete Kovacs."

"When he refused to cooperate, you sent a letter threatening legal action. When that didn't work, you lobbed a rock through his window." I was having trouble picturing the oh-so-elegant lady exec scrabbling around the banks of the Sacramento River for a rock, lugging it back to Retro Alley, and pitching it through the window. I mean, what if she broke a nail? On the other hand, she had a hair-trigger temper, judging from that little incident with the designer handbag. "You followed Pete when he left town and snapped that Polaroid of him pumping gas along the highway. By the way, where was that gas station?"

"Interstate 5, just south of Tracy."

"You used that picture to try to intimidate Pete and Mrs. Romswinkel."

Rose studied her manicure. "I'm not admitting to any wrongdoing. But my agency will be happy to pay for the window if that will put a stop to all of this unpleasantness."

I was ready to grab that silly designer handbag that had probably cost her way more than a replacement window and bean her in her bouffant in retaliation for all the worry she had caused me and Mrs. Romswinkel. I reminded myself to stay focused on the big picture, which did not include facing charges of assaulting a fashion victim.

I broke all my rules about devoting one hour of prep time for every hour on the air, barreled into the on-air studio, the headphone cord trailing behind me, and leaped over the ditch in the floor just as the network announcer launched into the last story of the top-of-the-hour newscast. "Get Vance Ballard lined up to do a phoner," I shouted to Josh into the intercom just before I punched the cart machine with my theme music and flipped open the microphone.

If there was one person in Sacramento who'd know all about the licensing of hit songs for commercial use, I'd put my money on the owner of the city's biggest production studio. Sure, I'd promised Cherise Rose I'd keep our little encounter confidential. But there was nothing stopping me from jawing over the issue with Ballard and my listeners on a what-if basis.

The radio gods were smiling on me. Josh was able to catch Ballard between recording sessions and he was gracious about spending more time on my show. "Sure, the licensing of hit songs for use in radio and TV commercials can be very lucrative," Ballard said after I'd set up the topic and reintroduced him to my listeners. "Both for the owner of the publishing rights and, often, for the recording artist."

"As in, how much?"

"That depends on many factors. If you're talking about a huge hit, a real classic that's never been used in advertising up until now, and you want to feature it in a national television campaign, shoot, you're looking at half a million and upwards."

"No kidding!" Now I could understand the temptation to sell out. Five hundred thousand smackers for a tune that was a hit twenty years ago could help pay for a lot of face-lifts and trips to rehab for an aging rock star, even after taxes.

"How about someone who might want to use the song just statewide in a radio campaign?" I continued.

"Oh, gosh, that still just depends. Again, how big of a hit was this song? Are you talking exclusive rights for all advertising, or just product exclusivity? What's the size of the market? San Francisco and L.A. will cost you more than Sacramento. And how long do you want the rights? Just for the Christmas season? A whole year? In perpetuity?"

"Could you at least give us a ballpark figure?"

Ballard paused for a moment. "I'd say a low of twenty-five grand, a high of seventy-five, maybe a hundred thousand, if it was a number one hit that your target consumer still loves and remembers."

"Cruisin' on K Street" had only made the charts in Northern California, and never hit number one. So the Dee Vines, if any of them were still around, might be looking at, what? Ten grand? A tidy little windfall, but not exactly life-changing.

I broke for traffic and weather—jackknifed big rig on southbound Highway 99, forecast continues pleasant with highs in the seventies—then asked Ballard, "Who profits, exactly, from the sale of these licensing rights? The original recording artist?"

"Interesting question," Ballard began.

"I know, I know. It depends, right?"

"Right. If you're looking at just the tune itself, just the composition, and you're going to do a new recording with your own musicians and your own singers, you'd get in touch with the publisher. But if you want master recording rights—in other words, the original artist—you'd need to cut a deal with the record company."

I paced in the control room, the headphone cord and mike keeping me on a short leash. Cherise Rose and Lloyd Ellwanger had written new lyrics for "Cruisin' on K Street" and given it a whole new feel, uptempo with a calypso beat. They obviously weren't planning to bring back any of the original Dee Vines to participate in the recording. So only the publisher would benefit.

Rather than pursue a topic that seemed to have crashed into a dead end, I thanked Ballard for his time and introduced surefire themes guaranteed to start the phones ringing with callers: the fall TV season, Sacramento's worst speed traps, crop circles. And, of course, the hottest topic of the day, Jasmine sightings.

A listener identifying herself as Torita on a cell phone landed on the air just before the 4:20 commercial break. "I wanted to call in when you were interviewing that guy from the recording studio," she said, "but I was at work and couldn't get to a phone until now."

"What's your point, Dorita?"

"Toe-reeta, with a T," she said with a touch of impatience. "Not the chips."

"The clock's ticking, Doe-reeta, Toe-reeta. What's your point?"

"My Grandpa Turner was in a group that cut a record once, a long time ago, right here in Sacramento."

I was pretty sure the topic was comatose, but there was one angle that might defibrillate it back to life. "Any chance you know the name of the studio where Grand-pappy cut the record?"

Her cell phone crackled, but I was positive I heard her say it.

El Jay.

"Stay on the line, Torita," I said. "Let's chat off the air, during the break."

"You did say El Jay, right?" I said as soon as I activated the tape cartridge with the Senator Ford commercial.

"Uh-huh." The cell phone reception improved. "El Jay Records on Stockton Boulevard. The Sounds of Sacramento."

I wasn't sure what any of this had to do with finding Jasmine, or the death of Johnny Venture. But some instinct told me it might be worth setting up a meeting with Torita's grandfather and discovering what he remembered about the recording studio where Jasmine had cut the demo tape that launched her into stardom. Or better yet, put him on the show.

"Grandpa Turner died before I was born," Torita continued.

Damn. Still, there might be a faint trail to follow. "How do you know about your grandfather's recording career, then?"

"I was helping my mother clean out her house and move into a condo a few months ago. I found this box full of my grandfather's records in the hall closet. She didn't care about that old stuff, but I thought it was cool. So I took it home."

"This stuff your granddaddy left you, what, exactly, are we talking about?"

"Publicity photos, old 45s, tapes, things like that."

Pete Kovacs had a similar box of El Jay memorabilia given to him by someone's granddaughter. Suddenly the trail seemed slightly more distinct, though I still had no idea where it was leading me.

"Any chance I could take a look at your granddaddy's legacy?"

She paused to deliberate and spoke with caution. "I guess it's all right."

"Could you stop by the station at six, when I'm off the air?"

Through the glass leading to the call screener booth, I could see

Josh pointing to the clock, signaling the rapidly approaching end of the stop set. My cue to go back on the air.

"I don't think that's a good idea." This time Torita sounded firm and in control. "Go to the parking lot at the Mansion Inn, southeast corner, six-thirty. Look for a guy driving a silver Lexus IS."

I closed the Sacramento telephone directory with a slam and swore.

"What's the trouble, hon?" Glory Lou said, emerging from her office and planting herself next to my desk in the newsroom.

"There's no such place as the Mansion Inn."

"The Mansion Inn?" Josh Friedman looked up from the pile of fan mail he'd been attempting to organize. "I haven't heard it called that since I was a little kid."

"You haven't heard what called that since you were a little kid?" I said.

"The Mansion Inn. This hotel, downtown at Sixteenth and H. They changed it to a Clarion a long time ago, and now it's a Holiday Inn. Whoever called it the Mansion Inn must be a real old-timer."

"What's this about, hon?" Glory Lou planted one hip on the edge of the desk and folded her ample arms over her equally ample chest. "You aren't planning to meet some caller at a hotel bar, are you?"

"You know me better than that." I make it a rule not to fraternize with listeners, no matter how cute, or even sane, they sound on the phone.

"You keep your cell phone handy, hear?" Glory Lou said. "If anything seems the slightest bit hinky, call 911."

The Mansion Inn/Clarion Hotel/Holiday Inn turned out to be an overgrown motel taking up an entire city block between H, I, Fifteenth, and Sixteenth. I must have driven past it hundreds of times heading out of downtown toward Highway 160 and never really took notice. It was that unremarkable. A low-slung fifties-era box softened by ivy trailing up the stuccoed walls and intertwining the balconies. Plus, it was hard to compete for attention with the Old Governor's Mansion, a glorious Victorian castle just across H Street. That was the house Nancy Reagan refused to live in, branding it a firetrap and lamenting a lack of neighborhood children suitable for son "Skipper" to play with. No California governor has lived in it since the Reagans decamped. The mansion is now part of the state parks system.

The tour groups had long departed when I pulled into the hotel lot and parked the Volvo just before six-thirty. One thing about downtown Sacramento, it's easy to figure out directions. The numbered streets run north-south, while the lettered streets form a perfect east-west grid. Boring, but hard to get lost. The southeast sector of the parking lot plunked me at the corner of Sixteenth and H.

A late-model silver sedan that I assumed was a Lexus IS, the engine running, hovered in a parking space near the appointed rendezvous, nose out. In the fading sunlight, I watched as a young African-American male emerged from the driver's side. "You the lady from the radio?" he said in a cautious voice.

"Who wants to know?" I shivered and pulled my sweater more tightly across my chest.

"Just get in the car." I'm guessing he was trying to sound menacing, but he was having trouble pulling off the act.

But he did hold something small and rectangular in his right hand.

I recoiled when he pointed it in my direction.

15

NOW, IF HE'D BEEN A WHITE GUY INSTEAD OF AFRICAN-AMERICAN, would I have reacted with such caution? I consider myself liberal, open-minded, and an enthusiastic supporter of diversity. Shoot, as a female in an industry that for years was a boys-only club, I owe my very career to affirmative action. But let's be honest. I'm also the product of childhood conditioning, years of exposure to outmoded cultural stereotypes.

To answer the question, probably not.

"Hey, chill," he said. "I'm just here to drive you over to meet Rita." He raised both hands over his head, surrender-style. He was dressed in a polo shirt with an embroidered designer logo, windbreaker, Dockers, and clean sneakers. Hardly ghetto attire. He continued to hold something about the size of a pack of cards in his right hand. It appeared too small, not pointy enough, to be any sort of weapon.

I edged closer until I could identify the object. A state of California employee ID badge. He moved into the illumination of the car's interior light and extended his arm so I could compare the photograph on the badge with the round face in front of me. The card introduced me to Wilmott Slade, information technology specialist with the Fair Political Practices Commission. Now there was an oxymoron if I ever heard one.

"Why don't I just follow you over to wherever this Rita person is," I said.

"That's not how Rita wants it."

"Why all the secrecy?"

"You'll have to ask Rita."

The guy looked harmless, and I had my cell phone fired up and clipped to my waistband for easy access, just as Glory Lou had instructed. This excursion had a remote possibility of providing a lead on Jasmine's whereabouts. That cinched it. I climbed into the passenger seat of the Lexus and fastened the seat belt.

"Here. Rita says to put this on." Slade handed me a leopard-print sleep mask.

Even though the vehicle was more luxurious and the blindfold way more stylish, the situation was starting to feel like a rerun of Luis and Hector and the jaunt to Castroville in the Catalina. "Look," I said, "I'm not going to rat you guys out, okay? I promise not to give out Rita's address or let on to anyone where she lives. I won't even pay attention to where you're taking me."

"I tried to tell Rita she was being too paranoid." Slade tossed the sleep mask into the glove box and smiled at me. I realized that he was little more than a kid, mid-twenties maybe, only a year or two older than Josh. Barely mature enough to be one of those old-timers who still referred to this hotel as the Mansion Inn.

He steered the Lexus out of the downtown district and onto I-5, heading south. About twenty minutes later, he exited onto Laguna Boulevard and into the labyrinth of new suburban streets that lay atop the cow pastures, wheat fields, and hop yards in the onetime farming hamlet of Elk Grove. Even if I'd been trying to pay attention, I would have been lost. These new housing developments all look alike to me, cheapo projects sprouting up from interchangeable blueprints. The Lexus twisted and turned through the narrow, treeless streets, finally stopping in the driveway of a one-story wood and stucco abode at the end of a cul-de-sac. I think it was a detached home, but it was hard to tell for certain in the darkness. The yards were that tiny and the dwellings were that snuggled up to each other.

The front door opened the instant Slade and I set foot on the porch. A petite African-American woman with a cap of short hair, roughly the same age as Wilmott Slade, stood framed in the light of the entry. She wore the female version of a state worker's dweeb uniform: denim jumper, cotton turtleneck sweater, Birkenstocks with tights. "Thanks for coming." She stuck out her hand. "I'm Torita Slade. You can call me Rita."

She ushered me in and offered lemonade, giving me time to snoop while she fussed in the kitchen. Like most new construction, the Slade home featured an open-floor plan, with living room, dining area, and kitchen occupying one vast space. The great room, I think the developers call it. As I gave the place the once-over, I realized this was no post-college starter home with hand-me-down mismatched furniture and do-it-yourself projects from IKEA. The Slades all but announced, *Adults live here.* The look was substantial and sturdy: dark polished wood and earth-tone fabrics, walls decorated with expensively framed photographs of architectural details from world landmarks. I recognized the onion domes of the Kremlin, the girders of the Eiffel Tower, and granite columns from, I think, the Lincoln Memorial. I wondered if they were souvenirs of the Slades' international travels. Several thousand dollars' worth of electronic gear, including a plasma-screen TV, occupied the entertainment center that dominated one wall of the living room.

Not bad for a couple barely out of college. Cozy new home in the suburbs, snazzy furniture, expensive vacations, the latest high-tech toys. Not to mention that thirty-thousand-dollar car in the driveway.

I studied the clutter on the kitchen counter: car keys, supermarket coupons, postage stamps. And Rita Slade's employee badge identifying her as an IT specialist with the state library.

Not long ago, *Time* magazine named Sacramento the most integrated city in the United States. Everyone's in the minority here, with non-Latino whites like me making up just forty-four percent of the population. State government employment acts as the great equalizer, a recession-proof industry providing fat paychecks and a treasure trove of fringe benefits regardless of which box you check off on those equal employment opportunity surveys. It's hard to remain bigoted when you toil side by side every day with a rainbow coalition of co-workers. I was surrounded by the proof in the home of Rita and Wilmott Slade.

Rita handed around tumblers of lemonade and led me down a hallway, Wilmott following, into a spare bedroom divided by a fabric-covered panel. As if the Slades didn't spend enough time eight-to-five in cubicles, they'd brought the look home, his 'n' her computer cubbyholes filled with terminals, monitors, keyboards, speakers, scanners, printers, and various electronic gadgets I was unable to identify. Wilmott took his place on the "his" side and immediately began tip-tapping on the keyboard. Rita motioned for me to have a seat on "her" side, cleared papers and books from the desk by pushing them to one side, pulled a thick scrapbook from a bookshelf, placed it on the desk, and seated herself next to me.

"You're the person who came into Retro Alley with a box of memorabilia from a local pop music group, aren't you?" I said before Rita Slade could start her show-and-tell.

"Grandpa Turner left duplicates of a lot of his photographs, and even records and tapes. I told Mr. Kovacs I wasn't interested in making a lot of money. I just want to find a museum or a private collector who would appreciate our family's heritage. He said he felt certain the city archives would be interested, and maybe even the Rock and Roll Hall of Fame."

"Have you heard from him since you dropped off the box of stuff?"

"No, but Mr. Kovacs told me I would need to be patient. He agreed to take on the project on a consignment basis, and told me that finding just the right buyer might take a little time."

It sounded like something Pete would say, and a cause he would take on. The pleasure he would take in finding an appreciative home for ephemera from the mid–twentieth century would far outweigh any chump change he might make in commissions.

Rita opened the heavy cover of the scrapbook and pointed to a black-and-white eight-by-ten mounted on the first page. "See? That's my grandfather. Otis Turner."

Four young men with processed 'dos, sharkskin suits, and pointy-toed, hep cat shoes, identically posed with one hand on hip, the other hand thrust forward in a finger-snap. I read the printing across the bottom:

THE DEE VINES

Clarence Willets • Ferdinand Simpson • Otis Turner • Douglas "The Duke" Donlon

"The Latest Hitbound Sound from the El Jay Label!"

"Did they really have a hit?" I asked. I'd never heard of the Dee Vines.

"Oh, sure. At least, a regional hit." Rita reached into the back of the scrapbook and pulled out a plastic sheet protector. She carefully slid a black disc, roughly seven inches in diameter, onto the edges of her fingers, then deftly transferred it to my upraised fingertips.

It looked just like the 45 record Pete Kovacs had proudly displayed to me a week ago. I peered at the red, yellow, and black El Jay label. "Cruisin' on K Street" by the Dee Vines, followed by the songwriter credits in tiny type. Some fellow named Lou Jelniak.

"Want to hear it?" Rita said.

"This?" I pointed my chin toward the disc that was still balanced on my fingertips, certain she wouldn't want to risk scratching the record by actually playing it. Assuming she and Wilmott even had a turntable among all those expensive new gadgets in their entertainment center.

"I've downloaded it onto my hard drive." She executed a few keystrokes in almost perfect imitation of LeVon Rogers's performance in the Sacramento Talk Radio production room earlier that day. A few seconds later, a familiar tune poured from the computer's speakers, the same doo-wop ode to cars, cruising, and young love that Pete had played for me. I'd heard that K Street had had a cruise scene right out of *American Graffiti* in the late fifties and early sixties, before they turned the boulevard into a pedestrian mall, in yet another urban renewal scheme. This tune brought the era back to life.

"I can burn you a copy if you'd like. As long as you don't tell anyone where you got it." Before I had a chance to respond, Rita placed a blank CD into a slot in the computer and clicked the mouse. While she fiddled with the cyber gizmos, I slipped the 45 back into its protective sleeve and continued to leaf through the scrapbook. I found a KROY Tunedex survey from September of 1961 placing "Cruisin' on K Street" in the local Top Ten, handbills from appearances by the Dee Vines at the State Fair and opening for the Shirelles at Sacramento Memorial Auditorium, a browned and crumbling *Sacramento Bee* advertisement for a gig at Momo's Lounge. And more photographs, including several candids that looked as if they'd been shot at a recording session.

I waited until Rita had finished making the CD copy of "Cruisin' on K Street," then held open the scrapbook and asked, "Who are these guys, any idea?"

"Lucky for us, Grandpa Turner wrote names on the back of most of the photos." She pointed to a young fellow with a crew cut and Buddy Holly glasses on a chubby face. He appeared to be sharing a joke with one of the Dee Vines. "That's Lou Jelniak, the owner of the recording studio. Here, I'll write it down for you so you get the spelling correct."

Lou Jelniak. El Jay.

Rita Slade jotted the name on a notepad and I contemplated the black-and-white photograph. Jelniak looked barely out of his teens, young to be running a recording studio. "How about him?" I indicated a slightly older fellow seated at the mixing board. He had a shaggy mustache and an unruly mop of hair, unusual in the buttoned-down early sixties. Either he was affecting some sort of Beatnik look, or he was just a hayseed.

"Sorry, I couldn't find a name for him, just a notation that he was the recording engineer."

I turned a page to a picture of another sound studio, the Dee Vines surrounding a young man sporting a neat goatee. "Oh, him," Rita said. "That's Johnny Venture, the disk jockey that gave the Dee Vines their first radio airplay."

The Johnny Venture who signed off underneath a pillow in a motor court in Monterey? The Anton Greb/Johnny Venture? I gave the photograph a closer examination, focusing on the eyes and mouth, mentally comparing the image of the fresh-out-of-broadcast-school DJ with the codger whose face had been splashed across the tabloids. Maybe it was just an overactive imagination, but I was pretty sure I detected a resemblance.

"I can scan anything you'd like, if you want a copy," Rita said. "As long as you don't let anyone know where you got it."

"The photos for sure," I said. "And that Tunedex survey. Oh, yeah, the handbill from Memorial Auditorium, if it's not too much trouble."

"Won't take but a minute or two." Rita removed the candid photo of the Dee Vines and Lou Jelniak in the recording studio and positioned it facedown on the glass plate of the scanner.

"So what happened?" I asked as I watched Rita Slade create her magic. "The Dee Vines seemed to be ready to break through with a national hit. I mean, they make the local Top Ten, they're playing Memorial Auditorium."

"My mother didn't know much about it, just that there was some sort of falling-out. She told me Clarence Willets and Ferdinand Simpson both got drafted within a few months of each other, and The Duke went back to Texas. Something having to do with a girl. Grandpa Turner had a family to support and he couldn't make it on what they were earning as entertainers. He went back to school and learned how to install and repair two-way radios, got a job with the state."

"Are any of the rest of the group still around?"

"Let's see." Rita Slade frowned a moment in thought. "According to what Mom remembered, The Duke was killed in an auto accident not long after he moved back to Texas. Ferdinand Simpson never came back from Vietnam—MIA. Then Grandpa Turner got leukemia in 1971."

"Man." I shook my head, not knowing what else to say.

"Yeah. Clarence Willets is still with us, though. He became a preacher, changed his name to Zakiyyah Mazama."

"The Reverend Mazama? The guy who runs the after-school center in Oak Park? I've heard of him."

"The same. If Mr. Kovacs is able to make any money off those old tapes and records, that's where I plan to donate my share. After all, Reverend Mazama helped earn that money."

Not only had I heard of Reverend Mazama, I'd interviewed him on the show this past Martin Luther King Day. Interesting fellow, spent most of the seventies in the Peace Corps—western Samoa, as I recall—then came back to Sacramento to do what he could to help the Oak Park community. He impressed me as one of the strongest flickers of hope in a neighborhood facing more than its share of challenges.

"Did your mother ever mention Jasmine in connection with the El Jay studio?" It was a long shot for sure. The girl who would become Jasmine would have been picking out the letters in her *Fun with Dick and Jane* reader about the time the Dee Vines made the Top Ten on the KROY Tunedex.

"Jasmine? Did she record on the El Jay label? I didn't know that." Rita Slade kept her gaze on the computer monitor as she spoke to me. "Should I e-mail the scans to you or download them onto CD?"

"E-mail, I guess." I was pretty confident about opening e-mail attachments, less sure about figuring out how to look at pictures on a CD. I gave her my e-mail address.

She responded by saying something that sounded like "Jaypeg, tiffs, or giffs?"

"Come again?"

"What kind of graphics files do you normally use? JPEGs, TIFs, or GIFs?"

Like I'm supposed to know? "JPEGs, I guess." It was the only option she'd given me that sounded like it could be a real word.

Rita handed me a CD, which she said contained both sides of the Dee Vines 45, plus the sheet of paper with IDs and correct spellings of the young men in the photographs. The pictures themselves were winging their way through cyberspace, where, if the electronic gods were on my side, they'd be waiting in my e-mail box the next time I logged on. My hostess gathered up the empty lemonade glasses and ushered me back to the entryway.

"Why all the secrecy?" I asked her as Wilmott shrugged back into his windbreaker in preparation for schlepping me back to the Mansion Inn parking lot.

The two Slades exchanged glances. Wilmott nodded, as if encouraging his wife to respond.

"Have you heard of the Original Artists Justice Committee?"

"I think so," I said. "Some sort of coalition of music industry people who are trying to provide redress to singers and songwriters who were defrauded of their rights back in the fifties and sixties? The 'Louie Louie' case, for instance."

"I don't think I've heard of that one."

"The fellow who wrote 'Louie Louie' sold the publishing rights for five hundred dollars to pay for his wedding. It went on to become one of the world's greatest party songs, making hundreds of thousands of dollars for the new owner."

I don't blame Rita Slade for looking puzzled. "Louie Louie" was way before her time. "It happened a lot, especially in the fifties," I continued. "And surprise, surprise, it was almost always a black artist who ended up being cheated, and a white singer who ended up having the big hit record."

Rita Slade nodded. "That's what the man from the Original Artists Justice Committee told me. He wanted to know if there was a chance the Dee Vines had been defrauded like that."

"Were they, do you think?"

"I don't believe so. According to what Grandpa Turner told my mother, the Dee Vines just recorded other people's songs. Shortly before he died, he told her he wouldn't trade the memories for anything. No regrets."

A sound philosophy of life, in my opinion.

"I don't understand why you feel as if you have to keep everything secret," I said.

"I don't know either, but that's what Mr. Sinclair told me."

"Mr. Sinclair?"

"The man from the Original Artists Justice Committee."

"That wouldn't be Donovan Sinclair, would it? White dude, late sixties, early seventies? Would have been coming over from the coast?"

"That sounds like the man. He said he was the committee liaison with some broadcaster's group in San Francisco."

"The Northern California Broadcast Legends," Wilmott put in. "C'mon, let's go."

"Mr. Sinclair is the one who told us we should be discreet while the committee conducted its investigation," Rita said. "He told us that you just never know what might turn up."

16

MRS. ROMSWINKEL SHOOK HER HEAD AND RAISED HER SHOULDERS and outstretched palms in a shrug. She was busy with a customer at the Retro Alley counter, but the body language she directed my way wasn't difficult to translate: *No news. Nothing.*

I let myself through the swinging gate to the business side of the counter and seated myself at Pete's rolltop desk. Mrs. Romswinkel appeared to have entangled herself into a sticky debate with the customer over a consignment of retired Beanie Babies that had been entrusted in Kovacs's care two weeks ago. The customer, a pudgy, sunburned thirty-something woman, wore a pullover sweater bearing the likenesses of Disney's Seven Dwarfs. She seemed to be taking her cues from Grumpy, definitely not buying it when Mrs. Romswinkel continued to insist that only Pete Kovacs could make a decision about the resale value of the Beanie Babies, and he was unavailable at the moment.

A wad of unanswered mail and faxes poured out of one of the desk's cubbyholes, while a stack of correspondence waiting to be filed crested over the top of a wire basket. I took pity on Mrs.

Romswinkel and decided to pitch in. I could at least file the correspondence without creating too much chaos with her organizational system.

Personally, I don't see the point in making paper copies of routine business correspondence. Last night's encounter with Rita Slade drove home the vast gulf that separates the casual computer user like me from the true geek. But still, even I feel savvy enough to store most files on my hard drive and to ditch the paper copy. Save a tree, and all that. As long as I remember to make a backup disc every so often.

Mrs. Romswinkel, though, came from an earlier generation, where smart girls were shunted off to secretarial school to learn the fine art of handling carbon paper and changing typewriter ribbons. And how to file. So I indulged her insistence on printing out a duplicate of every letter she wrote using Kovacs's signature and placing it in a manila folder with a tab indicating the first letter of the recipient's last name. Alphabetized by last name, first name, within the folder, of course.

I had to admit, there was something satisfying about watching that pile of correspondence grow smaller as I stored each piece of correspondence neatly in the correct folder in the file drawer. As an added bonus, scanning the contents of those letters gave me the chance to indulge in one of my favorite pastimes, snooping, as well as learning more about my boyfriend's business.

Some fellow named Stan Greco wanted to know if the first edition of Stephen King's *Carrie* that he'd snatched up at a library discard sale was worth big bucks. Alas, no, Kovacs had written back. All those library rubber stamps, plus years of wear and tear, had rendered it virtually worthless except for reading.

I leaned into the file drawer, opened the "G" folder and fingered through the contents. Gordon, Grayson, Greb.

Greb?

I yanked the letter from the file.

Anton Greb of Modesto had written to Kovacs last March. Would Pete be interested in being a featured performer at a pianorama sponsored by the Stanislaus County Traditional Jazz Society in May? Kovacs had declined the invitation, citing commitments to the Sacramento Jazz Jubilee in May. "Some other time, definitely," he'd ended the letter.

I couldn't recall Kovacs playing a gig in Modesto this past summer. Still, he and Anton Greb might have spoken by telephone, traded e-mails.

What was left of Anton Greb now rested under a stone in the San Francisco Presidio cemetery. His alleged killer had disappeared. Pete Kovacs was acquainted with Anton Greb. And now he too had vanished.

I felt a chill that had nothing to do with the blast of autumn breeze that whirled through Retro Alley as Grumpy stormed out the door.

"You missed the FedEx guy this morning." Glory Lou tossed a red, white, and blue envelope onto my desk in the Sacramento Talk Radio newsroom.

I zipped open the nine-by-twelve cardboard envelope and let the contents spill out onto my desk.

Glory Lou snatched up a piece of folded card stock and looked inside. "As I live and breathe!" she squealed. "Look, hon, they've got your name and picture right in the program."

"Where?" I stood and leaned over her shoulder for a closer look.

A page headlining Honored Inductees featured my mug square in the center. I knew about the other five honorees—a TV anchor who was planning to retire at the end of the year, a veteran Bay Area traffic pilot, the host of the longest-running local kiddie show in the U.S., northern California's first Hispanic television news reporter, the morning host at the top-rated San Francisco hip-hop station—but didn't realize the Broadcast Legends organization was planning to induct someone posthumously this year.

Johnny Venture.

The notes under his photograph spoke of his long career in San

Francisco and Central Valley radio, and of his recent activity on behalf of the Original Artists Justice Committee. The Broadcast Legends' official liaison with the committee, Donovan Sinclair, was quoted as urging the membership to continue the good work of broadcasters like Johnny Venture. "Let's all pull together to ensure that the talented men and women who have contributed so much to the fabric of popular culture, and to the vitality of the radio industry, receive the recognition and remuneration they so justly deserve."

It was an intriguing cause for a broadcast group to take on, for sure. For years, the recording and radio industries maintained an uneasy truce, feeding off each other—the record companies depending on radio exposure to push their products, and radio relying on the recording industry for a never-ending supply of product that kids want to listen to, and that advertisers are willing to support. Now the Internet threatened to upend the game board and change all of the rules. I wondered what the music industry—and radio—would be like in another ten years.

In the meantime, the Original Artists Justice Committee seemed to me like a terrific cause. A similar organization, Artists Rights Enforcement, had recovered the publishing rights for that fellow who wrote "Louie, Louie" back in 1955 and sold the rights a couple of years later for, well, a song. Richard Berry—I knew I'd flash on his name if I concentrated hard enough!—finally received the money and recognition that was rightfully his for creating one of the most heavily recorded songs of all time.

I folded the program open to the page of Honored Inductees and propped it up on my desk with a self-satisfied smirk. "I feel like a kid waiting for Christmas. Friday night is going to be so fun."

"You go, girlfriend!" Glory Lou said. "Here I was afraid you might be thinking of canceling."

"Why would I do that?"

"You know, Pete Kovacs bailing. No date. . . ."

"Are you kidding?" I waved away Glory Lou's doubts with a

laugh and flick of my right hand. "I'm going to that Hall of Fame ceremony, come hell or high water."

"Still no sign of Jasmine as the manhunt continues. Authorities report no new leads."

I focused my attention on the four TV monitors mounted above the edit bay in the newsroom. The Jasmine update followed Dewey Hopper's weathercast on Channel 13, not even rating lead story status. A full week had passed since my visit with Luis and Bobette in the trailer in Castroville, and the last confirmed sighting of the fugitive pop music star.

If something didn't break soon, the public would lose interest in Jasmine and find some other celebrity scandal to chew up and spit out, and there would go my chance at a career-making story. The adjustment to Standard Time was scheduled for this Sunday and Halloween was the following week. Before you knew it, the Christmas decorations would go up and the fickle public consciousness would shift to shopping, holiday movie blockbusters, and endless cookie-baking. Barring a break in the story, the Jasmine case risked becoming just another footnote in the annals of true crime, like D. B. Cooper.

The media and the cops had a round-the-clock stakeout of Jasmine's condo in Santa Monica, her agent's office in Century City, her lawyer's digs on Wilshire Boulevard, and the *Yo Mama!* production company in Burbank. Even her last boyfriend, a kickboxing instructor fifteen years her junior, had a constant entourage. So it was doubtful she'd gone back home to L.A.

She hadn't responded to the message to "call home" on my fliers in Santa Cruz and the Monterey Peninsula, so she'd either fled the coastal scene or didn't want to—or couldn't—communicate.

By now, the eighty bucks she'd lifted from Aunt Velma would have been long gone, and Jasmine must have ditched Hector's truck somewhere as being too visible. She must be hungry and tired—and desperate for someone to talk to.

I leaned back in my desk chair and contemplated the newsroom's fluorescent lights and ceiling tiles. What would I do if I were in a jam and on the lam like Jasmine? If I couldn't return to my home, or risk hanging around the community where I was last seen?

I'd go home. Not my current city of legal domicile. My real home, my childhood home. A familiar neighborhood where I knew every tree, every dog, every nook in the local park, and every cranny of the elementary school; a place where I held a vague memory of comfort, security, and love. In my case, that would be the west side of Silicon Valley and my old haunts: Valley Fair Shopping Center, Sunnyvale Plaza, Country Lane Elementary, and the hiking trails of Villa Montalvo Arboretum.

For Jasmine, home would be right here in River City.

It was time to take matters into my own hands.

"Jasmine, baby," I said into the microphone as soon as my theme music started to fade. "I know you're out there. I know you're listening. Come home to Sacramento, Jasmine."

Josh Friedman stared at me through the window of the call screener booth. His jaw didn't exactly drop, but his eyes widened.

"Cynthia Pepper, yes, you, baby, this is for you, class of 1971, El Camino High School. Sacramento loves you, Cynthia. Sacramento loves you, Jasmine. We don't care what you call yourself. We just loves ya, baby."

Through the double-paned glass separating the on-air studio from the newsroom, I could see Glory Lou, the traffic secretary, the entire sales department, and my boss, T.R. O'Brien, lined up and giving me high fives and thumbs-up.

"Jasmine, I know you're listening. I know you're hungry and tired. And I know that, more than anything else in the world, you just want someone to talk to. You want to tell your story to someone who will understand. Trust me, Jasmine. Call me."

Naturally, every wacko in our listening area called in. Even Ferretman Bob, one of the regular kooky callers, somehow managed to slip past Josh Friedman and sneak onto the air. He insisted Jasmine never would have "gone bad" if state law had only permitted her to keep a pet ferret as a child.

For those callers who sounded like they might be legit—something in the voice, a combination of weariness, wariness, and a diva-like imperiousness—I devised a quiz. What was the brand name of Aunt Velma's purple sweats? What did the sign over the door of the trailer in Castroville say? What radio station decal was in the back window of Hector's pickup? This information was in the public record, as in *People* and the *National Enquirer,* not some dry court document, so these should have been easy questions. The purple sweats had achieved a special status right up there with Monica's blue Gap dress in the celebrity clothing hall of infamy. Yet it was amazing how stupid these schemers were, how easy to winnow out the fakes.

Details. It's all in the details.

I saved one more question, off mike during a commercial break, for those few who survived the first round of questioning. A little detail that hadn't yet been leaked to the media. Private information, shared only by Jasmine and me.

So far, they'd all flunked.

"I have all your answers," the caller on Line One told me. It was just past the commercial break at twenty 'til five. "Target's Cherokee line. Protected by Angels. Radio Romantica. So you can call a stop to the interrogation."

The voice had the pitch and intensity that I remembered from her recent jailhouse interviews. She had that gritty thing working that you'd expect for a life-in-the-fast-lane rock 'n' roll chick pushing fifty. And just the right combination of trepidation and defiance.

"Fine by me, Jasmine," I replied. "Can I call you Jasmine? Or do you prefer Cynthia?"

"Cut the small talk or I'm out of here. The only reason I'm on the line is to inform you and the goddamn lady sheriff in Monterey County and her goddamn district attorney that I didn't do it, okay?"

"I believe you." Say anything to keep her talking.

"They set me up, framed me, played me like a violin."

"Who's they?"

"If I knew the answer to that, do you think I'd be shooting the breeze with the likes of you?" Jasmine—or a pretty good impersonator—let out a dramatic sigh.

I paused for another stop set, early for once. As soon as I'd closed the mike and punched up the first commercial that I could grab from the stack of cartridges, I posed the deal-breaker question.

She aced it.

"Told you I was the real deal," she said.

She interrupted me just as I gave my listeners the time, temperature, and call letters. "If I turn myself in, can you guarantee I won't go back to jail?"

"You know I can't do that."

"Well screw you, then."

"C'mon, Jasmine. Be reasonable. That's up to a judge down in Monterey County."

"I thought I could trust you. You're just like all the others."

"Look, if you're innocent like you say you are, you have nothing to fear from the legal system." I wasn't even sure if I bought into that line of reasoning. I couldn't imagine a gal as world-weary and street-smart as Jasmine falling for it.

She responded with a time-honored term traditionally uttered to indicate carnal knowledge. My hand bolted for the censor button to delete the expletive before it made it through our seven-second tape-delay system and over the airwaves. Just in time! My reflex was so automatic, I spaced on the fact that hitting the censor button also automatically boots the caller off the air and disconnects the phone line.

Fuck, indeed.

Sheriff Maria Elena Perez rang me up on the studio hotline the instant the five o'clock network newscast rolled. "Don't you even think of doing something like that again without running it by me first," she said without introduction.

"Gosh, and here I thought you were calling to congratulate me on a killer show."

"I am not amused." She paused between each word as if biting them off. "If you'd let us know what you were planning to do, we could have traced the call. By now Jasmine might be back in custody. I hope you realize you've screwed up big time."

I admit, that gave me pause. Had I let my ambition run out of control, forgetting my promise to cooperate with the investigation? Should I backpedal and salvage what I could of the situation? Save my ass? Apologize, grovel, promise Sheriff Perez I'd be a good girl and never do it again?

Nah.

"In case you haven't noticed, I've come closer than any of Monterey County's finest to actually locating your fugitive," I said. "So why don't we both pull in our claws and call a truce."

"How about sharing with me that question you were asking the callers off the air." Her voice softened, which I took as a tacit acceptance of my offer of the white flag. "Your secret question to determine if the caller might be the real Jasmine."

"Oh, that. I just asked them where they were in the summer of 1970."

"Go on."

"The real Jasmine, Cynthia Pepper, attended a music camp in the Sierra during the summer of 1970." I didn't feel the need to share the information about my mother being on the faculty. "To my knowledge, that tidbit never made it into print anywhere. That last caller had the correct answer. Camp Mel-O-Dee."

"Interesting." Sheriff Perez paused, and I could hearing the scritch-scratch of a pen against paper. When she resumed speaking, she was back in scolding mode. "Remember what I told you before."

"Yeah, yeah, yeah. Don't pull anything without letting you in on it first."

"I have half a mind to call my colleagues with the Sacramento PeeDee and the sheriff's office and have them keep an eye on you, just to make sure you aren't planning another little media stunt. In fact, I think I'll do it right now." She hung up before I had a chance to think up a snappy comeback.

Josh Friedman sent a yearning look my way as I signed off the program logs and gathered up my show notes and headphones.

"Aren't you going to need some help tonight?" He dogged me into the newsroom.

"How do you know what I'm planning to do this evening?"

"Like, duh? Go find Jasmine?"

I plopped my gear onto the desk and turned to Josh. "But that would assume I know where she's hiding out." I turned both palms outward and tilted my head, all coy and innocent. "Like, duh?"

"Oh, you know, all right." Josh trotted ahead of me and blocked the door to the parking lot. "You're going to cut me out of the action, just when things are getting good."

I expected any minute he'd burst into a refrain about how I wasn't playing fair. Under normal circumstances, I find Josh's nerdy enthusiasm to be his most endearing quality, so out of sync with the blasé aura of studied cool exhibited by most of his peers. But tonight I didn't have the time or the patience.

"The situation right now is very delicate. If I bring an extra person along, it might spook her and ruin everything." I gently eased Josh away from the exit. "I promise you can come along next time."

I strode out the door and over to the Volvo, fired up the engine, and tore out of the parking lot. As soon as I felt sure I was out of Josh's line of vision, I pulled over on the frontage road to Highway 160 and idled, trying to figure out where to go next. Despite my producer's confidence, I had no idea where Jasmine might be hiding out. She'd called the show on the local listener line instead of the 800 number, which likely meant she pulled in the station over the air instead of listening to the streaming audio on our Web site. At night, our over-the-air listening area blanketed most of California and all of the Pacific Northwest. But in the daytime, it would place

Jasmine within roughly a hundred-mile radius of downtown Sacramento. A metropolitan area with a million-plus residents to sift through.

I steered the Unmarked Vehicle onto Marconi Avenue, heading east in the general direction of El Camino High School and Jasmine's childhood suburban haunts, crossing a grid of avenues named for some inexplicable reason in honor of inventors: Howe, Bell, Wright, Fulton, Morse, Watt. I mean, none of these guys are Sacramento natives or have any connection to California's capital. My first day in Sacramento, I busted up when I heard a traffic reporter yammering about a big slowdown on U.S. 50 between Howe and Watt. I felt as if I had fallen into an old Abbott and Costello routine.

The first few blocks of Marconi, the homes that lined the boulevard and side streets represented the postwar jerry-built bungalow era, now shabby and rapidly downscaling, one of those neighborhoods where every street boasted at least one car up on blocks on the front lawn. Definitely a classy touch. Local legend has it some of the houses in this area had originally been built from crates used to deliver jet engines to McClellan Air Force Base. One look at the dumpy hovels and I was a believer.

As I continued east, the homes became larger and the yards neater, more boats in the driveways and fewer strings of out-of-season Christmas lights drooping from the eaves. Centuries from now, archaeologists will be able to chart the progress of the American dream in the last decades of the twentieth century by carbon-dating the suburban rings surrounding cities such as Sacramento, like the concentric sets of walls surrounding medieval cities: the aged postwar cottages just outside the core to the far-flung suburbs like Elk Grove, so new you can still smell the chemicals in the wall-to-wall carpeting.

A quarter mile past the intersection of Marconi and Watt, I hung a right into a maze of narrow, twisting, tree-lined streets. Jasmine's childhood home was at the apex of one of the curves, a classic California rancher straight out of the pages of *Sunset* magazine circa 1962. It had what looked like a newer second story tacked over the garage. I parked on the street and took a few steps down the cement walkway toward the front door.

I heard the crash first, the impact of something large flinging itself against the wooden fence separating the front yard from the back. Then the barking, a wake-the-dead chorus of woofs and growls. I couldn't see the beast, but if the bark was any indication, the bite would belong to something big and square-jawed, complete with dripping fangs.

The curtain over the front picture window parted a few inches. A sour-looking woman peered out and flicked her hand in my direction, as if she were trying to rid herself of an annoying insect.

I didn't blame her. She was a classic case of the innocent bystander, thrust into the media circus by the accident of owning a piece of real estate that had once provided home and hearth to a notorious celebrity. I was hoping to be able to check out the backyard to see if there might be a pool cabana or tree house where Jasmine could curl up for the night. But even if she were able to sneak past the welcoming committee at the front curtain, there's no way she could avoid Bruiser. I backed up the sidewalk, hands raised, surrender-style.

I cruised past a couple of convenience markets within walking distance of Jasmine's onetime crib, circled them twice. Nothing in or around the drab square structures leaped out and grabbed my attention as a possible shelter for a fugitive. I'd already visited El Camino High School and hadn't picked up any vibes. Anyway, if El Camino was anything like most high schools these days, it would boast security worthy of a medium-security prison when school was in session. Not a likely place to hide out from the law.

Tower Records! The Watt and El Camino branch of Sacramento's biggest homegrown industry after state government would definitely have been within a young Cynthia Pepper's turf, and what better hangout for a girl with stars in her eyes than a huge record store?

A right turn on Eastern and another right on Watt took me to a low-slung strip mall that housed the music-video-book chain. I parked the Volvo and walked slowly around the cement structure, peeking into empty boxes and Dumpsters. Not a clue, not even any remaindered books to pick over, certainly no shelter for a homeless desperado. I watched a clerk, hair a shade of chartreuse I was sure didn't originate with Mother Nature, stamp out a cigarette and tap a string of numbers into a keypad next to the back door. I did my best to peek in as she heaved the door open, but all I could spy was a glimpse of fluorescent lights and brown corrugated boxes.

I circled back to the front of the building, pushed open the glass doors, and stepped inside the vast music emporium. No actual records, of course, just row upon row of bins holding square CD jewel cases. A bone-rattling hip-hop tune blasted from the store's sound system. There was a time—not that long ago, I swear—when I could hum every tune on the Top Forty and recite the lyrics *and* the artist's discography. I studied the display of new releases and realized I wouldn't recognize at least half of these recording stars unless they managed to make the news by getting themselves arrested or becoming Jennifer Lopez's latest squeeze. I browsed enough aisles to convince myself that (1) Tower Records was still a hot teen gathering spot, (2) there was no place in this store to provide refuge for a desperado, and (3) I was too old for this. It was time to face facts. I was edging dangerously close to becoming an Oldie But Goodie, a pathetic aging hipster whose only CD purchases are those nostalgia compilations they advertise on *Jeopardy!*

That last thought depressed me so much I fled Tower Records and gunned the Volvo south on Watt Avenue and west on Fair Oaks Boulevard, out of suburbia, across the American River, and back into what I consider *my* Sacramento: the prewar neighborhoods loaded with charm and eccentricities: the Fabulous Forties, Sac State, Alkali Flats, Old Sacramento, Lavender Heights, the state government hub. My home.

So far, my trek into Jasmine-land had proved to be a bust. But there was one more childhood landmark worth checking out. Too far away from Watt and El Camino to be within bicycling distance for a kid, it nonetheless symbolized the site of her first breakthrough, her first taste of applause and adoration.

The two-story wooden structure, abandoned and dark, still stood at Fifty-seventh and J streets. A battered sign attached to a metal pole pointed to "Ye Public House." A contractor's chain-link fence circled the building. As I slowed, I read a banner tied to the fence announcing the future home of the East End Bar & Grill. I made a right on Fifty-seventh, parked the U.V., and hiked back to the corner.

The temporary fence consisted of sections of chain link attached to poles set in cement blocks. Someone had already moved one of the poles, creating a slip of an entrance. I pushed against the fence, creating a larger opening, and managed to squeeze my way through without snagging my clothing or scratching myself. One of these days, I really was going to have to add butt-burning exercises to my workout routine.

I strode around the building slowly, keeping one eye on the traffic on J Street for possible cop cars or private security patrols, the other on the plywood boards nailed over the first-floor windows. One of the boards over a low window in the back hung slightly askew. I studied it closer, and noticed the holes where nails had been pried loose. I gave the plywood sheet a slight tap, and it came close to falling forward, bopping me in the head. I halted the board's descent with both hands and moved it to one side, creating a slit of a few inches. Enough to peer through the glassless window into the abandoned building.

A tiny figure huddled on a pile of tattered blankets in a corner next to the fireplace. Female, as far as I could tell, either asleep or passed out. In the fading sunlight, it was difficult to pick out any identifying features.

But it was still light enough that I could discern her clothing, rumpled sweatpants and a baggy zippered hoodie.

The color purple.

17

I RACED HOME THROUGH THE LIGHT TRAFFIC OF POST-COMMUTE downtown Sacramento, parked the Volvo in the underground garage at Capitol Square, bounded up the stairs two at a time, and bolted through the second-floor apartment door. I paused just long enough to scratch Bialystock under the chin and dump some fish by-products into his bowl, then grabbed a bottle of Two Buck Chuck's from the fridge, two plastic glasses, and a flashlight, and stuffed them in my backpack. I'd opened the Trader Joe's sauvignon blanc the previous evening and sipped only half a glass, just enough to take the edge off my trip to Elk Grove and the meeting with Rita Slade. So the bottle was almost full. Plenty, I estimated, for tonight's mission.

A familiar figure waited for me on the landing when I flung open the front door. Young, male, frizzy mop of hair, wire-rimmed glasses. "There's an unmarked cop car outside your building," Josh Freidman said.

"So?" Capitol Square is home to a number of VIPs from state

government, so it wasn't all that unusual to see law enforcement lurking on the premises. "And since when have you taken to following me around?"

"Another unmarked cop car followed you when you left the station," Josh continued, ignoring my question.

"How do you know it was a cop car?"

"White? American-made sedan? This year's model? Two-way antenna on the roof? One of those geometric symbols on the license plate. An octagon."

The license plate probably also carried the words CA EXEMPT, meaning the car's owner—in this case, state, county, or local government—missed out on the fun the rest of us endured in passing a vehicle smog test every two years.

Had one of those CA EXEMPT automobiles been stalking me ever since I left the station an hour ago? I hadn't noticed, but then I hadn't been on alert. Sheriff Perez had just been making an empty threat, hadn't she? I knew for certain no one noticed me when I parked on Fifty-seventh Street and walked around the empty building on J. At least, I was pretty sure.

"I'm parked over on P Street," Josh said. "They don't know my car."

Damned if the kid hadn't figured out a way to get himself into the thick of the action. I had to give him points for tenacity. "Just let me swing by the garage first and get the tape deck out of the U.V.," I said.

I directed Josh to stop at the KFC at Thirty-eighth and J, where I ordered a Ten Piece Feast and sides of mac-n-cheese, mashed potatoes and gravy, and cole slaw. Don't forget the biscuits, and throw in some extra napkins. Comfort food. Bait to lure a fugitive out of her lair.

Josh started to whimper, as I knew he would, when I ordered him to park on Fifty-seventh Street around the corner from J and stay with the car.

"I already told you, she's going to be cautious enough just having one uninvited guest. She sees two of us, and she'll run for sure." I thrust the bucket of chicken in Josh's direction. "One piece. Okay, two. And stop looking at me like that."

Truth is, I could have used a helper as I retraced my steps, this time laden with backpack, bucket of chicken, and tape deck, through the gap in the construction fence. I placed the burdens on the cracked, weed-encrusted asphalt next to the window with the loose board and slowly removed the plywood sheet. I edged my torso through the empty rectangle and flicked on the flashlight. I deliberately aimed the light in the opposite direction from the fireplace where I'd spotted the prize on my first visit. My thought was to allow her to awaken slowly, gently, with indirect illumination instead of harsh electric light staring her in the face.

The white beam danced over a pile of picnic tables and benches and a four-foot-high counter that must have once been the bar. The shaft of light caught something in back of the bar, a wooden sign dangling at a crooked angle. I squinted to read the hand-painted letters.

FUN IS SERVED HERE

The light wavered and dove to the dusty floor as my grip on the ridged metal barrel of the flashlight sagged.

God, how many Saturday nights had I spent in a joint just like this one, my child's eyes picking out the letters on an identical sign that promised fun would be served here? The pizza was just so-so, but my father dug the Dixieland bands and the beer. Kids and unaccompanied females weren't supposed to venture into the backroom where the bands wailed and the bartender reigned over the taps, but my old man had enough pull, thanks to his one term in the state senate, to make sure his daughter was always treated like an honored guest. That pizza joint bore the same name as the abandoned hulk in front of me: Shakey's.

All of this zapped through my brain in seconds. A moan and rustle of bedclothes from the general area of the fireplace caused me to swing the flashlight beam in that direction. A bedraggled creature tottered to her feet and screened her face against the light with both hands.

"Don't shoot!" she shrieked.

"It's okay," I said in my friendliest tones. "It's just Shauna J. Bogart. I'm alone. No cops, I promise." I hoisted the cardboard bucket to the window, where I hoped the irresistible aroma of fried chicken would waft in her direction. "Had dinner yet?"

The woman gasped and inched forward, tentatively at first, then making a quick lunge for the bucket. "Not so fast," I said. Only after she helped me lift the backpack and tape deck into the dark chamber did I allow her to snatch the bucket of chicken out of my hands. She retreated to the pile of blankets and made scarfing noises while I clambered through the window. I uprighted a picnic bench, sat, placed the flashlight on the bench, and pointed it in the general direction of the figure on the nest of ratty blankets. Enough illumination to allow me to study her without making her feel as if she were in an old-time police interrogation.

It wasn't the first time I'd seen her in person. She'd dropped in on the rock music stations where I was working back in the eighties, promoting her latest comeback attempt. But it was my first look since she'd assumed the mantle of America's Most Wanted. Smaller than I'd remembered, but then, celebrities always lose stature when they're not projected onto a screen or holding court in the halo of a concert arena spotlight. She'd hacked off her hair so that it barely covered her ears and dyed what was left of it brown. Dyed it, or dumped a bottle of shoe polish over her head. But the eyes were the same as I remembered, amber and luminous, and the full lips were still set in the same pouty frown, lines carved deeply on either side of her mouth.

That is, when her lips weren't engaged in tearing apart a chicken breast with all the gusto of a feral cat devouring a pigeon.

I removed the bottle of wine and the two plastic tumblers from my backpack, uncorked the bottle, filled one glass to the top, and put a finger or so into the other. I passed the full glass to Jasmine and kept the short one for myself. Even though I had a designated driver, I wanted to keep my wits about me. She accepted the wine with an eager grab and gulp.

"You might think about some new threads," I said. "I don't know if you're aware, but everyone has heard about those purple sweats. You might as well pin a target to your back."

"I've got a fabulous new wardrobe." She jerked the half-eaten chicken piece in the direction of a heap of rags on the hearth. "Church charity box, and just my size. I just wear these to sleep in. It gets cold in here nights."

"I can imagine. I don't suppose you dare use the fireplace."

She shook her head and continued to gnaw on deep-fried poultry parts. I watched, fascinated, as she devoured a drumstick and thigh and tossed the stripped bones into the fireplace. She popped the lid on the container of macaroni and cheese and tipped her head back, letting the cheesy pasta slide into her mouth, not even bothering to root around in the bucket for a plastic fork.

"I haven't had a thing to eat in two days except bagels, muffins, and Danish." She leaned back with a combination sigh and belch.

"Bagels?"

"There's this coffeehouse over on Alhambra that gives away their leftovers to the homeless at the end of the day."

"So you're managing."

She laughed without hint of mirth. "Oh, sure. Cleaning up in the sink in the women's john over at Sac State. Did you know, if you time things right the students will be in class, and you'll have the place all to yourself for almost an hour? Begging for handouts from restaurant kitchens. Hanging around the self-service laundry on Folsom Boulevard to listen to your station on their sound system. Scrounging through trash cans for bottles and cans to trade in for a few pennies. Keeping my head down, skulking in the shadows, hoping no one recognizes me. Yeah, I'm managing."

Jasmine lurched toward the cardboard chicken container, retrieved another drumstick, then slid the bucket across the floor in my direction. I did my best not to appear too eager as I hefted the bucket and helped myself to a thigh and a handful of napkins. Jeez, I thought she would never offer!

I held the chicken thigh in my left hand and with the right hit the RECORD button on the tape deck, snaked the microphone over to the hearth, and waited to see if my quarry would throw a divalike hissy over my attempt to have her speak on the record.

She lobbed another set of bones into the fireplace, licked her fingers, plucked up the microphone, and began to warble.

"Meet me at the casbah
The incense will light our way
It's twelve steps over a light wave
Then mellow out in a bright cave . . ."

Wow! Even after all she'd been through—and with no accompaniment—that girl could *sing*. I placed the chicken thigh on a napkin and applauded.

"Do you know, I was standing on this very spot thirty-five years ago when I first appeared with my father's band," she said. "Just goes to show you what the ravages of time can do."

I peered around the murky light of the abandoned cavern and for a moment I could almost hear the faint echo of a Jelly Roll Morton tune and smell a hint of grease, tomato sauce, and brew. I'd forgotten exactly what happened to the Shakey's empire except that it had all but disappeared from the American scene. There'd been a time, though, when the pizza parlor chain had tied Tower Records as Sacramento's most beloved homegrown product. Shakey's, Tower Records, and a young pop singer calling herself Jasmine.

"I've always wondered what all that is supposed to mean," I said. "Twelve steps over a light wave? Mellow out in a bright cave?"

"Who knows? Ask Lou Jelniak. He wrote the song." She kept the mike held firmly within a few inches of her mouth to make sure she provided clear, concise sound bites. A real pro.

Lou Jelniak. Owner of the old El Jay recording studio. The songwriter/producer who discovered Jasmine performing in this very pizza parlor and launched her career. "Any idea where a person could find this Jelniak these days?"

Jasmine shook her head. "I haven't seen him in, like, thirty years. Not since I signed with a major label. He was a good guy, though."

"No hard feelings between the two of you when you decided to switch labels and go national?"

"Hell, no. He was cool, told me he totally understood how I'd gotten too big for Sacramento, and how he was just glad to have been a part of my career, and that if I ever needed a hand, I should give him a call." She looked around the derelict hall and sighed. "Sure wish I could take him up on that offer right about now."

"Really," I said in agreement. Privately, I had doubts. Jelniak's attitude, as described by his onetime protégée, seemed uncommonly magnanimous for an executive in an industry as cutthroat as entertainment. Even if it did come from a producer at a two-bit outfit like El Jay.

"You said on my show today that you didn't kill Johnny Venture, that you were framed," I said. "How do you mean, exactly?"

"If I knew the answer to that, do you think I'd be hiding out in a dump like this?" She was back into her princess mode.

"Why don't you start by telling me how you ended up in Monterey at the same time as Johnny Venture."

"I decided at the last minute to drive up the coast a couple of days before the gig at the San Jose Arena. I just wanted to lie back and relax for a few days before starting the tour, that's all." She sounded bored, as if she'd repeated the story many times to the cops and to her attorney. "I had no idea Johnny Venture or any of those other has-been radio people were going to be in town at the same time."

"How did someone like you end up in a dump like Casa del Pulgas? I would have figured you more for the Lodge at Pebble Beach."

"I didn't make any reservations. Like I said, this trip to Monterey was a total whim. Turns out, it was the same weekend as the Monterey Jazz Festival."

"Yikes. So all the posh places had been booked up months in advance."

"You got it. Casa del Pulgas wasn't that bad, though. I thought it was cute. All those little adobe cottages with the tile roofs. Mine even had a fireplace."

I paused to suck the last of the meat off the chicken bones and pitch them in the direction of the fireplace. "When did you first realize the Broadcast Legends group was staying in the same cute little motor court?"

"I ran into Spyder Webb in the lobby. He told me about the Broadcast Legends and the hospitality suite, and invited me to drop on by."

"No kidding. I didn't know Spyder Webb was still around." He'd been part of my stable of childhood radio idols, the host of a late-night rhythm and blues show on a station in Oakland.

"Next thing you know, he's introducing me to his friend and colleague, Johnny Venture." She continued her tale, ignoring my enthusiasm for a retired local DJ, a celebrity so minor I'm sure he barely registered on Jasmine's radar.

"Do you recall who else was there in the lobby? Besides you and Spyder Webb and Johnny Venture, of course."

"Man, I wasn't memorizing names for a pop quiz, you know? There must have been around a dozen people in the lobby. Just a bunch of old, retired radio and TV people from San Francisco, plus a couple of geezer tourists and the desk clerk." Her voiced changed to a girlish pitch. "You wouldn't happen to have any moisturizer on you, would you? That public rest room soap is hell on a girl's complexion."

"Sorry." Actually I was pretty certain I did have a tube of face cream floating around in my backpack, but now that the tape was rolling, I needed to keep her on track. "Tell me what happened when you were introduced to Johnny Venture. This fight you supposedly had."

"Sure, I called him a sonovabitch and a few other choice names. I may have even said I was going to 'get' him or that I hoped he'd rot in hell for what he did. And you know me, I'm not a shy girl. I was shouting. Everyone in the lobby heard me."

"What was that all about?"

She gave me a pained look, creating a pair of creases between her eyebrows. "A disc jockey named Johnny Venture promised he'd make sure my follow-up to 'Meet Me' would get plenty of airplay and make the charts in Sacramento. All I had to do was give him a blow job. This was backstage at a show at the Oasis Ballroom in July of 1976. I remember because it was right after the Bicentennial."

"Did you do it?" I felt a combination of fascination and revulsion.

"What do you think? I'd had a taste of stardom and would have done just about anything to stay on top of the charts. But he didn't keep his part of the bargain. The tune never made it into the Top Twenty in Sacramento, or anywhere else."

"What happened next?"

"Right away, I realized I had the wrong Johnny Venture. This guy was way too old to be that disc jockey in Sacramento in 1976. I apologized, and we got to talking. He told me he had some interesting research he wanted to share with me, and invited me to come to the Broadcast Legends hospitality suite that evening."

"Let's skip forward to the party. What were you drinking that night?"

"White wine. Two or three glasses, maybe four. I wasn't keeping track. I mean, my cabin was just a few yards away, so it wasn't like I had to drive somewhere." She uncorked the bottle of the one-dollar-and-ninety-nine-cents Charles Shaw sauvignon blanc and helped herself to another glassful, as if all this wine talk had whetted her thirst.

"So you were a bit drunk," I prompted.

"But I wouldn't kill anyone, drunk or sober. I know all those tabloid people are trying to say I murdered the old man just because of that misunderstanding in the lobby. Even if he had been the Johnny Venture from Sacramento in 1976, I'd never kill anyone over something so trivial." She sat up straighter, placed both hands on her knees, and leaned forward to look me in the eyes. "I mean, if I went around murdering every disc jockey and concert promoter and pop music critic I went down on in the past thirty years, I'd be the biggest female serial killer in history."

I glanced at the tape recorder to make sure the tiny gears were still turning. This was great stuff. "What happened next?"

She balanced the mike on her knees and spooned mashed potatoes and gravy into her mouth between sentences. "I hung out at the hospitality suite for an hour, maybe two. Made the rounds, chatted up the old farts, made them feel important, had a few laughs. Next thing you know, I'm waking up the morning after on the floor in a room next to a corpse."

"You have no idea how you ended up in Johnny Venture's cabin, and how he ended up smothered with a pillow, and you ended up passed out on the floor with the pillow in your hands?"

"I remember feeling a little woozy and disoriented toward the end of the party. I don't remember anything after that."

"Do you suppose someone could have slipped something into your drink? A date rape drug?"

"Like, duh?" She sounded like Josh Friedman for a moment. "People were coming in and out of that hospitality suite all night. Remember the party scene at the beginning of *Breakfast at Tiffany's*? It was like that for a while. Anything could have happened. But just try getting the Monterey cops to even consider that possibility."

"I know you don't have any proof, but you must have some theories. What do you think really happened?" I raised my hand, indicating for her to wait until I ejected the tape cassette and popped in a new one. No way was I going to risk losing the biggest interview of my career by pulling a novice stunt like running out of tape.

"Only that this old guy Johnny Venture had some information, some research I think he called it, that he wanted to show me and he never got the chance. And that whoever set it up must have had some help from the hotel staff."

"What makes you say that?"

"At some point, they would have had to drag me into Johnny Venture's cabin. That points to someone with a passkey. And the maid showed up way early the next morning to make up the room, like right around sunrise. That's how they were able to make sure someone discovered me still passed out on the floor."

"Good point. Whoever heard of a maid showing up at six in the morning?" Easy enough, I figured, for someone to bribe the staff into cooperating. If Casa del Pulgas was anything like every other hotel and motel in California, the housekeeping staff would consist of minimum-wage immigrants with limited English-speaking skills. "But still, why would anyone want to eliminate you and some has-been radio personality you'd never met before?"

"If I knew the answer to that—"

"Got it," I said before she had the chance to inject another sarcastic comment. "Let's move forward now to the moment you managed to escape from the trailer in Castroville. You told Bobette Dooley you were going to find Johnny Venture."

"My first thought was that whoever set this thing up had killed the wrong guy. I figured this Anton Greb just happened to be in the wrong place at the wrong time. I thought if I could find the real Johnny Venture, the one who was supposed to have been murdered, I might be able to clear myself."

"In other words, that guy from 1976 in Sacramento. The one you thought you were fighting with in the lobby."

"But now I'm not so sure."

"Oh?"

"One thing about hiding out, you have a lot of time to think. What I'm thinking is, this had to have been set up by someone who didn't want the old Johnny Venture, this Anton Greb, to have the chance to show me this information he supposedly had."

"When you had the fight in the lobby, someone saw the opportunity to get rid of him and point the finger at you."

"Yeah. And I played right into their hands. I suppose if it hadn't been for the fight, whoever did this would have invented some sort of romance-gone-bad angle, planted a love letter on the corpse or some such thing."

"But still, you're going to have to come up with something plausible to explain how you ended up in that room in the motor court next to a corpse."

"Now you're starting to sound like my attorney." She folded her arms across her chest and pouted.

I was about to tell her that I was just being realistic when something more urgent caught my attention. The wail of an approaching siren.

18

I SUCKED IN AIR SHARPLY, FUMBLED FOR THE TAPE DECK AND MY backpack, and poised to bolt for the window. Fine for Jasmine to get herself nabbed and hauled back to the Monterey County lockup, but no way did I want to share a cell with her for harboring a fugitive.

"Chill out." Jasmine spoke from the heap of blankets, where she lolled like an Egyptian princess. "You'll get used to them after a while. There must be a hospital real close by."

"Three of them, actually. Mercy General, Sutter Memorial, and the Med Center," I babbled to cover how rattled I actually felt.

"I don't imagine they'll use sirens when they come to get me," she said. "I'm guessing the first warning I'll have is when I hear the bullhorn telling me they've got the place surrounded and I should come out with my hands up."

"You won't do anything foolish, will you?" I had a sudden terrible vision of the pampered pop princess dying a messy death in a hail of police bullets. What do they call it? Suicide by cop?

"Hell, no. For one thing I don't have any equipment for doing 'anything foolish,' as you put it."

"How about that handgun you managed to snatch from Bobette Dooley when you made your mad dash for freedom?"

"Oh, that. I might as well make it easy for everyone and spill. I ditched Hector's pickup truck in the long-term lot at Sacramento International three days ago and took the bus back downtown. You'll find the gun in the glove box."

"There is no Regional Transit service to and from the airport." I latched on to the first inconsistency I could find in her story.

"There is if you don't mind a little detour to Woodland, Davis, and West Sacramento, last stop Seventh and J in downtown Sac."

"Ouch. The Yolo Bus. That must have taken all day."

"Felt like it, especially hiding behind a newspaper the whole time. But actually it took only around two hours."

The direct route from the airport to downtown, a straight shot south on I-5, would have taken fifteen, twenty minutes max instead of a two-hour slog through the boonies on the Yolo County transit system. That's Sacramento for you. Delusions of grandeur by insisting on calling its airport "international" due to one daily Mexicana Airlines flight to Guadalajara, yet unable to figure out how to provide something as basic as public transportation to and from the "international" airport.

I lowered myself back onto the bench and repositioned the microphone. "You're not going to be able to run and hide forever, you know."

"I'm aware of that fact. You know what's interesting?"

"What's that?"

"I wasn't really planning to make a run for it and start this big interstate manhunt when I managed to get out of the trailer. I just wanted to escape from Luis and Bobette, and especially Hector."

"For real. I couldn't get away from those three fast enough. Especially Hector."

"They seemed to think I had some sort of magical power that could purge their criminal records, and get them all movie contracts, and guarantee a perfect baby for Bobette, and clear up Hector's complexion. Just because I'm famous."

"You must have been afraid that once they realized you couldn't even keep them from going back to the Salinas jail, they'd turn on you."

"Damn straight. I know what you're going to ask next. Once I escaped from those creeps, why didn't I head right back to Salinas and turn myself in? I should have, if I had any common sense. But you know? Once you're on that open highway, and you feel that taste of freedom again, you've just got to make a run for it. And once you've put that karma in motion, you've just got to hang on and ride the wave."

I wasn't sure if I grasped her logic, but then I'd never been in quite the same pickle in which Jasmine currently found herself.

She yawned and sank deeper into the rumpled bedclothes, feeling the effects, I assumed, of a belly full of fried chicken and two glasses of wine. She appeared ready to drop into dreamland, and I had yet to ask the most important question.

"Why me? Of all the media people you could have talked to, why me?"

"I thought you knew." Jasmine sat up straighter and reached for the wine. This time she didn't even bother with the glass, just swigged from the bottle. "I was one of your mother's students at Camp Mel-O-Dee in the summer of 1970."

"Yeah, but there's one small problem with that whole scenario."

"What do you mean?" Now that she was well toward polishing off the entire bottle, it came out more like *Whaah yah me?* "I was there, she was there. Helen Hudson taught me everything I know. End of story."

"Not quite." I leaned forward and enunciated clearly, to make sure she picked up on the facts I had to convey. "I didn't go on the radio and become Shauna J. Bogart until years and years after your summer at Camp Mel-O-Dee. And I've never, ever mentioned publicly being Helen Hudson's daughter. That little fact has never appeared in any of my press materials. Even if Helen Hudson ever mentioned having a kid—which I doubt—you would have had no way to connect her with me."

"Helen Hudson never mentioned having a kid? You are joking, right? She talked about you constantly, how you were on the honor roll, and how you made it to the district spelling bee, and how you won the science fair. She was so damn proud of you!"

"Get real. You can't be talking about my mother."

"She used to tell us how she was sure you were going to be a huge success someday, somebody important, not some washed-up saloon singer like she turned out to be." Jasmine forged ahead, ignoring my sarcasm. "That's how she used to talk about herself, a washed-up saloon singer. She told us your name and showed us your picture, and said you were so smart, you'd probably find a cure for cancer or become an astronaut, or maybe even be the first woman president. That's how proud she was of you."

I wished I hadn't let Jasmine hoard the wine. I could have used a little liquid assistance to digest the information I'd just been given. This was Helen Hudson? The woman who never let me forget she gave up the chance to appear in a Doris Day picture because of me? The martinet who insisted on dragging me up onstage even after I thought I'd made it painfully obvious that I hadn't the talent or temperament to make a good half of a mother-daughter act?

"How interesting." I wondered if Jasmine sensed the agitation behind my act of neutrality. "But I still don't see how you connected the daughter of Helen Hudson with Shauna J. Bogart."

"I learned a few things when I was making the rounds of the radio stations. For one thing, try to find out as much as you can about the people who can make or break your career. I made it a habit of checking out the FCC licenses hanging on the walls of the control room."

I nodded slowly, sensing where this was going. Before the deregulation of the broadcast industry in 1987, on-air announcers had to pass an FCC test on broadcast law and electronic theory, and posted their licenses on the control room wall of the station where they worked. The license was made out in the disc jockey's legal name.

"So you found out my real name and squirreled away that information in case it might do you some good someday."

"And guess what?" She leaned forward to give me a grin. "It did." The grin froze into a grimace. The odd shadows created by the flashlight gave her an eerie Norma Desmond-esque appearance, waiting for a close-up that would never come except in a mug shot.

Jasmine dropped the melodramatic pose, lifted the bottle, and passed it to me. An inch or so of liquid swirled in the bottom. "Go ahead, finish it off. You sound like you could use a hit."

I followed Jasmine's lead, chugged straight from the bottle and let the tepid beverage slide down my throat. "What else do you remember about my mother? What was she like?"

"Man, she was the best. Funny, smart, and strict, but in a nice way, you know? She didn't just do vocal exercises and that stuff. She taught us how to work a crowd, and how to style a song to make it all your own. She made my career possible, just as much as Lou Jelniak and 'Meet Me at the Casbah.' All of us at Camp Mel-O-Dee who went on to have careers in the music industry have lots of good reasons for saying Helen Hudson taught us everything we know."

I studied the dirt-encrusted floor as I mulled over the last several minutes of conversation. "Back up a minute or two. All these radio stations where you were spying on the FCC licenses of the announcers and figuring out the real person behind the on-air name, didn't you ever run into the real Johnny Venture?"

"Not that I can remember. The only DJ calling himself Johnny Venture that I recall is that bastard backstage at the Oasis Ballroom." Jasmine made another huge yawn and sagged back onto a ratty sofa cushion. Gray stuffing tumbled out of a jagged tear on one side. "I didn't even get a real good look at him that night at the show. When a girl's giving head, she's not exactly making eye contact, know what I mean?"

I determined it best not to respond to that last question.

Jasmine's eyelids drooped and I could tell in another minute or two she'd be making z's. I shut off the recorder and coiled the mike cord, then put what was left of the chicken and side orders in a neat pile on the hearth. Breakfast, perhaps.

"Thanks. I mean it," she said in a boozy voice.

I was the one who should have been thanking her, but I just grunted, "You're welcome," and arranged the tattered blanket over her limp form.

"You know what?" she mumbled.

"No, what?"

"I used my last quarter to call your show today."

I watched her until her eyes remained shut and her breathing slowed to an even rhythm. Sweet dreams, Jasmine. Dream while you still can.

Josh leaped out of the Geo Metro the minute he saw me round Fifty-seventh Street. "So? I'm all? Like?" he demanded while I stowed the tape deck and backpack into the trunk and folded myself into the front passenger seat.

"Keep your voice down and start driving."

"I don't think so." He slid into the driver's seat, but dangled the keys in front of me. "Not until you spill."

"Since when do interns get to call the shots?"

"The cops would have been all over this place if it hadn't been for me and my powers of observation. And my wheels. I think that puts us on equal footing, wouldn't you agree?"

"Okay, okay. But you've got to promise no blabbing. Not to your girlfriend, not to your roommate. Nothing goes beyond this car."

"You can count on me." Josh stuck the key into the starter.

"It's her, all right."

Josh let out a low whistle. "Hiding out in the old Shakey's pizza parlor. Who would have guessed?"

Obviously, only yours truly, but I decided to let my chauffeur come to that conclusion on his own. "How about getting those wheels of yours turning toward the station. We've got a ton of tape to edit."

I gazed out the window as the darkened streets of East Sacramento flitted past. I should have been jazzed about the incredible scoop I was about to unleash on the dozing denizens of Sacramento when their clock radios jerked them awake the next morning. But something heavy weighed on my soul.

"You don't seem all that excited," Josh said as the tiny economy car crossed Alhambra Boulevard.

"Just thinking, that's all."

Helen Hudson taught her everything she knows.

The thing is, I believed Jasmine. Her story rang true, and I couldn't detect any obvious flaws, not even the bit about catching the bus at the airport. It wasn't a stretch to picture a not-much-younger version of myself in a similar predicament. How many radio industry parties had I attended where I drank too much, flirted too broadly, laughed too loudly, and picked too many verbal fights? How hard would it have been to dope me up and cart me off to the bedroom of some guy I didn't even know? Or find myself waking up in a jail cell? I could only thank the god or goddess that watches over careless young women for sparing me from such a fate.

Then there was the whole professional ambition and pride thing. I craved nothing so much as the luxury of time to continue my investigation and unmask the real killer of the disc jockey who called himself Johnny Venture. I'd keep Jasmine under wraps for another few days, stopping by the old Shakey's every evening with more eats. Maybe next time I'd bring pizza and beer.

Except . . . she was a fugitive, charged with a felony. I'd made a deal with the Monterey County sheriff. If I didn't keep my end of the bargain, I'd wind up in that jail cell after all. If I kept the bargain everyone would know I'd made a secret pact with law enforcement, and my credibility as a journalist would be forever tarnished. Not even Diane Sawyer could emerge from such a sticky mess with her reputation intact.

But, dammit, Jasmine was innocent! The authorities in Monterey County had pinned their entire case on the wrong suspect and they didn't seem interested in pursuing alternatives. What counted more, justice or my silly career?

Except . . . I'd be breaking the law. Aiding and abetting. Harboring a fugitive.

I faked the need to visit the ladies' john when Josh and I arrived at the station. It was the only place I could think of where no one would overhear what I was about to do. I hid myself in one of the stalls, pulled the cell phone out of my backpack, and slowly tapped a number in the 831 area code.

In a terse voice to dam an impending flood of tears, I told the dispatcher at the Monterey County Sheriff's Department where they could go to pick up their escaped inmate.

19

"YOUR BOYFRIEND DROPPED IN ABOUT AN HOUR AGO."

I looked up from the editing station in the news production room where a stack of tape cartridges held highlights from my Q&A with Jasmine for use during tomorrow morning's news block. I planned to make the listeners—and the competing news media—wait until my show in the afternoon to hear the entire interview. A fat reel of tape held a clean version of the recording I'd made in the abandoned pizza parlor, minus the pauses to gorge on KFC and swill wine.

"Your boyfriend. The gray-haired ponytail." Steve Garland, the host of the nightly sports talk show, stood in the doorway to the news production room.

"Pete Kovacs? Pete was here?"

"Either him or his twin." Garland let himself into the soundproof cell. Pretty much anywhere he stood would make for tight quarters, like two people sharing a phone booth. It was definitely close enough for me to pick up the aroma of peanut M&M's that

Garland chomped during commercial breaks. "I hope I'm not delivering bummer news, but he had a woman with him. A real babe."

"A young, sexy blonde, I suppose. Who cares?" I tried to sound as if I didn't.

"Yeah. Wearing one of those tight T-shirts, you know—" Garland cupped both hands at chest level, the universal male sign language to indicate a gal with a rack.

"I just hope he doesn't still owe you money betting on the World Series, because I'm not responsible for his gambling debts."

I must have sounded more abrupt than I'd intended, because Garland began to back away toward the door.

"Wait. What did Kovacs want, did he say?"

Garland shook his head. "It was hard for me to tell what was going on. Don't forget, I was in the middle of a live radio show. He and this blond babe just barged into the control room like they owned the place right when I'm doing a phoner with the new coach of the Hornets basketball team. They stayed maybe a minute or two, just looked around. Then they split."

"I wonder how they got in without a key."

"Probably followed the janitor. Or a sales guy working late. Security, what a joke, right?"

"You're sure it was Pete Kovacs."

"Definitely the gray-haired ponytail."

I resisted the urge to direct Josh to detour past Fifty-seventh and J streets when he drove me home. If the cops were already on the scene, he might put two and two together and figure out I was the one who tipped them off. If the place was deserted, I'd feel compelled to make more phone calls to the authorities. Either my professional credibility would hang in tatters, or I'd suffer more internal agonies over ratting on someone who trusted me.

Either way, I'd lose.

It was almost ten when Josh dropped me at the N Street entrance to Capitol Square. I waited until the Metro's taillights winked into the distance, then jaywalked across N, away from home, across the grass-and-asphalt expanse of Capitol Mall. I threaded my way through the crowds waiting for the late movies in Downtown Plaza, strode through the gloom of the pedestrian tunnel under I-5, and emerged on the cobblestone streets of Old Sacramento.

Retro Alley had long been closed for the evening, the plywood sheet still tacked over the broken window. I made a mental note to give Cherise Rose a call the next morning and tell her she'd better put a rush on the order for replacement glass, hang the expense. I let myself in with the key Kovacs had given me, punched in a series of numbers on a keypad to disarm the burglar alarm, fished the flashlight out of my backpack, and crept past shelves and display cases crammed with knickknacks and collectibles from the mid–twentieth century: Metal lunch boxes, lava lamps, bowling shirts, Japanese transistor radios still in their original leatherette cases. I eased my way around the upright piano where Kovacs pounded out ragtime and Dixieland tunes between customers, and headed up the staircase in the back of the store.

Another turn of a key brought me into a sparsely furnished apartment above the store. Kovacs's bachelor pad.

I wasn't proud of what I was doing. The whole point of exchanging apartment keys was to symbolize our mutual trust, *mi casa su casa,* and all that. I don't think Kovacs ever intended for trust to turn into spying the night he presented me with the keys to his castle. Still, what did the man expect me to do? He disappears, sends a postcard leading me to believe he's in the L.A. area, then comes back to town without even calling? And sporting a piece of arm candy? Don't even get me started!

I hovered in darkness for around two minutes, straining to hear any sounds that might indicate the apartment was occupied by someone other than myself. Nothing other than the raucous laughter of late-night revelers on the wooden sidewalk below. I cupped my hand over the lit end of the flashlight to diffuse the light, on the off chance Kovacs might be in the neighborhood and spot the bobbing light through the window.

A quick sweep of the combined living-dining-sleeping quarters, kitchen alcove, bathroom, and guest bedroom didn't yield any obvious suggestions of either foul play or adult fun-and-games. Don't detectives always discover the best clues by going through the suspect's garbage? My fingers felt something squishy and damp in the kitchen receptacle. Eeew! I snatched my hand away, brought my fingers to my nose, and sniffed. Coffee grounds. And fresh enough not to have dried out.

Nothing in the bathroom trash can. I snapped open the door to the medicine cabinet. Toothbrush, tube of paste, shaving gear lined up in their usual places. Just as if he'd stepped out for a moment to buy a newspaper. I fingered the cake of soap next to the sink. Damp, just like the coffee grounds.

I gave the closet the once-over, even though I was all but positive of what I'd find. Suitcases stacked in one corner. Check. Jeans, slacks, dress shirts, and T-shirts on their hangers. Check. Tuxedo protected in a plastic zippered bag. Check. Favorite pair of sneakers on the floor. Check. Navy blue terry-cloth bathrobe hanging from the hook on the inner side of the door. Check.

The faint light played against a piece of cloth crumpled on top of the hamper. A T-shirt, carelessly discarded by its wearer. I held the black cotton knit shirt to the light and recognized the silkscreened logo of the Hot Times Old Town Dixieland Band. Pete's group. I swear, I could still feel the warmth of body heat and smell the scent of the sandalwood soap Pete always used. I folded the T-shirt and gently placed it inside my backpack.

"Jasmine's back behind bars! Join us live at Fifty-seventh and J streets. . . ."

"A dramatic capture of the fugitive TV star Jasmine. We go live to East Sacramento. . . ."

"Authorities are crediting an anonymous tip with leading them to Jasmine's hideout. Reporting live from East Sacramento. . . ."

"Your eleven o'clock news team will be back with more live reports from Fifty-seventh and J streets right after this . . ."

I lounged on the couch with Bialystock curled beside me and thumbed the channel button on the remote. I'd been scooped by the three network affiliates, the two independents, even the Spanish station, and I didn't care. Tomorrow morning, the highlights of my exclusive-to-top-all-exclusives interview would make everyone forget about the live shots on the late evening news the night before. Especially when we broadcast Jasmine's *a cappella* version of "Meet Me at the Casbah" and teased our listeners with that little quote about being the biggest female serial killer in history if she "went around murdering every disc jockey and concert promoter and pop music critic I went down on in the past thirty years." By the time I played the interview in its entirety during my show tomorrow afternoon, everyone from the BBC to the local college station would be clamoring for a copy of the tape.

Just so long as that lady sheriff in Monterey County remembered to keep her end of the bargain and resisted the temptation to reveal the depth of my involvement in her department's investigation.

I continued to flick from one TV newscast to the next, creating a shifting patchwork of crime-scene tape, pulsating police cruiser light bars, solemn-faced reporters reciting into handheld mikes, spotlights trained on the boarded windows of the abandoned pizza parlor, curious neighbors bobbing in the background, kiddies in their jammies. I was glad no one had footage of Jasmine being led away in handcuffs and stuffed in a patrol car. At least she was spared that public indignity. On the other hand, considering who we were dealing with, she might have welcomed the attention. I zapped through the available stations one more time. Only the PBS outlet offered any respite. Pledge Guy again, pleading with us to call now to support fine programming like tonight's *Great RV Adventures of North America.*

I fell asleep with the remote held loosely in one hand and the cat stretched out on my tummy. And with Pete Kovacs's T-shirt clutched in my left hand, close to my heart. Pathetic, I know. But until the real thing came along, it was better than nothing.

The telephone jangled me awake just before dawn. "Girlfriend, you've got to shake your booty down here ASAP." Glory Lou, calling from the station.

I mumbled something incoherent.

"Everyone's calling, wanting to know about this interview with Jasmine we're promoting on the morning news. CNN, NPR, the *New York Times, People.* All the local TV stations and the *Bee* are camped out at the front door. As I live and breathe, the BBC's on the studio hotline."

"What time is it, anyway?" I asked through a yawn.

"Ten after six. Hon, you go get yourself some coffee and then hustle that booty down here." She spoke with her usual southern peaches-and-magnolia sweetness, but I still knew when I was being issued an order.

I splashed cold water on my face, brushed my teeth, tossed on sweats, strapped on Tevas. I didn't waste time making the coffee that Glory Lou had recommended, and I didn't hustle my booty to the radio station as she had ordered. Instead, I retraced my steps from the previous night. Back to Old Sacramento.

A shroud of darkness and silence enveloped the western-style storefronts, as if the historic district had been placed in a state of suspended animation until the tourists showed up a few hours later. Even the imitation gaslights from the street lamps had been doused in the predawn hours. I saw only one hint of life, a square of light from a second-story window above a shop in the middle of Second Street between K and J.

Pete Kovacs's apartment.

The hell with it. "It" encompassing everything that had transpired in the past twelve hours: tracking down the most wanted fugitive in America, slowly gaining her trust and then forcing myself to betray it, scoring a career-making interview, discovering a whole different take on the entertainer who was my mother. For the past week, my entire professional being had honed in on one goal: finding Jasmine before anyone else did. Okay, I did that. Now what was I going to do for an encore?

Then there was the little issue of my boyfriend and the blonde. This last reconnaissance mission into Old Sacramento sealed it. He was obviously back in town, sneaking into his apartment late at night, just long enough to catch some sleep, clean up, fix himself a cup of coffee, and then leave well before Mrs. Romswinkel showed up to open the store. Why all the subterfuge?

Forget roller coasters. This felt more like an emotional bungee jump, plunging my soul over an abyss, bobbing helplessly, tethered to reality only by the narrowest of cords.

I slunk out of Old Sacramento and plodded across Capitol Mall, only vaguely aware of the headlights of the early morning commuters. Eventually, I'd have to return home, put on some real clothes, tame my hair, and resume my expected role of the smart and sassy media personality. But before the inky sky turned gray and then blue, I craved at least a few more minutes of solitude to sort out my thoughts and get my groove back.

Aimless wandering took me past the Fremont Wing at Capitol Square, across the expanse of cement sidewalk where the cops had discovered the tape magazine from Pete Kovacs's antique recorder earlier in the week. I couldn't help but notice a light glowing from the town house being rented by that lobbying firm. Nor the fact that the vertical blinds had been pushed to one side of the sliding glass door.

What was I supposed to do? Just walk by and ignore the invitation to snoop? I ducked around the wooden fence enclosing a small patio area on the cement pad in front of the sliding door, cupped my hands on either side of my head, and placed them on the glass. I surmised I was peeking in on what was supposed to be the dining room, judging from the chandelier positioned in the middle of the ceiling and the built-in hutch against one wall. Two folding banquet tables pushed together dominated the space, both covered with expanding file folders, computers, tape decks, video cameras, and—yes!—the MacKenzie Repeater from the showcase at Retro Alley.

"Swear to God, if I'd known there were this many nosy people in this apartment complex, I never would have rented here, for sure."

I froze at the sound of the voice, female, brassy, with the hint of a Minnesota accent. Thick plate glass in front of me, wooden fence in back and opposite. An angry Midwesterner blocking the one way out of the patio. Trapped, like a cow in a cattle chute.

She grabbed me by one shoulder and forced me to face her. "First that snoopy old lady with her damn dog and now you." She gave me the once-over, from bed head to well-worn sweats to unpainted toenails peeking out from sturdy sandals. "Do you even live here? Or did you just wander in off the streets?"

I didn't answer, just returned her in-depth study of my physique and attire with one of my own in her direction. Mane of dense blond hair tousled just so, blue eye shadow, thick black mascara, pillowy lips stained magenta, pink sweater hugging a figure just as lush as Steve Garland had described, hip-hugger white capris, thin-strapped sandals with two-inch heels, toenails painted pink. She held a cardboard container of coffee in one flawlessly manicured hand.

"I think I know you," I said. "You're the woman they made the movie about—Traci Kapolsky."

The film had swept every major award when it came out two years ago. Scrappy young reporter at a small-town newspaper ends up exposing a major product liability scandal involving one of the nation's biggest automakers. It didn't hurt that the real Traci Kapolsky knew how to make maximum use of her God-given assets, nor that Hollywood had cast a bleached-tressed Sandra Bullock in the title role.

Kapolsky, one smart cookie, had capitalized on the popularity of the movie by going on the motivational lecture circuit and, most recently, by signing on to host a network TV reality series based on the premise of investigating and righting wrongs that had been ignored or given short shrift by the legal system. *Hammer of Justice.*

I was also virtually certain she was Pete Kovacs's mystery babe.

"You're still trespassing. I've got a lot of work to do, so why don't you run along back to the homeless shelter and I'll forget about calling the cops." She made a move toward the cell phone perched on her hip, just to emphasize the point.

Common sense said I should have retreated when she gave me the opportunity, but the desire to continue snooping won out.

"I really do live here." I pulled a set of keys out of the sweatpants pocket and dangled them in front of her face. "In case you've forgotten, there was a report of a burglary in this very apartment a few days ago. We long-term residents don't think of ourselves as nosy. We prefer to call it watching out for our neighbors."

She studied the clutch of keys, paying particular attention to a gold charm shaped like a classic RCA microphone. "I think I know you too. You do a little radio show here in town, yeah?"

"Shauna J. Bogart, and that little radio show happens to be the top-rated afternoon program in the nation's twenty-seventh largest radio market."

She took a sip of steaming liquid from the cardboard cup and relaxed her wary stance. "You're certainly the woman of the hour. Everyone's talking about Jasmine, and the juicy stuff she said on your exclusive interview."

Kapolsky unlocked the glass door, pushed it down the track, and motioned for me to enter. "If I'd known I was going to have a visitor, I would have picked up two coffees, for sure." She pulled out two folding chairs and seated herself at the head of the banquet tables. I followed suit, sitting to her immediate left. The power position in a traditional conference table setting.

"Here's the deal," she said. "I've got a live show to do in around thirty-six hours. I'm planning to build an entire segment around your interview with Jasmine. You could tell the entire nation how a local talk radio host managed to outsmart Larry King and Barbara Walters. Yeah?"

"Doesn't *Hammer of Justice* usually conduct its own investigations?" I was tempted by her offer, no question. But my b.s. detector was sniffing a hidden agenda.

"It's my show. I can do whatever I want with it."

I studied the array of notepads, file folders, laptop computers, recording gear, and the scattered debris of fast-food containers spread before me on the folding tables. "Looks to me like you were in the middle of quite a production here. I'm assuming Advanced Legislative Dynamics is just a cover."

"For sure, I can't run an undercover investigation under my own name or the name of the show."

Never mind that this so-called undercover investigation is being conducted by someone prancing around town looking like a Hooters waitress.

"You had something else planned for tomorrow night's show, didn't you? Something based here in Sacramento, something you had to keep under wraps. What happened? Your big investigation fell through, and now you're looking at me to cover your butt?"

"The point is, we could help each other out here." She leaned forward conspiratorially. Up close, I could pick up on the fine lines around her eyes and mouth, and realized she was close to my age. In other words, pushing forty. "We've both been basically following the same story, yeah?"

"So you were hoping to land an exclusive interview with Jasmine and I got to her before you did. Them's the breaks."

"Not exactly." Kapolsky opened a file folder. I suspected it was just to give herself something to do with her hands instead of in pursuit of any actual information. "Have you heard of something called the Original Artists Justice Committee?"

"Not only have I heard of them, the chairman is an old radio pal of mine. In fact, we're both members of the Broadcast Legends Hall of Fame." Well, technically I wouldn't be a member until tomorrow evening's ceremony, but it still sounded impressive, at least to me.

"That's just the point. On tomorrow night's show, we're planning to include a live shot from the Broadcast Legends ceremony. You'll be there, so will we. It's perfect, yeah?"

An inside door opened and a young man stepped into the dining room. His skin was the same color as the cardboard of Kapolsky's coffee cup, and I was able to see a lot of it. The fellow was clad only in pajama bottoms.

He gasped when he saw me, mumbled something about not realizing Traci had a guest, and scuttled back into an inner hallway.

"Maurice Parnell, one of my field reporters," Kapolsky said by way of explanation.

I responded with a skeptical look.

"I always set up headquarters in a residential hotel or a setup like this whenever we're on the road. We get so much more done that way. For sure, the team that works, plays, and stays together is the team that wins an Emmy."

I leaned back, letting the chair touch the wall, clasped my hands behind my head, and balanced my feet on the table. "How does Pete Kovacs figure in all of this?"

"He's the whole reason I brought the investigation to Sacramento."

"How about the trip to Los Angeles last week?" Just try explaining the photo that Cherise Rose snapped of Kovacs gassing up his van on I-5, and the postcard mailed from L.A.

"We were shooting promo spots at the network. Now it appears I'm going to have to pull them and replace them with generics."

"How come?"

"For months now, I've wanted to devote a show to the cause of recording artists who were cheated out of the rights to their creations, especially minority artists. We'd been working with Anton Greb. He told us about a case in Sacramento involving a doo-wop group called the Dee Vines."

"The Dee Vines?" Everything Rita Slade had told me pointed to her grandfather being treated fairly by the recording industry.

"For sure. He told me that an antiques dealer in Sacramento by the name of Pete Kovacs had a box of historic material, tapes, records, and contracts concerning the Dee Vines. He said I just had to take a look at it."

"Did he?" I brought the chair down with a thunk. "And did you?"

"Kovacs had the equivalent of a smoking gun."

"How wonderful for you." How could Kovacs stumble across the evidence for a hot story and then offer it to this TV floozy instead of good ol' Shauna J.?

"Yeah, until the break-in. Whoever did that knew exactly what he was looking for. All he took was that box of Pete's stuff. Without the source material, we have no show."

My heart bled for her. "I thought you told security there was no break-in, that it was all a misunderstanding."

"We didn't want to draw any more attention to ourselves than we had to, for sure. The cops would never have been involved if it hadn't been for that nosy old lady and her damn dog."

I half expected her to morph into Margaret Hamilton and start ranting about ". . . and your little doggy too."

"Who's in charge of the engineering down at your station?"

"Huh?" The change in topic was so abrupt, I didn't know how to respond.

"I might need to bring in some additional engineering staff for tomorrow night's show. Just thought you might know of someone who'd be interested in some freelance work."

"Gil Loomis, and normally he'd be up for it. But not right now. The station's in the middle of converting to digital and he's swamped."

Kapolsky digested this information, then pasted on a phony smile, all white teeth and pink gums. "So what do you say? Come on *Hammer of Justice* tomorrow night, help me fill time, and get some national exposure for yourself."

"No way. No effing way."

"This is national TV. Live, coast-to-coast. You can't be serious." She acted as if no one had ever turned her down before.

"Oh, yes, I can. For sure."

Three messages on my home answering machine, all from Glory Lou, each demanding I report immediately to the station, each in succession expressing more urgency and less honey.

I took a quick shower and donned my best "business dressy" outfit: black linen slacks, matching blazer, teal silk blouse that brought out all the best accents in a hazel-eyed redhead. I smoothed my locks into something presentable, slipped on a pair of black pumps, dabbed on lipstick and mascara. I normally don't wear makeup to do a radio show. I mean, what's the point? But I had a suspicion that I'd be facing the TV cameras at some point today.

I picked up the phone and dialed the newsroom hotline.

"As I live and breathe—"

"Not to worry," I told Glory Lou. "I'm back."

20

"THEY'RE GOING TO TURN OVER THE PRISONER TO THE MONTEREY County authorities at ten," Glory Lou said. "The story's yours if you want it. Or I can get someone else."

"Are you nuts? Of course I want it."

"You'll call in for the ten-thirty news update."

"Got it. Hey, you've still got that source over at the DMV?"

"That depends."

"I'm trying to locate a fellow named Lou Jelniak."

"It's not as easy as it used to be to get information out of the DMV, hon. These days, you need a court order or the permission of the person you're trying to find."

"I have the utmost faith in your abilities." And in Glory Lou's network of sources, snitches, spies, and moles that I knew she had in every law enforcement agency and government office in the capital city. "That's J-E-L-N-I-A-K."

"Got it. What do you want me to do about all the media calls I'm getting about your interview with Jasmine?"

"Tell them they can wait until three and hear the entire interview along with everyone else. Wait, even better. Tell them there'll be a photo op and Q&A immediately following. They can make like they're callers and ask anything they'd like."

"I love it, hon."

"Make 'em wait, build up the suspense. By the time my show starts this afternoon, those media people are going to be whipped up into a frenzy of anticipation." It sounded like advice Helen Hudson might have given the young Cynthia Pepper on how to work an audience.

"There is one other thing." Glory Lou spoke slowly, picking out each word with care.

"What's that?"

"Dorinda Delgado asked me to remind you about the grand opening of Lloyd's this evening."

It wasn't Glory Lou's fault she had to be the bearer of unpleasant news. Still, it was a struggle to keep the sarcasm out of my voice. "I bust my chops getting the hottest tape this station has ever aired, and they still expect me to show up at a goddamn sales event?"

Dorinda Delgado was the latest general sales manager at Sacramento Talk Radio. High-strung, driven, and demanding, as most of them are. She'd been hounding me for what seemed like weeks now to show up at the grand opening wingding of some big-shot restaurant client.

"I know, hon. I'm sorry. I just told her I'd pass it along, and that I couldn't make any promises."

That's radio for you. No matter how terrific your voice, how witty and informed you may be, how many exclusive stories you bring in, the sales department always ends up calling the shots. If you're an on-air talent, your mission in life is to hook and reel in listeners who will stick around long enough to hear the advertisers' messages. Bait to attract sets of ears.

I'd been in the industry long enough to know it was futile to put up a fight. At any rate, there was likely to be good food and an open bar at a restaurant bash.

. . .

I knew I'd want to race back to the station with whatever sound I was able to pick up at the prisoner transfer at the Sacramento County Jail, so, instead of walking, I drove the few blocks between home and the slammer at Sixth and I. I lucked out on a parking spot right across the street, another white Volvo pulling out just as I zipped in, and with time still left on the meter, no less. I joined the gaggle of reporters and camera shooters clustered around the back door of the modern high-rise house of incarceration. A Monterey County sheriff's sedan idled in the loading zone.

Normally, I detest these media gang bangs, but I felt I owed it to Jasmine to show up. When she faced that quivering mass of flashbulbs and microphones, she deserved to see one sympathetic face in the crowd. Even though I was probably the last person in the world she wanted to see right now.

A cry of "Here she comes!" and the pack descended on a knot of humanity struggling to make its way through the exit to the waiting patrol car. No red carpet on the perp walk for our diva, no Versace gown or screams from adoring fans. Only the flashbulbs to remind her of what she'd once had and lost. I made note of a half dozen tan uniforms of both the Monterey and Sacramento sheriff's departments surrounding the captive, as well as Sheriff Perez, the Monterey DA, and a short, bald man in a gray suit who I assumed was the counsel for the defense. And in the middle of it all, a tiny, dazed figure, shackled and in an orange jumpsuit.

"Did you do it, Jasmine?"

"Why'd you come home, Jasmine?"

"Hey, Jasmine, look over here!"

She ignored the shouts, kept her head ducked, and tried to shield herself with cuffed arms.

I only got one good look at her, just as she was being manhandled into the backseat of the Monterey County sheriff's vehicle. She looked up, spotted me, and shot me a look of pure venom. I didn't blame her. I tried to send her a look that said not to give up, that she could count on me to continue the search for the real killer. But I was overshadowed by taller, brawnier men and women of the fourth estate, elbowing me out of the way with their cameras and boom mikes. I jumped repeatedly, attempting to see over the crowd, and added my voice to the yammering demands for a comment. Only in my case, I hollered out a statement not a question.

"I'm sorry! I'm sorry!"

I cranked the wheel of the microfilm reader, sending the *Sacramento Bee* from the summer of 1976 spinning past in a blur of black-and-white, slowing to a lurch as the dates just after the Bicentennial neared. I'd just finished filing a report about the prisoner transfer over the cell phone, not bothering to hurry back to the station to edit tape. What was the point? All I or anyone else in the media pack had been able to do was record the roar of our own incessant babbling. Sacramento's Main Library was only two blocks away from the county slammer. I felt as if my spirit needed cleansing after participating in a media circus, and a trip to the cool silence of the library might provide just such a sanctuary.

That, and information.

I adjusted the wheel at the bottom of the machine and brought the black type of the advertisement into sharper focus.

Exclusive Sacramento Appearance!

JASMINE

"Meet Me at the Casbah"

The Oasis Ballroom, Midtown at 20th and I

Sponsored by KROY AM 1260

The facing page of the entertainment section included the weekly radio schedule. A Johnny Venture held down the noon-to-three slot at KROY AM 1260.

I pumped a couple of small coins into a vending machine to make copies of the advertisement and radio listings, folded them into neat squares, and placed them in my backpack. I cranked the wheel of the microfilm reader in reverse, removed the reel, packed Sacramento's Bicentennial summer back into a gray cardboard box, and handed it to the clerk behind the periodicals desk. I left the literary repository with proof that Jasmine and one of the Johnny Ventures had indeed occupied the same city one evening in July 1976, and could, theoretically, have participated in a semi-scandalous sex act.

Vance Ballard made me cool my heels for forty-five minutes in the lobby of his recording studio, but that was understandable. I hadn't made an appointment or even called to alert him I was on my way. I figured an informed source like Vance Ballard was worth the wait, saving me time in the long run, and I enjoyed the opportunity to study his collection of local rock and radio memorabilia.

Ballard burst through the door of the reception area, a white towel draped around his neck, prizefighter style. "Sorry to make you wait so long." He mopped his face with the towel. "It's been another marathon session over the Mine Shaft campaign."

I outlined the mission: to locate any information that might still exist about the Johnny Venture who worked at a station called KROY AM 1260 in July 1976. It was the longest of long shots, the off chance that a brief encounter at a defunct nightclub almost thirty years ago had sparked the events that led to the death of an over-the-hill disc jockey and the arrest of a TV sitcom star. Jasmine herself had said as much in her already-famous quote about murdering all those disc jockeys, promoters, and pop music critics that she'd gone down on during her career.

Ballard led me through the narrow halls and cubbyholes of the recording studio, parked me on one of the butterfly chairs in his office, and began rummaging through a bookcase.

"You know Lou Jelniak, the guy who owned the El Jay studio?" I said, while he searched. "Any idea what happened to him after he sold the business?"

"I heard he landed in San Francisco, and later on ended up in the Monterey area. Something about making a killing in real estate." Ballard removed a binder, placed it on his desk, and began riffling through the pages. "Too bad you didn't get to grow up in Sacramento. You would have dug the old KROY. They had the hippest talent in town and played the hottest new releases."

Sounded a lot like the Top Forty stations I worshiped when I was a kid: KYA and KFRC in San Francisco, and hometown KLIV in San Jose. "I've never even heard of KROY. What happened to it?"

"FM happened, that's what." Ballard snapped open the binder, removed a plastic sheet protector, and passed it to me. "Those AM music stations just couldn't compete with FM. AM 1260 went Spanish more than ten years ago."

The eight-by-ten card Ballard handed to me looked like part of a sales kit from the 1970s, a one-sheet featuring photographs of the KROY air talent. "Let Johnny Venture fill your midday with fun, prizes, and the best in music power, weekdays from noon to three!" The Johnny Venture in the photograph looked around twenty years old, with a wispy Keith Partridge hairdo and bristly muttonchop sideburns. A glance at the pictures of the entire on-air stable showed three other announcers sporting the same unfortunate male facial hair fad from the era.

"Do you have any idea who he really was, this Johnny Venture, and where he might be now?"

Ballard moved around the desk and stood next to me to study the half-tone. "Sure, that's Gary Drager. He's around, works for the state last I heard, still keeps his hand in the business. Community theater, voice-over work, stuff like that."

The intercom on Ballard's desk squawked something unintelligible. Rats, just as I was poised to make the obvious request for an address or phone number for this Gary Drager.

"Sorry, this is just not a good day." Ballard tugged at the ends of the towel still coiled around his neck and bolted for the door. "Cherise Rose doesn't know the definition of the word patience. See Whitney on your way out, have her schedule something for tomorrow."

"Any luck with the DMV?" I stood in the doorway of Glory Lou's office at the station.

She looked up from her desk and pushed long hanks of shiny black hair out of her eyes and over her forehead. "Sorry, hon. My source is taking a personal day and won't be back until tomorrow."

"A personal day? How many days off do state workers get, anyway?"

"Tell me about it." She leaned forward, placing two meaty forearms on the desk. "Curious, isn't it?"

"Curious what?" I sensed what was coming next.

"Curious how you were able to land that interview with Jasmine just before the law caught up with her. Or was it after? Did the cops give you access before they notified everyone else in the media about the bust?"

"It's like you've always told me, Glory Lou. A good reporter never reveals her sources."

CNN carried live coverage of Jasmine's return to the Monterey County Jail just after two. I watched on the overhead newsroom monitor as she repeated her exit from Sacramento some four hours earlier in reverse: her removal from the patrol car, the media riot, the perp walk, the disappearance through the heavy doors of the Salinas jail. Sheriff Maria Elena Perez told the media she credited the capture to "top-notch investigative work by my team here in

Salinas and an anonymous good citizen in Sacramento who doesn't want to take any credit."

Oh, puh-leeze. I waited around thirty minutes to give Sheriff Perez time to shake the media pack and return to her office, then picked up the phone and dialed her number.

"You know as well as I do that I can't get that information without an order signed by a judge," she said as soon as I'd told her what I was after. "And even if I could, I'm not about to turn that information over to a civilian."

"Spare me. It's all public record. Property ownership, business licenses, voter registration, arrest record, if any, civil suits. I'd do it myself, but, hey, you're already in Monterey County."

"Hire a private investigator, then."

"Aren't you forgetting something? You owe me big time, lady. I found your fugitive for you." God, it felt good to tell her that! "The name is Jelniak, Lou Jelniak. Short for Louis, I assume. J-E-L-N-I-A-K."

"You done good, missy," said T.R. O'Brien, paying a visit to the control room just as I finished signing off for the afternoon.

I had done good, dammit. The Jasmine interview in its entirety opened the show at three and was repeated at five. The impulse to allow the TV cameras and print reporters live access to the control room had been positively inspired, giving my exclusive instant exposure on every media outlet in the city and across the country. In between airings of the Jasmine tapes, I fielded questions from reporters and lobbed quips and comments from callers. Even engineering had cooperated, finally finishing the digital conversion and covering the ditch in the control room. So there was plenty of room for the camera crews and all their heavy gear to maneuver in the tight quarters of the on-air studio.

At moments like this, I can't imagine any high more thrilling than live radio.

I led T.R. out of the control room and down the hall toward the business offices and away from the lingering reporters. Not to mention our own busybody in the news director's cubicle. I was almost positive of what he was going to say next.

"It's like I said, you done good," T.R. said. "So spill. How is it that the very same night that you get exclusive access, the cops make the bust of the most notorious murder suspect since O.J.?"

I'd repeated the comment about a good journalist never revealing her sources. But I knew T.R. would never let me slide so easily. He was the boss, after all, the man who let me have fun on the radio for three hours every day. Even paid me to do it.

I pulled O'Brien into the lunchroom and looked around, making sure no one was within eavesdropping range. "I found her first. I did the interview, got the tape. Then I placed a call to the Monterey County Sheriff's Department."

"I knew it! My little Shauna J. is the anonymous tipster."

"Keep your voice down." I placed both hands at the small of my back and leaned against the soda machine. "I don't feel good about it, and I'd rather not have the whole world knowing."

"Seems to me you made the right decision. Shoot, what were you supposed to do? Find that little gal, get her to talk on tape, and then just sit on it? Or put the tape on the air, but not tell the cops how and where you got it?"

"Yeah, but I gave Jasmine my word she could trust me."

"You also gave that lady sheriff your word you'd cooperate with the investigation. Don't forget, I sat in on your little breakfast meeting. You did what you had to do. So stop frettin'."

"I suppose you're right."

"Damn straight. You just keep doin' good like you did this afternoon, missy, and it'll all work out. It always does."

I would have given a lot to have spent the evening at home, flopping around in sweats, doing nothing more strenuous than cuddling the cat and lifting the remote. But years in the radio industry had taught me that I'd pay later on, if I blew off that restaurant's grand opening the sales manager insisted I attend. I probably should have changed into something spiffier for the event. But I knew that once I actually walked through the front door of my apartment, I'd be a goner. So I had Josh drop me off in front of Capitol Square, made a straight line for the parking garage, and climbed behind the wheel of the Z-car.

No question, it felt terrific to be driving my own car again. The white sedan from Sweden had served its purpose well and definitely offered more in the way of amenities and safety features. But there was no point in keeping the station's Unmarked Vehicle for my own personal use now that Operation Find Jasmine was over. I'd turned over the Volvo keys to Glory Lou just before leaving the station.

This was another case where I could easily have walked from home to my destination, a new high-rise near the Convention Center. But that deserted stretch of the K Street pedestrian mall between the end of Downtown Plaza at Seventh and the Convention Center at Twelfth could be dicey after dark for a lone female. I pulled into an underground parking garage on J Street, took the ticket a machine spat in my direction, and found an empty spot two levels down.

I retrieved the invitation from my backpack and gave it one more glance, just to refresh my mind as to what I was getting myself into.

Lloyd Ellwanger cordially invites your presence at the grand opening of

LLOYD'S ON TWENTY-NINTH

The Capital City's newest dining destination

The date, time, and address followed.

Oh, great. I'd forgotten this was Lloyd's as in Lloyd Ellwanger. That meant Cherise Rose was sure to be holding court. On the other hand, Vance Ballard might put in an appearance, assuming he could get away from the studio long enough, and he could be fun to hang around with. And I might have the opportunity to mine his memory bank for information on the 1976 version of Johnny Venture, that state worker who does voice-overs and community theater on the side. Gary Drager.

I pulled my business card case out of the backpack and slipped it into the pocket of my slacks. You never know when there might be the opportunity to schmooze, or a drawing for door prizes. I figured I wouldn't be needing anything else for the short time I planned to spend at the party, so I hid the backpack under a beach towel in the back compartment of the Z-car, taking only business cards and keys. And the parking ticket, just in case I could get it validated.

An elevator crammed with a dozen other Sacramento VIPs wearing party duds took us on a stomach-dropping express ride to the twenty-ninth floor. The lift's doors parted to the aroma of roasted garlic, the mellow sounds of a smooth jazz combo, a quick peek at black-lacquered wooden tables, plump taupe cushions on banquettes, and a heart-stopping view of downtown Sacramento and beyond.

Twenty-nine stories is tall by Sacramento standards, topped only by the thirty-four-floor Wells Fargo Tower as the tallest structure in the city limits, if you don't count my station's transmission tower, that is. I gazed out at the winking lights of the vast suburbs spread out before me. Closer in, I easily identified the downtown skyscrapers that had enshrouded the state capitol in recent years: the Darth Vader building at Eighth and K, with its silhouetted resemblance to the *Star Wars* bad guy, the cylindrical, dome-topped Ban Roll-on building at 1201 K Street, the Wells Fargo Nutcracker with its curved copper roof, and the green glass of Emerald City at the far end of Capitol Mall. I accepted a glass of wine from a strolling waiter and wondered if this penchant for giving nicknames to high-rise buildings was unique to Sacramento, or if it represented a universal need to humanize those mega-sized structures. I also wondered how long it would take before the building that housed

Lloyd's got stuck with a nickname, and tucked the idea away to toss out to my listeners on a slow day.

A collective sigh from the west-facing windows prompted me to weave my way through the crowd in that direction. The sun was just sinking past the Tower Bridge, Interstate 80, the Delta, and the far-flung suburbs of San Francisco in the barely visible distance. The show was so spectacular I joined in on a round of spontaneous applause when the final sliver of orange disappeared behind the horizon.

My plan was to make the rounds just long enough to congratulate Lloyd Ellwanger on his latest enterprise, to make sure Dorinda Delgado saw me and knew I'd done my duty to the sales department, and to avoid Cherise Rose. That, plus one glass of wine and one pass by the buffet table, and I'd be home in time to catch *Will and Grace*.

Along the one wall not facing a bank of windows I found a row of easels, each holding a twenty-four-by-thirty-six-inch show card. I perused the poster to the far left. A color photograph depicted Ellwanger and a woman in a white coat and chef's hat. "And now Lloyd Ellwanger is proud to present the crowning achievement of his career," the two-inch-high block letters informed me. "Lloyd's on Twenty-ninth, The Capital City's Most Exciting Dining Destination. The finest in California fusion cuisine served to you on the glamorous top floor of the new Millennium Tower." A copy of the menu filled the rest of the show card.

I ambled over to the next easel, which contained photographs of various versions of the Mine Shaft Restaurants in suburban communities in the Sacramento area. "Lloyd Ellwanger continues to expand his family restaurant chain, opening soon in Southern California." The poster also featured photos of Ellwanger doing the grip-and-greet with Governor Deukmejian, President Reagan, Charlton Heston, and Ross Perot.

The easel to the immediate right showcased a faded color photograph of the ribbon-cutting of the first Mine Shaft. "In 1982, Lloyd Ellwanger opens his flagship Mine Shaft Restaurant on Arden Way. The fun, casual family atmosphere and the mouthwatering ribs proves to be a winning combination, and the following year, he opens a second Mine Shaft in Rancho Cordova."

I was beginning to sense a theme: Lloyd Ellwanger, This Is Your Life. Only I'd apparently been reading the posters in a backward order. Instead of breaking my stride to detour to the beginning, I continued to sip wine and strolled to the next easel. Its poster gave me a capsule version of Ellwanger's canny real estate investments in the sixties and seventies.

Another few steps rewound the Lloyd Ellwanger saga to 1958. "Twenty-year-old Lloyd Ellwanger takes $1,850 he'd saved from delivering newspapers and makes his first strategic investment with high school chum Lou Jelniak."

The black-and-white photograph was similar to the one Rita Slade had shared with me. The chubby, Buddy Holly–spectacled Jelniak and a scraggly-haired, mustachioed young man, both behind the buttons, knobs, and reels of a recording console. Rita Slade hadn't known the identity of the Beatnik-slash-hayseed. But now I did.

Lloyd Ellwanger.

The El in El Jay.

21

"QUITE A STORY, WOULDN'T YOU SAY?"

I was so intent on my inspection of the 1958 photograph of Lloyd Ellwanger and Lou Jelniak, so engrossed in the implications of this discovery, that I'd sealed myself into oblivion from the festivities whirling about me. I tensed at the sound of a familiar voice and almost sloshed wine down the front of my best blouse.

"It's just that I never expected this." I spoke more to myself than to the man standing next to me.

"Aren't you even going to say hey to an old pal?"

"Donovan Sinclair!" I yanked myself away from the Lloyd Ellwanger pictorial review and turned to greet the man behind the voice. "What brings you to Sacramento?"

"Looking after some real estate investments. I happened to run into Cherise Rose in the lobby of the Sheraton and she promised to add me to this evening's guest list. She told me everyone who's anybody in Sacramento will be at the grand opening of Lloyd's. Looks like she was right."

"Will I see you tomorrow night at the Broadcast Legends thing?" It was just cocktail party chitchat. I'd already inspected the program and knew Sinclair was scheduled to make a presentation.

"Wouldn't miss it for the world." Sinclair took a sip of mineral water. "Especially the chance to see Shauna J. Bogart inducted into the Hall of Fame."

I made a quick scan of the crowded eatery and spied the bouffant brunette hairdo, pink designer suit, and gold chain jewelry of Cherise Rose bearing down in our direction.

"Lookin' good." I gave Sinclair's lower arm a pat. He did look pretty fine, if you go for older guys, black cashmere turtleneck sweater tucked into narrow black slacks in an expensive fabric, clear eyes, thinning brown hair pulled neatly back into a knot at the nape of his neck. The loss of at least fifty pounds and a mound of facial hair had taken at least ten years off his age. He could pass for a corporate executive in his early fifties instead of the super-sized over-the-hill hippie I recalled from my San Francisco radio days.

I took a step back, poised to flee from the approaching ad agency lady. "Gotta run. Be seein' you tomorrow in San Francisco."

The mob scene surrounding the buffet table discouraged me from sampling the cuisine at Lloyd's, even if it meant never discovering exactly what "California fusion" might be. These VIPs were doing a better-than-passing imitation of Jasmine with the bucket of chicken last night. What, did they think they were never going to get free food again? My ears picked up the booming cracker accent and hee-haw laugh of the restaurant's namesake as our host glad-handed his way through the crowd. Perfect. Shake hands, exchange pleasantries, and then I'm outta here.

"Shauna J. Bogart! I'm delighted to see your purty little face." Lloyd Ellwanger pumped my arm like he was drilling for oil. "Have you tried out them shrimp things with the almond crust? Them's hot diggity dog."

Ellwanger draped a long arm around my shoulders and steered me away from the feeding frenzy. "Got my own private dining room set up in back, just for special people like this little lady," he announced as he cleared a path and walked me in the direction of a swinging door that led, I assumed, to the kitchen.

I followed along, still holding the wineglass, as Ellwanger led me through the door and down a short hallway. I inhaled a wave of spicy cooking odors and felt a blast of hot air as we passed the kitchen.

Ellwanger pulled open another door. "Welcome to the new headquarters of Ellwanger Enterprises."

I found myself in a Hollywood fantasy of an Old West bunkhouse. We're talking lassos, cattle brands, and spurs mounted onto walls paneled in knotty pine. Navajo rugs flung over the backs of heavy log sofas and chairs upholstered in brown leather. More examples of indigenous weaving on the tongue-and-groove flooring. Two chandeliers fashioned out of wagon wheels, and what appeared to be the chassis of a chuck wagon forming the base of Ellwanger's massive desk. A credenza constructed out of more pine logs held the only nonauthentic western gear: an iMac, printer, fax machine, and shredder. The computer's mouse pad was made of faux cowhide. Yippie-ti-yo-ki-yay!

The full-length windows on the far wall offered a view not of cowpokes on the range, but of Sacramento's southern exposure. French doors opened onto a small terrace. I followed Ellwanger out the doors, across the tiled floor to a chest-high solid cement guardrail. I looked out onto the twilight cityscape, tracing the red and white winking lights on Highway 99 until they disappeared into the deepening darkness.

"I chose this view for my new corporate headquarters for a special reason." My host stood at my side. I noticed, now that he had an audience of only one, he dropped all but the slightest trace of the hillbilly act. "My ma and pa drove their jalopy up that very highway, all the way from Oklahoma in 1937. I like to stand out here and look, remind myself of where the Ellwangers started, and how far we've come."

"It must be quite a tale," I agreed. My boss has a similar family saga, as do many of the second- and third-generation white residents of the Central Valley. You can still hear a trace of the Dust Bowl in local speech oddities, not just from the Okie descendants but pretty much everyone who's lived here for any length of time. I catch myself saying "Sackamenna" more and more these days, and I'm a relative newcomer.

"I didn't know you were involved with El Jay Records," I said, in what I hoped was a neutral voice, as if I were commenting on the weather. "That must have been interesting."

"You're talking a long time ago. Jelniak bought me out in 1964 and I used the dough to start my real estate investments."

"But you held on to your share of the building." I thought of my visit this past Monday evening to the Attention Deficit Zone, Lloyd Ellwanger's little family togetherness project.

"The Med Center is going to continue to expand and a parcel at Fourteenth and Stockton will be worth a bundle someday. In the meantime, it's a nice plaything for my grandchildren."

"Whatever happened to Lou Jelniak?"

"Shoot, I haven't heard from that ol' boy in at least twenty-five years, not since he closed the studio and left town. You know how it goes, people get older and drift apart."

"Sure." Lou Jelniak had been Ellwanger's boyhood chum, though. And his first business partner. You'd think they'd still at least exchange Christmas cards.

The French doors opened and two men appeared, one a uniformed waiter, the other a vaguely familiar fellow in a business suit, white shirt, and rep tie. It took me a moment to place the gangly guy with the dour disposition. Oakley Plummer III, Monterey County's chief deputy district attorney.

The waiter had to ask twice whether madame would like her wine refreshed. I declined and placed the half-empty glass on his tray. Even though the chardonnay he was pouring was a cut far above the buck-ninety-nine stuff I'm used to swilling, I had a sudden instinct I'd fully require functioning brain cells and coordination before the evening ended. "Just water, please," Madame told him.

"Shauna J. Bogart is the hottest voice on Sacramento radio," Ellwanger said by way of introduction. "And Oakley Plummer has a big future ahead of him in state politics."

"We've met before," Plummer said without changing his expression.

"Well, that's just swell!" Ellwanger clapped Plummer on the shoulder. "Like I say, Oak here is going places. He's tough on crime and a strong booster of business and agriculture. I plan on supporting him when he runs for state senate in two years."

The waiter silently handed me a bottle of designer water. I twisted off the cap and swallowed. I couldn't figure out where this conversation was headed. Even the most oddly gerrymandered senate district originating in Monterey County wouldn't cover my listening area.

On the other hand, if Oakley Plummer III managed to win a conviction in a highly publicized and televised felony case, the state senate would hardly be big enough to contain him. Think governor or U.S. senator. First, though, if he was going to be electable he would need a makeover in the smile and personality department.

"Time for me to get back to mingling." Ellwanger gave me a little bow. "I'll leave you two to get better acquainted." He and the waiter disappeared through the French doors.

"In the next few weeks my department will be initiating discovery in the Jasmine case," Plummer said as soon as Ellwanger was out of hearing range. "That means you need to turn over your tapes, notes, and any other documentation you might have that pertains to the case."

"Not without a subpoena." I pretended to ignore Plummer and continued to gaze over the balcony, feigning fascination with the satellite dishes on top of the telephone company building at Fifteenth and J. The wind from the Delta had kicked in, causing me to constantly push my hair out of my eyes.

"I can still have you arrested for obstruction of justice."

"Get real." What, did this guy think I just fell off the turnip truck?

"I can arrange all the jailhouse access to the accused that you'll ever want. Exclusives, right up to the day we lock her up for life."

Now there was an offer worth at least considering.

"So let's make it easy for both of us." Plummer's narrow lips twitched into something that might have been a smile. "You give me the original, uncut tape of your interview last night, recordings of any and all programs in which Jasmine may have called in, and your notes and background material. Also, any records or tapes or documents that you might have concerning the career of the Dee Vines."

"The Dee Vines?" I stared at Plummer, watched his knobby fingers gripping a half-full tumbler of scotch and ice. "What do the Dee Vines have to do with the Jasmine case?"

"That's confidential."

"Then come back when you've got a subpoena."

Plummer flipped back one side of his suit jacket and placed a hand on his hip, revealing a holster and butt end of a gun. Swell. Here I was getting my hair whipped into shreds on a perch twenty-nine stories above the city, facing an armed man with political ambitions. I didn't seriously think he'd do anything. I mean, put a bullet in my head, pitch me over the side? Or leave my lifeless body for the waiter to find when he came around for last call? But I thought it best not to encourage Plummer to act impulsively.

"As you can see, I don't have any records or tapes on me," I said in a conciliatory tone. "I'm not even carrying a purse. I'd be more than happy to go down to the station and make copies for you. You can pick them up first thing tomorrow morning."

"Originals, no copies."

"Sure thing." Say anything, just get away from him and off this damn balcony. I stuck my hand in my pants pocket and pulled out a business card. "Give me a call tomorrow and we'll work something out."

Plummer took the card and gave it a glance. I used the opportunity to slip away from the balcony's edge and through the French doors into Ellwanger's deserted dude ranch den. I didn't hear any footsteps following me, but I ran anyway, not pausing until I passed the kitchen and burst through the swinging door, back into the laughter, music, culinary aromas, and body heat of Lloyd Ellwanger's swank new restaurant.

A team of waiters was placing fresh nibbles on the buffet table, but I was going to have to skip the opportunity to try those shrimp things with the almond crust. I rode the elevator to the second level of the underground parking garage, trotted over to my car, and placed the key into the driver's-side door of the yellow Z-car.

"Leaving so soon?"

This time, Plummer showed teeth when he smiled, a frosty grin below a set of steel-gray eyes. Damn! how did he manage to get down here so fast? The freight elevator?

"You can't leave now. The party's just getting good." The heels of his wing-tips clipped against the reinforced concrete of the parking garage as he strode closer to me.

"They're expecting me back at the station," I lied.

Plummer repeated the little action with the suit jacket and the hand on the hip, making sure I didn't miss his little holstered persuader. "Just give me what I want."

"And that would be . . . ?" I leaned against the door of the Z-car, folded my arms, and made a quick visual sweep of my surroundings. No one in sight, no one to hear me scream. Just cement, white lines, and a regiment of silent vehicles.

"Don't get cute." He stood close enough that I could smell the scotch on his breath. "You know damn well what I want."

"This recording that I supposedly have from a group called the Dee Vines."

"Now you're starting to talk sense."

"What's it to you, a bunch of old, forgotten doo-wop singers from 1961? And what does it have to do with Jasmine?"

"That's for me to know and for you—"

"Okay, okay." I cut him off, afraid he would try to smile again after his weak attempt at witticism. What was I going to do to get rid of this guy and get out of here? Throw him a bone. Just like dealing with a mean dog.

"I've got just what you're looking for right inside the car. I'm not going to try anything, honest." I opened the car door while keeping an eye on Plummer. He moved in closer, still keeping both hands on his hips.

I reached into the back compartment of the sports car, retrieved my backpack, undid the drawstring, plunged my hand into the canvas interior. I fished around until I found a plastic sleeve holding a four-and-three-quarters-inch silver disc. The CD copy of the Dee Vines' one hit, "Cruisin' on K Street," that Rita Slade had burned for me the other night. I hated to give it up, but I could always ask Rita to make another copy and e-mail it to me.

Plummer snatched the CD out of my hand and snapped it in two. "This isn't what I'm after and you know it." He flung the pieces to the ground.

Tsk, tsk, such behavior. Vandalism *and* littering.

"I don't know what the hell you're talking about." I started to lower myself onto the black leather of the driver's seat.

"Not so fast." He grabbed my upper arm and dug his bony fingers in deep. "You've either got the record or you know where it is. You and your boyfriend. Give it up."

My boyfriend? I writhed under Plummer's grasp and tried to think. Something in that box of old records and tapes that Rita Slade turned over to Pete Kovacs? But what? It had to be vital enough for Traci Kapolsky to base an entire episode of *Hammer of Justice* around, and to hastily revamp her plans when the box got stolen. And now this clown was after it too. Whatever it was, it must be important. But what did this thing—this record, according to what Plummer just said—have to do with the Jasmine case?

"I don't know where any of that stuff is, I swear," I said. "Pete Kovacs had a box of memorabilia from the Dee Vines, if that's what you're looking for. But it got stolen from an apartment over at Capitol Square." I gave him the address and apartment number. "Go ahead, knock on their door. Ask Traci Kapolsky if you don't believe me."

Plummer acted as if the information were old news. "You know where it is." The fingers tightened.

"First, take your greasy fingers off me. If I have to get this blouse dry-cleaned, I'm sending the bill to the Monterey County's DA office." I hoped I came off sounding braver than I felt.

The elevator dinged and the doors slid open. Three men and two women emerged, still chattering brightly in party mode. They air-kissed good-byes and one of the women began walking in my direction. When she drew closer, I noticed she carried a plastic plate loaded with goodies scrounged from Lloyd's smorgasbord.

Plummer loosened his grip on my upper arm. I wasted no time sliding into the driver's seat, slamming the door, pushing down the lock, and roaring the engine to life. I put the gear in reverse and slammed on the gas pedal, not even bothering to see if Plummer—or anyone else—was in my path.

I took the turns to the ground level with a screech and lurched forward to the exit gate. Two cars idled ahead of me. I fidgeted as the first driver turned over a ticket to the attendant, then money, then reached out for change. The guy in the booth pushed a button and the wooden gate began to ascend.

The second vehicle, a silver Honda minivan, inched forward to the small enclosure. I followed on its tail. I heard the rumble of a large engine and looked in the rearview mirror. A white Crown Victoria sedan, two-way radio antenna sticking from the roof, hexagonal design on the license plate. CA EXEMPT. A sour-faced, angular figure behind the wheel.

I wriggled the parking ticket out of my pants pocket, grabbed my wallet from the backpack, wrapped a five-dollar bill around the parking stub, and secured the package with a rubber band I found in the glove box.

The gate rose. The minivan eased out of the parking garage and hovered on the driveway. I swear, I've never done anything like this before. I tossed the parking ticket and cash in the direction of the booth and depressed the gas pedal. The Z-car stuck to the silver

Honda as if we were chained together. It slowed to wait for a break in the traffic on J Street. The gate began to descend, a direct line to the hatchback window of my car. I tore around the minivan, barely escaping the guillotine, jumped the curb, and slammed the palm of my hand on the horn as I steered into the flow of traffic.

I turned right onto Seventeenth, hung another right onto L Street. Heading not toward home, but to the one place in the city where I felt I might be safe.

One more swerving turn on the downtown streets. I was pretty sure I'd lost him. A straight shot north on Sixteenth Street would take me out of the downtown district. My heart continued to hammer as Sixteenth merged into Highway 160.

A pair of headlights followed.

I didn't bother to signal as I exited onto the frontage road, pulled into the parking lot, and stopped in the red zone next to the back door of the radio station.

The headlights of the white Crown Victoria stuck right to my tail.

22

"DON'T EVER PULL A STUNT LIKE THAT AGAIN." OAKLEY PLUMMER barreled out of the unmarked county vehicle.

"Now you're starting to sound like my father." I stuck my keycard into a slot next to the newsroom door.

"I could have you arrested for petty theft, reckless driving, endangerment of others, speeding, crossing a double-yellow, and failing to signal. And that's just for starters."

"Petty theft?" I gave Plummer an insulted pout. "I paid the parking guy." Or tried to, anyway.

I had no idea what I was going to do next, but I'd made note of three cars in the station parking lot in addition to Steve Garland's Miata. Plummer wouldn't dare try anything funny with witnesses. I'd stall Plummer until inspiration came to the rescue. I pulled open the newsroom door and waved my arm at Plummer, motioning him to follow me. "You want your record, don't you?"

I stopped at my desk, picked up a file folder of notes and background material on the Jasmine case, and ushered Plummer into the green room. The only thing green about the tiny waiting room was a vase filled with plastic ivy. I thrust the folder into Plummer's hands and motioned toward the brown vinyl-covered couch. "Make yourself at home." I counted on the reading material to keep him occupied while I concocted my strategy.

The red light above the door to the on-air studio dimmed, signaling the start of a commercial break in Steve Garland's show. I strolled in and almost pitched into the open ditch running across the studio floor. My backpack went tumbling to the floor, coming to rest in front of the transmitter control panel.

"What the—?"

Gil Loomis, the chief engineer, poked his head from around the back of the broadcast console. "Tell me about it. This new digital system crashed the first time we tried to do a test. So now we've got to dive back in and change one of the routers."

"Ouch," I said in sympathy.

"Yeah, all that overtime was great for a while, but now it's getting old."

Garland raised his hand, alerting us to the end of the stop set and the need for silence. I seated myself in one of the guest chairs and listened with only partial attention as Garland gave his name, the station call letters, the time and temperature, and introduced his next caller.

Pete Kovacs and I had lingered in this very on-air studio a week ago Monday. It was the first and so far only time I'd seen that box of memorabilia from the short career of a doo-wop group called the Dee Vines. Kovacs had told me he had something "interesting" to show me and something "important" to talk about. Then he had unveiled a 45 rpm record from a bubble-wrap cocoon.

That evening had been the last time I'd seen Pete Kovacs live and in person.

Thoughts tumbled around my mind, connecting, disconnecting, then flying around in new formations. That old vinyl disc had to be the key. But to what? Rita Slade inherits it from her grandfather, one of the original members of the Dee Vines. She turns it over to Pete Kovacs. Kovacs offers it to Traci Kapolsky to use on her TV show.

The apartment rented by Kapolsky and the *Hammer of Justice* crew is burglarized. The box of Dee Vines memorabilia is stolen.

I was positive that same ditch had bisected the control room floor the last time I talked with Kovacs. I was also certain that I'd turned my back on Kovacs for a few moments, while I fiddled with the knobs and meters on the transmitter control panel.

The crevice was normally covered with metal plates and carpet sections, only revealing itself when the engineering staff needed access to the yards of wire snaking under and around the on-air and production studios.

At six inches deep and a foot wide, might there be room among all that wire to hide something small? Like, say, a flat disc roughly six and three-quarter inches in diameter?

On the far side of the broadcast console, Gil Loomis unearthed a tangle of cable and spread it on the carpeted floor, like a physician performing intestinal surgery. I knelt in front of the ditch a few yards away, trying to keep out of his way, and lowered my head.

Something shiny and clear lay barely visible under a covering of cable. Way back, in a section of the ditch still covered by the metal plate and carpet. I stretched my arm as far as it would go. My fingers made contact with something cool, smooth. I gave it a poke. It deflated with a slightly squishy feel. Yes! Bubble wrap!

I could have asked Gil Loomis to help me pull up another section of carpet and the metal plate, but I hated to interrupt the chief engineer in the middle of another all-nighter. I stretched out on the carpeted floor and lowered my torso into the ditch, thrusting my arm farther into the cavity. This time I was able to wrap my fingers around the package. I inched it forward slowly, careful not to disturb the cables that rested on top. Finally I managed to maneuver the bubble-wrapped package to the open section. I wriggled it around the wires, slid it up one side of the rectangular hole, and raised the object with both hands.

Still kneeling in front of the ditch, I glanced at the plastic-wrapped square just long enough to confirm that it did, indeed, encase a 45 rpm record. Then I grabbed for my backpack, untied the drawstring, and carefully placed the package inside. I retied the strings of the colorful hand-woven bag.

The control room door opened. A pair of wing tips planted themselves at my eye level.

"This is all public record stuff, and you know it." Oakley Plummer slapped the file folder against the palm of his hand. "Now give me what I want."

I scrambled to my feet, grabbed Plummer by the elbow, and steered him out of the control room. "The red light means we're on the air," I scolded in a whisper, resisting the urge to add various descriptive titles calling into question his mental capacity and parental antecedents. Steve Garland shot me an annoyed glance while he continued to chat with Marvin from Rio Linda about the World Series.

"Just give me the record. I don't have all night."

"Of course." I piloted him back into the green room. "I go on the air live with a news update in less than two minutes," I vamped. "As soon as that's all wrapped up, I'll get your record and everybody's happy. In the meantime, put your feet up and relax." I traded the file folder for a copy of last week's *Radio and Records* and gave Plummer a gentle shove toward the couch.

"I need you to help me out of a jam," I said to Steve Garland as soon as he switched off the mike and punched up the tape cartridge to segue into a commercial break.

"What's in it for me?" He eyed me with suspicion, groped into a bag, and popped a peanut M&M into his mouth.

"Okay, I'm sorry about that bit the other day about guys who call in to sports talk shows being a bunch of evolutionary throwbacks."

"What kind of favor are you looking for?" Garland folded his arms across his chest and leaned back in the announcer's chair.

"There's this guy in the green room—"

"That guy? He barged into my show! This is supposed to be a closed studio. Whatever you want me to do, if it involves that doofus, forget it."

"Look, this guy is really important. He's going to be the lead prosecutor in the Jasmine case. Very newsworthy. All I need is for you to interview him for about a half hour on your show. Right now." A half hour would give me enough time to grab the backpack, race home, bolt all the door and windows, and call security to request an extra watch on my apartment tonight.

"In case you haven't noticed, this is a sports show. The sixth game of the World Series is coming up. What's more important, some lawyer going after some whacked-out TV star, or the showdown in Chavez Ravine tomorrow night?"

Garland glanced at the clock, and I could hear the final commercial in the stop set winding down with a breathless reminder that these special values will end on Friday, don't miss out! I stepped behind the console, next to Garland. Before he could open the mike, I grabbed a taped public service announcement reminding us about Spare the Air Days, slammed it into the playback machine, and hit the start button.

"I swear I'll never blow off your promotional announcements ever again," I said. "This guy is really newsworthy and I promise he'll be a terrific guest. Fun personality, lots of laughs."

Garland raised both palms in surrender. "Fine, whatever. Bring him on in. But a half hour, that's all he gets."

"You won't regret this," I said over my shoulder as I exited the newsroom.

"Great news!" I announced as I flung open the door to the green room.

"It better be." Plummer had doffed his suit jacket and rolled up his shirtsleeves, revealing the twin knobs of his wrist bones.

"Our topnotch political analyst is on the air right now. When he found out Oakley Plummer III was right here at the station, he insisted on having the opportunity to interview you. Right now."

"Really?" Plummer's mouth twitched into a grin, and this time it looked almost genuine.

"For real. Steve Garland is especially eager to talk to you about the state senate race." I guided Plummer out of the green room and into the on-air studio.

Politicians and entertainers. They just can't resist an opportunity for media exposure.

I eased the vinyl disc from the protective plastic covering and the paper sleeve, and held it by its edges with both hands. It appeared to be a duplicate of the 45 disc Rita Slade had shown me the other night. "Cruisin' on K Street" by the Dee Vines on the El Jay label. Then I took a second look, at the smaller type on the yellow and black label:

Otis Turner • Clarence Willits

I gently slipped the record back into its paper sleeve, placed it on top of the bubble wrap, took a sip of wine, and leaned back on the living room couch. Lou Jelniak had been listed as the composer of "Cruisin on K Street" on the 45 disc I saw at the Slade home. I was sure of it. Not only that, Rita Slade was under the impression Jelniak wrote the song. Her grandfather and his pals simply provided the vocal talent.

Could this be an early pressing, with the error corrected later on? Or vice versa, a later release that somehow resulted in a screw-up on the label?

I flicked on the power to the stereo system and placed the 45 on the turntable's spindle. I pride myself on maintaining a functioning turntable and keeping my LPs in playable condition, even though I've converted most of my favorites to CDs. There's just something about original vinyl, the gorgeous artwork of its covers, and liner notes in type large enough to actually read.

The stylus dropped onto the opening groove of "Cruisin' on K Street."

It was the exact tune I'd heard at Rita Slade's house. I played it again. No question, absolutely, positively the same song.

I dropped the needle onto "Cruisin' on K Street" one more time, sank into the couch, tickled the cat under the chin, and gave the tune another listen while I pondered the situation.

Let's say "Cruisin' on K Street" really had been penned by Otis Turner, Rita Slade's granddaddy, and Clarence Willits, now the Reverend Zakiyyah Mazama. What if, later on, they sold the rights to the song to Lou Jelniak for a few bucks? Jelniak then gave himself songwriting credit on the second pressing.

So what?

"Cruisin' on K Street" had been only a minor regional hit, had never gone on to make any serious money for anyone. In my opinion, the tune was every bit as catchy and danceable as the releases from the Shirelles and Everly Brothers that topped the national charts in 1961. Only a lack of luck, timing, and money for promotion kept the Dee Vines from busting out of the regional ranks and hitting the big time.

I'm not the definitive expert, but I've worked in the radio industry long enough that I have more than a passing knowledge of the pop music scene for the last half of the twentieth century. I'd be willing to make it a true daily double, Alex, and bet all of my winnings that "Cruisin' on K Street" had never been rerecorded by a white band and turned into a hit. Nor had the ditty ended up as a jingle for an automaker, breakfast cereal, or feminine hygiene product.

Okay, Lloyd Ellwanger and Cherise Rose had toyed with the idea of using the "Cruisin' on K Street" melody as a theme for the Mine Shaft Restaurant chain. Ellwanger had strong ties to the old El Jay studio, as in the "El" in El Jay. But his name wasn't listed on the Dee Vines' 45 as the composer of "Cruisin'," and according to his story he and Jelniak had long ago parted company. So he wasn't due any special treatment when it came to obtaining the rights to use the ditty as an advertising jingle.

And yet, he'd sent his ad lady on a mission to get that box of Dee Vines memorabilia back from Pete Kovacs. To avoid paying chump change for the rights to an all-but-forgotten regional hit? And for an advertising campaign they'd decided to drop?

It all added up to a big zero.

Now "Meet Me at the Casbah," that was a different story. This Lou Jelniak, whoever he was, would have pocketed a nice chunk of change after *Yo Mama!* turned out to be the surprise hit of the summer season, and the show's theme song, a remixed, hip-hop version of the original, had topped the national charts.

"I don't know, Bialy, I just don't know." I gave the kitty one last scratch behind the ears and hauled myself up from the couch. I stood in front of the sliding glass door, sipped wine, gazed at the twinkling lights of Old Sacramento, and tried to think.

This particular record, the one listing Turner and Willets as the songwriters instead of Lou Jelniak, had to be important to the prosecution's case against Jasmine. Why else would Oakley Plummer desire it so desperately? Damned if I could determine why an obscure recording from 1961 was so important to a current homicide case. The El Jay studio was the only common link that I could discern. Yet a good ten years separated the time frame of the Dee Vines' short recording career at El Jay and Lou Jelniak's discovery of Jasmine.

And how did Lloyd Ellwanger tie in—if he played a part at all? Other than adopting Oakley Plummer as his political protégé, that is.

I was close. I could just sense it. I traced a crude timeline in my mind. The Dee Vines record with Ellwanger and Jelniak at El Jay in 1961. Jelniak discovers Jasmine and launches her career in the 1970s, Ellwanger out of the El Jay picture at this point. Fast-forward to the present. Jasmine meets Anton Greb/Johnny Venture, member of the Original Artists Justice Committee. Donovan Sinclair steps in on the committee after Greb/Venture is killed. Sinclair gets in touch with Rita Slade about her collection of Grandpa Turner's old recordings. Rita Slade has already given the box to Pete Kovacs. Kovacs hides the Dee Vines 45. I find it, play it, begging the harmonious homage to teen cars and crushes to give up its long-hidden secret.

The images swirled around my brain, but refused to click into place. Only after I tracked down Jelniak would I have the answer.

First thing tomorrow morning I'd check with Sheriff Perez and with Glory Lou. See if either had had any luck locating a Lou Jelniak in the Monterey County or DMV databases.

I drained the wine, closed the curtain, and returned to the living room. I removed the 45 disc from the spindle, carried it by its edges to the coffee table, and slid it back into the paper sleeve. A circle cut in the center of the paper wrapper allowed the label to show while protecting the vinyl grooves. I placed the relic facedown on the bubble wrap.

The B-side, that free song you got when you bought a 45, the one that never was played on the radio, stared back at me.

The same red, yellow, and black El Jay label. Another Dee Vines tune. Songwriting credits to Otis Turner and Clarence Willets.

The title: "Meet Me at the Chapel."

23

Meet me at the chapel
Our true love will light the way
Just twelve steps takes us to the altar
Then rejoice on our golden wedding day. . . .

I SANG OUT LOUD, POSITIVELY BELTING, AS I PACKED MY OVERnight bag for the trip to San Francisco and the Broadcast Legends Hall of Fame ceremony. Bialystock, curled in sleep in a patch of morning sunshine on the bedspread, jerked himself awake, laid his ears back, and scuttled under the bed.

"Seems to me Lou Jelniak ripped off the Dee Vines twice." Yeah, I was talking to the cat. Pathetic, I know. "Not only in stealing their song in the first place, but by twisting the lyrics of a simple and sincere love ballad into a drug culture anthem."

Bialystock answered by sticking one paw out from under the bed skirt.

"No wonder Anton Greb had to die. He must have discovered the truth through his work on the Original Artists Justice Committee, and threatened to expose Jelniak," I told the cat. When there's no other human around, any pair of ears will do.

I opened the sliding door of the closet and removed a black velvet dress. Glory Lou had helped me select the fifties-inspired gown a few weeks before at a chichi boutique at Sacramento's exclusive Pavilions shopping center. I'd balked at the price tag, close to what I shelled out in monthly rent. "As I live and breathe, that dress will make you look like a carrot-topped Marilyn Monroe," Glory Lou had promised. "Pete Kovacs won't know what hit him."

Pete Kovacs! Why did that man continue to keep himself so scarce? I placed the gown into a garment bag and worked the zipper. I'd make the scene tonight no matter what and look fabulous. Damn right Kovacs won't know what hit him.

I resumed warbling. The orange tabby retreated under the bed. I didn't blame him for fleeing. No matter how hard I tried, this white gal would never match the velvety tones of the four Dee Vines as they harmonized on "Meet Me at the Chapel."

The biggest decision I'd need to make this day—besides which shoes to wear with my evening gown—was how to break the story.

I was scheduled to show up at the hotel at five for a quick run-through before the ceremony. I planned to arrive fourish, to avoid the worst of the Bay Area rush-hour traffic. That meant leaving Sacramento around two. I'd be spending the entire three hours of my show either on the road or at the rehearsal. Glory Lou had already agreed to fill in at the station, with the idea that I'd report in periodically on the cell phone from the road. "Hon, you don't want to pass up this chance to remind your listeners that their very own Shauna J. is winning a major broadcast industry honor, do you?" she'd said to me.

I could make the announcement via cell phone on an afternoon radio show in Sacramento.

Or I could go on prime time, live, coast-to-coast network television.

Right about now, Traci Kapolsky was probably engaged in the same routine as I, tossing nightie and makeup into an overnight bag. Assuming she wasn't already on her way to Los Angeles and the network studio where she planned to broadcast *Hammer of Justice* this evening. I stopped in the middle of folding spare underwear, snatched up my keys, and sprinted down the stairs. I didn't even need to travel as far as the Fremont Wing. I found Kapolsky and that field reporter—Maurice Parnell—loading suitcases and cameras into the trunk of a rental car idling in the passenger loading zone on N Street.

Kapolsky was dressed in what she must have considered appropriate attire for travel: pink satin shorts, another clingy, midriff-baring knit shirt, and platform sandals. At least, it would be obvious to the airport security screeners that she wasn't carrying any concealed weapons.

"Are you still looking for someone to fill time on your show tonight?"

"Possibly." She placed one hand on the trunk lid and regarded me with suspicion. My curt dismissal of her offer the previous morning must have still rankled her.

"What if I told you that I've figured out who really killed Johnny Venture?" It was a gamble, but if Sheriff Perez and Glory Lou both came through with their sources, I was pretty sure I'd be able to deliver.

"I'd say you'd better be able to prove it." Kapolsky bent to shove a suitcase deeper into the trunk, giving me a view of butt cheeks that I really didn't need to experience.

"Just be sure to have that camera crew standing by at the Broadcast Legends Hall of Fame ceremony," I said.

"That was already part of the plan."

"Terrific." I waved as Kapolsky slid into the driver's seat of the sedan and started the engine. "Be prepared to cut away for a live pop at a moment's notice."

As she peeled away from the curb, I noticed a third member of the *Hammer of Justice* crew seated in the front passenger seat. I caught just a glimpse of him, but it was enough. A baseball cap was pulled low over his forehead. Something dangled from the back of the cap.

A gray-haired ponytail.

I was really glad I'd let Glory Lou talk me into plunking down all that cash on a dress. A stunner in black velvet, shawl collar, low-cut wrapped bodice secured with one velvet-covered button at the waist. Narrow skirt ending just below the knees. A sensual yet classy look.

Not like the hootchie-mama getups some people insist on wearing.

I'd attended the Broadcast Legends Hall of Fame ceremony as a guest for the past two years, and was fairly certain that I recalled the basic setup. A high-rise hotel on the east end of the San Francisco–Oakland Bay Bridge. Banquet hall covering the entire top floor. Reception area in front of the elevators, built-in bar at one end, risers and podium at the other. A DJ booth and portable dance floor in a corner at stage left.

Just to be sure, I dove into the packet of information the Broadcast Legends had FedExed to me, found the hotel phone number, gave the front desk a call, and confirmed that I'd remembered correctly. A DJ booth and dance floor did indeed exist in that stage left corner in the banquet hall, and dancing was, indeed, planned at the conclusion of the ceremony.

I placed two bubble-wrapped phonograph records into my overnight bag. The 45 disc with the Dee Vines' "Meet Me at the Chapel" on the B-side, and Jasmine's first LP, featuring her smash hit, "Meet Me at the Casbah." I cushioned them with a bathrobe and zipped up the bag.

Now for something to wear for the road trip, comfortable for driving, yet neat and covered-up enough for walking into the lobby of a grand big-city hotel. I dug through the contents of my closet and settled on the same costume that had served me well on the jaunt to Castroville with Luis and Hector: navy canvas slacks, red-and-white-striped cotton knit top, black leather flats.

"Hold down the fort, old boy," I instructed Bialystock as I hefted the overnight case and slung the garment bag over one shoulder. What I didn't tell the kitty was that I'd already made arrangements with security to have someone check in on him tonight and tomorrow morning. Wouldn't want the little fellow to get lonely or run out of kibble, now would we?

"You just missed her!" Josh Friedman buzzed with excitement when I arrived at the newsroom to tie up a few loose ends before the drive to San Francisco.

"Who's that?" I scrolled through my e-mail and gave Josh fifty percent of my attention.

"Traci Kapolsky."

"Oh." I raised my vision from the message inviting me to lose ten pounds in thirty days, guaranteed!

"I got her autograph and everything. See?" Josh held out a sheet of paper ripped from the wire service machine. It contained a huge, curlicued black felt tip signature. I took a closer look. Yep, she'd penned a tiny heart over the "i."

"What did she want?" As if I didn't already know.

"She said she's thinking about doing a show on the corporate consolidation of the radio industry, and she's scouting around our shop as an example of one of the last of the family-owned stations in America. She wanted to take a look at the on-air studio to see if it would work for a live shot."

The consolidation of the nation's radio stations into the hands of a few mega-corporations is a hot topic, well worth investigation. But I seriously doubted that was what brought the *Hammer of Justice* bombshell to the station. More likely, she wanted to take one last look at the control room floor and see if she could find the old record she needed as the showpiece for tonight's episode.

"Did she have anyone with her?" Another example of a question I could have answered myself.

"One of her field reporters. Maurice Parnell." Josh adjusted his wire-rimmed glasses and looked uncomfortable. "And Pete Kovacs."

Glory Lou called me into her office. "The Monterey County sheriff phoned for you three times this morning," she said. "The final time, she told me she had more important things to do, and told me to pass along the information to you." She handed me a sheet of notepaper torn from a steno pad.

I studied the notes Glory Lou had jotted as dictated by Sheriff Perez.

An address on Bird Rock Road in Pebble Beach.

A business license for an enterprise on Alvarado Street in downtown Monterey.

Fifteen parking tickets in the past twelve months, all dismissed by the Monterey PeeDee.

Registered to vote at the same Bird Rock Road address. Republican. Didn't vote in the last election.

I memorized the information, folded the scrap of paper, and slid it into my pocket.

"Any luck yet with your source at the DMV?" I asked.

"I was able to reach her this morning. She said she'd get on it as soon as she could and call me back."

"Let me know as soon as you hear back." After getting two confirmations on Jelniak's residence and a business address, I really didn't need the information from Motor Vehicles. Still, it might come in handy to have a description of his vehicle and a license number.

Glory Lou and I worked out the final details for this afternoon's show, approximate times for my cut-ins from the road, introductions, and out cues.

"What else are you supposed to remember?" Glory Lou prompted as I closed my notebook and prepared to leave.

"Spritz my hair with water when I get to the hotel, then use the round brush and blow dryer to smooth out the frizzies," I recited.

"Very good. Nails?"

I displayed my ten digits, palms down, for inspection. Glory Lou had taken me on as her special makeover project, passing along the dos and don'ts most teen girls get from a sympathetic older sister or youthful aunt. I'd grown up with neither. I had to admit, it was fun rediscovering the allure, lost since the end of childhood, of playing dress-up. I balked, though, at the constant upkeep required of nail lacquer.

Glory Lou nodded her approval. I'd shaped my nails into gentle curves and buffed them this very morning. "And?" she continued.

I frowned in thought.

"Stage lights?" Glory Lou hinted. "You're going to do what to make sure you don't look like death warmed over?'

"Oh, yeah. Put on way more makeup than I think I'll ever need. Especially blush and lipstick."

It was all I could do to stop myself from leaping into the Z-car and zooming south on I-5 toward Monterey so I could barge into that office on Alvarado Street and collar Lou Jelniak. If he wasn't there, then blow through the gates at Pebble Beach, find that house on Bird Rock Road, pound on the door until someone answered.

But it was a good three-and-a-half-hour drive from Sacramento to the Monterey Peninsula. Here it was almost two in the afternoon, and I was due in San Francisco no later than five. I couldn't skip out on the Broadcast Legends this late in the game. They were nice guys and it was a tremendous honor they were about to bestow on little me. Then there was the commitment I'd made to Traci Kapolsky to do a live shot on *Hammer of Justice*.

I was so deep in thought during the walk across the parking lot to my car, I didn't pay any attention to the vehicle parked next to it.

A white Crown Victoria.

Two men emerged, the lanky frame of Oakley Plummer and a uniformed Monterey County deputy, a compact-sized Latino.

"I have a warrant for the arrest of Shauna J. Bogart," the deputy began.

I ignored the officer and planted myself in front of Plummer. "Not you again." I was beginning to feel as if I were a character in a continuous-loop tape, like Bill Murray in *Groundhog Day*.

"Didn't you hear the officer? You're under arrest."

"On what charges?" I tilted my head upward, so I could look Plummer in the eyes.

"Withholding evidence. Interfering with an investigation. Obstruction of justice."

"I haven't done anything illegal and you know it. I cooperated fully with the county of Monterey's investigation. Just ask Sheriff Perez." What was up with the Monterey County sheriff, anyway? First she calls not once but three times to help me out with background information, then she turns around and sics this goon on me.

"There's a simple way you can avoid all this unpleasantness. Just turn over that piece of evidence we discussed last night and I'll cancel the warrant."

I forced myself not to glance at the back compartment of the Z-car, where the 45 vinyl disc of the Dee Vines' "Meet Me at the Chapel" reposed in its cocoon of bubble wrap and terry-cloth robe, and to keep my gaze fixed on the emotionless gray eyes of the Monterey County district attorney.

"Maybe if you told me what relevance this old record has in building your case against Jasmine, I might be more inclined to cooperate." Arrogant, demanding types like Plummer bring out all my defiant tendencies. If he wanted that record, he'd have to fight me for it.

"I don't have to tell you anything." Plummer nodded at the deputy, who gave me an embarrassed look, fumbled for the handcuffs hanging from his belt, and began doing the you-have-the-right-to-remain-silent bit.

I made a quick survey of my surroundings for someone, anyone, I could flag down for help. Some twenty cars in the lot, no humans. Beyond the asphalt, a packed-earth berm separated the businesses along the Highway 160 frontage road from the American River floodplain. On the horizon, a line of cottonwoods, branches wafting in the gentle fall breeze, marked the actual riverbank. A needle of steel rose from the floodplain in front of the foliage. The radio station tower, the for-real tallest man-made structure in the city limits, the high-rise developers' hype notwithstanding. If I were able to make a 180-degree turn, I knew I'd see the windowless stucco wall and solid steel door of the rear entrance to Sacramento Talk Radio. Unless a reporter racing out to a story, or a salesperson chasing after a hot prospect, happened to leave by the back door and head in my direction across the parking lot, I was on my own.

"Just let me see that warrant." I folded my arms, daring the deputy to forcibly cuff me.

The rumble of an engine masked Plummer's attempt at a response. A screaming red Mercedes-Benz two-seater, top down, zipped into the parking lot and jolted to a halt in a T-formation in front of my Datsun and the county of Monterey's unmarked sedan. I noticed the vanity plates first—TUNE IN—then the trim figure of Donovan Sinclair bounding over the driver's-side door.

"What seems to be the problem here?" he asked in a pleasant tone.

The deputy took a step back and moved his fingers away from the cuffs. Even Plummer seemed to deflate slightly.

"No problem here," Plummer said. "Everything's under control."

"That's terrific," Sinclair said, "because this is just the little lady I came to see." He stood in front of me and gave me a salute. As usual, he was lookin' fine, in a polo shirt the same color as the car, pressed black jeans, and tasseled loafers. I didn't see even a hint of a potbelly where the knit shirt tucked itself into the waistband of the jeans. At his age—shoot, at any age past twenty-five—you don't get abs like that by diet alone. Donovan Sinclair must have been putting in some serious time at the gym.

"It's great to see you too." Great? I couldn't remember the last time I'd been so happy to see anyone. I began edging my way toward my car, sensing an opening for a getaway. "But I've got an appointment in San Francisco in two hours, so I'll have to catch up with you later." In fact, shouldn't Sinclair be hitting the highway right about now if he wanted to be on time for the Hall of Fame rehearsal?

"That's exactly why I'm here," Sinclair said. "I got to thinking, after I ran into you at Lloyd's last night, why should we take separate cars when we're both going to the same place? Wouldn't it be more fun to travel together?"

Plummer and the deputy hovered at the open passenger side door of the Crown Victoria, Plummer barking something I couldn't make out into the two-way.

Under normal circumstances, I much prefer the freedom of traveling solo on a long road trip, gas savings be damned. Today, I gave Sinclair an enthusiastic, "You're on!," lifted the hatchback of the Z-car, and removed my overnight case and garment bag from the back compartment.

"Hey, I wasn't finished here yet," Plummer said.

"It's okay." Sinclair gave him a look.

"Yeah, it's a Spare the Air Day," I said. "Carpooling encouraged. Haven't you been listening to the radio?" I handed my bags to Sinclair and watched as he snuggled them next to his own duffel and a tuxedo encased in a dry cleaner's bag in the trunk of the Mercedes.

I hopped into the passenger side of the jaunty sports car, not even waiting for Donovan to open the door for me. He strapped himself in to the driver's seat and placed a snap-brimmed cloth cap over his balding dome. What was left of his hair was tied back in a button-sized knot at the bottom of the cap. I never really understood that particular look, but a lot of older gents who consider themselves hip, creative types seem to go for it.

Sinclair started the engine, idled in front of the Crown Victoria, and leaned out through the open side window to have one last word with Plummer. "Like I just said, everything's cool." Then he slammed the gas pedal and gunned it out of the parking lot and onto the Highway 160 frontage road.

I turned to wave bye-bye to Oakley Plummer, III. He didn't respond, just stood, slump-shouldered, on the asphalt, the two-way microphone still dangling from its cord in one hand.

24

"YOU CAME ALONG JUST IN TIME," I TOLD SINCLAIR. "YOU HAVE NO idea."

"Glad to be of service, my dear. There should be an extra cap in the glove box. You'll need it once we hit the freeway."

I flipped down the lid of the in-dash compartment and found a forest-green baseball cap embroidered with the lone cypress logo of the Pebble Beach Company. Perfect—I was secretly hoping I wouldn't be saddled with a twin of Sinclair's geezer headgear. I perched the cap atop my mop of red frizz and bunched as much of it as I could through the hole in the back, ponytail-style.

"If you're thirsty, you'll find cold drinks in the fridge."

I followed the direction of Sinclair's gesture to a Sharper Image cooler tucked between the two seats and plugged into the cigarette lighter.

This was the life, I decided. Ensconced in the soft tan leather of a luxury sports car, top down, escorted by an attractive older gentleman, sipping Italian designer water and watching the scenery go by, on my way to the big city to be feted and fawned over by my peers.

Even though at this point the scenery consisted only of the discount warehouses and drab office buildings of the connector route between Highway 160 and the westbound Business 80 loop, I still felt like a princess.

Sinclair shifted and merged his SL500 onto Business 80, zipping across the American River. "What was that all about, anyway?"

"I hardly know where to begin." I had to raise my voice to be heard over the thunder of the freeway traffic.

"Good thing we have a long drive ahead of us."

A plan was beginning to form in my mind, a way to tie together the Hall of Fame ceremony, Donovan Sinclair's scheduled tribute to Johnny Venture/Anton Greb, and my live shot on *Hammer of Justice*.

"You should find this interesting," I said, "because it all relates to your work with the Original Artists Justice Committee."

"Do tell."

"It goes back to 1961 and this doo-wop group in Sacramento called the Dee Vines. You've heard of them, right?"

"Sure. I was working Sacramento radio in the early 1960s. They had a regional hit, 'Cruisin' on K Street.' Interesting, I met with the granddaughter of one of the Dee Vines just a few weeks ago."

"Exactly. And she probably told you the same thing she told me. As far as she knew, her Grandpa Turner had been treated fairly by El Jay. But get this. The B-side to 'Cruisin'' was a tune called 'Meet Me at the Chapel.'" I crooned the first few lines. *Meet me at the chapel/Our true love will light the way*. "Sound familiar?"

"'Meet Me at the Casbah.' Jasmine's big hit from the seventies."

"Bingo. Officially, some guy named Lou Jelniak takes songwriting credits for both. But I have reason to believe two members of the Dee Vines actually wrote 'Meet Me at the Chapel' and deserve to share in the profits of 'Meet Me at the Casbah.'" I wasn't quite ready to share with Sinclair the proof I had in the 45 disc listing Otis Turner and Clarence Willets as the composers and lyricists of "Meet Me at the Chapel." Nor the fact that the record reposed in an overnight bag in the trunk of his Mercedes.

"The point is," I continued, "'Meet Me at the Chapel' and 'Meet

Me at the Casbah' are the same song. All Lou Jelniak had to do was tweak the lyrics a little when he turned it into a number one hit for Jasmine."

"I remember Lou Jelniak. Chubby little fellow with horn-rimmed glasses. He was always dropping in at the station, pestering us to play the latest release from El Jay. Some of them weren't bad and could have made the national charts, given enough promotion."

"Just luck and timing." I gazed at the panorama of steel and glass towers of downtown Sacramento and thought of my mother's lifelong struggle to hit the big time in the music industry. "And knowing the right people."

"Don't forget the race issue," Sinclair said. "It wasn't until the Motown sound came along a year or two later that white teenagers were willing to buy records by black artists in big numbers."

"What happened to Lou Jelniak, any idea?"

"Gosh, I haven't thought about him in years. I'm sure I wouldn't even recognize him if I bumped into him on the street."

"He lives in Pebble Beach on Bird Rock Road, and has a business on Alvarado Street in downtown Monterey. I thought you might have run into him."

"Anything's possible. Like I say, so much time has passed, he could be sitting one barstool away from me at Club Nineteen and I wouldn't even recognize him. Or him me, for that matter."

"The Dee Vines broke up not long after they released 'Cruisin' on K Street.' " I picked up the thread of the story. "A dozen or so years later, the B-side resurfaces as 'Meet Me at the Casbah,' sells a million-plus copies, goes platinum, Jasmine's this huge star. Lou Jelniak claims songwriting credit and makes a bundle. The question is, what happened between the two 'Meet Me' songs? Did Jelniak buy the song from Turner and Willets back in 1961 for a few hundred dollars, or did he just steal it outright after the group broke up?"

"Well, did he?"

"I'm not sure about that part." The red convertible arced over the Sacramento River on the Pioneer Bridge, which is steeply pitched to allow clearance for ship traffic. With the open air whipping past me and the roller-coaster rise and fall of the freeway, I could have been screaming on a ride at the State Fair.

"It was wrong either way," I continued. "Even if he paid Turner and Willets a pittance for their song, he was taking advantage of a couple of naive young men who had no resources for fighting back."

"I can see where this is leading." Now that we'd crossed the Sacramento River and left the city traffic behind, Sinclair relaxed his right arm from the steering wheel and began groping in the mini-fridge. "The Original Artists Justice Committee. Someone tipped us off that the Dee Vines may have been cheated, and that they might be a good cause for the committee to champion. But when I talked to Turner's granddaughter, she gave me the same impression she gave you: Everything had been on the up-and-up in their dealings with El Jay."

I leaned toward the console to assist him, and to make sure Sinclair kept his attention on the eighteen-wheelers and SUVs schooling around us on the interstate. "Orange juice? Mineral water? How about a diet Coke?" In these exclusive surroundings, I felt like a flight attendant on a private jet.

"You're a doll. Diet Coke, please."

"But Rita Slade hadn't paid any attention to the B-side of Grandpa Turner's record." I popped open the soda and placed the icy can in Sinclair's right hand. "So she's not aware that it's virtually identical to the song Jasmine turned into a hit."

"But the members of the Dee Vines would still have been around in the seventies," Sinclair said. "They must have heard 'Meet Me at the Casbah' on the radio and recognized their own tune."

"Two of the four were dead by then, one in a car crash in Texas and Otis Turner by leukemia. A third member is still MIA in Vietnam, so we can't ask him. Clarence Willets was overseas in the Peace Corps in the seventies. When he came back stateside, he got religion, changed his name to the Reverend Zakiyyah Mazama. Maybe he renounced all secular concerns like rock 'n' roll music." Regardless of the reverend's feelings about his former life as a doo-wop singer, the profits from "Meet Me" ought to pay for a lot of snacks and basketballs for his after-school youth center in Oak Park.

The red Mercedes zoomed across the Yolo Causeway, the stubble left from the rice harvest lying on the Sacramento River floodplain far below, waiting to be either torched, plowed under, or flooded and left to decompose. Most growers had abandoned the use of fire, but there were still days when the burning rice fields belched huge plumes of smoke and left the Central Valley choking in an orange-brown haze. That, plus natural atmospheric conditions and thousands of gas-guzzlers, gave Sacramentans far too many Spare the Air Days in the autumn months.

Today's Spare the Air smog alert barely registered on my consciousness, so intent was I on the story unfolding in the ergonomically correct, climate-controlled cockpit of the Mercedes. "Don't you see?" I told Sinclair. "Anton Greb represented the Broadcast Legends on the Original Artists Justice Committee. He must have discovered the same thing I did, that Lou Jelniak cheated the Dee Vines out of their song, and threatened to expose him."

"You may be on to something," Sinclair said.

"Of course I'm on to something. Jelniak is living and working in the Monterey area. I'm guessing he was in the lobby of Casa del Pulgas when Jasmine met up with Johnny Venture. He must have heard the fight, and maybe he even overheard Anton Greb tell Jasmine he had some interesting research that he wanted to show her that evening."

"And that research would have to do with the real creator of 'Meet Me at the Casbah.' "

"Precisely. So Anton Greb had to die, and who better to blame it on than Jasmine?"

"Makes sense. Obviously, this Jelniak would have a vested interest in making sure no one ever learns the truth about his cash cow."

"You got it. I figure Lloyd Ellwanger is involved in this somehow. Don't forget, he was Jelniak's original partner, the 'El' in El Jay."

A barely formed thought took shape in my mind. "Ellwanger must have known the true origin of 'Meet Me.' He was in on the recording session. I'll bet he's still in cahoots with his old pal Jelniak. I'll bet he planned on not paying any licensing fees for using the Dee Vines' one hit tune for an advertising jingle for the Mine Shaft chain. Then Jasmine is arrested for the death of Johnny Venture. Jelniak and Ellwanger realize their sleazy activities might come to light during the investigation."

"I'm afraid you've lost me."

"Just thinking out loud. See, Ellwanger probably counted on getting the rights to 'Cruisin' on K Street' for free through his old pal and partner Lou Jelniak. Then he finds out a box of old discs, tapes, and paperwork has surfaced from the early days of El Jay. Why else would he send Cherise Rose out on a wild goose chase to get that box back from Pete Kovacs? Except to retrieve that record that gives songwriting credits to Otis Turner and Clarence Willits?"

"In other words, evidence that might cast doubts on the business ethics of Lloyd Ellwanger and Lou Jelniak."

"Exactly. Ellwanger's loaded, so he must have bought off the Monterey County DA, promised a huge contribution for his political campaign in return for suppressing certain evidence and sending Jasmine to prison."

"And that's why I found Oakley Plummer giving you a bad time in the parking lot back at the station. You know too much."

"You have no idea how glad I was to see you drive up."

We sped past the Cal Aggie water tower marking the location of the University of California's agriculture school at Davis, and continued southwest on Interstate 80 through the only stretch of farm country left between the greater Sacramento region and the rapidly expanding sprawl of the San Francisco Bay Area. Only a few homemade signs advertising pumpkin patches and the ubiquitous "gas food lodging" billboards broke up the wide expanse of tomato and rice fields.

"What I'm thinking is, Traci Kapolsky wants me to do a live shot on *Hammer of Justice* from the Hall of Fame ceremony tonight and reveal what I know," I said. "You were already planning to do a tribute to Anton Greb and his work on the Original Artists Justice

Committee during the ceremony. We could join forces, pool our resources—"

"Excellent idea!" If Sinclair's hands hadn't been occupied in steering and sipping diet cola, I'm guessing he would have applauded.

"*Hammer of Justice* airs at nine, so the timing will be perfect."

"Nine o'clock West Coast time. That means shooting live at seven."

"Run that by me again?"

"They'll shoot at six out here for a live broadcast at nine on the East Coast. Then they'll turn around and roll the tape at nine for the West Coast feed."

"Well, hell."

"I know, I know. Why does the television industry always cater to the prime time needs of New York? We get to watch the Academy Awards in the daytime just so East Coasters can tune in during prime time.

"It could still work," Sinclair added. "We'll do the live shot for *Hammer of Justice* during the cocktail reception. There's a big-screen TV in the banquet hall. I'll work it into the script to make the segment featuring you a part of the ceremony when it airs at nine."

"Awesome!" Well, it wasn't quite as exciting as appearing onstage in a fabulous dress to make a bombshell announcement about a notorious murder case over live TV, but it would have to do.

"You keep hinting around about the label on some record that gives songwriting credit to Otis Turner and Clarence Willets," Sinclair said. "I take it you've actually seen this record?"

It was the key, all right, the piece of evidence around which my entire theory stuck together or fell apart. The smoking gun, the jewel-encrusted bird statue, the second shooter on the Grassy Knoll, the bloody glove.

I wasn't about to give it up. Not even to someone who'd been as helpful and sympathetic as Donovan Sinclair. What, do I look that stupid?

"I haven't actually seen it, but I've heard about it and talked to enough people who have seen it." I counted on a lot of fast talk and a little b.s. to keep Sinclair from losing faith in my theory and booting me from the award program. "Rita Slade saw it first, in the box of memorabilia she inherited from her grandfather. She didn't realize the importance of the small print on the label and thought all of the records in the box were the same."

"Didn't realize there were two different pressings," Sinclair agreed.

"Rita Slade took the stuff she wanted to keep for the family. One copy of every song the Dee Vines recorded, one set of photographs, and publicity materials. The rest she boxed up and turned over to Pete Kovacs with the idea that he would research the value and see if there might be a museum or archive interested in it."

"So Pete Kovacs has seen the record."

"And not to forget, he was acquainted with Anton Greb." I told Sinclair about the file of correspondence between the two I'd stumbled across in Kovacs's desk in Retro Alley. "There's every good chance Kovacs shared information with Greb at some point."

"Especially if he knew Anton Greb was on the Original Artists Justice Committee."

"Enter Traci Kapolsky. She's on the trail of the same story, she's heard about what happened to the Dee Vines from you, and comes to Sacramento to enlist Kovacs's help." I took a sip of mineral water. Why he agreed to help *her* instead of letting me have the story was still a sore subject.

"Do you think Kapolsky caught on to the connection between the Dee Vines and the Jasmine case?"

"I don't believe so. She never mentioned it when I talked to her, and I'm sure she would have been all over something that hot. As far as I know, her only plan was to devote a show to an investigation into black artists who were cheated out of the rights to their creations by the white recording industry in the fifties and sixties."

"A worthy cause in and of itself."

"Then someone breaks into the apartment Kapolsky had rented for the *Hammer of Justice* crew and steals the box."

"And that's the last anyone's seen of the record," Sinclair concluded.

"Yeah." Thank goodness Kovacs had had the presence of mind to squirrel it away in the underground wiring of the radio station a week ago Monday. I still hadn't figured out who or what had tipped off Kovacs to the value of the record, or why he hastily stashed it under the control room floor. It was as if he knew it was in imminent danger, and he scrambled for the first hiding place he could find.

I glanced at the clock on the dash. Almost three. "Do you mind if we put the top up? I'm supposed to do a series of live cut-ins during the three and four o'clock hours. I'm afraid it'll be too noisy with the top down."

"Your wish is my command." He pulled off at the next exit and parked the red Mercedes in the deserted, weed-choked lot of the defunct Nut Tree Restaurant.

"This won't take but a sec." Sinclair began to fiddle with a button on the dash.

I was glad we wouldn't be lingering long, even though I could have used a stretch. The sight of the abandoned roadside attraction, the peeling paint and browned, overgrown gardens, filled me with melancholy and a vague sense of unease.

The retractable hardtop settled into place with a barely perceptible click. "Feel free to borrow my cell phone to file your reports if you'd like." Sinclair opened the lid of the storage compartment between the seats. "It should be right on top."

"Thanks, but that won't be necessary. I come self-contained and fully equipped." I snapped a cell phone off the waistband of my slacks.

"The station's finally going digital, and they traded out cell phones for the entire on-air staff. All the latest bells and whistles, even text messaging. See?" I held up the phone so Sinclair could take a gander at the tiny screen.

I had one message waiting, according to the electronic gizmo. I punched in the proper combination of pound symbols and numbers to retrieve it. Glory Lou, finally hearing back from her contact at the DMV. I let out an excited gasp.

Sinclair raised one eyebrow. "I've been waiting over twenty-four hours for this information," I told him. "My news director just came through with another clue to help me track down Lou Jelniak."

I cupped my hand around the screen, shading it from the sun pouring through the windshield, and read the terse message.

Two vehicles registered to Jelniak, Louis F., on Bird Rock Road in Pebble Beach. A 1998 Isuzu Trooper, blue, license number INVJ699.

And a current-year Mercedes-Benz SL500 convertible. Red.

Personalized license plates: TUNE IN.

25

I SNAPPED THE CELL PHONE SHUT AND STUFFED IT INTO THE RIGHT pocket of my slacks. Had Donovan Sinclair seen the message on the screen? The tiny letters would have been difficult to pick out in the bright sunlight. But not only had I done nothing to prevent him from peeking, I'd actually encouraged him to admire my new toy.

Sinclair/Jelniak steered the Mercedes onto the westbound I-80 ramp. "Shall we proceed, then?" he inquired in a bland tone. I didn't answer, just made quick glances at his profile. If he was tense, distracted, or upset, he was disguising it pretty well behind Ray-Bans and a relaxed upward curve to his lips.

I'd done it this time, no question. Blabbed everything I knew about the case I'd built against Lou Jelniak, only to end up sitting next to the one and the same Lou Jelniak in a sports car hurtling at seventy-five miles an hour down the interstate. If my hunches were right, this dapper fellow in the geezer cap had slipped a date rape drug into Jasmine's drink, smothered Anton Greb with a pillow, and let Jasmine take the fall.

That whole confrontation in the radio station parking lot

between Oakley Plummer and me must have been scripted and staged right from the get-go. Scare me and soften me up, so I'd hop into Donovan Sinclair's cute little roadster without thinking twice.

And here I thought I was so smart. That's what they ought to put on my tombstone: "She thought she was so smart."

At least I'd had the presence of mind not to reveal the fact that not only had I seen the Dee Vines record, but it was in my possession, riding along with us in an overnight bag in the trunk of the Benz. The thought was small comfort.

There had to be a way out of this jam, besides throwing open the car door and flinging myself into four lanes of traffic. I could punch in 911 on the cell phone, blurt out my location and the description of the vehicle. But by the time the Seventh Cavalry showed up, Jelniak could easily exit the freeway, find an abandoned warehouse or business like the boarded-up Nut Tree, and dispose of me in some fashion. Maybe this time he'd use a drug overdose instead of a pillow, so I could at least look forward to going out on an incredible high, following the well-trod path of entertainers too numerous to name. I wouldn't be the first radio personality to shed this mortal coil with a little help from a needle and the fruit of the opium poppy, and I undoubtedly wouldn't be the last.

I gave myself a little shake to force a stop to these morbid thoughts. It wasn't helping the situation, you know?

Jelniak wouldn't stop me from doing my live cut-ins back to the station on the cell phone. He wouldn't dare. It would look suspicious if I didn't call in as scheduled. A plan began to form in my mind. What if I worded my reports carefully, inserted the most clever turn of phrase, so a knowledgeable person who tuned in might figure out what's really going on? Say, someone savvy and powerful, like Monterey County Sheriff Maria Elena Perez? A bright gal like her would certainly figure out I was in jeopardy and send a posse to the hotel, ready to intercept Jelniak and rescue me just in time for the Hall of Fame ceremony.

The plan hinged on two major assumptions: that Sheriff Perez found my show so fascinating she continued to listen via the station's Web site, even though she'd already recaptured Jasmine. And that she wasn't as corrupt as the Monterey County district attorney.

My watch read 3:12 P.M. I was scheduled to go live with Glory Lou in two minutes. I dialed the studio hotline, identified myself to Josh, and listened for my cue.

"Normally, from three to six, you'd be tuning in to Shauna J. Bogart," I heard Glory Lou say over the air. "Today, she's on her way to San Francisco for a very prestigious honor, to be inducted into the Broadcast Legends Hall of Fame. We're catching up with Shauna J. on the road. How's it going out there?"

"I'd venture to say I'm having a divine time," I said into the cell phone.

"Where are you, hon?"

"We just passed Fairfield. What a divine town."

"Is everything okay?" Glory Lou sounded concerned. It was working! "Divine" is not an adjective that comes tripping over my tongue on a regular basis. Glory Lou, yes, but not me.

"Like I told you before, I'd venture to say I'm having the most divine time."

Glory Lou segued into a commercial break and I made another study of Lou Jelniak. He appeared as if he were focusing all of his attention on the thickening Bay Area traffic, and that he was barely aware of my antics on the cell phone.

"I've got a killer topic for my next show," I said during my next live report.

"What would that be?" Glory Lou prompted from back in the studio.

"Date rape drugs. It's a very serious problem. Did you know that women of all ages are being constantly victimized by these horrible drugs?"

"I've heard about it, yes."

"Especially in hospitality suites in old motor courts in resort cities like Monterey. The problem is of epidemic proportions."

"I'm sure it is." This time, Glory Lou sounded confused.

Jelniak eased up on the gas as we crossed the Carquinez Bridge, where the waters of the Sacramento River flowed into San Pablo Bay. I gazed in envy at the lines of vehicles halted behind the toll booths on the northbound lanes. Damn, why did we have to be traveling on the free side? A stop to pay a bridge toll might have distracted Jelniak just enough for me to issue a cry for help on the cell phone. Or even bolt from his car, throw myself into the arms of the toll-taker, and beg for help.

"Give us an update on the Hall of Fame ceremony this evening," Glory Lou said by way of introducing my next live report. I could tell she was doing her best to prevent any more odd or delusional comments on my part from going out over the air.

"The tribute to Johnny Venture is sure to be a high point of the program," I said. "I personally plan to take part in that tribute and to make sure his colleagues are aware of his work on the Original Artists Justice Committee. He gave his life speaking up for the rights of fellow members of the radio and recording industries."

"Johnny Venture did that? I thought Jasmine killed him over some sort of quarrel they had at a party."

"You'll have to tune in tonight. Just tune in."

Did Glory Lou get any of it? Or did she—and Sheriff Perez, if she was listening—just assume Shauna J. was a little off today, tired, perhaps, or distracted in anticipation of the upcoming awards ceremony?

I had to send a clear, unmistakable message. *He's here, Sitting right next to me. He killed Johnny Venture and made Jasmine take the blame. I could be next. Look for a red Mercedes, license plate* *TUNE IN*, heading south on I-80.

Massive storage tanks and sprawling industrial fortresses passed by as we skirted the oil refineries of Hercules and Pinole, the stench of fuel mixed with a faint odor of salt from San Pablo Bay. Think: How can I get away from Jelniak—or distract him—long enough to get through to the station?

When in doubt, employ a tried-and-true tactic.

I tapped Jelniak gently on the right shoulder. "I'm sorry, but I need a pit stop."

For the first time since our journey began, he dropped the pleasant facade. "Can't it wait? We're almost there and I want to beat the commuter traffic if I can."

"I've really, really got to go," I whimpered.

"We'll be there in less than a half hour. You can hold it."

"I can't wait another five minutes. It's, you know, that time of the month. . . ." I let my voice trail off in a sigh indicative of barely suppressed discomfort, allowing his imagination to fill in the rest. I counted on the universal male squeamishness over the slightest hint of "female problems" to triumph over his impatience.

"Oh, all right." He cut across four lanes of traffic and left the freeway in El Sobrante.

Hah! Works every time.

I assumed he would stop at a fast-food restaurant, where I could run into the women's restroom, lock myself in a stall, and punch up the station on the cell phone. Instead, he parked in the back of a dilapidated service station where the door of the unisex john opened directly to the grease-slicked asphalt.

"That lock looks like it's broken," Jelniak said. "I'll stand right outside the door and make sure you're okay."

Oh, swell. Holed up in a tiny cubicle, separated only by a flimsy door from a killer. I should have tried my luck jumping from the Mercedes in the middle of the freeway.

Thank God I wasn't really suffering from a "female emergency," because there's no way I would have taken care of any business in this filthy cell. No t.p., of course. Just years of grime, mineral deposits, and graffiti informing me that Richmond High sucks. I depressed the handle of the decrepit toilet with one finger, hoping the flushing gurgles would cover the sound of my voice.

Josh Friedman picked up the control room hotline.

"Listen good, because I don't have a lot of time," I whispered into the phone. "I've been kidnapped by Donovan Sinclair. Call the Monterey Police Department and the county sheriff. Tell them to meet me at the Emperor Norton Inn, ASAP."

"You're breaking up bad," Josh said. "I can't make out what you're saying."

Damn, damn, damn. I gave the cell phone screen an impatient glance. The minuscule battery icon showed full strength. This miserable pit of a gas station must be in the middle of a cellular no-man's-land, just beyond the fringe of one service area and before another began. It would figure.

I redialed. "Can you read me now?"

A muffled "Whaaaah?" and an electronic crackle were my only answers.

Pounding on the thin wooden door. "Everything okay in there?"

"Just finishing up," I said in a cheery voice. I ran some water in the sink just for authenticity's sake and emerged from the restroom, blotting my hands on the sides of my slacks. No paper towels, of course.

Even though everyone connected with the Broadcast Legends talked about the Hall of Fame ceremony as if it were taking place in San Francisco, the host hotel was actually located on the Oakland side of the Bay, just north of the Bay Bridge. It's like the way "L.A." encompasses dozens of cities and neighborhoods in the Los Angeles Basin. San Francisco is as much a region and state of mind as a municipality.

The high-rise Emperor Norton Inn had anchored the east end of the Bay Bridge since the sixties. From the beginning, its convenient location and fabulous views of the Bay Bridge and San Francisco skyline made it a favorite stopover for athletes and musical groups playing the Oakland Coliseum. The inn had been named for a legendary character from San Francisco's early history, Joshua A. Norton, the self-proclaimed Emperor of the United States and Protector of Mexico. An apt choice, because among his many decrees was the order, in 1872, to construct a bridge between Oakland and San

Francisco. Norton was considered insane at the time, but the lovable lunatic's vision came true in 1936 when the first car drove across the double-decked engineering marvel between Oakland and "Baghdad by the Bay."

I followed Jelniak across the polished marble floor of the hotel lobby, clutching the overnight case in one hand and hoisting the garment bag high in the other. I dawdled, pretending to trip over something in the revolving door, to make sure Jelniak ended up ahead of me in the check-in line. I placed my overnight case on the floor and gently draped the garment bag across it, careful not to crease the velvet gown inside.

The clerk behind the counter requested a credit card. Jelniak dropped his duffel bag to the floor, moved his tuxedo from his right hand to the crook of his left arm, and fumbled for his wallet.

I pulled the cell phone from my waistband.

Jelniak scribbled a signature on a computer-printed card.

I dialed the station hotline and gave my name. "You're not scheduled for a report now. Call back at four-twenty," Josh said.

"Double-check the log. I'm sure you're mistaken." I tried to keep my voice calm enough not to alert Jelniak, but still convey a sense of urgency to the intern. Not an easy trick.

It must have worked, because Josh patched me through to Glory Lou in the on-air studio.

The young woman behind the counter placed a map and key card on the shiny wood surface and began describing to Jelniak the location of guest parking, the easiest route to his room, and the location of the elevators and fire escapes.

"I've just arrived at the Emperor Norton Inn, about to go into rehearsal for the Hall of Fame ceremony," I reported to Glory Lou. I scrutinized the activity at the counter. Jelniak's attention seemed to be riveted with the checking-in ritual. "And I've just learned a very special guest will be making an appearance tonight. The legendary record producer Lou Jelniak."

As if on cue, Jelniak pocketed the key card and map and turned toward me.

"So that's all for now from San Francisco. Reporting live for Sacramento Talk Radio, I'm Shauna J. Bogart."

Jelniak lurked at my side as I handed my credit card to the clerk—Sholanda Wilcox, according to the brass name badge pinned to the lapel of her polyester maroon uniform jacket—and let her explain about the elevators, key cards, security bolts, fire escapes, and earthquake evacuation plan. "Shall we?" he said when I'd finished, indicating a registration table set up by the Broadcast Legends at the opposite end of the lobby.

I stuffed the key card and map into my pocket, hefted my bags, and followed. I could have run at this point, of course. Found the nearest ladies' room—a real bathroom, not that Turkish prison cell in the gas station—and dialed the station, punched in 911. But, now wrapped in the comforting security of the Emperor Norton Inn—all those locks and escape routes!—I sloughed off the edgy panic from the road.

For one thing, I wasn't certain Jelniak knew I'd figured him out. As far as he was aware, I still thought of him as good ol' Donovan Sinclair, the veteran San Francisco disc jockey who'd managed to scrape together enough money to buy a little jazz station in Monterey. Just an old radio pal. Wouldn't it be more fun to expose him tonight, in front of his peers and the crew from *Hammer of Justice*? If I called the cops now, the bust would take place in an almost-deserted hotel lobby, with the bell captain, Sholanda Wilcox, and the fellow at the Broadcast Legends registration table as the only witnesses.

Jelniak led me to a cloth-covered banquet table next to the concierge desk. I gave my name to the man behind the table. He danced his fingers through cards alphabetized in a shoe box and handed me a name badge. It was almost a twin of the identification cards worn by state employees, minus the mug shot and plus the logo of a major manufacturer of digital broadcast equipment silkscreened to the lanyard. The registration guy retrieved something from under the table and looped it over my wrist. A paper gift bag in a gold color with purple tissue frothing from the top.

I thanked him and made eye contact with the ID badge hanging from his neck.

Gary Drager.

Silver-haired, in a gray business suit, light blue shirt, and diagonally striped tie, he bore only a passing resemblance to the Johnny Venture in the photo of the 1976 KROY AM 1260 staff that Vance Ballard had shared with me yesterday. He'd ditched the muttonchops and the hair was no longer brown and wispy, but he had managed to maintain the lean, dancerlike physique.

He looked familiar, somehow. I'd seen him around town recently at some media event. I just couldn't hone in on exactly where or under what circumstances.

"You're Johnny Venture, right?" I said as if I were greeting an old buddy. "Sacramento, KROY AM 1260, 1976?"

He stuck out his hand for a shake. "I was Johnny Venture, one of the Johnny Ventures, but not *the* Johnny Venture. Lucky for me, right? Nice to meet you."

"Didn't I used to see you backstage at the Oasis Ballroom?"

"Possibly. It was a long time ago." He craned his neck toward the person behind me in line. "May I help you?"

Okay, he didn't want to talk about it in public. I wouldn't either, if I'd been the one having oral sex with juicy young performers who passed through the backstage of the now-defunct music hall. Especially if the sex acts came with a promise on which I'd failed to deliver. I rearranged my name badge, the goodie sack, satchel, and garment bag and schlepped across the lobby floor toward the elevators.

"Here, let me help you with that." Jelniak swooped next to me and placed his hands on the garment bag.

"It's okay." I gripped my possessions firmly and took a step back. "Anyway, you've got enough to carry as it is."

"Suit yourself, then." Jelniak placed his free hand between my shoulder blades and steered me to the bank of elevators.

The sound of chatter and the clump of heavy equipment dropping to the marble floor caused me to look toward the revolving front door. A party of five had just bustled in to register at the Emperor Norton. A young man and woman, both in jeans and T-shirts, burdened with a professional-caliber video camera, TV lights, boom mike, and three aluminum-sided cases, then Maurice Parnell, the field reporter for *Hammer of Justice*, Traci Kapolsky, and the oldest member of the fivesome, an all-too-familiar male figure with a gray ponytail.

The elevator doors parted.

"You go on up," I told Jelniak. "That's my boyfriend over there. We haven't seen each other in over a week."

"We don't have time for that." Jelniak gave me a little push toward the waiting lift. "We don't want to be late for the rehearsal, now do we?"

I didn't even waste time thinking of a response. Just jerked away from his touch and strode across the lobby toward the revolving door. I dumped bags, dress, and badge into an overstuffed chair, then scampered the rest of the way and flung my arms around the neck of the man with the gray ponytail. "Smile and pretend you're having fun," I commanded in a whisper.

He let me guide him into the bar next to the lobby, the camera crew, Parnell, and Kapolsky trailing behind. I made sure to keep one arm around his waist and a perky grin on my face. Just two old friends hooking up with each other after a long absence. Jelniak followed a few yards behind. That red polo shirt was difficult to miss, even in the muted light of the cocktail lounge.

I slipped behind a round, glass-topped table and seated myself on a curved banquette. On the wall, a framed black-and-white photograph from 1935 depicted the Bay Bridge while under construction, the girders ending abruptly just past Treasure Island. I tugged my companion into place next to me and gave a little wave of dismissal to the entourage from *Hammer of Justice*. "Be sweet, and give us a few minutes to catch up," I said to them with a flirtatious wink. Three of the four immediately picked up the message and departed.

To Kapolsky, I directed a terse jerk of the head, body language for *Beat it, bimbo*. She took the hint and backed away.

Jelniak seated himself on a stool at the far end of the bar.

For the first time in one week, four days, and twenty-two and a half hours, I was alone with Pete Kovacs.

26

WHERE TO BEGIN? THE BOX . . . THE RECORD . . . THE HIDING PLACE under the radio station floor . . . the secret overnight stays in his own apartment . . . Traci Kapolsky. Especially Traci Kapolsky. What the hell was she doing here, anyway? Wasn't she supposed to be in the network studio in L.A., preparing for the final countdown for tonight's show?

"We should invite him to join us," Kovacs said.

"Who?"

"Donovan Sinclair."

I grabbed both of Kovacs's hands and held them tightly. I kept that charming smile on my face and wriggled seductively. As Jelniak observed us from the barstool, I wanted him to see nothing more than a couple enjoying a late afternoon tête-à-tête. In reality, I needed to restrain Kovacs's arms to keep him from waving at Jelniak.

"How do you know Donovan Sinclair?" I asked.

"He's a member of the Original Artists Justice Committee. He's been helping us out with an investigation for *Hammer of Justice*."

"Don't you know who he really is?"

As soon as I blurted, I regretted it. My big mouth had gotten me into enough trouble this afternoon. I didn't seriously believe Kovacs would align himself with a character as foul as Lou Jelniak if he knew the truth. But I could see Kovacs had been duped into believing "Sinclair" was one of the good guys. Jelniak had even me fooled until just over an hour ago.

Then there was the matter of trust. I'd had enough faith in Pete Kovacs to share with him my most intimate desires and fears. And to let him see me naked. He'd always returned that level of honesty and good faith. I had to place my trust with that solid core.

I draped my arms around his neck. "Remember, keep smiling, and act like we're just fooling around. Donovan Sinclair is not your friend, trust me. His name isn't even Donovan Sinclair, for starters."

Kovacs seemed to finally catch on and to relish his assigned role. He returned the embrace, placing his hands around my neck and leaning forward so that our foreheads almost touched. I all but purred. I had waited much too long for a moment like this.

"So his name isn't really Donovan Sinclair. That's a problem?" Kovacs said. "I mean, your name isn't really Shauna J. Bogart either."

"But I didn't go around for years cheating recording artists out of their rights. Donovan Sinclair is more than just a disc jockey name. It's a cover-up for a killer. Lou Jelniak."

"Donovan Sinclair is really Lou Jelniak? The guy from El Jay Records?"

"Yes. And keep canoodling."

A chunky woman wearing a too-tight ruffled white blouse and black stretch pants and sporting a multicolored frost job materialized before our table. "Can I get you folks anything?"

God, yes. I hadn't realized how much I needed a drink until the opportunity presented itself. I disentangled myself from the clinch and ordered a gin and tonic. Kovacs said he'd have a beer.

"That's just hard to believe," Kovacs said after the barmaid melted back into the shadows of the cocktail lounge. "About Donovan Sinclair, I mean. If he's not who he says he is, then why would he go out of his way to help us on *Hammer of Justice*?"

"To keep his eye on you. What better way to control the investigation than to make himself a part of the team?"

"I suppose. It still blows my mind, though." Kovacs made a hangdog face, then remembered his instructions and threw his head back as if in laughter.

"Tell me about it. But it all makes sense when you think about it. Donovan Sinclair is in Monterey and is tight with all the movers and shakers. Jeez, he had enough pull to get fifteen parking tickets dismissed. He even dated the sheriff for a time. Someone like him wouldn't have had any trouble scoring date rape drugs and dragging a doped-up Jasmine into Johnny Venture's cabin."

Kovacs kept a crooked grin on his face, but I could tell he was unconvinced.

The waitress returned with our drinks and at the same time three men swaggered into the bar and began glad-handing Lou Jelniak. I recognized the traffic pilot who was being honored this evening for a lifetime of service, but wasn't sure about the identity of the other two. I welcomed their presence. Anything to stop Jelniak from constantly giving Kovacs and me the gimlet eye. The three men, and the arrival of two alcoholic beverages, meant I could finally drop the sweetie-pie pose and be myself. The muscles in my cheeks were starting to ache from all that smiling.

"There was no real burglary at the *Hammer of Justice* apartment," I said. "Jelniak did it himself, or he hired someone, maybe one of Lloyd Ellwanger's busboys, to go in and get that box."

"You think?"

"It all makes sense. You guys trusted Donovan Sinclair, so how difficult would it have been for him to make a copy of the key to the apartment? Or just snatch the box when the rest of you went out to lunch or whatever. He scatters a few things around—like the tape magazine to that old recording machine of yours—to make it look like a burglary. What were you doing with a treasure like the MacKenzie Repeater in Kapolsky's apartment, anyway?"

"Some of those tapes in the box of material from the Dee Vines could only be played on the MacKenzie Repeater, so I brought it over from the store one evening."

"You're lucky it didn't disappear when Sinclair faked the burglary."

"Damn right." He took a swallow and clunked the beer bottle onto the Formica-topped table.

"What is she doing here, anyway?" I realize there were more important things I should have been asking Kovacs, but dammit, I just had to know.

"Who?"

"Traci Kapolsky."

"We were on the way to dropping her off at the airport when she gets a call on her cell phone from her producer in L.A. I didn't follow all they were talking about. All I know is, we're turning around from the airport and heading for San Francisco. They apparently decided it made more sense to broadcast the show from this hotel."

"All of her best sources will be right here on the fifteenth floor tonight." I had to admit, Kapolsky's producer's scheme had logic behind it.

"We spent the last couple of hours getting set up over at the network affiliate in San Francisco," Kovacs said.

"I understand you're broadcasting live at six for the East Coast."

"That's what they tell me. They apparently feed a taped version of the live broadcast for the Pacific time zone."

"Do me one favor. Make sure the camera crew sticks around, no matter what. I guarantee I'll have an update for their West Coast feed that'll make those New Yorkers wish they hadn't gone to bed so damn early."

"I'll do my best." Kovacs took a swallow of beer.

"Tell me, how did you first get involved in all this? When Rita Slade walked into your store with a box full of her grandpa's memorabilia?" I was certain Kovacs had met Anton Greb well before his encounter with Rita Slade, but I wasn't ready to 'fess up I'd been snooping through his files.

"Actually, I met Anton Greb a couple of months before his death. We started out trading letters about my doing a guest appearance with the Stanislaus County Traditional Jazz Society. He happened to mention in some e-mails his work on the Original Artists Justice Committee, and how he was looking into an interesting situation in Sacramento involving a doo-wop group called the Dee Vines. The last I heard from him he was saying the case looked even bigger than he'd first realized, and that he was getting in touch with *Hammer of Justice*. That was in late August."

"Why didn't you come forward when Anton Greb was killed in Monterey? You could have at least told me about it."

"I didn't realize Anton Greb was Johnny Venture at first. He never told me he had an on-air name, and I don't follow all those celebrity crime stories like most people do. Sure, I'd heard of the Jasmine case, and Johnny Venture, but I didn't connect the two until much later."

Yeah, like when a certain TV host sashays into your store and sweet-talks you into sharing your information with her.

"And then Rita Slade asks you to help find a home for her grandfather's collection of records and photographs," I said.

"I recognized the Dee Vines right off. When I went through the box and found that record naming Otis Turner and Clarence Willets as the songwriters, I knew this was the missing link Anton Greb had been searching for. There were fourteen copies of 'Cruisin' on K Street' in that box, but only one with the label giving songwriting credits to Turner and Willets."

"Back up for a minute. How did you end up hiding that record under the floor at the radio station?"

"Some annoying woman wearing too much makeup had been nosing around the store, just way too curious about the Dee Vines' box and especially the record. She even followed me over to your station that night."

"Cherise Rose. You're sure she followed you?"

"She drives a pink Beemer. How many of those do you suppose there are in Sacramento?"

"You've got a point."

"I should have hidden more of the stuff in that box."

"Like what?"

Jelniak slipped off the barstool and, along with his three buddies, sauntered in my direction. I returned the seductive smile to my face and began tracing circles with my index finger on the palm of Kovacs's hand.

Jelniak stopped in front of our table. "Rehearsal's in five minutes." He pointed upward, indicating the top-floor banquet hall. "That is, if you two can tear yourselves apart."

"I'll be right there, don't worry."

I sipped my drink until the last of the foursome left the cocktail lounge. "You were saying? Hiding more of the stuff in that box?" I reminded Kovacs.

"The original contract in which Turner and Willets sold the rights to 'Cruisin' on K Street' and the rest of their compositions to El Jay," Kovacs said. "Even a copy of the check. Two hundred dollars each."

"And now Jelniak's got it." Damn, this would have been good stuff, crucial evidence. By now, I was sure Jelniak had turned the contract and check into confetti in Lloyd Ellwanger's corporate headquarters shredder.

"But he doesn't have the record," Kovacs said.

"You're right. He doesn't have the record."

The record!

I'd carelessly dumped the overnight case, along with the rest of my gear, in a chair out in the lobby and hadn't given it a thought since. I'd been that excited about seeing Pete Kovacs after all this time. I'd left my stuff sitting out there in public for how long? Twenty minutes? Thirty?

I raced out of the bar and skittered across the marble floor of the lobby to a cluster of upholstered chairs grouped on an oriental carpet. Empty. Every damn one. I clapped both hands to the sides of my forehead.

Stupid, stupid, stupid!

Lou Jelniak. He must have snatched my stuff on his way to the Hall of Fame ceremony rehearsal. I ran to the elevator, jammed my thumb against the UP button, and bounded in as soon as the doors slid open. The elevator seemed to jerk to a halt at every floor as guests laden with suitcases struggled through the doors. Canned music serenaded us with a syrupy version of the *Flashdance* theme.

The elevator finally deposited me on the fifteenth floor. I slowed to a walk so as not to draw unwanted attention and entered the banquet hall. On the risers at the far end, the president of Broadcast Legends instructed the inductees on the importance of walking from left to right across the stage, and of limiting their remarks and thank-you's to three minutes. Lou Jelniak and two of the men from the bar clustered in one corner and made notes on a clipboard, while a pair of techs conducted a sound check from the DJ booth at stage left. The center of the hall remained empty, the round banquet tables and chairs stacked along the walls, waiting to be set up.

I strolled along the long east wall, peering into corners and behind curtains for any sign of my luggage. Nothing but a few dust bunnies and, beyond the heavy drapes, a view of congested commuter traffic on Interstate 80. I repeated the process behind the risers and along the west wall with the bank of windows overlooking San Francisco Bay. I couldn't resist stopping to admire the sparkling view of the bridge and the city skyline in the late afternoon sunshine. Closer to the hotel, just north of the Bay Bridge toll plaza in the mud flats, an array of radio towers thrust their way into the sky.

"It's somehow fitting, wouldn't you say?"

I turned to see a figure in a red polo shirt and black jeans at my side.

"What's fitting?" I said.

"The towers."

"Yeah."

We didn't need to say anything else. Two radio people instinctively got it, the symbolic presence of the radio towers watching over the ceremonies of the Northern California Broadcast Legends, their red lights pulsating in two-beat harmony, reminding us who we were and why we were here.

Maybe Lou Jelniak wasn't as sinister as I'd thought.

I left the fifteenth floor and stopped at the front desk. "I left my luggage on that chair over there." I waved my arm in the direction of the conversational cluster on the oriental carpet. "And now it's gone."

Sholanda Wilcox furrowed her forehead in concern. "That's terrible! We pride ourselves here at the Emperor Norton for providing the utmost in security for our guests. But these days you just never know. Have you checked with the bell captain?"

Of course not. That would have made too much sense.

The bell captain's freckled face split into a wide grin. "Got your gear right here. I saw it sitting there all alone and figured I'd better set it aside for safekeeping."

He led me into a storeroom in back of the bell captain's podium. My garment bag dangled neatly from a rod holding a dozen or so similar bags, the overnight case at its feet. The bell captain had even rescued the goodie bag and name badge.

I bent my knees and took a closer look at the satchel. "That zipper wasn't undone the last time I saw my bag."

"Are you sure? That's how I found it. We pride ourselves here at the Emperor Norton—"

"Yeah, yeah." I knelt on the floor for a closer look into the bag. The white terry-cloth bathrobe that I'd placed on top was a rumpled mess, no longer neatly folded like I'd left it this morning. I eased the robe out of the bag and carefully unfolded the length of soft cloth. The Jasmine LP still nestled deep inside. But no bubble-wrapped 45 disc. I thrust both hands into the bag and rooted around, on the off chance the record had slipped out of its cushion and worked its way to the bottom.

Gone.

"I don't suppose you saw anyone messing around with my luggage while it sat there on the chair in the lobby." I rose and dusted my knees with my hands.

"Sorry, no, and I feel just terrible. We pride ourselves—"

I didn't stick around to listen to the rest of his gushing apology. Jelniak must have broken into my bag on his way to the rehearsal. Who else? Logic told me he'd stash the record in his room. I had no idea how to determine which room he'd been assigned, let alone how to break in. Plan B: I could check every other possible hiding place first and narrow the field. Like the red Mercedes out in the guest parking lot.

A white van with a satellite dish on the roof and the logo of one of the San Francisco network TV affiliates hogged a good half of the passenger loading zone in front of the Emperor Norton. The side doors of the van stood open, revealing a TV monitor, transmitting equipment, and yards of cable. The young camera and sound crew that had arrived with Pete Kovacs earlier this afternoon had the tools of their trade trained on Traci Kapolsky.

From what I could tell, Newscaster Barbie was in the middle of a live tease for tonight's edition of *Hammer of Justice*. She'd upgraded her look from the satin shorts and clingy top of this morning, and now wore a miniskirt the blue shade of a Tiffany's box, a matching jacket, a cream-colored tube top, and spike-heeled pumps.

"Tonight at nine *Hammer of Justice* exposes the sound of money, years of exploitation of black artists by the white recording industry." She stuck out one hip and used both hands to hold a round object at shoulder level, like an infomercial hostess displaying a new bust enhancement device. "This is just one of many examples."

The camera zoomed in on the object. I stared in horror at the monitor as the six-and-three-quarters-inch disc with the black, red, and yellow El Jay label came into focus. "Cruisin' on K Street," listing Otis Turner and Clarence Willets as the songwriters. *My* record!

She didn't even bother to hold the disc by the edges, just let her pancake-makeup-encrusted fingers wander all over the grooves. The bubble wrap and paper sleeve reposed in a crumpled ball next to one of the van's tires where it had been carelessly discarded. If there's one thing that really bugs me, it's someone who doesn't care for her vinyl.

"So be sure to join me, Traci Kapolsky, and the entire team tonight at nine for another provocative edition of *Hammer of Justice*." The crew snapped off the portable lights and began detaching cable as soon as she'd finished talking.

I marched up to Kapolsky and grabbed at the record. "Give me that."

"Why should I? It was never yours to begin with."

"You stole it from my luggage." I made another attempt to snatch the round black wafer.

"So what if I did?" She jerked her hand back. I flinched, picturing the precious vinyl disc tumbling to the paving stones of the hotel entryway and shattering into a thousand pieces.

"I knew you had it, for sure," she continued, "ever since Pete and I went back to your little radio station this morning. When we looked in that open trench, surprise, surprise, our record was gone. Who else would have taken it but you, right?"

"So you saw my bag sitting there on that chair in the lobby and decided it was fair game."

"For sure, you really shouldn't leave the luggage tag with your business card hanging out there where anyone can see it."

"I ought to call the cops."

"And tell them what? That Traci Kapolsky, America's favorite crusader for the underdog, found and retrieved something that belonged to her in the first place?"

"It doesn't belong to you. It belongs to Pete Kovacs, and to Rita Slade."

"Pete Kovacs works for me now, so it's a moot point, for sure." She dropped the record into a leopard-print tote bag. I winced again at the mistreatment of the fragile relic. I mean, what if it got scratched by her nail file?

She was right, though. I had no claim of ownership to the 45 disc, other than finders keepers. If Pete Kovacs had chosen to throw his allegiance to this piece of TV trailer park trash, then so be it.

I scrounged the protective wrapping from its resting place next to the van's tire and smoothed the wrinkles from the paper sleeve. "Here." I thrust it and the bubble wrap into Kapolsky's hands. "At least take decent care of it, okay?"

It took most of another gin and tonic in the lounge before I felt as if I'd recovered sufficiently from this latest run-in with Traci Kapolsky. "America's favorite crusader for the underdog." Yeah, right. She apparently hadn't figured out the significance of the B-side of the record, didn't get the connection to the Jasmine case. So I still held the trump card, even though she possessed the one remaining piece of evidence.

"No worries," the bell captain told me when I stopped by his podium to retrieve my luggage. "We've already delivered it to your room and upgraded you to a Bay view, compliments of the house and with our apologies for any inconvenience."

I was still fuming as I marched down the corridor of the ninth floor toward my room. I had over an hour left before the cocktail reception to shower and perform all that hair spritzing I'd promised Glory Lou I'd do, paint on makeup, tuck myself into a push-up bra, and zip myself into one bombshell of an evening dress.

Couldn't you just see me up at the podium during the awards ceremony, exposing Donovan Sinclair as a ruthless fraud to his peers, and to Kapolsky's TV crew? Her puny story would fade to a footnote next to the megaton weapon I was about to unleash tonight, the identity of the real killer of Johnny Venture. If the Monterey County sheriff had listened to my reports from the road this afternoon, decoded my messages, and was on hand to lead Sinclair/Jelniak away in cuffs, so much the better.

I was starting to feel better, so much so that I found myself humming the opening bars of "Meet Me at the Chapel" as I located my room and thrust the key card into the lock.

Something round, hard, and cold jammed its way between my shoulder blades.

27

"SHUT UP AND DO EXACTLY AS I TELL YOU."

The remains of that last gin and tonic rose to my throat as I recognized the baritone of Lou Jelniak. My knees turned to something mushy.

"Be a good girl and maybe you won't end up in a grave like Anton Greb."

An electric current of adrenaline raced up my spine, flooding my brain with a barrage of conflicting commands: Run! Freeze! Fight back! Do what he says! Scream! Get the hell out of here!

"Now just open the door and walk into your room like everything's normal." Jelniak spoke softly, as if soothing a frightened child.

My overnight bag rested on a folding luggage stand, and in the open closet alcove I spotted my garment bag hanging from the rod. Whoever had delivered my luggage had flung open the curtains, revealing the promised Bay view. In another half hour or so, I'd be able to watch the sun drop behind the San Francisco skyline. That is, if I was still around a half hour from now.

Jelniak slammed the door shut. "Go sit on the bed, next to the nightstand." He gave my back another prod with the gun barrel.

The nightstand held a lamp, a TV remote bolted to the surface, a telephone, pen, and notepad inscribed with the logo of the Emperor Norton Inn. I did as instructed and seated myself on the bed next to the pillows, where a four-color printed card invited me to partake of the Emperor's royal breakfast specials.

"Now pick up the pen and write the following on the notepad." He stood over me and dictated a local phone number and address on Fruitvale Avenue. I penned the numbers with a shaky hand.

"Very good." Jelniak sounded like he was praising work in a third-grade penmanship class.

"Now pick up the phone, get an outside line, and dial that number. No funny stuff." He leaned in close and followed the movement of my trembling digit just to make sure I didn't do anything desperate. Like, say, dial 911. "That's a good girl, get your fingerprints all over that number pad. Is it ringing?"

I bobbed my head, too scared to say anything.

"Wonderful! Now hang up the instant you get an answer."

Someone picked up on the fourth ring. No greeting, just raspy breathing.

I dropped the receiver into its cradle.

Jelniak grabbed my arm, forcing me from the bed. "See this?" He let me have a quick glance at the handgun, shiny and ugly, then stuck it into the right-hand pocket of the tan windbreaker he'd donned over the red polo shirt. "I'm going to have this little baby aimed at you and my hand on the trigger the entire time we're together, so just do as you're told and no one gets hurt."

"Right. No funny stuff," I squeaked.

Jelniak escorted me into the elevator and pushed the button for the lobby. I was still so flummoxed over the incessant internal signals to fight, flee, or freeze that I kept my gaze on the floor for the entire ride.

The elevator doors parted. Jelniak put his left arm around my shoulder and steered me toward the revolving door. "You run into anyone you know, just say something polite and keep moving," he commanded in a soft voice.

"Traci Kapolsky is expecting me to meet with her and the *Hammer of Justice* crew any minute now," I improvised.

"Well, they'll just have to be patient, won't they?"

The entryway to the Emperor Norton, almost deserted when the red Mercedes pulled up two hours ago, throbbed with activity. Tuxedoed and evening-gowned couples pushed their way through the revolving doors and grouped themselves in chattering clusters of small talk in the bar and around the overstuffed chairs on the oriental carpet. They all had dutifully looped their name badges around their necks, and many clutched gold paper gift bags. I recognized veteran Sacramento broadcaster Harry Warren holding court on the very chair where I'd impulsively dropped my bags. I had to fight back the urge to wave hello.

Jelniak managed to pilot me through the revolving doors, into the parking lot, and down a long aisle to the red Mercedes.

Do not get into the car! I'd heard the advice dozens of times, recited it over the air, in stories about kidnappings and child snatch cases. Once he's managed to stuff you inside his car, ninety percent of the time you're a goner.

Phalanxes of cars, trucks, and buses rumbled past us on the raised deck of Interstate 80, while a steady trail of vehicles crept into the hotel parking lot. A Jeep cruised to a stop a half dozen spaces away from the Mercedes and a woman sporting brown hair with golden highlights, and wearing a vibrant, sixties pop art print cocktail dress stepped out.

"Shauna J.!" She whooped as she drew close. "You guys just get here too?"

I recognized Maxine Carlin, news director at a radio station in the Napa Valley wine country. We'd bonded at previous broadcast industry shindigs, two smart gals with wicked senses of humor struggling to make it in a business still male-dominated after all these years.

"Something like that," I said.

"Who's your friend?" she asked with a little wink-wink, nudge-nudge.

I made introductions and explained, "Donovan happened to be in Sacramento on business and we decided to carpool. That's all."

Try as I might, I just couldn't think of any secret verbal or hand signal I could send to Maxine. Not when a man with a gun stood right in front of me. She wasn't involved in the case like I was, wouldn't pick up on a subtlety. Anything obvious, and Jelniak would be all over me. He'd probably take out Maxine as well.

Jelniak kept his hand in the pocket of his windbreaker. "Nice to meet you," he told Maxine, while making a thrusting motion in the pocket in my direction. "We'll catch up with you over dinner."

"Fab!" She wiggled her fingers in our direction and continued her stroll toward the hotel entrance.

"Weren't you listening to anything I told you?" Jelniak said from between clenched teeth as soon as Maxine was out of hearing distance. "Don't make conversation. Keep moving."

"Jeez, what did you expect me to do? Ignore an old friend? That would have looked even more suspicious."

Jelniak said nothing, just yanked open the passenger door of the Benz and made a gesture with the hand in the pocket toward the seat.

I had no choice. I climbed in.

He sped onto the I-80 on-ramp, then downshifted to a crawl and threaded his way into the glacially moving traffic. The car crept into one of the lanes that peeled off to the Bay Bridge and inched its way to the toll plaza, joining hundreds of other cars making their way toward a Friday night in the big city. I felt my panic ebb slightly for the first time since Jelniak got the jump on me in the corridor of the Emperor Norton. He'd have to stop at the toll booth. No way could he bust through without paying, not with all this traffic. Once he braked and turned to hand his money to the toll taker, I was home free. Stranded in the middle of rush hour on the Bay Bridge, but free.

Just before reaching the toll plaza, the Mercedes veered to the right, off the interstate. "Last Oakland Exit," according to the green and white directional sign. The roadster bounced over a potholed frontage road, passing a faded board announcing the future site of Eastshore State Park, a joint project of the California Department of Parks and Recreation and the East Bay Regional Parks District.

The car jolted around piles of rebar, broken concrete, and clumps of pampas grass, coming to a halt before a low-slung wood structure. The ramshackle building squatted on cement blocks to protect it from high tides. Billboard-sized red neon letters attached to the front of the overgrown shack spelled out for the Bay Bridge travelers the call letters of the radio towers in back. I recognized the call sign as belonging to the Oakland rhythm and blues station I used to listen to late at night as a kid, where disc jockeys like Spyder Webb introduced this white chick from the suburbs to Etta James, B. B. King, and John Lee Hooker. These towers, and the four giant neon letters, had anchored the eastern terminus of the Bay Bridge almost as long as the bridge had existed. Though not as famous or picturesque as the cantilevered structure, they were still a familiar part of the local landscape, just like the Emperor Norton Inn.

Jelniak opened the passenger door and ordered me to get out.

Just before sunset in autumn and it was still warm enough to linger outdoors in shirtsleeves. Or, in my case, a red-and-white-striped cotton knit pullover. The California coastal climate is like that, blustery winds and bone-chilling fog in the summer months, then glorious sunshine after the throngs of tourists have vamoosed. Usually we get treated to one last week of Indian summer in late October, a grace note from Mother Nature before the winter rains lash out. It was a balmy late afternoon in October 1989 when the Loma Prieta earthquake struck, crushing forty-two people to death in the collapse of the Cypress viaduct only a mile or two from where I now stood.

This evening felt just the same, warm and with an odd stillness to the air.

Waiting for something to happen.

Jelniak grabbed a plastic grocery bag from the back compartment of the Benz, herded me to the front door of the dilapidated structure, and used a key to let us inside the deserted engineering shack. The building had a damp, musty smell and carried a foggy chill that made me instinctively wrap my arms around my torso. One glance at the inert meters and dimmed buttons on the dusty transmitter equipment and I knew this station was dark, hadn't been on the air in months if not years.

"Sit." Jelniak pushed me into a wooden chair. It was then that I saw the items in the plastic bag he'd retrieved from the back of the car. Bungee cords. He used two to lash my legs to the bottom of the chair, and with a third commenced to tying my wrists together in back.

Swell. He probably intended to leave me here to starve. Unless I figured out a way to smash the chair. Maybe I could thrash my way out the door and clump onto the frontage road. There was a chance someone from the bridge, a toll taker maybe, might see me.

"I suppose you own this station too," I said as Jelniak finished binding my wrists. I figured it was better to keep him talking, drag things out as long as I could, maybe even make him like me, think twice about harming such a nice gal.

"A piece of it. My partners and I will be putting it back on the air after the first of the year. All Indian, all the time."

"All Indian?" I pictured tribal chants and drumming.

"East Indian. India Indian."

Silicon Valley has a huge workforce from India. The last few years, the multiplex in downtown Sunnyvale where I used to hang out as a child had devoted itself exclusively to Bollywood, and I'd heard there was a similar theater complex in Fremont. These days, the only people willing to listen to music on AM radio are seniors, the fifty-five-plus demographic group who grew up before FM, and newcomers yearning for tunes and news from their native land. "All Indian, all the time" could work in the San Francisco Bay Area market.

Jelniak opened a metal storage locker. An eleven-by-seventeen sheet of paper was taped to the outside door of the locker. A tide chart.

"I get the bit about putting my fingerprints all over the phone," I said. "And about having me actually place a phone call so it'll show up on the hotel records when the police start checking. I'm just curious, who did I call?"

Jeliak didn't answer, just removed something long, black, and rubbery-looking from the locker.

"I'm guessing it must have been a drug dealer. I mean, we all know Fruitvale Avenue is just the nicest part of Oakland. So we've got the phone number and address of a drug dealer, in my handwriting, on the notepad. Won't that be convenient for the cops? They'll just write off my disappearance as a drug deal gone bad."

He scowled and began climbing into that rubbery thing from the storage locker. A pair of fisherman's hip waders.

"Another thing I've wondered about. El Jay. I get Lloyd Ellwanger as the El. But shouldn't your half be Yay, like Yelniak? The name is Slavic, isn't it? Or Slovenian?"

"Don't you ever shut up?"

"Nope. Talk is what I do for a living."

"Well, if you want to keep on living, you'll shut up."

I kept quiet while Jelniak untied the bungee cords, stuffed them in a pocket in the hip waders, and jerked me to my feet. He pointed me in the direction of the door and jammed the handgun into my back. "Move it."

Jelniak guided me out the door, past the Mercedes, picking our way around clots of weeds to the back of the abandoned engineering shack. Rickety catwalks crossed the silt and salt water, barely clearing the tide line, to the concrete blocks that anchored the steel towers.

I didn't like this. Not one bit. There had to be a reason Jelniak had pulled on hip waders, and I guessed it wasn't a good one. Already I could feel my flimsy pumps being sucked into the muddy shoreline beneath my feet. Why, oh, why, today of all days, didn't I wear my trusty river sandals?

"You could still skate on the Johnny Venture thing," I said. Time to start bargaining, if not outright begging. "You could plead involuntary manslaughter and probably get just probation and community service. I'm willing to keep quiet about what I know, honest."

Jelniak shoved the gun barrel deeper between my shoulder blades. One more step forward, and my toe would actually dip into the brackish water.

Just then my cell phone chirped a greeting.

Jelniak whirled to the front of me, splashing into the tide, and aimed the gun in the direction of my head.

"Don't!" I raised both arms in surrender as the phone gave a second ring. "It's not my fault someone's trying to call me."

I glanced down to where the phone was clipped to my waistband. Even reading the screen upside down, the caller ID was easy to discern. I'd received many, many calls from that cell phone number in the past.

"It's Pete Kovacs," I told Jelniak. "He'll think something's wrong if I don't answer."

The phone trilled a third time.

"Oh, all right," Jelniak said. "But get rid of him fast. If I have the slightest suspicion you're pulling a fast one, there's a bullet going right between your eyes."

I whipped the phone off my waistband and held it to my ear. "Sweetie?" I tried to speak without a quiver in my voice.

"Honey, is that you? I can barely hear you."

"It's me." I hollered to be heard above the roar of the traffic on the Bay Bridge. "Can you hear me now?"

"Hey, glad I found you," Kovacs said. "We're doing the final setup for the live feed and wondered where you were. I rang your room but there was no answer."

"I must have been in the shower. I'll be there in a minute." Think, think! Don't waste your last chance to send a signal for help. But how?

"The steering committee from the Broadcast Legends has been looking for you too. They said you missed almost all of the rehearsal."

"Everything's fine." I paused and I let my finger tap against the mouthpiece. Dot-dot-dot, dash-dash-dash, dot-dot-dot. SOS. As in:

Save my sorry ass! Then I drummed in the call letters from that big neon sign facing the freeway.

"Where are you?"

"I forgot to pack panty hose and had to make a run to the drugstore. Wasn't that silly of me?" I stopped to fake a giggle, and to allow the nail I'd so perfectly shaped and buffed this morning to repeat the message on the mouthpiece.

"You're sure everything's okay?"

Did he sound concerned? Or was I just deluding myself?

"Never been so fine in my life, sweetie." Dot-dot-dot, dash-dash-dash, dot-dot-dot. Then the four letters making up the call sign. Get it, Pete, get it! Pick up on that cue I'm desperately trying to slip! You were an Eagle Scout, weren't you?

"Got it." This time he sounded firm, ready to take action.

I think.

Jelniak wrested the cell phone from my hand and tossed it into the bay. "Enough, already!" He roared to be heard over the noise of the highway.

He placed the gun at my back and forced me to venture forward, following one of the catwalks. I sucked in air as the cold water soaked through the thin leather of my flats and seeped around my toes. At around sixty degrees, the waters of San Francisco Bay weren't necessarily life-threatening, but not a lot of fun for recreational swimming except for polar bear types. The thought of what might be *in* the water worried me more than how cold it could be. The East Bay MUD sewage treatment plant was directly opposite on the south side of the Bay Bridge, and the marshy waters were undoubtedly home to God knows what in the way of sea creatures: crabs, snails, slugs. Sharks? I'd heard of shark sightings in San Francisco Bay, and added that to my list of anxieties.

The gently lapping waves rose slowly, first over my knees, then—another gasp—the water crested crotch level. We continued to slog toward the cement block and tower at the end of the catwalk. Jelniak, damn him, stayed cozy and dry in his hip waders. I had to curl my toes to keep my slip-on shoes from sliding into the silt. I seriously considered ditching them, then decided to cling to anything that could conceivably be used as a weapon.

"The Dee Vines were only the beginning, weren't they?" I said. The time to be nice and to bargain had long passed. Now my thought was to piss him off enough to make him drop his guard. "How many other musicians did you cheat over the years? There must have been quite a few for you to be able to afford a house in Pebble Beach, and spend eighty grand on a sports car, and buy all those radio stations. Oh, yeah. Let's not forget your spiffy new wardrobe and a personal trainer to help you get in shape for it, and laser eye surgery so you don't have to wear those Buddy Holly glasses."

"Shut up and keep moving."

I reached the end of the catwalk, the trapezoidal cement anchor to the tower directly before me. A chain-link fence topped with barbed wire surrounded the base of the tower, and a red, white, and black aluminum sign bolted to the fence warned of high voltage. No trespassing!

Jelniak stretched his arm over his head and placed the gun on the wooden plank of the catwalk.

Now! Take the chance and go for it!

Before I could even think, let alone react, Jelniak placed his hands on both of my shoulders and pushed straight down, ramming me into the murky water up to my shoulders. I thrashed frantically and sputtered as the turbulent liquid washed over my head. Jeez, what was he trying to do, drown me?

Somehow, Jelniak managed to yank the bungee cords from the pocket of the hip waders, pin my hands behind my back, and lash them to one of the tar-coated catwalk pilings. I struggled and scratched, but he had the advantage of size, muscle mass, and the element of surprise. I screamed and managed to gash his cheek with a fingernail as he wrapped another cord around my waist to secure me to the piling. I floundered in an awkward crouch, the water lapping at my chin and my legs churning uselessly in the silt.

Trussed and helpless like one of those silent movie heroines on the railroad tracks.

Jelniak grabbed me by the hair and gave a painful yank, forcing my head to make a ninety-degree turn. "See that?" He pounded his index finger against a dark line on the next piling. "Know what that is?"

"The high watermark?" I quavered.

"Smart girlie." He released my head. "Know what else?" Gone was the debonair older gent who'd given me a lift in his luxury car. I faced a water-splattered madman, strands of hair that had worked loose from the knot in back pasted to his forehead, blood creeping down the side of his cheek, a cold gleam from narrowed eyes.

"I'm tired of playing games," I said. "Just get on with it."

"The top of your head is at least three inches below the high watermark."

"Why not just shoot me if you want to get rid of me?"

"This thing?" Jelniak took the gun from its temporary resting spot on the catwalk. He aimed at the concrete anchor, about three feet distant, and pulled the trigger. The handgun made a nice bangy noise and a wisp of smoke emitted from the barrel, but created not one tiny chip in the old block.

"Merely a theatrical prop." Jelniak gave a harsh laugh and lobbed the fake weapon into the Bay.

My third error in judgment in less than twenty-four hours. First in hopping into that red Mercedes and spilling everything I knew about Lou Jelniak. Then leaving my suitcase out in plain sight in the hotel lobby where anyone and everyone, including Traci Kapolsky, could get their paws on the Dee Vines record. And most recently in assuming something round, cold, and metallic poking me in the back was really a deadly weapon.

Bad luck comes in threes, so they say. Using that logic, my fortunes should be about to take a turn for the better.

That is, if that third error in judgment didn't prove fatal.

Jelniak patted me on the head while I continued to strain against the bonds. "According to the chart, high tide is less than two hours away. That'll give you plenty of time to think about what a foolish girl you've been, and how you could have avoided all this unpleasantness if you'd just minded your own business."

He waded to shore and tramped around the corner to the front of the engineering shack. A few moments later, his figure reappeared and climbed into the Mercedes. The lights flicked on and the car began to move.

I watched the taillights bob along the frontage road, then disappear into the twilight.

28

NO USE SCREAMING. I'D TEAR MY VOCAL CORDS TO SHREDS BEFORE anyone would detect a cry over the never-ceasing thunder of Bay Bridge traffic.

No chance of anyone spotting a tiny bundle of red hair bobbing under the catwalk. The engineering shack hid the pilings and bases of the towers from the freeway.

Thousands of cars carried many more thousands of souls, all going somewhere on a bridge within walking distance of my watery prison. I had never been more alone in my life.

It would take weeks, even months before anyone found me. Possibly not 'til next year, when some schnook of an engineer ventured out on the catwalk to put "all Indian, all the time" on the air. By then the residents of these waters would have had me for Sunday brunch, and the coroner would have to send for my dental records to identify the remains.

I continued a frenzied struggle and strained against the bonds. Jelniak had stretched the bungee cords tight, no give. He'd fastened them not only around the piling but over a crossbar as well, so there was no chance of wriggling myself upward. I'd have better luck trying to split the rotten wood piling. I dug my heels into the silt as best I could and began butting myself against the post. Break, damn you! The catwalk shuddered and something slimy fell from the underside of the planks, but the structure held.

The high-rise slab of the Emperor Norton Inn rose before me on the eastern shore of the Bay, less than a mile away. The uppermost floor blazed with light. Right about now, the cocktail reception would be in full swing, Traci Kapolsky would be in the middle of her live broadcast of *Hammer of Justice*, and Donovan Sinclair, freshly showered and buttoned into a tux, would soon be making the rounds. I sent a mental message to Pete Kovacs across the tidal flats and up to that penthouse ballroom, marked it urgent: Dot-dot-dot, dash-dash-dash, dot-dot-dot. Get it, for God's sake, get it!

The tiny squares of light from the hotel windows gazed back at me in silence.

I felt like one of the doomed passengers on the *Titanic,* staring from the rapidly tilting deck to the lights of a ship on the horizon. The ship that refused to stop. *The Californian.* Well, California, here I come. Before midnight, this daughter of the Golden State would be heading right back where she started from.

The final blush from the setting sun had faded and the waters of the Bay had turned an inky black. The night sky took on an unnatural orange glow, too much man-made light in the metropolis for the heavens ever to go completely dark. The air smelled of exhaust, salt, tar, and moldy wood.

The gravitational pull of the sun and moon drove the tide relentlessly inland. I had to tilt my head backward to keep my mouth, nose, and eyes out of the water.

Won't be long now.

I arched my head farther back and gasped for air. The planks of the catwalk extended a foot from the pilings, restricting my vision. Through a gap between the ancient boards, the red beacon at the top of the radio tower winked at me. When I was a child, I thought those lights were an actual physical representation of the sounds going out into the air. Even now, knowing full well the lights were merely warning signals to low-flying aircraft, something about that old imagery of visible sound waves, like the concentric rings throbbing from the tower in the old RKO Pictures logo, felt familiar and oddly comforting.

I'd heard once about an Eastern belief that the last image you see in this world will be the picture you carry with you through all eternity. It was fitting, then, that my final focus would be on that pinpoint of red light from a radio station tower. Beating like a broken heart.

A thud.

Then more thuds from the catwalk directly above me. The piling trembled.

The hallucinations of death throes?

I shifted my eyes to the right, toward the shore. At least three sets of headlamps and—God, yes!—the pulsating red, blue, and amber light bar of a law enforcement vehicle.

More thunks on the catwalk. The beam from a flashlight danced on the waves not a yard away from me.

I thrashed and shouted.

The footsteps grew fainter.

No! Come back, you idiots!

A wave swept over my head. I sputtered and floundered, my legs fluttering uselessly, stirring up more silt. In frustration and anguish, I reared my right leg back, then gave a mighty kick with the last ounce of my fading strength. I guess I thought my foot might possibly break the water's surface and get their attention.

Just as my leg reached the peak of the arc, my black leather flat freed itself at last, rocketing out of the murky depths. I heard a soft plop as it landed on the catwalk.

The footsteps returned, faster this time.

More flashlights, then a splat as a figure clothed in black threw himself into the muddy water.

Next thing, Pete Kovacs was thrusting his hands under my arms and trying to lift me. "Hang in there, baby, hang in there." He was able to raise me only an inch or two, but it was enough. I gulped and took in air.

Another heavy splash, and another male figure sloshed his way toward the piling. A uniformed police officer, who began hacking away at the cords with a knife.

I don't remember much about the next few minutes, just lots of lights, shouting, and confusion as the blade finally severed the last of the restraints and I was able to fling my arms around Pete Kovacs's neck. I mostly recall alternating between sobbing out thanks and scolding him for ruining his tux.

Kovacs held me upright, half carrying, half dragging me through the marsh to shore. The vehicles clustered around the engineering shack came into sharper focus: a Monterey County sheriff's cruiser, a patrol car from the Oakland PeeDee, and News Unit Five. I made out two more uniformed officers and Sheriff Maria Elena Perez waiting on the shoreline. Glory Lou leaned against the side of News Unit Five and spoke into the two-way. And was that really Josh Friedman waving from the water's edge?

I felt dry soil beneath my feet and relaxed my grip slightly from around Kovacs's chest and neck.

"We'd better get you to a hospital," he said.

"Are you nuts? There's nothing wrong with me that a hot shower and a tall, cold one won't cure."

I broke away from Kovacs and tottered toward the headlights, one foot still in the soggy black flat, the other bare, pullover and slacks heavy and dripping with water and silt. I must have looked like a prehistoric creature emerging from the sea in some cheap science fiction movie. I planted myself in front of the welcoming committee.

"Which one of your vehicles will get me back to the hotel the fastest?"

"I should have gotten there sooner." Kovacs snuggled next to me in the backseat of the Oakland PeeDee patrol car and tucked a thermal blanket around me.

"You got there on time. That's what counts."

"I shouldn't have wasted so much time redialing your cell phone, and then searching all over the hotel for you. When I finally called the Oakland cops, they knew where you must be the minute I gave them the call letters. At least some people have their act together."

"Stop beating yourself up about it. You know who really deserves all the credit tonight, don't you?" I teased.

"Who's that?"

"Samuel F. B. Morse."

I cuddled closer into Kovacs's soggy tuxedo. Just now, I wanted to be no place else but here, safe in the arms of a man I cared deeply about, floating past the lights of the city in the back of a police cruiser, warm and cozy behind the wire mesh where the prisoners usually sit.

I stood in dry underwear and a black push-up bra in a steam-filled bathroom. I had probably just used up the Emperor Norton's entire supply of hot water.

"So who figured it out first?" I asked Glory Lou as she helped zip me into the black velvet dress. "You or Sheriff Perez?"

"Both of us about the same time, actually. She called me during the five o'clock network newscast just as I was about to call her. We both knew something wasn't right about those reports you were filing. You, having a divine time? Lordy! Then Josh noticed your car was still in the parking lot. The minute Steve Garland showed up at the station, we told him he was starting his show early tonight. Then we took off."

Once again the sports talk guy gets dumped on. I made a mental note to stop at Costco on the way home and pick up a barrel of peanut M&M's for Steve Garland.

"No way you could have kept Josh from tagging along," I said with a laugh.

"As I live and breathe," Glory Lou agreed.

"The last I saw Josh, he was trying to help Pete get the water out of his tuxedo with my blow-dryer."

"He what?" Glory Lou marched out of the bathroom and attempted to wrest the handheld hairdryer from Josh's grasp. "Sorry, hon, but we need that more than you."

"Forget it," I told them both. "There's no time." I'd already toweled most of the drips. The rest could dry *au naturel.*

Sheriff Perez, meanwhile, wore a path in the carpet between the door and the Bay view window of my hotel room. She was clad in black athletic shoes, tan slacks, a yellow cotton shirt, and navy blazer, and had her silver-streaked hair piled in a knot on top of her head. "I can't believe I actually dated that slimeball. I ought to pop him right now. Put the cuffs on him myself." Counting the lady law enforcement official, her pair of deputies, the two Oakland cops, Kovacs, Josh, and Glory Lou, we had more than a quorum crowded into the room.

"I know, I know," I told her. "But just give me a few more minutes. Won't it be more fun to publicly humiliate him and drag him away in front of his colleagues?"

I slipped on the strappy, open-toed high-heeled shoes that Glory Lou insisted I wear with the black velvet gown, then grabbed the Jasmine LP from the overnight bag. "Here. You're in charge." I thrust the record into Josh's hands.

"As for you," I said to Kovacs, "your assignment is to get that 45 disc back from Traci Kapolsky. I don't care what you have to do." Within reason, that is.

I left the hotel room and made for the bank of elevators, an entourage dogging my footsteps.

"Bend over and shake your head," Glory Lou told me as the elevator began its ascent. I obeyed, careful not to jostle the other seven passengers. She used her fingers to fluff and scrunch my damp hair. "There. With any luck at all, you'll have curls instead of frizz when it finishes drying."

The elevator came to a halt at the top floor. "Hold the door!" Glory Lou ordered. She pulled lipstick and blush from her shoulder bag and began painting my face. "You are not going out there under all those hot lights looking like death, and that's final, hon."

I managed to escape her on-the-fly makeover and tiptoed to the back of the ballroom. Some three hundred guests seated at round banquet tables had their attention focused on the action on the risers at the far end of the hall. Five Hall of Fame inductees stood in a row on the stage and clutched gold statuettes depicting a broadcast tower with lightning bolts emitting from the apex.

"We regret that Shauna J. Bogart is unable to join us this evening," the president of the Broadcast Legends intoned, "but moving right along—"

"Stop the wedding!" I bellowed from the back of the room.

Heads turned and the crowd began to murmur. I heard several outbursts of nervous giggles and a clap or two of applause as I danced my way around tables and chairs, bounded up the stage stairs two at a time, and elbowed the president away from the podium.

"Shauna J. Bogart is back!" I said into the microphone.

I paused to let my breathing catch up. Lou Jelniak, showered and in a tux, shared a table with his cronies in the front. He flinched for a moment and glanced around the room, then shrugged and took a swallow of mineral water. One cool cucumber, I had to admit. Traci Kapolsky was still camped out in a corner with her crew, the shooter fumbling with camera and lights. I vamped with a thank-you to the Broadcast Legends for bestowing such a tremendous honor, giving the cameraman time to assemble his gear and capture my finest moment for posterity.

Through the windows to my left, the red light atop the radio tower under which I almost drew my last breath twinkled a greeting.

"Ladies and gentlemen," I said, "I stand before you tonight to remind you of the important work being conducted by the Original Artists Justice Committee to protect the rights of the creative geniuses in the music industry who have added so much to the American culture."

The four law enforcement officers and Sheriff Perez stationed themselves quietly in front of the passageway leading to the elevator and stairway landing, the only escape route from Emperor Norton's rooftop ballroom.

"Many of you may not be aware of the hard work of our own Donovan Sinclair in that fight for justice. For years as a disc jockey and later as a station owner, he has constantly championed the rights of artists, so often minorities, who created our nation's most popular music. After we lost Anton Greb so suddenly, it was none other than Donovan Sinclair who stepped in and gave unselfishly of his time and considerable talents to complete the work Anton Greb began."

Glory Lou and Josh slipped into the room and seated themselves in two of the few empty seats scattered in the hall. Kovacs followed and positioned himself against the back wall, apparently deciding not to inflict the damp tux on any dinner guests.

"What you don't know—what none of us knew, until now—is that Anton Greb, our own Johnny Venture, gave his life because of his work on the Original Artists Justice Committee. The court of tabloid opinion would have you believe Anton Greb was killed because of a quarrel with the pop music star known as Jasmine. They're wrong. Anton Greb died because he came too close to learning the truth about the origin of Jasmine's hit song."

The audience began murmuring again, and the cameraman from *Hammer of Justice* moved in closer to the podium.

"I've got the proof and I'll share it with you right here tonight, but as we like to say in the business, stay tuned and don't touch that dial."

That comment elicited a few polite chuckles. Lou Jelniak lowered his head and whispered something to the man seated next to him.

"I've told you about Donovan Sinclair and Anton Greb, but there's a third member of this little drama who deserves equal recognition."

Jelniak rose from his seat.

"An almost forgotten figure from the early days of rock 'n' roll, a record company executive who had easy access—too easy access, some might say—to the creative output of talented young songwriters."

I held on to both sides of the podium and teetered in my ridiculous shoes. Up 'til now, I'd operated on sheer adrenaline and instinct, not stopping to think things through. What if Jelniak had a gun in his pocket? A real one this time, not a stage prop?

"That man is Lou Jelniak, from the old El Jay recording studio in Sacramento. Lou Jelniak took a song written by one of his young black vocal groups, changed the lyrics just slightly, and turned it into a number one hit for a white singer named Jasmine."

Jelniak began threading his way through the closely packed banquet tables toward the back of the hall.

"Anton Greb can't tell us the truth any longer. But there is one man in this room who's very close to Lou Jelniak. You might say he knows him like a brother. That man is Donovan Sinclair."

Necks craned in the direction of the figure known to everyone in Broadcast Legends as Donovan Sinclair. He'd reached the back third of the room. He hurried now, dropping all pretense at finesse, not even bothering to utter an apology as he stepped on toes, elbowed shoulders and backs of heads, and upended a busboy's tray.

The shattering of china and clattering of silver sent a signal of sorts. The uniformed officers burst into the room, guns drawn. One of them tackled Jelniak, who managed to grab the corner of a tablecloth as he toppled to the floor. More crashing of crockery and a sharp female cry as an urn of coffee overturned. A hollered command of "Freeze, sucker!" from Sheriff Perez.

"Ladies and gentlemen." My dramatic enunciation reverberated from speakers positioned at each corner of the hall, covering the pandemonium. "May I present for your entertainment and edification, a true Legend of Broadcasting, the one and only Lou Jelniak."

29

I SAT ON THE EDGE OF THE STAGE AND LET MY LEGS DANGLE OVER the edge. Relief at last from the toe-pinching, ankle-twisting footwear. Sheriff Perez got to wear sensible shoes on the job. Why couldn't I?

A tide of humanity eddied around me, snapping photos, thrusting microphones at my face, and offering hugs, handshakes and atta-girls. At some point, Glory Lou had pressed that tall, cold one I'd been craving so long into my hand. I watched the hotel crew fold down tables and chairs and lay down a portable dance floor. The crowd that wasn't clustered around my corner of the stage huddled around the bar, waiting for the dance party segment of the evening's festivities to begin.

A shapely woman with cascading blond locks blustered her way to my roost on the edge of the stage. "Not bad," Traci Kapolsky said.

"Aren't you glad you took my advice and stuck around with your camera crew?" I couldn't help crowing.

"Not bad, for sure." She handed something round and flat to me. "I guess this belongs to you after all."

I placed the record on my lap, the only place where I felt confident it wouldn't be crushed by a clumsy footstep. Kapolsky had at least remembered to place the Dee Vines 45 disc into its protective paper sleeve. The bubble wrap was long gone, though. She'd probably used it to wrap her vials of Botox.

Maxine Carlin was hard to miss in that zany pop art dress, like one of the Beatles' wives, circa 1965. She broke away from a conversation she'd been having with a lean, silver-haired man.

"What a sleaze!" She sighed dramatically, then took a gulp from a glass of white wine.

"Who, Jelniak?"

"Him too. No, I mean that guy I was just talking to. Gary Drager." She pronounced the name as if the wine had just turned sour.

"I've heard about him. Worked at a radio station in Sacramento, used to trade professional favors, record promotion and the like, for sex. Then he refused to deliver. Right?"

"Used to? Get this: He just told me he could arrange a guest host gig for me on that public affairs program Friday nights on the PBS station. If I was willing to cooperate, that is."

I took another glance at the silver-haired man. A PBS station? Now I knew why he looked familiar. Gary Drager—the Johnny Venture who'd so cruelly used Jasmine backstage at the Oasis Ballroom in 1976—was Pledge Guy.

"You said no, of course."

"I told him his act was old twenty-five years ago, and it's still old. What a sleaze!"

We raised our glasses in a toast to the sisterhood of WWDJ. We Won't Date Jerks.

This could be fun, I thought as the cool liquid slid down my throat. I'll get every female I know to jam the phone lines during the next pledge drive. Even recruit Jasmine from whatever TV soundstage or concert arena she'll happen to be performing on to make some calls. Tell the operators, sure, we'll sign up for a membership to public television. But first you've got to deliver on one little favor. Make Pledge Guy shut up and go away.

Fun? This will be downright delicious.

Pete Kovacs squished across the ballroom floor in muddy shoes and seated himself next to me on the edge of the risers. Now that the tuxedo was starting to dry, it looked even more pathetic, the salt leaving a pattern of white squiggles and semicircles. The bow tie hung in two limp ribbons and the folds of the cummerbund held traces of silt.

As far as I was concerned, he was the best-dressed man in the room.

"I see she gave you the record," he said, when he saw the vinyl disc sitting on my lap.

I nodded and chewed my lower lip, unsure what to say next.

"Answer one question for me," I said slowly. "Why her instead of me? Why'd you go to Traci Kapolsky with the story instead of me?"

Kovacs pretended to squeeze water out of the cuffs of his shirt, but I knew he was just trying to buy time. "Remember that night I came by the station with the box of memorabilia from Rita Slade's grandfather? The night I hid the record under the floor?"

"Of course."

"I tried to get you interested, remember? I showed you the box and even took the record out of the bubble wrap. You acted like it was a bunch of boring old stuff. I could tell, you weren't as excited as I was."

There was nothing I could say. He was right. I'd been so confident he was stopping by with a ring, so wrought up in trying to decide whether I'd say yes or no, I'd all but ignored the box and the record.

"Meanwhile, Traci Kapolsky had called me three times and visited the store twice. She was extremely interested and excited about what I could contribute to her show. She can be very persistent when she wants something, in case you haven't noticed."

"I noticed, I noticed."

"The next thing I know, she's swearing me to secrecy, and having me sign all these documents giving *Hammer of Justice* exclusive rights to the story, and agreeing not to divulge anything about the investigation before the program aired. This is network television. It's hard not to get caught up in all the excitement."

"Tell me about it."

I must have sounded more sarcastic than I intended because Pete grabbed my shoulders and gently twisted my torso, forcing me to look him in the eyes. "I swear, that's all there was to it. A professional arrangement. She tried to get me to move into that apartment with the rest of the crew, but I refused. I went home to my own bed every night."

He was telling the truth. My late-night breaking-and-entering spree into his apartment had proven that.

"Anyway, you know I'm not attracted to phonies like that."

"It's all right, sweetie. Let's just forget about it, okay?" Once you've stared down death, petty emotions like jealousy suddenly seem exactly that. Petty.

"You haven't even opened your gift bag."

For the first time, I noticed Pete had been carrying the silly gold paper bag with its fluff of purple tissue peeking from the top.

"Who cares?" I shrugged. "I'm sure it's just junk." They don't exactly give out Harry Winston diamonds and keys to Jaguars at regional broadcast industry events. Usually the goodie bags contain CDs from unknown groups desperate to get played on the radio. Some things never change.

"You won't know 'til you look, now will you?" Pete spoke playfully as he slipped the record from my lap and replaced it with the paper bag.

No harm in going along with the gag. I groped past the crinkly tissue and wrapped my fingers around a small box. Not the plastic CD jewel case I expected. A square cube covered in soft velvety fabric. Could it be? I withdrew my hand and held the tiny jewel box in my palm.

The real thing, not a plastic case for a CD.

I lifted the hinged lid and saw what was inside.

"Dude," I said with a shaky whisper.

"Is that all you can say?" Kovacs's voice sounded equally quivery.

It was a ring. Not the diamond I expected. Something even better. Kovacs had hired a jeweler to fashion a gold ring in the shape of the Broadcast Legends Hall of Fame statuette. A two-dimensional radio tower curved so that the top touched the base. A circle just the right size for my ring finger. Where the lightning bolts should have been, perched one knockout of a ruby.

"This is absolutely, positively the most meaningful thing anyone has ever done for me," I said as Kovacs helped me slip the ring on my trembling finger. Then I placed my mouth over his to prevent him from demanding I say anything more.

The lights in the ballroom dimmed and a silver disco ball descended from the ceiling. The hotel staff had finished clearing away the banquet tables, replacing them with a scattering of small cocktail tables around the edge of the room. The portable dance floor covered the center. The members of the Broadcast Legends and their spouses and dates began flooding back into the hall, filling it with chatter and laughter.

A spotlight illuminated the DJ booth at stage left, and a young man with a shaved head, multiple ear piercings, and the tattoo of a dragon on his right arm. "DJ Derek," according to a small plastic sign leaning against the front of the booth. A number in the 415 area code followed, along with the notation "Weddings—Reunions—Corporate Events."

I eased myself off the stage, cautious in those damn heels, and took the Dee Vines 45 from Pete. "Be a sweetie and go find Josh," I said, already halfway to the DJ booth. "Get the Jasmine LP and bring it right back."

"Do you mind?" I asked DJ Derek as I seated myself behind the console.

"Whatever." He barely looked up from a plastic crate, where he was sorting through a selection of techno dance music discs. "It's your party."

"It sure is." I placed the Dee Vines 45, B-side up, on the second turntable, then reached across the console to snatch the LP from Pete's outstretched hand.

I removed the long-playing record from its cardboard cover and set it on the first turntable.

Cover my ears with headphones, start the turntable to rotating, place the needle at the start of the correct cut, listen through the headphones for the opening note. The technique all came back. Flick the switch that will send the notes from the right-hand turntable through the amp and out the speakers. Gently place my thumb against the edge of the record to keep it from rotating.

"Ladies and gentlemen," I said into the microphone. My assembled peers and colleagues from the Northern California broadcast industry halted their conversations and zeroed in on the DJ booth.

"I promised earlier this evening that if you stayed tuned I'd give you an example of how two unknown black artists in a group called the Dee Vines had their creation stolen by the white recording industry. This is the very tune that led to the death of Anton Greb, our own Johnny Venture, to the near destruction of Jasmine's career, and to the arrest that you witnessed this evening. First we'll listen to a song I'm sure you all know very well. Then we'll hear the original."

I removed my thumb from the LP. Jasmine's powerful voice filled the hall with her anthem from the seventies.

Meet me at the casbah
The incense will light our way

Glory Lou and Josh had crept to the front of the room and joined Pete in giving me encouraging smiles and thumbs-up. Even DJ Derek stopped his futzing around and sent a look of surprised admiration my way. Yeah, this almost-forty broad still has all the right moves!

I repeated the procedure on the second turntable, gently dropping the needle and finding the opening note. I let Jasmine finish one verse, just enough to make sure my audience recognized the tune, then slid the control on the console downward, letting the notes fade to just the right moment.

The ruby sparkled as I lifted my hand from the second turntable, performing a perfect slip cue to the first-ever public performance of "Meet Me at the Chapel."